Patrick L. Strathmore

The Book of Record

A diary written by Patrick first earl of Strathmore and other documents relating to

Glamis castle, 1684-1689

Patrick L. Strathmore

The Book of Record
A diary written by Patrick first earl of Strathmore and other documents relating to Glamis castle, 1684-1689

ISBN/EAN: 9783337115586

Printed in Europe, USA, Canada, Australia, Japan

Cover: Foto ©Raphael Reischuk / pixelio.de

More available books at **www.hansebooks.com**

PUBLICATIONS

OF THE

SCOTTISH HISTORY SOCIETY

VOLUME IX

GLAMIS BOOK OF RECORD

September 1890

PATRICK, FIRST EARL OF STRATHMORE AND KINGHORNE.

THE BOOK OF RECORD

A DIARY WRITTEN BY PATRICK FIRST EARL OF STRATHMORE AND OTHER DOCUMENTS RELATING TO GLAMIS CASTLE

1684-1689

Edited from the Original MSS. at Glamis with Introduction and Notes by

A. H. MILLAR, F.S.A. Scot.

EDINBURGH

Printed at the University Press by T. and A. Constable for the Scottish History Society

1890

CONTENTS

ILLUSTRATIONS

INTRODUCTION

The papers contained in this volume have been chosen as illustrative of the social life of Scotland two hundred years ago. They consist of the *Book of Record*, an autobiographical diary, written by Patrick, first Earl of Strathmore, between the years 1684 and 1689; a Contract betwixt the Earl of Strathmore and Jacob de Wet for the execution of decorative pictures used in the enrichment of Glamis Castle; the Account for this artistic work rendered by de Wet, with the deductions made thereon by Lord Strathmore; and an Estimate for the repairing of Lord Strathmore's Organ at Glamis Castle. It was intended to include in this volume the Itinerary of Thomas Crombie, the valet who accompanied Lord Strathmore's son to the Continent, but as it would have carried the subject-matter of the volume to a much later date than was contemplated, this document has been reserved. It was also intended to have published with the *Book of Record* the Household Account-Book of Lady Helen Middleton, wife of the first Earl of Strathmore, but the original manuscript has unfortunately been misplaced, and could not be obtained in time to be published in this volume. The Editor has to acknowledge the valuable assistance he has received in the transcribing and annotation of these papers from the Right Hon. the Earl of Strathmore, the Rev. S. G. Beal, M.A. Oxon., Rector of Romald-Kirk, who was for many years chaplain at Glamis Castle, and A. C. Lamb, Esq., F.S.A.Scot., Dundee. It is hoped that the comprehensive index appended to this volume will make it useful as a book of reference.

The Book of Record.

The manuscript of the *Book of Record* is contained in a vellum-bound folio, consisting of unruled pages of antique paper, extending to 300 folios. It has evidently been prepared for the purpose of being used as a daily journal of events, both of private and public life, and as a record of business affairs, payments made by tenants, cash transactions, and memoranda such as one would expect to find in a modern day-book. During the course of the period over which it extends the original intention has been altered though not abandoned, and Lord Strathmore has written a large portion of his own life in the volume, giving minute and interesting particulars as to the earlier incidents in his career. Especially has he entered into great detail regarding the alterations effected by him upon Glamis Castle and Castle Lyon (now Castle Huntly), and to students of the period his book is extremely valuable as showing the cost of work of this kind, the method of payment adopted, and the relationship betwixt capital and labour at a time of transition.

The whole appearance of this volume shows that it was constructed in a way which made it convenient for transportation from one place to another with safety. The strong vellum cover is made with an elongated flap, which comes up over the front edges of the book and is tied to the top cover, thus encasing the whole of the manuscript within an indestructible covering. The portion of the volume written upon extends to 129 pages, the rest of the folios being left blank. The earlier part of the volume, up to folio 110, was written by Thomas Crombie, who seems to have been a confidential servant of Lord Strathmore, and who was afterwards, as already stated, intrusted with the charge of the Earl's second son when on his travels. Crombie's writing is in the crabbed style of the period, and is frequently indistinct, whilst the orthography, though faulty, is really much better than one would expect from a mere valet. In 1685 Crombie's work in the *Book of Record* ceased, and the remainder of the volume is written in the clear, bold, legible handwriting of Lord Strathmore himself. Between the period of Crombie's departure for Paris until the Earl resumed the function of diarist three years elapsed, and it was with a feeling of regret that his lordship found that public affairs had prevented him from continuing the writing of the *Book of Record* with regularity. The remarks which he makes, on taking up the pen himself on 28th March 1688, are most interesting, as showing the feelings which had actuated him in conceiving the idea of making such a volume, and as indicating that sentiment of profound responsibility towards posterity which was one of the salient features of his character :—

'Here is a long surcease of what I am very unaccountable for ; for this three years I have neglected to wreat memorialls of my transactions. But I conceave it is a thing very necessar both for the ease of one's own memory, and ther present satisfaction, to the end when all is recorded posterity may see and be convinced of ther not being unprofitable in there generation, and may be induced by good example to follow the good and to eschew what may be amiss in the management, Tho. I take God to witness it has been and is the outmost indeavour of my life to order all my affairs both for the honour credit and preservation of my family.'

From this period the Diary was written with some attempt at regularity, the commercial items being interspersed as formerly with recollections of the past and opinions on the current events of the day. It is probable also that one of the principal reasons which Lord Strathmore had for continuing the *Book of Record* in his own handwriting was the troubled state of public affairs. It was not then safe for one in his position to confide his inmost thoughts to any one in his employment, as he might thereby place life, liberty, and goods in the power of a menial, who might prove a traitor. This idea is at least suggested by the following allusion to his position on page 92 :—

'The servant who wrote the former part of this book went abroad w^t my second son, after wch Having six moneths at leave, and in some more disuse of pains and application from that tyme till now I was instant enow and at the head of my own affairs, but delayed making or continuing the record of what I did, trusting the same to my memory. But that now finding myself at a loss therby, and being resolved to sett all down w^t my own hand and not to committ it to a serv^ts wreating, who may be here to day and away the morrow, I hope by being punctuall therin, and by what is writ'ne before and hereafter shall make up the loss of thes three years memor's, for from the tyme I left and discontinued my wreating till now it is no less then full three years and some odd moneths.'

The *Book of Record* comes to an abrupt termination on 18th June 1689. The reason for this sudden stop may be found in the fact that in that month Lord Strathmore was engaged in a conspiracy with the Earl of Southesk, the Earl of Callender, Lord Livingstone, and his own son, Lord Glamis, for the purpose of raising troops to create a diversion in the north of Scotland in favour of James II. Of this project there is not the slightest hint given in the volume, unless it be found in the purchase of horses for the levy of horse, referred to on page 102. After his return to Glamis as a reconciled supporter of King William, Lord Strathmore wrote nothing further in his Diary, and we are thus deprived of his opinions regarding the new state of affairs and the leading men who ruled Scotland from the time of the Revolution till the death of Lord Strathmore in 1695.

In transcribing the manuscript great care has been exercised to preserve the original spelling and phraseology, and the printed copy is an exact *facsimile* of the original. The side-headings are given exactly as in the manuscript volume, and the folios are indicated in the text, so that cross references made by his lordship to written pages in his manuscript may be easily followed.

The Book of Record—Its Author.

Patrick Lyon, third Earl of Kinghorne and first Earl of Strathmore, was the only son of John, second Earl of Kinghorne, by his second wife, Lady Elizabeth Maule, only daughter of Patrick, first Earl of Panmure. He was born on 29th May 1642, and succeeded to the title of Earl of Kinghorne on the death of his father on 12th May 1646. From a reference on page 16 it appears that his father died of the plague, with which he had been infected at St. Andrews, whilst in the house of his ward, the Earl of Errol. The infant nobleman succeeded to an unfortunate inheritance. Shortly before his death the second Earl of Kinghorne had been engaged with the Presbyterian party, and had held a commission under the great Marquess of Montrose when that general had command of the Covenanting Army. In the expedition against the Marquess of Huntly Lord Kinghorne was actively engaged, and was present at the Battle of the Bridge of Dee. A contemporary ballad relating to this engagement associates the names of Montrose and Kinghorne in a very peculiar fashion, and indicates the high esteem with which Kinghorne was regarded by the Covenanters :—

> 'God bless our Covenanters in Fyffe and Lothean,
> In Angus and the Mearnis quho did us first begin
> With muskit and with carabin, with money, speare, and shield,
> To take the toune of Aberdeen and make our Marques yield.
>
> God bliss Montrois our General,
> The stout Earl of Kinghorne,
> That we may long live and rejoyce
> That ever they were borne.'

The connection of the Earl of Kinghorne with the Presbyterians brought great misfortune, not only upon himself, but upon his innocent child, and there is something pathetic in the judgment which Lord Strathmore pronounces upon his father's career, whilst he was himself suffering from the punishment with which it was visited. As a pronounced Royalist and Episcopalian, Lord Strathmore had little sympathy with the

Presbyterians, and vigorously denounced their dealings with the martyred king. But he exonerates to some extent his father for the share which he unwillingly took in the doings of the Presbyterian Army, and indicates that it was through his facility and desire to please his first wife, Lady Margaret Erskine (who was a daughter of the Earl of Mar) and his younger brother, James Lyon of Aldbarr. The passage in the *Book of Record* is interesting as a historical incident, and as exhibiting the devoted loyalty of Lord Strathmore.

'But of all the actions of my father's life there was on which I am sorrie to mention since he is so inexcusable for it, but that the fault was truly more his brother's, The Laird of Aldbarr, then his, who was in his owne nature a man of a noble dispositione and feared no ill designe from any man, because he had none himselfe, only it was his misfortune to be easie to be intreated, and it was painfull for him to refuse to relieve his freind when in distress, not considering the hazard of the event, for indeed he was a man not fitted for the time he lived in, fraud and deceit rageing in the transactions of privat busines, and the purpose of rebellion in the publick. All which prov'd too true by the ruin of many good families in their privat fortune and the murder of the best of Kings, but my father was preveen'd by death and did not behold this Tragedie, but was sufficiently convinced of the error of the times—tho. att the beginning he was carried away by the speat and by the influence of his first Lady and his brother Aldbarr, two mightie Covenanters, was induced to goe on too far, and was ingaged in persone with his regiment of Angus to march four severall times and companyed with many of his freinds to the North, which expeditions and the buying of arms I have seen by the reall accompts thereof stood him no less then Fourtie thousand merks. This and the lyke advancements for the propagating the good cause (for the rebellious covenant was so called at that time) were thought meritorious, and no less then heaven was the purchase, tho. it was the Divill in

Masquerad, and my father's wyfe, who was the E. of Marr's daughter, dyeing and his brother Aldbarr soon after did discover the wicked designs against King and Kingdome which were carried on under the pretence of Religione, and in the parliament sometime before his owne death declared no less, and opposed as much as in him lay the preventing partie at that time, and when his countrie-men (an unpardonable sin in those who received the pryce q^{ch} will certainly prove a snare and a curse to their posteritie and does remain an everlasting reproach to the natione, tho. many there was in it honest and blamless) sold there King and voted in Parliament to delyver him up to the Inglish att Newcastle, and not only past his vote against it, and there was but a feu in Parliament did so, but entered his protestatione thereupon boldlie enough but honestlie done att that time.'

The facile disposition of the Earl of Kinghorne not only led him into political difficulties but brought him into extensive commercial obligations which plunged his family deeply into debt. Lord Strathmore throughout the *Book of Record* refers to many instances of this over-obliging disposition on the part of his father, and blames him severely for incurring debts and granting bonds of caution for which he obtained no equivalent and which were incurred merely for friendship's sake. From the brief yet trenchant remarks which he makes it is easy to understand the character of his father, and though Lord Strathmore was too young to have any personal recollections of his parent, his own sufferings and privations led him by bitter experience to appreciate the weakness of his father. Left thus an infant of four years, and with the prospect of a long minority, it might have been imagined that the young Earl of Kinghorne would in ordinary circumstances find himself a wealthy nobleman on attaining his majority. Such, however, was far from being the case. His father's military actions had roused the resentment of Oliver Cromwell, and a fine of £1000 was imposed by the Protector upon the estate that belonged by inheritance to this helpless infant, that he might endure the punishment due for his father's crime. The Royalist predilections of the author are firmly expressed with reference to this fine. He writes—'It was my misfortune being a child at that time not to be in that capacitie to act against him [Cromwell] wch had I been a man I would have done to my utmost hazard.' The long period of dissension and unrest that afflicted Scotland for the thirty years preceding the Restoration told severely upon the estate of the Earl of Kinghorne. Both his father and grandfather had been compelled to raise money for the exigencies of war by borrowing upon the security of their real estate, and every available piece of ground, even to the very Mains of Glamis, was mortgaged or pledged in some form to numerous creditors throughout the land. The magnificent pile of Glamis Castle was almost denuded of furniture, and the noble house of Castle Lyon in the Carse of Gowrie was literally uninhabitable. The guardians who had charge of the young nobleman were unwilling to undertake on their own responsibility the rescue of a property so deeply involved; and though his uncle, the Earl of Panmure, did much to preserve a remnant sufficient to start him in life, it seemed an almost hopeless task to secure an income adequate to his rank in society. To add to his misfortune, his mother married a second time, in 1650, whilst he was only eight years of age, and her new husband, the Earl of Linlithgow, treated his step-son with harsh cruelty and unconscionable extortion. Throughout the earlier portion of the *Book of Record* the dealings of the Earl of Linlithgow are severely animadverted upon, although the writer does not greatly blame her for her second marriage. Under all these discouragements the boyhood and youth of Patrick Lyon could not have been a happy time, and only a mind well-principled and just, courageous and upright, could have faced the difficulties with which he was confronted. The spirit in which he regarded them long years afterwards is thus indicated:—

'I had a verie small and a verie hard begining and if I had not done so great and good things as I might or willingly would have done I desyre that my posteritie whom God has bless'd me with may excuse these my endeavours for the reasone before mentioned.'

Having completed his studies at St. Andrews University Lord Kinghorne returned to his estate in 1660, when he was seventeen years of age, and even at this time he had formed the resolution of restoring as far as possible the honours and estates of his family. With this end in view he refrained from making the tour of the Continent, which was then considered necessary for the completion of the education of a young noble. The lamentable condition in which he found Castle Lyon on his return from college is graphically described at page 29. There was literally not a bed in the Castle for him to sleep in, and he was compelled to borrow a bedstead from the minister of Longforgan to set up in the dreary waste of this uninhabited fortalice, and to wait patiently for the arrival of his humble student's furniture from St. Andrews. His inhuman step-father had taken possession of some of the paraphernalia that had belonged to Lord Kinghorne's mother, and his aunt, Lady Northesk, succeeded in buying back 'att a deere enough rate' from Lord Linlithgow the furniture of one room, and some pieces of silver plate that were immediately necessary for household use. It would be difficult to find in fiction a more touching or pathetic delineation of high life than is afforded by the simple description which the young nobleman gives of his early days at Castle Lyon. The heir of a name that had been famous in Scottish history for centuries was reduced to a condition of extreme privation through no fault of his own but through the crushing weight of circumstances over which he had no control. His barns, his byres, and his stables at Castle Lyon were alike tenantless, and, as he quaintly puts it, 'att that time I was not worth a four-footed beast, safe on little dog that I keeped att and brought with me from St. Andrews.' The empty chambers within the prison-like Castle were bare of furniture, and it was here that he and his only sister, Lady Elizabeth Lyon, began their first attempt at housekeeping on a most parsimonious scale. For his sister he seems ever to have had profound respect and affection, and she worked for him in this matter of furnishing with unselfish devotion. Having scrambled together from the deserted Castle of Glamis 'some old potts and pans q^ch^ were verie usefull,' and collected odd furniture which plenished two rooms in an incoherent fashion, he and his sister began to decorate with their own hands their lonely dwelling-place, and to make it, in appearance at least, fit for habitation. Looking back upon this period of his life twenty-five years afterwards, Lord Strathmore was as keenly impressed by the sisterly affection of Lady Elizabeth during this trying period, as he had been at the time of its occurrence. 'Her companie,' he writes, 'was of great comfort to me, so young as were both we consulted together, and partlie by our owne conclusions and partlie by advice, in two years time I gott togither as much of cours furniture as in a verie mean and sober way filled all the rowms of my house, some on way some another.' With his sister he remained until his marriage, which took place in 1662.

The Restoration in 1660 seemed to promise great advantages to one who had suffered so much for the Royalist cause, and the Earl of Kinghorne was induced to repair to the Court at Whitehall to kiss his Majesty's hand. He remained in London for six weeks, making the journey back and forward upon the three first horses he possessed, and he quaintly states that 'tuo of them as I was comeing hom and ryding thorrow ffyfe failed me even there and dyed poor beasts in the cause.' The whole journey to London and back, with a six weeks' residence there, cost him only £200 sterling, principally because he refrained from purchasing those works of decorative art towards which his fancy inclined. There is a touch of humour in the reflection which he makes upon the small expense of this expedition. 'Had I been as moderate in all my severall jorneys to that place since, from q[ch] I have brought things of great value for the furniture of my houses, I had saved many a pond and pennie, but I acknowledge a great dale of weakness in my humour that way, inclining to be verie profuse upon all things of ornament for my houses as I have been upon building. Let this only serve to excuse me if in this I have exceeded, that what has been bestowed upon the first, or expended upon the second has been acquyr'd with pains and industrie and performed with much care and labour and will be tok'ns of both (being things of long indurance) to my posterity who I hope shall enjoy the pleasure of it, whereas indeed I have suffered the toil.'

One of the epochs in Lord Kinghorne's life was his marriage, which took place on 23rd August 1662. Lady Helen Middleton was the second daughter of John, first Earl of Middleton, and of his first wife, Grizel, daughter of Sir James Durham of Pitkerro and Luffness. The career of her father, the Earl of Middleton, is sketched in the Notes to this volume, page 135, to which the reader is referred. Her elder sister, Lady Grizel, was married to the Earl of Morton, and on page 28, it will be seen that Lady Middleton was inclined to favour the suitor of her elder daughter rather than Lord Kinghorne, regarding Morton as the weaker of the two. The marriage of Lady Helen and Lord Kinghorne was in every way a happy one, though begun under such unpropitious circumstances. Wherever throughout the volume he has occasion to refer to his wife, he does so in the most affectionate terms, showing that he had found her not only a skilful housewife and manager of domestic affairs, but a wise counsellor in times of difficulty, and a devoted mother, who reared her family with discretion. He was himself of a disposition framed to appreciate highly the domestic virtues, and was ever ready to sacrifice his own pleasure and convenience for the sake of his children and their posterity. Thus we find him writing, a quarter of a century after his marriage, with reference to his family circle in these terms:—

'I have reason dayly to adore and magnify the name of my God who out of his infinit goodness to me, more than I deserve, and to my family, has blest me with good and vertewous sons and daughters, of good dispositions and frugall and moderat as much as my heart can desyre. Blessed be he who has made me happy by them, and make me thankfull and exemplar to them in what is good. Nor can I deny the great advantage I have by their mother who's care has been of her children and to stay at home and guide w^tin the house her part.'

The marriage took place at the Abbey of Holyrood, the ceremony having been performed by Archbishop Sharpe. The home-coming was made a kind of triumphal progress. During the first winter of their married life the Earl and Countess remained at Edinburgh, and there is a beautiful and characteristic sketch given of the surprise which he had prepared for his wife on taking her to her bridal-chamber. 'I caused bring home a verie fin cabinet, the better was not in the Kingdome in these days, which I never told my wyfe of till her comeing home, and upon her first comeing into her owne chamber I presented her with the keyes of the cabinet.' In March 1663 Lord Kinghorne and his Countess set out for Castle Lyon. They crossed the Forth to Aberdour, where her sister, the Countess of Morton, was then residing, and, passing through Fife, they remained for a night at Cupar, where many of the friends of the young couple were gathered to meet them. Thence they proceeded to Dundee, where they were entertained by the Provost and Magistrates, the Earl having been made a burgess of that burgh on 19th July 1660. Taking up their residence at Castle Lyon, they remained there for seven years, and here their eldest son, John, afterwards second Earl of Strathmore, was born on 8th May 1663.

A portion of the lands of Castle Lyon had been for ages in possession of the family, but the house itself with the remainder of the Mains and Kirktoun had been acquired from

Lord Gray by Patrick, first Earl of Kinghorne, his Lordship's grandfather. Despite the alterations in this building that had been made by his father, the Castle was far from satisfying the the refined taste of Lord Kinghorne, and he at once set about repairing it. Glamis Castle was then so desolate that he and his wife decided to bring such furniture as was necessary to Castle Lyon, and to make the latter their principal residence until their improved exchequer would allow them to put the larger Castle into a habitable condition. The alterations which he made upon Castle Lyon, and the improvements he effected in the grounds beside it, are very fully detailed in the *Book of Record*. Even now, after the lapse of more than two hundred and twenty years, his description of the changes which he made is perfectly intelligible. The feeling which caused him to avoid Glamis Castle was a very natural one. He says:—'For the first three years of my life, wch I only reckon since the year 1660, I could not endure allmost to come near to or see it [Glamis] when the verie Mains was possessed by a wedsetter, so, when my wyfe after the end of the first seven years considered that nothing contributs so much to the distruction and utter ruine of furniture than the transporting of it, I was induced by her to make my constant abode att Castle Lyon for some time longer till she gott togither some things necessary to be had before we could think of comeing to Glammiss, wch she provyded with so much care as that for our first comeing to Glammiss where I proposed to live for some time as reretcedly as I did att first when I took up house at Castle Lyon having scarce a spare rowme furnished to lodge a stranger in.' It was not until 1670 that the Earl and Countess found themselves in a position to remove to Glamis Castle, and in the following year he began those alterations upon the structure which ultimately resulted in transforming it into one of the noblest castles in Scotland.

It may be convenient here to refer to the two Castles of Glamis and Castle Lyon which are so frequently mentioned in the *Book of Record*, and the reconstruction of which formed the principal occupation of Lord Strathmore during many years, so that his descriptions may be understood by the reader who is unacquainted with the localities. Castle Lyon, or, as it was originally and is now termed, Castle Huntly, occupies a situation that is more picturesque than imposing, and the stern aspect of the lofty baronial tower which faces the south might suggest that the Castle was the residence of some predatory chief, were the building not surrounded by the smiling fields and fruitful orchards of the Carse of Gowrie. It is situated beside the village of Longforgan, which was evidently in early times the place where the retainers of the first proprietors of Castle Huntly had their residence. The landscape around the Castle has been transformed by centuries of industrious labour from a barren and marshy wilderness into a highly cultivated vale, and this gradual change has taken place beneath the shadow of its ancient walls. The original Castle, which still exists in its entirety, though now much enlarged, is said to have been built by the second Baron Gray of Gray in 1452, under a special licence granted by James II. in acknowledgment of his many faithful services. The accuracy of this statement, however, may be doubted. The earliest reference to this date as that of the erection of the Castle is to be found in the old *Statistical Account*, written in 1797, where the author alludes to a charter then in the possession of the family of Gray. No such charter is recorded in the Register of the Great Seal, where it would almost certainly have appeared, and the statement rests on very doubtful authority. The family of Gray first settled in the Manor of Longforgan in 1308, their original seat being the Castle of Fowlis in the neighbourhood. It is very probable that a fort of some kind existed on the site of Castle Huntly from an early period, as the rock on which it stands would make a building of that description valuable alike as a watch-tower and a defensive post, but no prehistoric remains of such an erection have been found. As Castle Huntly was much larger than

Fowlis Castle, it is likely that the Gray family had been settled for a long period in the vicinity before they would be in a position to erect such an extensive pile. The earliest document that has been found which distinctly refers to 'the tower and fortalice of Huntlie,' is a confirming grant by James IV. to Andrew, third Baron Gray, of the lands and barony of Longforgund on 7th January 1508-9. The architectural construction of the oldest part of Castle Huntly makes it likely that it was built not long before this date. Much dubiety has existed in the minds of topographers as to the derivation of the original name of Castle Huntly, said to have been bestowed by the second Baron Gray upon his new homestead. The tradition of the locality is still current which ascribes the origin of the name to the marriage of a Lord Gray to a daughter of the Huntly family. As Patrick, fourth Lord Gray, was married during his father's lifetime to Lady Janet Gordon, second daughter of George, second Earl of Huntly, *circa* 1492, and as he succeeded his father in 1514, this tradition seems to confirm the date of the Castle as being about 1500. The only other theory worthy of consideration is, that the appellation of Huntly may have been taken from the Berwickshire property of that name which belonged to the Grays before they settled in Perthshire.

The Lyon family first obtained property in the neighbourhood of Castle Huntly through the marriage of Elizabeth, daughter of Andrew, third Lord Gray, with John, sixth Lord Glamis, which took place in 1487. From Lord Strathmore's statement in the *Book of Record* this land consisted of a third part of the Mains, and two-thirds of the Kirktoun of Longforgan. The rest of the property remained in the possession of the Gray family until 1614, when Andrew, eighth Baron Gray, who had chosen the military profession and obtained an appointment in France, disposed of a large portion of his estate for ready money shortly after his father's death. At that time Patrick, first Earl of Kinghorne, and grandfather of the first Earl of Strathmore, purchased a part consisting of 'the place and seat of the house with the two part land of the Mains, and the third part lands of the Churchtoune,' and set about altering and repairing the Castle. It is unnecessary to quote here the description of the alterations effected by the first Earl of Kinghorne and by his grandson, as these are very fully detailed on pp. 32-37. From the time of its purchase until the estate was disposed of by John, seventh Earl of Strathmore, in 1796, Castle Lyon was made the jointure house of the Countesses of Kinghorne and Strathmore, hence it frequently happened that the early days of successive Earls of Strathmore were spent within its walls. In 1672 the first Earl of Strathmore obtained a charter from Charles II. erecting the lands of Longforgan into a free barony to be called the Lordship of Lyon, and it was probably at this time that the name of the Castle was changed from Huntly to Lyon. When the property was sold in 1776 it was acquired by Mr. George Paterson, who was married to the Hon. Anne Gray, one of the descendants of the Gray family, and he reverted to the original title, calling the place Castle Huntly, which name it still retains.

Glamis Castle stands a little way off the road from Dundee to Kirriemuir, and is about five miles distant from the latter place, and close beside the old town of Glamis. The main gateway is a triple-arched structure, battlemented and surmounted by carved lions, the heraldic emblems of the family of Strathmore. From the gate a spacious avenue, closely planted with trees, is led for a short distance through the umbrageous foliage until it suddenly enters upon a grassy plain, and is carried almost in a straight line for three-quarters of a mile up to the principal entrance of the Castle. The general appearance of the structure, as seen from the main approach, reminds one of a French château of the sixteenth century. Two wings extend at right angles to each other, and a quarter-circle tower which rises seven stories high, contains the staircase that affords access to these divisions. The chief doorway is at the base of this tower, and at its summit a wooden clock-dial, bearing the date 1811, usurps the place of an elegant triple window. Around the upper portion of the tower a numerous array of picturesque turrets has been grouped, and on the leads a spacious platform has been laid, protected by wrought-iron railings and terminated by two graceful open pagodas. The central part of the Castle, which is the oldest portion, rises much higher than the side-wings, and it forms one side of a spacious courtyard, the quadrangle being completed by the kitchen, stable-yard, and servants' apartments. The doorway at the base of the tower is flanked by pilasters with richly carved floral capitals. Immediately over it the bust of Patrick, first Earl of Kinghorne, is placed, whilst along the upper walls of the wings, the armorial bearings of the principal Earls since 1606 are marshalled with those of their separate wives. Above one of the main windows the initials of Patrick, first Earl of Kinghorne (died 1615), and of his wife, Dame Anna Murray, daughter of the first Earl of Tullibardine, are plainly visible. Over the door the Royal Arms of Scotland have been carved, and the heavy iron knocker on the oaken door bears the date '1689,' when the principal work of reconstruction was completed by the first Earl of Strathmore. Within this door a heavily grated iron gate has been erected, which doubtless formed the guard to the entrance of the original Castle, and may be about four hundred years old. Within the doorway three staircases appear, that to the left leading to the upper great hall, the one to the right descending by a few steps to the vaulted crypt or lower hall and then ascending to the old portion of the Castle known as 'King Malcolm's Room,' and the third or newest staircase, circling around the interior of the tower and giving access to all the flats from basement to roof. The last of these consists of a newelled stair of 143 steps, which was erected by Patrick, Earl of Kinghorne, between 1600 and 1606. At a later date the walls of the staircase were plastered, but the present Earl of Strathmore has had the plaster removed so as to show the dressed stone-work, which is more in keeping with the style of the building than the false stone markings with which the plaster-work was painted. The great hall is a vaulted apartment about 60 feet long by 25 feet wide, and is composed entirely of stone. The vaulting of the roof and cross-vaulting of the windows is managed by using numerous small wedge-shaped stones to form the archway. Much controversy has arisen regarding the architect who designed this staircase and great hall. The consistent tradition in the family is that when Patrick, first Earl of Kinghorne, was in attendance on James VI. in London, he employed Inigo Jones to prepare the plans for the proposed alterations. The first Earl Patrick certainly carried out many of his projected improvements before his death in 1615, but it was left to his grandson, who was also called Patrick, and who was *third* Earl of Kinghorne and *first* Earl of Strathmore, to complete the reconstruction of the Castle, and to enlarge and improve it. Critics have usually objected to the statement that Inigo Jones had any concern in Glamis Castle, as his death took place in 1652, whilst the first Earl of Strathmore was a mere child. So far as the Editor knows, there is no document in the Charter-room at Glamis which distinctly proves that Inigo Jones had any share in this work; but it is certain that Patrick, first Earl of Kinghorne, did make great alterations on the Castle, and that his grandson Patrick, first Earl of Strathmore, was also a reconstructor, so that the difficulty of the date does not militate against the tradition. The real cause of confusion probably lies in the fact that both noblemen bore the same name, and each was the first holder of his distinctive title. It should be borne in mind that the two outer wings of the Castle have been greatly altered in comparatively recent times.

A very remote antiquity is ascribed to the oldest part of Glamis Castle. It has been frequently asserted that King

Malcolm II. was carried from the scene of his assassination on Hunter's Hill in 1033 to one of the rooms in Glamis Castle, where he expired from his wounds; though less credulous historians maintain that the King died peacefully, and was buried at Iona, and have discredited the stories of his legislative reforms and murder as mere figments of monkish times. It is not impossible, however, that a royal keep of some kind occupied the site of the present Castle at a very early time, though the connection of the Lyon family with this place does not extend further back than the middle of the fourteenth century. No record has been found of the alterations and additions at Glamis Castle previous to the description given in Lord Strathmore's manuscript, but it is apparent from his account of Glamis that even in its ruinous condition, before he began the work of reconstruction, it was a noble and imposing pile. The details which he gives of the work undertaken by him are full of instruction, but it is unnecessary to do more than refer the reader to his narrative as contained in the *Book of Record*, pp. 37-42. It is not difficult, even at the present day, and despite the many alterations made during the last two centuries, to trace every item of his description, and to see where his improving hand has been at work. The dule-tree to which he refers cannot be identified, but the dial which he erected is still extant and presents more than eighty faces to the sun as heretofore. He alludes (page 44) to his intention that 'howsoon the walk and green plots are layed there will be statu's put into the gardin.' Not one of these now remains in its place, though the fragments of a leaden Venus, which lie in one of the basement passages, give some faint notion of the character of the decoration adopted.

It was in 1671 that the Earl began the work of reformation upon Glamis Castle, and it was not completed until 1689. Many strange incidents happened to him during this long period. His grandfather had been created Earl of Kinghorne in 1606, with strict limitation to his heirs-male. On 30th

May 1672 Patrick, third Earl of Kinghorne, obtained a new charter enabling him to nominate a successor in default of male issue. Five years afterwards he procured another charter, dated 1st July 1677, ordaining that his heirs and successors in tailzie should be designated in all time coming Earls of Strathmore and Kinghorne, Viscounts Lyon, Barons Glamis, Tannadyce, Sidlaw, and Strathdichtie, and this is the full style and title of his descendant, the present Earl of Strathmore. On 10th January 1682 he was sworn of the Privy Council, and on 27th March 1686 he was appointed an Extraordinary Lord of Session. When Argyll's rebellion broke out in 1685 he was appointed to provide the stores for the army, and was commissioned to bring the prisoners and spoil from Clydesdale to Edinburgh, and the artillery from Glasgow and Stirling (see page 84). By his commissariat transaction he lost a considerable sum of money, as a much larger quantity of provision was ordered from him than was required (see page 85), and this fact indicates that the government anticipated that Argyll's rebellion would be much more formidable than it really was. His connection with this rebellion proved a disastrous one for him. He obtained a portion of Argyll's lands in Kintyre, and, as the king desired to resume these lands and annex them to the Crown, a proposal was made whereby Lord Strathmore and the Earl of Errol were to obtain an equivalent from the town of Edinburgh. The description of this curious transaction, as given on pp. 89, 90, is somewhat confusing, though the following passage from a memorial presented to the Earl of Melville, then Secretary for Scotland, by the town of Edinburgh, renders the matter more intelligible. This memorial is quoted in the 'Leven and Melville Papers' (page 130). The town of Edinburgh was in debt to the extent of 150,000 merks in 1633. Betwixt that date and 1654, the coronation of Charles I., the building of the Parliament House and of several churches, the besieging of the Castle, and other public affairs had raised the debt to

1,200,000 merks. Cromwell granted an imposition of a plack on the pint of ale to assist in clearing off the debt, and this tax was continued till his death. At the Restoration this imposition was restricted to two pennies on the pint, and this was continued till 1682. In 1683, Sir George Drummond, Provost of Edinburgh, undertook the watching and warding of the city, which had been previously accomplished by train bands, and, acting upon his authority, the debts of the town were further increased. The tax upon ale had been farmed during its continuance to various parties, and in 1680 Charles II. made a new gift of the imposition for twenty-one years. Shortly before his abdication, James II. (apparently in 1686) entered into a contract with the Earls of Strathmore and of Errol, whereby he granted a portion of the tax to them in exchange for the lands of Kintyre. 'The two Earles parts of the contract was, to dispone to the King some lands in Argylleshire, out of which they had their relieff, the Earles of Errol and Strathmore being only cautioners in a bond to Heriot's hospitall of tuentie thousand pounds scottis of principall for Argylle. The Town's part of the contract was to undertake the said debt dew to the hospitall, which of principall and annual rents amounts to near 5000 lib. sterling, for which the Town has given bond to the hospitall; but it's hoped the Parliament will reduce this transaction as done to the grosse and palpable lesion of the Town.'

According to Lord Strathmore's account of the business, he could not obtain a just settlement of his claim against the town when he made application to James II. at London, and it was in consequence of the loss he thus sustained that he was made an Extraordinary Lord of Session on 27th March 1686, with a pension of £300 sterling (page 90). The arrangement of the 'tripartite contract' between the King and the two Earls was ultimately accomplished in the beginning of 1688, and thus Lord Strathmore got rid of one of the onerous charges which had been bequeathed to him by his father. He thus expresses himself regarding this affair: 'And so at last we are delivered from that greivous debt, wch first and last has stood me more by seeking releif of it then the thing would have been to my part if I had payed it in the year 1660 when I came from scools. O miserable and fatall cautionry, ffor my family has suffered more by the engadgements of my father, who, good man! thinking every one as honest as himself, and tender-hearted to his friends, refused scarce any one who ask'd of him, then at this day I enjoy of free estate over the pay^t^ of my present debt.'

The part which Lord Strathmore took at the Revolution has already been referred to. There can be little doubt that his first intention was to resist the Prince of Orange, and to associate himself with some of the leading Jacobite noblemen to accomplish the restoration of James II. to the throne. He implicated himself with the Earls of Southesk, Callender, and Breadalbane, and endeavoured to assemble in arms such of the militia as he had control over. He was present as a member of the Privy Council when intelligence of the proposed invasion by the Prince was received. 'This was the time,' he writes, 'of the first surprysing news of the Dutch invasion, and of the P. of Orange's designe of landing in England, wch he did afterwards w^t^ wonderful success. It was then scarce when harvest was done that the militia was draw'ne togither, and by one detachment after another thes expeditions dwynled into nothing, as everything else did wch concerned the king's service, all succeeding w^t^ the Prince to a miracle.' Finding it hopeless to resist the progress of the revolution, as King James had gone beyond the seas, Lord Strathmore deemed it prudent to make his peace with the Prince of Orange. He was nominated by the Privy Council to convey their address to the Prince to London, and in this task he was associated with his eldest son Lord Glamis. As he found it impossible to obtain from the Treasury sufficient money to defray the expenses of his journey, he was compelled to borrow £2000, and transferred the task of presenting the address to his son, who set out for London early in 1689. The Marquess of Athol, who was then commander of the forces in Scotland, deputed his office to Lord Strathmore, but this duty was felt by his lordship to be a dangerous one for him. He was strongly suspected of a leaning towards the Jacobites, and he was deprived of his office as a Lord of Session. By a curious circumstance Lord Cardross, whose misfortunes had increased the wealth of Lord Strathmore (see Note 80, page 169), was now in a position to receive the submission of that nobleman to the new king. A letter from Lord Cardross to Lord Melville, dated 9th September 1689, contains the following passage:—

'Being returned here this afternoon, and being since then in the Councile, I thought it my deucty to acquaint you that the E. of Straithmore, Southesk, Breadalbine, and some gentlemen came in and took the benefit of the indemnity. E. Callender, L. Livingston and Duffus, prisoners in the Castle, have also now petitioned for it, and the Councile is to give it them the morrow. I confess, since, they did not desire it at their first comeing in, but on the contrary stood upon their innocency, I was for remitting their case to the king that his mercy might flow in a particular manner to them since their circumstances seem to me to differ from those that were included in the indemnity.' From another letter written on the following day by Sir Alexander Bruce to Lord Melville, it appears that Lord Strathmore and his associates were induced to submit themselves through the remonstrances of the Duke of Queensberry, and to acknowledge their obligations to him for his advice. Though thus nominally submissive, there is evidence that Lord Strathmore had still hopes of overthrowing the Presbyterian party. Towards the close of 1689 he wrote a letter to his son Lord Glamis, stating that he and some of his intimates were 'hopefull to hough Melvill, and defeat all his Presbiterian projects.' Before many months had fled, however, he had abandoned this design, and on 25th April 1690 he took the oath of allegiance to King William. After this period he took little share in public affairs. His name only appears once in the Rolls of the Parliaments of William and Mary under date 18th April 1693. About this time Lord Strathmore made the draft of a deed in which, after setting forth the many difficulties which had beset his progress through life, and all the many blessings for which he had to be thankful, in consideration whereof he resolved to build four 'lodges' near the Kirktoun of Glamis for the use of four aged men of his own surname if they could be found, and, failing them, to such decayed tenants as had been reduced to want not through their own fault, to each of whom he intended to mortify yearly four bolls of oatmeal and 25 merks Scots money, with 'a new whyt coloured wid cloath coat lyned with blew serge once every thrie years.' His purpose was that these four men should attend the Parish Church, and 'wait alwayes at the Church door when we goe there, and at their own dores whenever we shall have occasion to pass by, if they be not imployed abroad. . . . And that they shall be holden (if sickness and infirmity do not hinder) to repair everie day, once at the twalt-hour of the day to our buriall place (whereof a key shall be given to each incomer), and a forme of prayer to be read by them by turns, by such of them as can read, and if they cannot read, that they learn the same by heart.' His lordship's intention seems never to have been carried out, and it remains merely in the form of a draft. He died on 15th May 1695, in the fifty-third year of his age, and was buried in the family vault at Glamis.

The character of the Earl of Strathmore may be easily deduced from the *Book of Record*. He was apparently a man of strict integrity and uprightness, with a profound respect for the honour of his ancestors and a deep sense of his responsibility to posterity. Succeeding in his youth to an estate heavily weighted with debt, he managed, through a long course of economy and self-denial, not only to relieve his successors of the burden he had inherited, but to leave to them an estate greatly enhanced in value, and two castles which will bear favourable comparison with any others of the time. He was just without penuriousness, generous with discretion, affectionate in the family circle, and tender and true to his friends and relatives. There are two portraits of Lord Strathmore and a marble bust at Glamis Castle, and to the student of physiognomy these show the features of a mild and amiable man, more fitted, perhaps, to shine in the court than on the field, and greater as a politician than as a warrior. His own description of his character is amply borne out by the facts which he relates in the course of his narrative. 'By Divine providence, which I may rather ascrive it to then out of any choise of my owne, being then so young and of no experience, I did then begin, and still have continued, with just and equall dealings to all men. I never defrauded the poor, nor had I ever any favour or ease from those who were powerfull, allwayes acknowledging my father's bonds when I saw them. And I hope, by the mercie of God, founding againe my familie upon the pillar of justice, I shall be able to transmitt a good pairt of my estate with much less of incumbrance and debt then I found att my entrie thereto.' It is not possible to read the simple story of his career which he has narrated, without feeling that he was in an eminent degree one worthy of the esteem of his own posterity and of mankind.

The Book of Record as Illustrating the Social Condition of Scotland.

In examining the *Book of Record* the first point which strikes the reader is the extreme scarcity of money at the period. Though the estate which Lord Strathmore inherited was one of the largest in Scotland at the time, the revenue derived from it was seldom available for the direct payment of debts in current coin. According to his own statement, the estate which his grandfather left was valued at 560 chalders victual and 100 merks annual rent. But through mismanagement, extravagance, and especially through the 'woful cautionries' which his father had undertaken, the debts upon the estate, when he came into it, amounted to £400,000. By careful financing and rigid economy Lord Strathmore succeeded in reducing the debt to £175,400, but the interest upon this sum in 1684 was an annual charge upon the estate of £10,524. The rate of interest upon the whole of the borrowed money was 6 per cent.; and when it is remembered that the most of the rents were paid in kind, and had to be sold in the market to procure ready money, it will be seen that the payment of this heavy annual charge must have been a great burden. During the six years between 1678 and 1684 Lord Strathmore succeeded in clearing off debts to the amount of £99,866, 13s. 4d., and this was at the time when he was most busily engaged with the reconstruction of Castle Lyon and Glamis Castle. To accomplish this stupendous task Lord Strathmore must have had a faculty for finance far exceeding many of his contemporaries. A modern actuary might find much instruction from the study of the clear and business-like way in which he has set down his debts, and the methods he took for liquidating them.

One of the principal difficulties in the financial system of the time arose from the frequent assignation of debts from one party to another. Bills and Bonds were then negotiable as the only substitute for a paper currency, but the incidence of this system often told severely upon the original debtor. The granter of a bond might have a verbal agreement with the holder of it that he was not to be pressed for payment within a certain time; but the necessities of the holder may have compelled him to assign this bond to a third party, who was under no obligation to delay the claim for payment. It is easy to see how a bond like this getting into circulation might come into the hands of an enemy, who would find in it an opportunity for revenging himself upon the granter by demanding instant payment. A peculiar instance of this is shown by Lord Strathmore's own family experience. After the death of his father, his mother kept a strict note of all the money which she expended for him out of her own liferent, intending, as he suggests, to claim for this money in the event of his dying without issue. She married the Earl of Linlithgow, however, and after her death, that nobleman, whose treatment of the young Earl was extremely cruel, compelled the repayment of all this money, and claimed upon the estate, though still under curators, for a debt to which he had only a secondary right (see page 17). Many other circumstances of the same kind will be found throughout the volume, and the value of the *Book of Record* is considerable because of the clear manner in which this method of assigning debts is shown to have brought about the ruin of many families. This is an aspect of the social life of the times which has not received due attention from historians of Scotland.

The two principal methods then employed for raising money were the pledging of land as security, or the assigning of the value of so many ploughs for the liquidation of the principal sum and interest. As an instance of the former, the transaction of Lord Strathmore with the Earl of Linlithgow, described on page 15, may be examined. When Lord Strathmore purchased some superiorities from the Earl of Crauford he borrowed £1333, 6s. 8d. from Lord Linlithgow. Shortly afterwards, when Linlithgow married Lord Strathmore's mother, he preferred a claim for the money she had expended during her widowhood in the manner already referred to. To meet this charge, which amounted to £14,666, 13s. 4d., Lord Strathmore was compelled to pledge the lands of Cardean and the third part of Lenross, and thus run the risk of losing a large portion of the most valuable lands in his estate. Fortunately he was able to clear off the debt shortly afterwards; but the fact that he was necessitated to make such an arrangement shows how difficult it was to obtain money on any save heritable security. It is interesting to notice that Lord Strathmore had frequent money transactions with Provost Coutts of Montrose, who was the direct ancestor of the late Thomas Coutts, the famous banker of London.

With very few exceptions, the whole rental of Lord Strathmore's estate was paid to him in kind, and the values of various farms were expressed more frequently under the form of their produce than in current coin. The Byreflat in Longforgan paid a rental of 'ten bolls of bear, besyds the teind sheave drawne.' The Templebank of Thorntoun paid an annual duty of 8 bolls bear, 8 bolls meal, and 12 poultry. These are examples of the yearly farm-rents exacted; but the entry-money had to be paid in coin. The factors appointed for the administration of the different portions of the estate received the grain paid in name of rent, and stored it; and the proprietor paid his debts by giving an order to one of the factors to deliver grain to the value of the amount charged against him. In many cases this must have been a most inconvenient method of payment, as it threw the onus of selling the grain upon the creditor, and its frequent use shows in a remarkable way the great scarcity of ready money throughout the kingdom. In short, it was a survival of the old system of barter which was in vogue in very early times. Another striking proof of the lack of a circulating medium is afforded by the way in which tradesmen's accounts were paid. Andrew Wright, the ingenious rural joiner at Glamis, who did much of the reconstruction work at Lord Strathmore's two castles, was paid in this manner. He received the farm of Byreflat at an agreed price, and was allowed to make up the cost of it by work spread over a number of years. The agreements with the masons and paviours always contained the stipulation that so much was to be paid in money, and so much in meal. A memorandum contained in a bundle of accounts relating to the mason work at Glamis exhibits the usual form of agreement, and may be here quoted, as showing the relations between employer and employed at that time :—

'At Glamis the 15th of Aprile, 1685.—After communing with the four messons here at Glammis such is their shameless greed and unthankfulness albeit of all the work and employment they have had of me these many years past, in which they have gotten mony a pound and penie, I find that they demande for laying the walk about the inner court with stone upon edge verie exorbitant, it being no less than eight pounds and ane firlot of meall for the rood, which would come to a most extraordinar and exorbitant wage—but that I, considering that I have noe such thing to doe againe, have condescended to give them eight marks, and ane firlot of meall for each rood, but that if I fynd any part of it worse done then that is alredie, or that they presume soe much as on stone upon its back unless it be more than a foot thick, I'll withdraw at least the one half of the price, but if it be well done they shall be well paid—only this—since I give them so liberally there's a little peice of wall from the corner of the door which is to goe in to that eastmost gate house, which most be taken down and rebuild by them in bounty to me, for it is but a verie small matter if they had the good manners not to grudge when more than reason is offer'd—but that I observe there designe is upon task work to take it always soe as that they may have wages thereby and a third part more; and for to give them daily wages, that is a thing which I'll doe no more in all my life, for no master is able to subsist by soe doing, unless they resolve to build themselves out of doors.'

On page 64 an agreement with the masons of Glamis for building a closet within the charter-room is recorded, the price being £50 Scots, and 4 bolls meal. The two masons at Castle Lyon were paid partly in money and partly in meal for the work of building the wall round the plantation at Castle Lyon (see page 80), and it is very seldom that a payment is recorded as being made to tradesmen wholly in money. The system of giving bounties on the completion of work was frequently adopted. From the above quotation it will be seen that Lord Strathmore expected some extra work to be done for him gratis as a bounty. On the other hand, George Ramsay, slater, received £94 Scots 'for dressing the roofe of the house of Cossens, and for theicking the new byres and sheep cott att my barns of Castle Lyon,' together with three bolls 1 firlot, 2 pecks of meal as bounty. One of the customs of the labouring classes, which was then dying out, but did not disappear entirely before the present century began, is alluded to on page 80. From April till the middle of October, the working day was from 5 A.M. till 7 P.M., the breakfast hour being from 8 till 9 A.M., dinner from 12 to 1.30 P.M., the half hour from 4 to 4.30 P.M. being allotted to what was called the 'four hours drink.' Against the latter custom Lord Strathmore rebelled, and he thus alludes to it: 'I chuse much rather to pay a very full and competent pryce to all kind of workmen than to be in use of waisting meall and malt and allowing them morning drink and four hours w[ch] was the custom long ago: but that I have worn it out of use, finding too tho. it was much, yet these kind of cattell being in use of it considered it very litle.' Though inclined to deal fairly with his workmen, Lord Strathmore found himself sometimes imposed upon, and the acute observations which he makes regarding workmen on page 93 shows his attitude towards the workpeople in his employment: 'Though I hold it as a rule to agree w[t] workmen so as not to have the trouble of feeding them, for in some cases if they know off no imploy[t] elsewhere they prolong the work for the benefit of having ther meat bound to their mouth, yet such as thes painters and the more ingenious sort of craftsmen coming from places at a distance, ther is a necessity of being liberall that way; and ev'ne of masons and wrights wher a man has much adoe, it is expedient to have a headsman over the rest who must also have something of this nature done to them. Tho. ev'ne its frequently losed that is done that way, for they are apt enow to receive the favour w'out any rebatement of the pryce of ther work. And the only way not to be cheated is to have no work.'

The ordinary work of the farm was at that time accomplished partly by oxen and partly by horses. Though breeding was not then so thoroughly understood as now, Lord Strathmore was ahead of some of his contemporaries in this respect, and his cattle account on page 63 is a suggestive one. He had then a hundred oxen, besides cows and young cattle, several of the oxen being utilised in the plough. Some idea of the price of horses is afforded by the later entries in the *Book of Record*, from which it appears that a dun gelding for riding cost £18, a saddle horse cost £2 sterling, and a cart horse £3 sterling.

The value of grain during the years 1684 to 1689 may be ascertained from the entries referring to sales made by Lord Strathmore. Oats ranged at from £3 to £4 per boll. Bear (barley) was sold at from £4 to £5, 6s. 8d. per boll, the latter price being charged for home grain sold to the brewers at Glamis. In dealing with the Glamis brewers, his Lordship had a peculiar custom for which it is difficult to account, and which he thus refers to :—'I usually sell a quantity of bear more or less to my own brewars everie year at 13 sh. 4d. of the boll att least more than the current rate, . . . the price accorded on with those in and about the toune of Glammiss is five pond six shill. eight pennies per boll, and those few of them who paid readiest money hes 13 sh. 8d. of ease in the boll wch is yet six shilling eight pennies more then the current pryce in common mercats.' The price of meal does not vary throughout the period covered by the *Book of Record*, being quoted at £4 per boll. Wheat rules at £6 per boll, though on one occasion, after a scanty crop, Lord Strathmore sold 200 bolls in Glasgow at £8, 6s. 8d. per boll. Taking these prices as the current rates in the markets of the time, we may easily calculate the stipend of the minister of Longforgan as detailed in the *Book of Record.* It was as follows:—5 bolls wheat, 46 bolls bear, and 44 bolls oats, which would amount in money value to nearly £350.

The rent roll of Lord Strathmore as given on pages 46-49 may be thus summarised:—

The Narrow Circle of Glamis.

260 bolls bear.
160 bolls meal.
£1160 money.

David Lyon's Factorage at Glamis.

800 bolls meal.
£2666, 13s. 4d. money.

Tannadyce.

253 bolls bear.
394 bolls meal.
£2240 money.
Yarn and poultry.

Little Blair.

20 bolls bear.
44 bolls meal.
16 bolls, 2 firlots oats.
£784, 18s. money.

Auchterhouse.

127 bolls bear.
160 bolls meal.
£3569, 17s. 4d. money.

Lordship of Lyon.

276 bolls wheat.
225 bolls bear.
62 bolls oats.
230 bolls meal.

36 bolls peas.
£1200 money.

Kinghorn.

176 bolls 3 firlots bear.
7 bolls meal.
15 bolls oats.
£403, 13s. 2d. money.

Malthouse at Glamis.

Annual rent, £33, 6s. 8d.

It is worthy of notice, that in this rent roll the greatest variety of grain is obtained from the fertile fields in the Carse of Gowrie. In connection with this subject, attention may be directed to the remark which the author makes on page 17 with reference to the valuation of property for purposes of taxation. His father seems to have left the management of his affairs very much in the hands of his servants, and they, through vanity, thinking thereby to increase the importance of their master, entered the valuation of his rental much above the real sum. The result proved disastrous to Lord Strathmore, for as the taxes increased, and were exacted upon an overstated rental, he had to pay a sum out of proportion to that contributed by his neighbours.

Many curious items of information are to be gathered from the *Book of Record*. In the matter of forestry, Lord Strathmore was in advance of his time. On page 32, he gives prudent advice as to the planting of new timber, both for decorative purposes and as a source of income. He calculates that the timber planted in his time at Castle Lyon would come to be worth from £6 to £12 per tree, 'but reckoning them all but att three pond the piece will aryse to a sowme exceeding the worth of the heretage of ane equal yearlie rent to it.' Alluding to the ground at Glamis Castle, he writes about 'the old chattered and decayed trees wch surrounded the house, yet there were not many, and the most of these that were, were to the southward, a comon mistake of our ancestors, whereas reasonably any thickets or planting that are about any man's house ought rather to be upon the north, northeast, and northwest.' His reformation in the plantations at Glamis did not meet with the approval of the 'commons who have a naturall aversione to all maner of planting, and when young timber is sett be sure they doe not faill in the night time to cut even att the root the prettiest and straightest tree's for stav's or plough goads.'

Amongst the miscellaneous items of information the following may be referred to. A tun of French wine cost £312. Taking the tun as equal to four hogsheads, or 252 gallons, this would make the price of it a little over £1, 4s. 8d. per gallon. On the occasion of the marriage of his niece to the son of Lord Tarbet, Lord Strathmore paid £66, 13s. 4d. for 'a parsell of dry sweetmeats,' which are distinguished from the 'wet sweetmeatts' that Lady Strathmore had in her store-room. There is some caustic humour in the remark he makes as to the account rendered by a Dundee apothecary. 'I have payed Robert Stratone, the apothecary, his acct. of 123 lib., which is long owing, and such accts. are ridiculous, and I pray God help them who have occassione to be much in there books, since ther drogs and pastiles are sett doune under such strange names and unknown marks that they cannot be weell controlled.' On page 95, where Lord Strathmore alludes to his purchase of silver-plate that had belonged to the Earl of Perth, he quotes the current value of silver at £3, 4s. per ounce, to which he adds 6s. per ounce on condition that the Perth crest is removed and the Strathmore crest engraved in its place. On the same page he notes the price which he paid for a cabinet for his 'fyne bed-chamber,' a large looking-glass for the dining-room, a table, and two glasses, all of which cost £80 sterling. Wheels for stone-carts, which were strangely enough purchased in St. Andrews, cost £4 the set. For 100 deals purchased from a Dundee timber merchant 'for the use of the church' he paid £38, and 30 twelve-ell trees used for building purposes were charged £1 each. The price of coal brought by water to the Burnmouth of Invergowrie for the supply of Castle Lyon is quoted at £26, 13s. 4d. per chalder, equal to £1, 13s. 4d. per boll. The Book will well repay the careful consideration of every one interested in the social life of Scotland two hundred years ago.

Contract for Artistic Work at Glamis Castle.

The refined taste of Lord Strathmore led him to make provision for the internal decoration of Glamis Castle after he had completed the alterations on the exterior. For this purpose he employed the Dutch artist Jacob de Wet, who had come to this country with his fellow-countryman, Jan Van Santvoort, the carver, for the purpose of executing some of the ornamental work at Holyrood Palace. It is not easy to tell the precise nature of the work which Santvoort did at Glamis, but it probably consisted of some of the carved chimney-pieces, and the picture frames which were made whilst he was at the Castle, and it is likely that the stone carving of the Royal Arms and the bust of Patrick, first Earl of Kinghorne, which is placed in a niche over the main door, were executed by him. On 23d February, 1684, there was 'paid to the Dutch carver, Jan Van Sant Voort,' the sum of £394, and it is very likely that for such an amount he had also carved the two life-sized gladiators and the satyrs and lions which adorn the two principal gates. The work of De Wet at Holyrood was begun in 1674, and was somewhat miscellaneous in character. Sometimes he was employed painting chimney-pieces in marble colour, at other times depicting 'peices of historie' for the King's chamber, or designing the Coats-of-Arms for the stone-carvers. Tradition has vainly attempted to fix the odium of inventing the Holyrood 'Gallery of Kings' upon George

Jamesone of Aberdeen, but it is now indubitable that these 'paltry forgeries' were the productions of this Dutch artist. De Wet's work at Holyrood was completed in 1686, and the contract betwixt him and the Earl of Strathmore was dated 18th January, 1688. The details are precisely laid down, and De Wet undertook to execute the whole of the work for £90 sterling, one half 'to be payed at such times as he shall call or have occasione for it at any time during the work, provyding that before the payt. of the full half three pairts of foure of the whole work be done, and the oyr. equall half of the sowmes so agreed on shall be thankfullie payd at his finishing and perfecting the same.' He was also to have his bed and board at the Castle whilst employed on the work, although there was no time stated for its completion. The Earl was to prepare the roof of the Chapel and of the dining-room, and such panels of the side-walls as were to be decorated with pictures, and was also to provide oil-colours, cloth, and canvas, where these were required. Before the end of 1688, De Wet had received the whole sum included in his bargain, as the dorso of the original contract contains a full discharge for the £90 sterling, dated 17th November in that year. After this time, however, he sent in a detailed account, bringing up the sum claimed by him to £150, 3s. sterling, deducting therefrom £111, 2s. 2d., and leaving a balance due by the Earl of £39. This account, with the characteristic remarks of Lord Strathmore upon the various items, will be found on page 107. De Wet had not acted fairly by the Earl in the executing of the work he had undertaken. There was a certain William Rennie, a painter from Dundee, who was employed at Glamis and Castle Lyon in some of the coarser decorative painting, and the Dutch artist gave him some of his own artistic work to do, much to the Earl's dissatisfaction. Annoyed at thus being taken advantage of, Lord Strathmore entered into litigation with De Wet, and a protracted law plea was the result.

Whilst this case was in progress De Wet had injudiciously engaged in the stormy politics of the time, and naturally sided with his countryman the Prince of Orange. A violent anti-Orange demonstration took place in Edinburgh, and De Wet was seized by the mob, and suffered severely at their hands. With noble magnanimity Lord Strathmore, though an ardent Royalist of the most pronounced type, came to the rescue of his hapless artist, and offered shelter to him and his daughter at Glamis Castle. His kindness in this respect was ill requited, for it was after this event that De Wet endeavoured to extort a large sum beyond his contract for the artistic work which he had executed. It is to this incident that the Earl refers (page 108), when he writes that he 'wishes w^t all his heart that Mr. d'Vit had made as good and profitable acct. of his tyme ever since as he did for the short tyme he was w^t the Earle of Strathmore.' No note has been found to show exactly how the disputed account was settled, but it seems probable that the very generous offer of Lord Strathmore would be accepted by the artist.

Of De Wet's work at Glamis a considerable portion still remains, although some of the portraits have been lost. The decoration of the Chapel, which was the part of the contract most interesting to Lord Strathmore, is in the same condition as he left it. The chapel is an oblong apartment, about thirty feet long by eighteen feet wide, with a raised dais at the east end on which the altar has been erected. The walls and roof are divided into oblong panels which are filled in with the pictures painted by De Wet. The subjects are full-length pictures of the Saviour, St. John, St. Matthias, St. Simeon, St. Matthew, St. James, major, St. Philip, St. James, minor, St. Thomas, St. Andrew, and St. Peter, together with pictures of the Last Supper, the Resurrection, the Nativity, and Mary in the Garden. The fifteen panels in the ceiling are thus arranged—

Shepherds of Bethlehem.
Nativity.
Angel and Joseph.
Flight into Egypt.
The Baptism.
Temptation.
Peter walking on the Sea.
The Woman taken in Adultery.
The Transfiguration.
The Syro-Phœnician Woman.
Entry to Jerusalem.
Gethsemane.
The Kiss of Judas.
The Scourging.
Bearing the Cross.

These have all been reproduced from the engravings in an old Bible still preserved at Glamis Castle. The decorations in the dining-room and hall have disappeared, and the portraits of King Charles the Martyr, St. Paul, and St. Stephen, which were to have been placed in the room off the chapel are no longer there. The chapel was erected by Lord Strathmore in 1688, and was dedicated in that year, but as the record of the original consecration could not be found, it was re-dedicated in 1865 to St. Michael and All Angels.

The estimate for the repairing of the organ at Glamis is especially interesting, as showing the range and combinations used by organ-builders two centuries ago. It is not known when this organ was brought to Glamis, nor when it was removed, but there is now no trace of it in the Castle. From the specification by James Bristowe it appears that it was a ten-stop manual organ very highly set, and limited so far as combinations were concerned. The largest wooden pipe would not exceed eight feet, and as the Thirteenth, which is now very rarely used, was included amongst the stops, the tone of the instrument would be very shrill and piercing. The sixth stop in the specification is described as 'Fifteenth Trible,' but this is probably a mistake for 'Nineteenth Trible' to correspond with the Nineteenth Bass; or otherwise it may have anticipated some of the later compound stops, in which there are two Fifteenths in the treble, with a Tierce or Tirza making the Seventeenth. The terms of the estimate suggest that this had been an old organ which Lord Strathmore had purchased, and which James Bristowe was prepared to put in order for the very moderate sum of thirty pounds sterling. The new stops which he was to make for this purpose amounted to more than one-half of those originally there, whilst the mechanism of both bellows and manual was to be renewed. The name of Bristowe does not appear amongst the eminent English organ-builders of the time, and no clew is given as to his place of residence. The great English organ-builders at that period were Bernard Schmidt (known as Father Smith), and Renatus Harris his rival, the former having come from Germany and the latter from France. Shortly before that time George Leslie, a Scottish organ-builder, erected the great organ in the church of St. Godard at Rouen, but the feeling against the use of the organ in public worship which was prevalent in this country had brought the instrument into disrepute. It is not likely that there was any similar instrument in the east of Scotland employed in the celebration of divine service besides this one in the private chapel at Glamis Castle.

The organ in the Chapel-Royal at Holyrood was repaired by order of James VI. in 1617, and doubtless it was the only instrument of the kind used at that time. At the coronation of Charles I., at Holyrood in 1633, this organ was in operation, much against the will of the Presbyterian party. The famous Assembly of 1638, which was held at Glasgow, abolished Episcopacy, and apparently the question of the use of the organ was under discussion, as the King was consulted on this matter by Lord High Commissioner Hamilton. In his reply Charles wrote: 'For the organs in the chapel, we leave them to your discretion when to be used.' In this year, however, the Presbyterians rose in revolt against instrumental music, and Spalding records in his *Memorialls of the Trubles in Scotland* that in 1638 'the glorious organs of the Chapel-Royal are masterfully broken down, nor no service used these, but the whole chaplains, choristers, and musicians discharged, and the costly organs altogether destroyed and unuseful.' In Dalyell's *Musical Memoirs of Scotland* the following notice occurs:—

'At a meeting of the Kirk-session of the parish of Holyrood in the year 1643, the matter being motioned concerning that organ which was taken down and put into the aisle, now lying idle, rotting and consuming; yea, moreover, the same being an unprofitable instrument, scandalous to our profession, whether the same might not be sold for a tolerable price and the money given to the poor. The session agreed that this would be expedient, but postponed the matter.' There is no further record of the fate of this instrument. Is it not possible that the instrument at Glamis was the veritable 'organes' from Holyrood? The theory is not incredible, especially when it is remembered how intimate was the connection of Lord Strathmore with Holyrood. He had employed James Bain, His Majesty's Master of Works there, to begin the alterations at Glamis; and the painter De Wet and the carver Santvoort had both gone from Holyrood to decorate his Forfarshire castle. Apparently the Kirk-session would be very willing to dispose of this dilapidated instrument on easy terms, and it would have a special attraction for such an ardent Royalist as the Earl of Strathmore. It is right to state that no documentary proof of this theory has been found, and it is merely put forward as a suggestion.

BOOK OF RECORD, Etc.

I

BOOK OF RECORD OF PATRICK EARL OF STRATHMORE

My Eldest sons bill.

I SENT a bill to my sone for on thousand thrie hunder and thirtie thrie pond six shi. eight penies. The on halfe of the money was raised by the effects of my compting with my tenents for the croft 1682. The other halfe was by the seal of bear cropt '83 at 4 lib 6/8 per bol.

Mr Ranken's @ rent.

I ordered the payment of two hunder pond as a years @ rent to Mr. Ranken[1] Catechist in Dundee q^h I owe by thrie thousand thrie hunder and thirtie thrie pond six shillings eight penies of stock mortefied by Mr. Pat. Yeaman to him and his successors bearing office as Catechist in Dundee.

I sold two hunder boll bear cropt '83 to the brewers in *fol. 2.* Dundee of the q^{ch} number there are fiftie bolls ordered to be delyvered out of the paroch of Glammiss, the like number out of Airlie, the third equal part out of Auchterhouse and the fourth out of Castle Lyon @ 4 lib. 6 sh. 8d pr boll readie money.

Brewars of Glammiss.

I sold about the lyke number of bols of the bear of the paroch of Glammiss to the brewars in the churchtoune @ 5 lib. 6 sh. 8d. pr boll payable at Whit: Lam: and Mert: be equal portions.

New tack to Ouer Yeards.

I gave a new tack to pa: Smith in Oueryeards of the said toune and lands for the payment of ten bols wheat ten bols bear ten bols oats and ten bols meal which is thrie bols of augmentation of the rental.

5th day.

I obtained from Frederick Lyon[2] ane assignement to Mr John Lambie[3] of Dunkennie's bond for four hundred ponds

[1] These figures in the text refer to the Notes at the end of the volume.

with the bygone @ rents thereof which with other of his bonds I have right to and other provisione I intend to make use of for paying him four thousand a hunder and thirtie thrie pond six shill: eight penies of privatt which I owe to him with bygone @ rents since Wittsonday '82.

Strathmartine and Dunkenny's thrie bonds assigned. I have also obtained ane assignement from ffrederick Lyon to the Laird of Strathmartine's[4] band for sixtie six ponds thirteen shill. four penies with its bygone @ rent which with other debts that I am Master of I designe to applie for the payement of twelve hunder pond q^h I owe to him and @ rents since Witt: -83 and this is remainder of the pryce of the lands of Pettpoyntie which I purchased from him.

fol. 3. Frederick Lyon. I gave bond to Frederick Lyon for a thousand thrie hunder and thirtie thrie ponds six shill. and eight penies, this sowme is made up pairtly be ane old debt q^h I owed him pairtlie by a debt of Bridgeton's whereto I am assigned by him and pairtly by those mentioned in the last two particlers of the other syde.

Alex^r Cram. I compted with Alex^r Cram, Mosend and have gott from him a clear receit of what payments are made to him preceeding Mertimas '83. All contained in a paper which lyes in my chamber below Together with the agreements I made with him for his work till the same be compleite.

8th Day. Major Stewart. I receaved from Major James Stewart's sone sixtie pond thirteen shill. four penies in part of pay^t of a smal debt of his assigned to me be Mr Tho: Wilsone and have gott his son's band of corroboratione for the remainder.

10th Day. Wins in the year 83 payed. I hawe sent James Elder doune to the M^r of Kinnaird[5] with compleit pay^t for a tunn of ffrench wine q^h I had from George his brother in the yeare -83 att thrie hunder and twelve pond the tunn with the deductione of the customes [in another hand] (James Divlan).

Whyt Wals compts cleared. Haveing the last moneth fitted and cleared w^t David Lyon of Wheat Wal The accompts of his intromissions with my rents at Tannadyce, The ffermes of Killemwire and oyr. places adjacent for the cropts '80 '81 and '82 I have taken bond from such of the tenents as were resting any bygone dewties, and have received payment from some of them all readie.

fol. 4. James Lyon[6] sometime Littster in Dundee having married to his wyfe Elspet the daughter of Donald Thorntene of Babenie and had four hunder pond of toucher promitted to him which he was altogether froustrat of and the said James his trade failing was reduced to great want quh moved me to run a hazard for him and to accept of ane assignement to the mony promitted by the said contract of marriag, and in liew thereof I have granted for his better subsistance ane oblidgement for payt of four bols. bear and four bols. meal to Mr Patrick Lyon,[7] minister of Rescobie, his brother, for his behove, it being safer in his name then in his owne. The payt of qch is of continuance for all the dayes of the said James Lyon his life and his wyfes the langest liver of them two. 11th day of January. Minr of Rescobie.

Memous Guthrie was resting to me thrie hunder and thirtie thrie pond. six shill: and eight penies by bond qch is this day payed by Wm Lyon of Easter Ogill and the bond is assigned by me in favour of a blank persone for his reliefe and John Lyon's fiar of Whytwall who has payed the bygane @ rents thereof by giving me signet for 96 lib. 13 sh. and 8d. payable on demand. 12th day. Memous Guthrie.

I was owing to Easter Ogill a thousand ponds with some bygane @ rents which is this day cancelled and I have given a new bond for six hunder and sixtene ponds thirteen shillings four penies bearing @ rent from Mert. last. Easter Ogill.

The Earle of Airlie[8] as having right from his daughter My Lady Couper now Lady Lendors[9] for certain soes of money upon the accompt of the augmentation of the minister's Stipend of the Church of Essie out of the lands of Castletoune of Inglishtoun disponed by the Earle of Buchan to the Lord Couper whereby the said lands was sold wt warrandice to be free of all augmentatione so occurring upon the warrandice it is certainly a burden qh affects the lands of Auchterhouse so that I must take course therewith provyding the Earl of Airlie show ane unquestionable right thereto since it may be doubted but that the Lord Balmerinoch who falls in right to that estate after the deceas of the Lady Lendors may have a better right to the same, but taking it as granted that the Earle of Airlie has right thereto qch yett must be further tryed. I resolved and with his owne consent I took a right from James Weems to 15 Day. Earle of Airlie. *fol.* 5.

two bonds of his for thrie thousand and two hunder pond, and two hunder and nynteine pond seven shill; two pennies of bygone @ rents, preceeding Witt: 1681 thereby to compense the Earle of Airlie's clame being unwilling to be addebter to him. In the meantime The Earle of Airlie being slow in business I am to look after the pay[t] of the @ rent out of the lands wherein James Weems, my author, had infeftment of Coddam and Polgavie.

I was also assigned be James Weems to eighteen hunder ponds or thereby resting to him be the Laird of Strathmartine which I applyed as a part of the pryce of the lands of Pitpoyntie q[ch] I latlie acquyred from him.

James Weems. And now after compt made with James Weems I find myselfe debiter to him in four thousand ponds q[ch] I gave new bond for payable att Witt: 1685 w[t] a years @ rent.

The said James Weems is taksman of the halfe of the Mains of Auchterhouse and hes by the tack allenarlie to retaine his current @ rent in firstend of his dewtie, and by the fitted accompt betwixt us is dischairged of his dewtie cropt 82 and 83, and he hes gott a proceys for a hunder and eighteen ponds payable by Tho: Hill in the bonytoun which was the just ballance due to him by the other accompt besydes the 4000 lib. for q[ch] I gave band so that the retentione of his @ rent is out of the duty excepting for paying the @ rent till Witt:

fol. 6. The minister of fforgan having departed this life in October 1683. The stipend payable out of my lands of the Lordship of Lyon being five bols. wheat, fourtie six bols. bear and fourtie four bols. of oats falls due to his executor M[r]. Alex[r]. Leslie[10] Minr, at Siris in ffyfe who married his sister. So I have this day bought the fornamed bols. and have gotten his discharge the wheat at 6 lib. pr. bol. the bear at 4 lib. per bol. the oats at 3 lib. and have given John Lyon provisione for the payment thereof, and his own bond mentioned on the fourth page of this book in the first end thereof. The rest of the provisione are bonds q[ch] I took when I fitted David Lyon of Whytwalls accompts crop 82 of Tannadyce and the fforiest so many of these bonds q[ch] I gott at that time from tenents who were resting to me mony according to the conclusione of the

M[r]. Leslie, Min[r]. att Siris.

said fitted accompt as well make up to John Lyon together with his own bond the soume of thrie hunder and fourtie sex ponds being the just pryce of the victual of the stipend q[ch] I bought and were all acceptable to the said John Lyon for enabling him to undertake the payment. The on halfe att Candlemas and the other att Wittsunday nixt to Mr. Leslie.

I compted with Alex[r]. Craw measone for his receit in the yeare 1683 but in regard the work is not finished the compt lyes till the same be done in a bundle with the contracts past betwixt him and me in my compting rowme as before noted. Lykeas I compted with the other four working masons att Glammiss whos staited accompt is their also but that of the messings payed off. 21 Day. Alex. Craw and the rest of the measons at Glammiss.

I have given a factorie to Robert Ogilvy of Glencallie to uplift the rents of Tannadyce and other my lands lying there abouts, with a paper apairt for his sallarie and such exact rentals taken up by concessione | of the tenants before him and diligently compared with the former rentalls I have also given him a warrand as for all for the payeing the yearlie @ rents to the creditors aftermentioned. 23 Day. *fol. 7.*

To witt first the sowme of 400 lib. as the @ rent of the prin[ll]. sowme of 6666 lib. 13 sh. 4d. due to the Laird of Rattra. @ rents to be payed be Glencallie.

More 120 lib. @ rent of the pr[ll]. sowme of 2000 lib. due to the Laird of Clunie.

More 80 lib. @ rent of the prin[ll]. sowme of 1333 lib. 6sh. 8d. due to Mr. Campbell,[11] minister at Menmure.

More thrie hunder pond @ rent of the prin[ll] sowme of 5000 lib. due to Provest Couts.

More the @ rent and prin[ll]. sowme of five hunder pond or theirby due to Provest Watsone in Dundee.

More the @ rent of 36 lib. of the prin[ll]. sowme of 600 lib. due to Lindsay of Glenquich.

More 56 lib. @ rent of 933 lib. 6sh. 8d. due to Robert Lindsay.

More 90 lib. @ rent of 666 lib. 13sh. 4d. due to the Laird of Easter Ogill.

More 64 lib. as the @ rent of 1066 lib. 13sh. 4d. due to Mr. Balvaird, Minr at Kirkden.

More 30 lib. as the @ rent of 500 lib. due to Thomas Clepan.

More 120 lib. @ rent of 2000 lib. due to Mr. Patrick Strachan,[13] Minr att St. Vigeanes.

More 80 lib. @ rent of 1333 lib. 6sh. 8d., due to Comissar Strachan.

More there is an annuity of 28 lib. yearlie to Andrew Cardean in Baldukie his wyfe for q^{ch} I have my releife of the equivalent from the Laird of Logie Ogilvy.

fol. 8. I have conforme to act of $parl^t$ warranding the heretor to tax those who live within their lands for the releife of the current supplie layed on this impositione upon the whole inhabitants of Glammiss and other places adjacent within the divisione of Wm. Nicol officier conforme to the stent roll given him q^{ch} he is to collect with all diligence and the compt for q^{ch} extends to the sowme of [*blank*].

The tax of Tannadyce and thereabout.

I have also tax'd the indwellers of and upon the lands of Tannadyce and others places thereto adjacent which is within Ro^t Ogilvy of Glencallies factorie and hes committed the collection thereof to David Rickart, ground officer, extending to the sowme of [*blank*].

25 Day.

Bond given by By Lewnay for 533 lib. 6s. 8d.

A generall discharge given to him.

I have after communing with Thomas Brown of Lewnay sometime my factor about Glammiss settled and agried with him about the additional charge which I gave to him this was provyded by the conclusione of his last compt cropt 1679. In caise of any error or omissione competent to be challenged be either of us that the same might have place within a twelve month efter the concluding of these accompts in caise it were given in w^t in that time q^{ch} accordingly wes done but nothing followed upon it till now that after all he was glad content to give me a bond for five hunder threttie thrie ponds six shill. and eight penies payable att Wittsunday nixt whereupon he hes gott a full and ample discharge but with this reserve there being bear delyvered out of my own lofts to the brewars of Glams and others within the years of his factorie with the money whereof he was supposed to have intromitted but by a discharge which he hes obtained on way or other from James *fol.* 9. Elder then grinter he alledges | that the effects of that bear so delyvered out of the lofts was within his province to have uplifted and that if he, the said Thomas Brown received any pairt thereof from the Brewers of Glammiss or others to whom it was sold be compted to the said James Elder for it and upon his general discharge ffor clearing of q^{ch} there is a process aggried upon to be intented before the Sherrif of fforfar that either the on or the other may be comptable upon the event of the actione. It being verie just that I sould have the returne and pryce of my own bear delyvered out of my Lofts, and that the brewars and others hes payed it it's most certaine and that the subterfuge in either the on or the other is most false and deceitfull. Perhaps both upon on acc^{t} or other are verie blamefull in it for q^{ch} causes I am resolved for the slowthfullness of the on by whom I suffered great prejudice in his service suffering tenents to run on in heavie and shamfull rests and to goe away in the yeare of their displenishing without payment of anything and many other gross mismanagements too tedious here to enumerate and for the other his litle tricks and underhand wayes having suffered abuses not ofen tho. not of so great value that ay never to trust further then what either of them at any time may by chance be employed in q^{ch} at night they must give ane accompt of wherein for a dayes service there can be very litle damnage don especially if a man be cautious which the former prejudices I have sustained cannot but render me, and I have a good many years of James Elders compts yet [to] canvass which must be done the more narrowly since justly I have jealousie of him.

But with a reserve of the pryce of such bear as was delyvered out of my owne Lofts.

James Elders accts yet to be taken in.

I have in lyke maner gottine a bond from James Elder anent the bear delyvered out of the lofts that in caise he should succumb in the actione betwixt him and Thomas Brown of Lewnay in that caise he must be lyable for the pryce of these bolls.

I have also made the Tax Roll for the lands and inhabitants of the paroch of Nether Airlie and Killemwre within the division of Alex^{r} Reid officer who is to collect the same and q^{ch} does extend to the sowme of [*blank*].

Tax Roll w^{t}in the division of Alex^{r} Reid officer.

fol. 10.

26 Day.

I have given a factorie to David Lyon the grinter at Glammiss to be factor for the wyder circle of the Lordship as Lykewayes to continue grinter conforme to the particular table rentalls signed and delyvered to him for the cropt 1683

David Lyon his factorie of the Lordship of Glammiss.

I have also committed to him the payment of such @ rents yearlie of the prin[lle] sowmes oweing to the persones after-named To witt.

A List of @ rents to be payed by him yearlie.

To David Crightoune in Kookston 80 lib. as the @ rent of 1333 lib. 6 sh. 8d. due to him.

To the childreine of Mr. James Crighton 240 lib. as @ rent of 4000 lib. due to them.

To Patrik Crightone in Breadstone 40 lib. as the @ rent of 666 lib. 13 sh. 4d. due to him.

To Alex[r] Hood in Reidie 40 lib. as the @ rent of 666 lib. 13 sh. 4d. due to him.

To James Bennie in Balmukety about 40 lib. as the @ rent of 666 lib. 13 sh. 4d.

To the Catechist in Dundee for the time 200 lib. as the @ rent of 3333 lib. 6 sh. 8d.

To Helen Symmer and her son in Dundee 200 lib. as the @ rent of 3333 lib. 6 sh. 8d.

To Katteren and Marie Pilmore 144 lib. as y[r] @ rent of 2400 lib.

To Henrie Craford of Easter Seton 120 lib. as the @ rent of 2000 lib.

To Rodgeres Mortefication 80 lib. as the @ rent of 1333 lib. 6 sh. and 8d.

To the Laird of Craigie 160 lib. as the @ rent of 2666: 13: 4d.

This debt is payed [in writing of L[d] Strathmore].

To the Laird of Nevay 240 lib. as the @ rent of 4000 lib.

To M[r] John Lambie of Dunkennie 248 lib. as the @ rent of 4133 lib. 6 sh. 8d.

To the Bishop of Dunblane[14] 160 lib. as the @ rent of 2666, 13 8d.

fol. 11.

To Thomas Blair 160 lib. as the @ rent of 2666 lib. 13 sh. 8d. and

He ordained at his death this bond to be given up [note in L. Strathmore's writing].

To Frederick Lyon 80 lib. as the @ rent of 1333 lib. 6 sh. 8d.

I am also to establish [blank] my factor att Auchterhouse who is to have a clear table rental, and he is to satisfie and pay yearlie the @ rents aftermentioned to the rex[ive] creditors to witt.

To the Countess of Buchan[15] dureing her lyftyme and to my Lord Buchan's assignay the prin[lle] of 7333 lib. 6s. 8d. the @ rent of q[ch] being 440 lib. is payed to her duety at Wittsunday and Mertimess and the first term that is due is Witt. next 1684.

To James Read in Auchterhouse 400 lib. as the @ rent of 6666 lib. 13s. 4d.

To James Weems there, 240 lib. as the @ rent of 4000 lib.

To Duncan [16] of Lundie 240 lib. as the @ rent of 4000 lib.

To Cristian Young 40 lib. as the @ rent of 666 lib. 13. 4.

To the Churche Sessioun of Auchterhouse about 533 lib. 6 sh. 8d. prin^lle and 32 lib. @ rent yearlie.

To on Farmer who lives in the Cottoun 200 lib. and the @ rent thereof yeirlie is 12 lib.

The six immediatlie above named at least five of them are the more easily payed that they have localities for their @ rents.

To Mr John Cambell of Denhead 160 lib. as the @ rent of 2666 lib. 13 sh. 8d.

To John Duncan, merchant in Dundee 200 lib. as the @ rent of 3333 lib. 6 sh. 8d. I owe him only 2000 heirof.

To the Earle of Panmure [17] 138 lib. as the @ rent of 2300.

To Mr Nathaniel ffyfe in Perth 240 lib. as the @ rent of 4000 lib.

To Mr Patrick Lyon [18] of Carnustie, advocat 120 lib. as the @ rent of 2000 lib.

To Mrs Hay in Perth 120 lib. as the @ rent of 2000 lib. *fol. 12.*

James Couper continues factor of Litle Blair and the feu duties and other rents payable thereabout conforme to his particular table rentall. James Couper factor for Litle Blair.

He is to pay out of his intromissiounes the @ rents of the debts after named to witt.

To the airis of James Crightone portioner of Couper Grange 560 lib. as the @ rent of 9333 lib. 6 sh. 8d. prin^ll.

To William Geeky of Baldowrie 120 lib. as the @ rent of 2000 lib. prin^ll.

To the Minister of Ketns [19] 40 lib. as the @ rent of 666 lib. 13 sh. 8d. prin^ll.

This Alexander Swin hes only his compts for the cropt 82 to clear and adjust. Alexander Swin factor att Kinghorn.

He hes the @ rents after mentioned to pay to the creditors particularly sett downe out of the inst. jm vi^c and eightie thrie.

List of @ rents to payed by him.

To Andrew Brown, merchant in Eden, 480 lib. as the @ rent of 3000 prin[ll].

To Bail. Reid in Eden. 240 lib as the @ rent of 4000 lib.

To Doctor Edward,[20] minister at Cryl 240 lib. as the @ rent of 4000 lib.

To Adam ffirnell, wreitter in Eden. 120 lib. as the @ rent of 2000 lib.

To John Whytt of [*blank*] besyde Kercadie about 100 lib. sterlin the @ rent of q[ch] is 72 lib.

Castle Lyon and the Narrie Circle of Glamis in my hand.

ffolloweth the List and accompt of such @ rents as I am determined to take course with yeirlie myselfe having reserved it into my own hands without any factor, my estate att Castle Lyon as Lykewayes such pairts of the Lordship of Glammiss as lye the nearest to the house which lands will pairtly by process of time be inclosed within the park in the way and maner as it *fol.* 13. is desyned to surround the house or does in some place or other touch the park wall and is commonly called the Narrow Circle. The managment hereof by myselfe was but undertakne some two years agoe—att the outtgoing of Thomas Browne my factor here att that time, but that att Castle Lyon hes continued no less then these twentie years and is a good and certaine rent albeit att my first entrie they were generally ill payers which indeed was not the fault of the Land but the Tenendrie their att that time were a race of evill doers desolate fellowes and mislabourers of the ground.

The @ rents to be payed yeirlie be myselfe.

A List of @ rents reserved to be payed by my owne care as is before said.

To M[r] Nicolson[21] minister at Erroll 80 lib. as @ rent of 1333 lib. 6 sh. 8d.

To the Laird of Leyes 80 lib. as the @ rent of 1333 lib. 6 sh. 8d.

To the minister of Inshture[22] 40 lib. as the @ rent of 666 lib. 13s. 4d.

To M[r] James Auchinleck's aires 240 lib. as the @ rent of 4000 lib.

To Andrew Dal tylour in Dundee 40 lib. as the @ rent of 666 lib. 13s. 4d.

To Sir James St. Clare of Kinnaird 360 lib. as the @ rent of 6000 lib.

To the minister of Newburn's aires 44 lib. as the @ rent of 733 lib. 6s. 8d.

To the aires of on Bonner in ffyfe 160 lib. as the @ rent of 2666 lib. 13s. 4d.

To Craigmillar[23] besyd his old sowme for q[ch] there was provision made by money in Merchants hands 180 lib. as the @ rent of 3000 lib. near payed [L[d] S.]

To my Lord Carse[24] about 240 lib. as the @ rent of 4000 lib. prin[lle] or thereby. The lands of Quilco desponed to him [L[d] S.]

To Sir James Rochhead[25] 240 lib. as the @ rent of 4000 lib. *fol. 14.*

To Hugh Wallace Cash Keeper 240 lib. as the @ rent of 4000 lib.

To M[r] Thomas Gordon about 180 lib. as the @ rent of 3000 lib. prin[ll] or thereby.

To M[r] Thomas Lermont about 240 lib. as the @ rent of 4000 lib. prin[ll] or thereabout.

To the Assigneyes of Bailzie Calderwood 160 lib. as the @ rent of 2666 lib. 13s. 4d.

To Sir John Maitland[26] 80 lib. as the @ rent of 1333 lib. 6 sh. 8d. payed [L[d] S.]

To the Tutor of on Lawder 80 lib. @ rent of 1333 lib. 6s. 8d.

To the relict of M[r] pa. Hay 20 lib. as the @ rent of 333 lib. 6 sh. 8d.

To Gourdie Kinloch[27] 40 lib. as the @ rent of 666 lib. 13s. 8d.

If there be any other debts its lyke they may be verie inconsiderable and for compts there are verie few it never having been my custome to let them run on to any hight.

There is indeed resting a considerable debt to some Inglish factors, but there is equal provisione to ballance it in the hands of Sir W[m] Sharp.

There is another debt due to Craigmillar and provisione for the payment of it.

The Laird of ffindourie[28] hes a Wadsett of Marquess and Milne thereof and Moorhillock, but the rent of the Wadsett lands is not in the factors rentall except only the superplus dutie so the on is at least as good if not better then the other. The sowme whereupon the Wadsett is redeemable is 5700 lib. Sicklyk M[r] David Lindsay has a wadsett redeemable for thrie thousand pond, and Mitchell Gray of Turbeg for two thousand thrie hunder and thirtie thrie pond six shillings eight pennies. Wadsett Lands. *fol. 15.*

Now to make ane exact survey of all the before written debts both for my owne clearness and to satisfie posteritie if they read this book, here follows The sowmes of the whole principale debts before enumerat:

The Sowme of the whole debts before enumerat.

1. First Robert Ogilvy of Glencally his division comes to twentie two thousand a hunder sixtie six pond thirtaine shilling four pennies.

2. By the second committed to David Lyon there is Thirtie seven thousand and two hunder pond.

3. By the third committed to the care of the factor of Auchterhouse There is of principall sowmes Thirtie eight thousand nyn hundred and sixtie six pond thirtaine shilling four pennies.

4. By the fourth committed to James Couper there is for his share the @ rents of 12000 lib. twelve thousand pond.

5. By the fifth committed to the care of Alex[r] Swin factor att Kinghorne there is nyntene thousand thrie hunder and thirtie thrie pond six shilling eight pennies.

6. By the sixth and greatest reserved to my owne care there is @ rents answearing to the principale sowme of fourtie five thousand seven hunder and thirtie thrie pond six shilling eight pennies.

The Total of the debt.

The whole sowme of the debts before mentioned in these six severall divisions extends to on hundreth seventie five thousand and four hundred pond.

The @ rent of which sowmes is yeirlie ten thousand five hundred and twentie four pond.

fol. 16. Followes a List of debts payed and discharged pairtly by the effects of my estate and partlie by the fewing of Lands and the pryce of them since the year jm vi[c]. and seventie eight, att which time I made that inventar of my debts and creditors who's names and sowmes I find new crossed and which I am sure will never stand in judgement against me or mine.

Debts payed and the bonds returned.

Since Januarij 1678 compts with Drybrough are not yet

Payed to Clunie two thousand pond . .	02000 00 00
To M[r] John Croket six hunder and sixtie six pond, thirtaine shilling four pennies . .	00666 13 04
To Drybrough ten thousand pond . .	10000 00 00
To Alexander fforester six thousand six hunder	

and sixtie six pond thirtaine shilling four pennies . . . . . . 06666 13 04 cleared tho: they most be payed.

To Bailzie Watsone four thousand pond . 04000 00 00

To John Pilmore nyn hunder thirtie and thrie pond six shilling eight pennies q^ch^ was att that time the remainder of as many thousand pond q^ch^ I wes once oweing him *inde* . . 00933 06 00

To Provost Watsone in Dundee five hunder pond, but I was once owing to him twentie thousand pond the papers Whereof Lye and ane assignment to the securitie to a blank persone 00500 00 00

To ffodringham[29] of Bandean three thousand thrie hunder and thirtie thrie pond six shilling eight pennies *inde* 03333 06 08

To Easter Powrie two thousand pond . . 02000 00 00

To Kinnaber two thousand six hunder and sixtie six pond thirtaine shilling four pennies *inde* 02666 13 04

To Lindsay of Glenqueich thrie hunder and thirtie thrie pond six shilling eight pennies, but his grandfather had a Wedset of Litlecoul and Dirachie within the paroch of Tannadyce for ten thousand merks . . . 00333 06 08

To Robert Lindsay in Coul on thousand and sixtie six pond thirtaine shilling four d. . 1066 13 04 *fol.* 17.

To William Lyon of Easter Ogill thrie hunder and thirtie thrie pond six shillings eight besyde as much the last day recorded upon the fourth page of this book but I was owing his father ten thousand merks on a Wadsett in Tannadyce which I redeem'd *inde* . . 0333 06 08

To the Minister of Cyrus on thousand three hunder and thirtie three pond six shilling eight pennies There was lykewayes more owen to his father *inde* . . . 1333 06 08 A mistake for there was never owen to Mr Leslie but to the nixt.

To Mr Patrick Lyon, Advocat, six hunder sixtie six pond thirtaine shill: four pennies *inde* . 0666 13 04

To severall Tenents of the Earle of Panmure of

old Cars-gray's debts two thousand pond and upwards *inde* 2000 00 00

To Auchterlownie of Guynd,[30] twelve thousand pond, *inde* 12000 00 00

To Thomas Nairn a thousand pond . . 1000 00 00

To Captain Lyon two thousand pond but he had lykewayes a wedsett in Tannadyce which I redeem'd and I lykewayes bought from him the lands of Westhill for this was a debt of old Cars-grays *inde* 2000 00 00

To Thomas Clepen five hunder pond his father had lykewayes a considerable wedsett in Tannadyce q^{ch} was redeem'd *inde* . . . 0500 00 00

To Sir William Binning of Walingford and others the assigneys of the aire of the Earle of Bramford who evicted from me, and q^{ch} was a sore blow, money with the interest thereof which my father gott of his fine att the parliament at St. Androws for just debt then owing him be the publick this wes done in on of the Duke of Lauderdal's [31] parlia^{ts} and violentlie carried on as indeed it was thought that his brother the Lord Hatton went snips and had a share, the sowme of sixtaine thousand six hunder sixtie six pond thirtaine shilling four pennies *inde* . . . 16666 13 04

fol. 18. To Salton[32] three thousand pond *inde* . . 3000 00 00

To Trumble of Stracathrow on thousand six hunder pond *inde* 1600 00 00

To Andrew Crawford, Sherrifs clerk att Linlithgow on thousand two hunder pond *inde* . 1200 00 00

To Bannerman [33] of Elsick three thousand three hunder and thirtie thrie pond six shilling eight pennies *inde* 3333 06 08

To my Lord Ross [34] four thousand six hunder and sixtie six pond thirtaine shill. four pennies *inde* 4666 13 04

To Hunter of Burnsyde two thousand four hunder pond *inde* 2400 00 00

To the Earle of Linlithgow[35] on thousand three hunder and thirtie thrie pond six shilling eight pennies qch I borrowed from him qn I purchased some superiorities from the E. of Craford.[36] This noble Lord having married my mother, who dyed in October 1659, had such clampers and pretences against me as by advice of my curators I was induced to impignorat the lands of Cardean and the third pairt of Lenros to him for the sowme of fourtaine thousand six hunder and sixtie six pond, thirtain shill: four pennies, qch I payed soon after *inde* 1333 06 08

To Mr. John Lyon Sherrif clerk of fforfare on thousand three hunder and thirtie three pond six shill: eight pen: 1333 06 08

To Sir George Lockhart[37] two thousand pond, *inde* 2000 00 00

To Craigmiller five thousand pond and there must be on thousand six hunder and sixtie six pond thirtaine shill: four pen: yet made out to him to compleat that payement *inde* . . 5000 00 00

To James Wilsone three hunder and thirtie thrie pond six shill: eight pen: . . 0333 06 08

To Mr. Auchterlownie and Wm. Nicolson being a pairt of Cossens debt five hunder and thirtie three pond six shilling eight pennies as lykeways considerable soumes of money more of this miserable man's debt not here compted in regard that the greatest pairt of the debts qch exhaust that estate wes payet be me before the year of God 1678 inde . . . 0533 06 08 *fol.* 19.

To Mr. Cheesly[38] att Edenburgh a bas uncivil raskel on thousand two hunder pond *inde* . 1200 00 00

The Total of Debts payed since the year 1678.

The sowme of the payments since the yeare 1678 according to the debts before narrated extends to the sowme of nyntie nyn thousand eight hunder sixtie six pond thirtain shill: four pennies, ... 99866 13 04

I cannot forbeare here to informe the reader who perhaps may peruse these writings after I am gone that from this time of my fathers death who dyed in the month of May 1646 when I

[note in pencil. She married the Earl of Lithgow 30 July 1650.]

was four year old till the year 1660 when my mother dyed in the October before. The debt q^{ch} my father left behind him was, by inventars whereof some are yet extant no less then four hunder thousand ponds much of which debt was contracted by him for paying great sowmes of money for q^{ch} he engaged himselfe cautioner for relations and others which I have been told that after I was borne he repented him much of but could not help it. This debt still increasing The @ rents exceeding the rents of the unlyfrented lands in so much as the verie Mains of Glammis was wedsett and in effect litle or nothing there was in Angus of the estate he left behind him not possessed by on creditor or another except the lands of Bahelvie in Aberdeenshyre q^{ch} I sold to my uncle the E. of Panmure and thereby returned to the possession of many of my lands in Angus and by the money of my Toucher with a

fol. 20. pairt of q^{ch} I | redeem'd the Mains of Glamms and other Lands and payed off the E. of Linlithgow. I receaved lykewayes about twentie seven thousand pond out of the hands of the E. of Morton[39] for who's father and grandfather my father was att great Loss even to the value of a hunder thousand pond and had it not been that the E. of Morton married att that time a sister of my wife and daughter to the E. of Midlton[40] I cou'd never have gott any releife att all. This with the return of my mothers liferent lands brought me againe allmost after a total eclipse of this family to live but still with the misfortune even to this day of some inpervenient cautionerie or other which puts me back allmost as farr as I press forward. I must lykewayes remember that the familie and hous of Erroll in the persone of Gilbert who's mother was my father's sister which relatione is now lost by his dyeing without airs of his bodie was verie fatal to my familie for the E. of Erroll[41] being a child when his father dyed was keeped in my father's hous and by his being att S^t. Andrews q^n the plague first broke out, it pleased God by the infectione q^{ch} the E. of Erroll's governour was attact'd with sadly to visit this familie whereof my father dyed Besyds divers and sundrie debts there were which my father as tutor to the E. of Erroll gave his owne bond for which in justice I ought to be relieved of but dair not awake sleeping dogs There being more hazard in the event by accompt and reckoning as tutor (q^{ch} is the most hazardfull imployment in the world a tutor being lyable not only for commissions but ommissions and for q^{ch} cause it's advysable for no man that can shun it to be a tutor and which I my selfe have declined both in my cusan Bridgeton's children and in the case of my sister's children by the Earle of Aboyn[42]) then anything to be expected and evicted that way. Albeit the soumes I lye out of are verie considerable.

It wes lykways a great misfortune of my family that in my *fol. 21.*
minority and nonage my mother being a verie young woman married and it was verie excusable in her so to doe who in the time of her widdowhead managed the intricat effairs of this familie with great prudence but in the year 1650 after she was married and cloathed with a new husband he repeated back these debts which she had payed in her widdowhead with the effects of her lyferent Land. There being assignat^{ne} wes taken all alongs by her to such debts as she did pay which I haue out of respect and charitie to the memorie of my mother reasone to beleeve she did of no such designe tho. after my Lord Linlithgow wes master of these papers she could not help it, and that the true designe in her of so doeing wes only that in case I had dyed and having no other son to succeed me that she might have receaved from My uncle Bridgtone who was the next aire male of the familie these debts, however it fell out cross to what I presume she designed and many families there are besyde mine who are reduced to a verie low conditione and seme quyte extinct by exorbitant joynters.

Ane other great evill to this familie was that my father not being cautious enough nor forseeing the evill consequences of it when the valuat^{ones} in order to publick burdens were first made in the shyre, he for his whole estate was rather valued above his real rent then under. And indeed it was the fault of his servants whom he trusted over much who's vanity in behalfe of their Lord moved them to too liberall a condescensione when others his neighbours more cuningly made concealments even to the halfe and some under that. Yet this was the rule and there was no help for it, the | troubles of the countrie increased *fol. 22.*
and so did the publick burdens and all was laid on according to the value^{ne} So were the outreicks and Levies And this

cuntrie being then as without a head it was the Paster and prey of the souldiers—marching back and fore from South to North and the allowances given to the tenents for their losses for quartering were verie great. Morover in the year 1650 when my uncle Bridgtone efter my mother's marrieg came tutor in Law it was a great Loss to my affaires that he was a most simple tho. a weell meaning man. And albeit there were gross ommissions as weell as commissions in his tyme who dyed in the yeare 1660 yet such was the affectione and pitie which I had for his sons who, the on succeeding to the other, and both leaving wyfs behind them, and the first daughters and the second a daughter besyde his sone and the estate being so incumbered not only with the lyferents with the provisione of the daughters and debts left by the grandfather who managed his owne no better then mine in my minoritie, that I have still forborn nor will I resume any thing of those mismanagements against his grandchild my kinsman, but in the time of his tutorie there was a verie notable roug who heired a factor called John Smith who dyeing Lykewayes made it not so easie for me Yet I repeated something most justlie from him which
fol. 23. helped me in some things att | that time when I purchased the lands of Thorntone in the paroch of Glammiss. In the year 1660 at which time I came from scools and upon the verie day of his Majestie who now reigns his birth and restoration to his Kingdom the twentie nynt of May, upon q^{ch} day I have been told I was born Lykewayes my selfe, and stayed in Dundee all night and the nixt day I went out to Castle Lyon from which place my Lord Lithgow had removed some time before when I found nothing but bare walls and had not so much as on bed to ly doune in, for all was carried away by him in the right of my mother whom my father left his executrix. And the place of Glammiss, the ancient seat of my family was no better for all that time it was not altogithir purged of the Inglish garrison who tho. they spoyled and damnified the house and all about it verie much yet some of the worst of the furniture of my father's two dwelling houses being left of designe be my mother in this place for my use was also left and spared by the Inglish garrison so that I was not so much spoil'd by them as I was by my owne father in Law. I had a verie small and a verie

hard begining and if I had not done so great and good things as I might or willingly would have done I desyre that my posteritie whom God has bless'd me with may excuse these my endeavours for the reasone before mentioned.

And tho. since the time of my father's death in the month of May 1646 I have brooked the Title and dignity yet to any considering persone who shall read what is before written that I was but a nominal Earle and in every mans apprehensione the estate was irrecoverable.

Yet being at that time but seventaine yeares of aige and *fol. 24.* inflam'd stronglie with a great desyre to continue the memorie of my familie, I looked upon nothing as too hard hopeing still to doe it and albeit there was nothing more frequent then frauds in conveyances by which appearing heires invested themselves with such titles by getting assignationes from such creditors as were first in diligence whereby the greatest part of their debts which were resting to the poorer sort or to the more ingenuous and less distrustful kind of people fearing no harme or ill designe as by this means altogether frustrate the payment of the greatest pairt of their debts. And by such practises I have been a looser my selfe who have payed of my father's cautionerie for the Earle of Seafort [43] fourteen thousand pond and for the Laird of Dun [44] upwards of ten thousand pond out of wch with the interest of this money I have lyen and am in no possibilite to recover it. But by Divin providence which I may rather ascrive it to then out of any choise of my owne being then so young and of no experience I did then begin and still have continued with Just and equall dealings to all men. I never defrauded the poor nor had I ever any favour or ease from those who were powerfull allwayes acknowledging my father's bonds when I saw them And I hope by the mercie of God founding againe my familie upon the pillar of justice I shall be able to transmitt a good pairt of my estate with much less of incumbrance and debt then I found att my entrie thereto.

But there are still some impending cautionries of my father which I fenced these twentie yeires with long weapons, and if those saise upon me it will infalliblie reduce this familly againe into a desperat conditione such as the debt of Herad's hospitall,

Sir Andrew Dick's great clame is now transferred to his children, another debt due by the Earle of Morton and his
fol. 25. cautioners | to Mr Samuel Jonstone and truly payed to him by the E. of Traquer[45] by the pryce of the E. of Morton's lands then sold as the bond was truly retired from the creditor and some yeares agoe out of a sinister designe by My Lady Traquer and on Veitch of Daick who strongly solicit the heir of that Jonstone and with great difficultie was at last prevailed upon to give them or some confident persone in their name a title to persue for that bond. In which there is a proces commensed but industriously againe wav'd of purpose that time may obliterat the foulness of the deed, waiting for a fair opportunity to renew that proces.

My father Lykwayes greatly suffered for the Lord Spinie[46] and payed considerable debts for him.

But of all the actions of my father's life there was on which I am sorrie to mention since he is so inexcusable for it, but that the fault was truly more his brothers, The Laird of Aldbarr,[47] then his, who was in his owne nature a man of a noble dispositione and feared no ill designe from any man, because he had none himselfe, only it was his misfortune to be easie to be intreated, and it was painfull for him to refuse to relieve his freind when in distress, not considering the hazard of the event, for indeed he was a man not fitted for the time he lived in, fraud and deceit rageing in the transactions of privat busines, and the purpose of rebellion in the publick. All which prov'd too true by the ruin of many good famillies in their privat fortune and the murder of the best of Kings, but my father was preveen'd by death and did not behold this Tragedie, but was sufficiently convinced of the error of the times—tho. att the beginning he was carried away by the speat and by the influence of his first Lady and his brother
fol. 26. Aldbar, two mightie | Covenanters, was induced to goe on too far, and was ingaged in persone with his regiment of Angus to march four severall times and companyed with many of his freinds to the North, which expeditions and the buying of arms I have seen by the reall accompts thereof stood him no less then Fourtie thousand merks. This and the lyke advancements for the propagating the good cause (for the rebellious covenant

was so called at that time) were thought meritorious, and no less then heaven was the purchase, tho. it was the Divill in Masquerad, and my father's wyfe, who was the E. of Marr's[48] daughter, dyeing and his brother Aldbarr soon after did discover the wicked designs against King and Kingdome which were carried on under the pretence of Religione, and in the parliament sometime before his owne death declared no less, and opposed as much as in him lay the preventing partie at that time and when his countrie-men (an unpardonable sin in those who received the pryce q[ch] will certainly prove a snare and a curse to their posteritie and does remain an everlasting reproach to the natione, tho. many there was in it honest and blamless) sold there King and voted in Parliament to delyver him up to the Inglish att Newcastle, and not only past his vote against it, and there was but a feu in Parliament did so, but entered his protestatione thereupon boldlie enough but honestlie done att that time.

I have made this digressione tho. it be out of the way of my privat concerns, only here to have the opportunitie to conjure my posteritie never to engage themselves upon any pretence whatsoever against the interest of their lawfull King, who certainly is Charles the second now reigning and his heire in the right and lineal descent. | But to returne to the particular *fol. 27.* actions so destructive to his familly which his brother Aldbar was in a great pairt to be blamed for. There was on John Rind a mean-born man in Angus, became of great trade and reputatione as a merchant att Edenburgh, yet it seems all was not gold with him that glistered, and att the verie nick of time before his breaking My father being caried by his brother Aldbar to a deer traitie prepared by John Rind for them, he was induced by the flatterie and insinuationes of the fellow to become suretie for him that night in bonds for the sowme of four thousand ponds sterlin which sowme John Rind soon after breaking and departing the Kingdome My father was necessitate to acknowledge as his owne debt and the toucher which my father gott by my mother his wyfe of the second marriage being the lyke sowme, and no small toucher at that time, which had lykewayes in return a great provision of Joynter was interlie imploy'd for the payment of John Rind's debt wherein my

father stood engaged, for q^{ch} there was never any releife obtained to the worth of a grott. This was a great blow to the familly. And I am sorrie that I behoove to transmitt the narrative of it, but Aldbarr the brother, was to blame for all, and who was a deer brother to this house, for he was a proud and forward man and a great Maister My father gave him the Baronie of Aldbarr of inheritance, but he never lived upon the rent of it, contracted debt yearlie which my father from time to time payed it till exceeded the worth of the land, neither did my grandfather appoyint so much as the halfe of the value of that estate to this his second son so that it was a free and a gratuitous thing done of my father neither did he ever live by himselfe or had the charge of a familly, but allwayes with my father. This estate was the second time given him and my father discharged him of all the debts he had payed for him, and had he lived he had certainly spent it againe, but he dyed
fol. 28. shortlie after and was | never married so the estate returned from whence it came, but my father having yet another brother, the Laird of Brigtone who is mentioned before, out of his good nature and innate justice, thought he ought not to be the sol heir of his brother's estate, albeit he bought it before and att that time made the purchase of a prettie roume convenient for his brother Brigtone called Kinnetls tho. it has been the mischance also of that house not to keep it long.

There was also on Lammie of Dunkennie good for telling of old storries and a familiar friend in the house who I cannot tell hou transported in the time but made a shift to spend up his owne litle estate My father still engaging for him till his debts exceeded the double of the worth of the estate. It was then sold and what the estate did not pay of his debt My father behooved to pay being ingaged for it; which did not serve, but my father also gratified him and his wyfe with a pensione of fiftie bolls of victuall dureing all the dayes of their life, and they out lived himself a long time. His brother was minister in Glammiss, which hes not such a provisione as could inrich any man but such were the advantages those had who were constantlie about my father that he, without any visible cause made a shift to purchase bonds of my father so as he obtained a wedsett for his money from my Tutor Bridgton to the value of Balnamoon and the sixth part lands of Drumgley, with which his son, I having redeemed these wedsetts, hes againe made a purchase of his uncles lands.

Now by what is written and by many mischances which I have not written tho. I know them, and by a great many more q^{ch} I doe not | know tho. I beleeve verily they were, The *fol. 29.* reader may see how debt was contracted by my father upon his familly for tho. he lived att a great rate and keeped a noble house tho. without order, and his servants were all liberteins and had famillies of their own, yet all that cou'd be spent that way cou'd never have exhausted his estate, for my grandfather left him full Twentie eight score of chalders victuall on hunder merks of mony rent without debt, except indeed the provision of his two brothers and the portion of his sister The Countess of Erroll, and so without raking up any more the old sores and the bruises given to my familly in the last age I returne to the staggering conditione I left it in the twentie third page of this book.

Had I keepit a yearlie account of all my busines and transactions I might have been able to have written something to better purpose then I can now doe after so long a time, and I acknowledge that I am verie much to be blam'd for not keeping a record of all my transactions and doeings I am so much convinced of the necessitie of any man of busines his doeing some such thing for their owne vindicatione to posterity of there not being idle and useless in their time (a verie unpardonable crime in any man that is so) that however short my life may be (q^{ch} is in the hands of the Lord) henceforth to continue this book of a daly account of all that I doe, and q^{ch} I did beginn the first of this moneth so tho. it be impossible for me to relate the ten thousandth part of what I have done I must make this on apologie for all, and that I doe intreat my successor to beleeve I have w^{t} my best and uttmost endeavours served my familly in my generatione and have been still uncessant goeing about the interest and advancement thereof with equall labour and diligence in the time past as I hope the method q^{ch} I now am to followe in setting doune the whole particulars as they are daylie transacted will | evince as to the *fol. 30.* future and as I have done hitherto all that I was able and am fully bent to continue so to doe it is my opinion that I am bound in duty to improve all which lawfully I can doe to the profit and behoove of my familly and that every man in his age is but ane administrator to the nixt of his familly, and if he doe no good deserves no less reproofe then the man in the Gospel which put up his talent in his napken.

And for the time past instead of A full account which is impossible for me to render, I shall sume it up in this short deductione.

In the year 1660 when I was some seventaine yeares of aige I did deny myselfe the satisfactione which the most pairt of youth of that aige desyre, of goeing abroad and travelling, considering pairtlie the narrowness of the estate that I was left in but especially being adicted to the restoring of my familly to some conditione of living, for which I was determin'd to spare no pains or travell, after which time I did verie seldome give my curators the trouble of meeting togither, tho. all of them were verie kind and affectionat to me, and had my business been as well managed in the time of my tutorie as it was after I chused my curators, it had been the better for me. Yet tho. I seldome brought my curators togither I did no matter of consequence without the advyce of such of them as I had occasione to meet with. Gilbert E. of Erroll, tho. greatly obliged to my father's kindness was so ungrate according to the proverb, That what is done to children and old men is most pairt lost, The on forgetting favours and the other dyeing before a requytall, that he refused to accept as a curator, albeit att the verie time of the election of my curators att fforfare, he was at Kinnaird in the E. of Southesque's house about his marriage busines.

fol. 3r. Others of my relations by my father whereof the new Marquess of Athol was the nearest in blood, Lay at such a distance as that in my private affairs I could not have so easely their advyce, so that the freind that I made most use of, and who rendered himselfe verie usefull to me was my uncle by my mother George E. of Panmure, who, studeing my interest more than his owne convenience of purpose to render my business the more easie for me, bought the estate and interest which I had in Aberdeenshyre, which was the whole paroch of Bahelvie in propertie or superiority, which lands continued in my familly verie long, even since the dayes and reigne of Robert the second and first King of the race of Stewarts, att a just and equall pryce and more then land giv's now in that countrie a hunder pond sterlin for each chalder of victual and a hunder merk o'erhead and made good payment thereof, but the time is so farr passed that I can give no more particular account thereof, then that att the time of the doeing of it that other of my freinds and I were fully satisfied by the payments made and exact collectione thereof. And I remember verie well that such of my creditors who's bonds he was oblidged to reteer to me, the same was done with that ingeneuitie and honesty by him that they upon payment made to them by him, were induced to give some small eas of some by gone @ rents which he verie kindly rendered to me and took no benefit of it himselfe.

He was lykewayes verie usefull by his presence constantlie with me when I took in any of my factors accompts, and being of himselfe a verie | understanding man, knew most exactly the *fol. 32.* right forme of a compt and was at the pains to instruct me in it, and gave me many good advyces so that when he dyed I had reasone as I did regrat his death verie much.

The kindness of my uncle did repair in some measure a cruel and an inhumane injurie q^{ch} my grandfather on my mothers syde did to me which was shortlie this. In my younger years when I was under the tuition of my mother, the necessity of my affairs requyred the vendition of Land, and my mother att that time entered into a bargon with the old E. of Southesque who was att that time to have bought the Baronies of Tannadyce Aldbar, Dod, and Tullies. The old E. of Panmure being a rysing man and fitt for conquess was somewhat emulous of the other to have so great a bargon and so prevailed with his daughter my mother that she was induced by him q^{ch} she sorely repented after, upon some pretence or other to give up the bargon with the E. of Southesque,[49] so there past a minute in the same terms betwixt my mother as tutrix to me and her owne father, but sometime shortlie after, he having the said Minute in his hand upon some smal occasione or other, for litle would have offended the old crabed man,

to ared his name from the minute, Which minute lyes yet in my cabinet so destroyed. Now the loss was verie irreparable to me for tho. these lands remained still with me till I found other merchants for them, since I becam a man, yet the times from the breaking of the bargon in maner before mentioned, till the yeare 1660 being a constant vicissitud of trouble, in which the duties payable be the tenents were all exhausted by the payment of Taxes, Levies, and quarterings that for the most part of those years these lands yielded no rent or profitt to me and in the meantime the @ rents of those
fol. 33. creditors debts which the pryce of the land should | have payed, runn on to a great hight and herein my prejudice is obvious to any considering persone in so much as in common discourse which I have had since I was a man with James E. of Southesque he hes told me frequentlie that the breaking of that bargone was of great service to their familly for that if it had holdne it wou'd certainly have ruined his familly. But I desyre to forgett injuries and with them I shall also forgett my grandfather of that syde. And to returne againe to the eldest son for respect to whom I must also narrate here another special good office done me. For when I was a minor some creditors of the E. of Morton to whom my father stood engaged as cautioner, notwithstanding that they had a good ground right upon the E. of Morton's Lands and estate of Aberdour, yet such was their cruelty even to me a minor and but the heir of a cautioner, that laying asyd their right to the estate of the prin^{ll} debitor as if they had it not, they persued me all of them in the persone of James Butter a stoical and regardless kind of a man, who prosecute the same so rigorously that in a short time he obtained decreets, and led and deduced ane apprysing upon my whole estate to seven or eight and fourtie thousand pond which was the first of that nature against me, but this was of great mischeife, others being alarm'd therewith, they immediatly persued in the same manner.

My uncle more in his owne nature then any merite that he could perceive in me for I was verie young, stopt the carreir of
fol. 34. their malice, | knoweing well that if he had not done it the consequence would a been my utter ruine. And after a

meeting or two with those rabid hell hounds agried with them and payed them there sowmes of money and took assignment from their common trustie James Butter to the rights of the debt and the diligence also done aganst me and had good reasone so to doe. Yet in this he used it only as if he had it not for laying up all these decreets against me safe in his custodie, he commensed process before the commissioners for the administratione of justice in the Inglish time and upon his rights evicted the lands of Aberdour and possessed them for his sowmes ay and while after the King's restauratione, he was payed of his sowmes and the lands were redeemed by the E. of Midleton commissioner then to the current parliment for the behoove of his eldest daughter whom the Earle of Morton had married, so att that time my uncle was payed and he took care at the same time in the conveyance which he made of his rights to have me discharged. A freindly and a reasonable good office to his distressed nephew.

This eviction by my uncle Panmure of the lands of Aberdour from the E. of Morton and the necessity Morton was in to comply wt. the payment of the moneys of his Toucher that way, for these were the lands his Lady was to be secured in for her joynter, exasperat the E. of Morton extreamly so that he and a number of his freinds contracted a great malice against my Lord Panmure for it, and there were of his freinds and relationes powerfull enough att that time and had no small interest with the Earle of Midleton then commissioner and many counsills wer held by | him and his freinds how to over- *fol.* 35.
take my Lord Panmure as if he had done some notable iniquity in rescueing his nephew and putting the sadle on the right horse back. So these devices against him ended in this That to be sure when the Committie of Parliment for imposing of fines should sitt they would informe so strongly against him as to gett him severely fin'd and put the Duke of Lenox [50] mightily in rage against him as being a rich man that he might gett a gift of his fine.

However in the meantime I was in suite of the Earle of Midleton's nixt daughter to have her in marriage which I obtained and the same I thank God hes been verie successfull to me. I was att that time some nynteen years old. Yet

this putt no period to the malice of the Earle of Morton and his freinds against my uncle, but as they insisted maliciously against him on the on hand I was so much the more concerned on the other and at last my dear Uncle gott free of the snare in which they thought to have intrap'd him. Freinds were then imployed to settle the matter betwixt the E. of Morton and me and after much adoe and with great loss to me, our business was settled and I quyt great sowmes that were owen me for the payment of what in some place of this book before I have recorded meerlie upon hopes that his engagement personally for my releife of such debts as were not yet payed, but stood in hazard of, and of this I was altogither frustrate and I
fol. 36. remember verie well tho. My Lady Midleton seemed | equall to us both, as indeed her Lord was, yet she imployed some of her owne particular Trusties to tryst for him against me, which I have after asked the reasone for who's answear to me was that the odds was only here, that she knew I was intent upon my busines and that he could not be, q^{ch} made her pitie him more then me. And indeed att that time had his L/p had any right conduct in his busines he was in a fair conditione to have restored his family to its ancient greatness for his father in law gott him againe from the king the gift of the Isles of Orkney and Shetland (no small thing for a subject) and because of his apparent rysing I quyt him much the more of what he was oweing me to gett him of new obleidged to releive me of my cautionries as I said before, but things succeeded not with the Earle of Morton for his first misfortune was by his Lady's death who was ane excellent good woman, and within some years after, her only son, a prettie child dyed also, his rights to Orkney and Shetland were also reduced and he himselfe in great straits and want before he dyed, who lived also to dispone and putt away his title to the reversions of Kinrosshyre, a noble Lordship, att ane under value to Sir Wm Bruce.[51] More of him could be said but this is enough to the purpose in hand and I'm affraid that his uncle now Earle of Mortone ane old man, and his son the Lord of Aberdour shall signifie verie litle either to the raising of that ancient familly and far less will be able to attribut anything to my releife of the s^{d} great debts which I stand yet unreleived off. And Sir W^{m}

Bruce being a contentious | and Teuch lawer will be verie *fol. 37.* troublesome to be overtaken upon that head tho. his right to Kinros be with the burden of my right of regress to the reversioune att least the equall halfe of the Wedsetts there and to the halfe of the feu duties about Kinghorne which belonged to the E. of Morton of which feu duties I am yet in possessione upon a decreet which I obtained by my right of regress.

Now after all this digression wherein I have told of my marriage which happn'd not till two years after my comeing from the colledge I must yet returne to my first comeing to Castle Lyon upon the thirtie of May 1660. I borrowed from the minister of Longforgan[52] a bed wherein I lay, but within a week my owne q^{ch} I made up att St andrewes came about in a boat to Dundee and immediatly was brought out by carriage horses to Castle Lyon. I did lykewayes imploy my aunt My Lady Northesque,[53] who bought for me the furniture of a rowme back againe from My Lord Lithgow att a deere enough rate, and a dusone of spoons and a salt att 3 lib. the ounce whereupon my fathers and mothers name were. It may be easily guesed I had even att that time sufficient impressions of the inconveniences of second marieges, which tho. in my case att that time was of the mother's being married to a second husband, yet upon good reasone I conclude that when husbands marrie upon the death of their wifes when they have children of the marriege it is yet more fatal and destructive to famillies, wherein it happens, then when wemen marries after the deceas of their husbands, | for they carrie away only a life- *fol. 38.* rent, but the former carries away heretablie some part of the estate less or more, for the children of the second marrieg and oft times for peace sake the husband must give more then he is able to doe or would willingly give to satisfie the importunities of a Clamorous wyfe and ane envyous woman of the children of the first marriage.

I behoov'd also att Middsummer mercat to provyde my selfe with three horses for att that time I was not worth a fourfooted beast, safe on litle dog that I keeped att and brought with me from St. andrews. These horses also qu^{ch} I caused buy were all three within twentie pond sterlin payed. by this time the Inglishes were all gone out of Glammiss so I sent and

brought from thence the remnant of what they had left behind them. And horses went from the Cars to bring it, for att Glammiss I could command no carrieges all there about being wedsett. amongst other things which cam from thence were some old potts and pans q[ch] were verie usefull, so within few dayes I gott two rowmes more dressed up as a begers cloak consists of many cluts of divers colors, so my furniture was verie disagreeable but being alone I was impatient and thought long and so sent for my sister who had been from the time of My Lord Lithgow's removall till the begining of July with her aunt, and her companie was of great comfort to me, so young as were both we consulted togither and partlie by our owne conclusions and partlie by advice in two years time I gott togither as much of cours furniture as in a verie mean and sober way
fol. 39. filled | all the rowms of my house, some on way some another. but in the begining of summer 1662 when I begane to forsee the probability of my marriage I sent to London a commission for two suite of arras hangings and some Inglish cloath for a bed and linen and frings to it which my sister made up, and some pewter for I was verie ill served before and severall other things to the value of tuo hunder and fiftie pond sterlin. And att their arrivall q[ch] happened soon after I was married I obtained leave of my wyfe in the latter end of September to come home where I busied myselfe in putting things in order the best way I could, and after my stay some six weeks which my young wyfe thought long enough I returned to Edēn. leaving my sister behind me att Castle Lyon. Att that same time also I caused bring home a verie fin cabinet the better was not in the Kingdome in these days which I never told my wyfe of till her coming home, and upon her first comeing into her owne chamber I presented her with the keyes of the Cabinet. but the whole winter past over att Edēn, so in the month of March 1663 when my wyfe begining to grow big of her eldest son could hardly stay any longer, we sett out and her mother with her and came by the way of Aberdour where her sister was dwelling, and from thence thorrow ffyfe and were all night att Couper attended with a great many freinds of her's as weell
fol. 40. as mine. The next day | divers more of mine mett us at Dundee and the Magistrats of the Town welcomed us verie

cheerfully, so again night we came safe home where I entertained My Lady Midletone and all her freinds I presume better then they could have expected, however I was concerned to doe no less, and after they were gon we lived verie contentedly and quietly till the month of Maj upon the eight day of q^{ch} month my wyfe brought furth her son, who being a verie weak child tho. the apprehensiones of the wemen of his dyeing was concealed from me I was contented to deferr his christining for some time And of purpose because I designed to invite a goodlie companie of freinds to his Christining as indeed I had a great many being verie joyfull upon the birth of my sone who after the time of the Christining grew stronger everie day, and in whom I thank God I had never reasone but to rejoyce he was carefully brought up in his younger yeares by his mother. thereafter there has been nothing wanting in me for his educatione and it is now two yeares near run out since I sent him abroad who's returne shall be allmost as joyfull to me as his birth was.

After all companie was gone att that time I returned to the thoughts of my private busines.

But I had allmost forgott as a thousand things will be ommitted after so long a time about Lambas in the yeare of God 1660 | Att which time the spirits of all Loyal hearted men *fol. 41.*
were revived and quickened to a great degree Upon the late restitutione of our Sovereigne Lord the King att q^{ch} time or shortlie after a great many from all quarters of the Kingdome repaired to London to kiss his Majesties hands, and I was verie desyrous to goe, but my freinds obstructed it, extreamly fearing that being once ther I might fall into ill companie or might be desyrous to goe furthur, but after I stayed some six weeks there the thoughts of my owne conditione prevailed so upon me that I was no less desyrous to returne then I was at first to goe and so I cam back in the month of October. I went jorney up upon those horses bought att Middsummer on q^{ch} I cam downe againe but two of them as I was comeing hom and ryding thorrow ffyfe failed me even there and dyed poor beasts in the Cause. I bought litle or nothing that time safe cloaths q^{ch} were necessary for me, yet even verie litle of that being still in mourning for my mother. Some things I

brought for my sisters use fitt for her when her mourning was over, so that I made all my jorney for two hunder pond sterlin, and had I been as moderate in all my severall jorneys to that place since from q^{ch} I have brought things of great value for the *fol. 42.* furniture of my houses I had saved many a | pond and pennie but I acknowledge a great dale of weakness in my humour that way inclining to be verie profuse upon all things of ornament for my houses as I have been upon building. Let this only serve to excuse me if in this I have exceeded that what has been bestowed upon the first or expended upon the second has been acquyr'd with pains and industrie, and performed with much care and labour, and will be tokn's of both (being things of Long indurance) to my posterity who I hope shall enjoy the pleasur of it, whereas indeed I have suffered the toil. I doe not mention my planting here, that being a thing not so expensive, yet so vast a number of trees as I have planted cannot be done without a dale of previous care and foresight, which will certainly ryse be process of time, and amount to, in value, a great sowme of money, if care be taken to preserve them till they come to that pitch of being readie to be cut downe; and there is no less vertue in improving old and ripe timber, by the seal [sale] thereof and to the best advantage which ought to be done in a good bargone togither by which money comes in and yeilds a sensible profitt, and not by single trees squandering the whole away into nothing, then there is at the first planting; provyding allwayes that caution be had where the timber is such as does not rise equally weell againe by the root, neither will that doe unless it be weell and exactlie hain'd, that at the seal thereof it be digg'd up root and all, by which the ground will be clear, and fitt againe to receive a new plantation, whereas if the old Roots be suffered to remaine in the ground, besyd that it is a great eyesore, no young and new planting will prosper in the place.

And I am verie confident there is about Castle Lyon timber *fol. 43.* planted out in my time some | whereof may come to be worth six pond the tree some worth twice so much, but reckoning them all but att three pond the piece will aryse to a sowme exceeding the worth of the heretage of ane equall yearlie rent to it, Besyds Charls-Wood which cannot be considered that

CASTLE LYON (NOW CASTLE HUNTLY).

[p. 32

way, and the Ozar planting in the Middows. But observe, I say to the value of as much rent but not to the value of Castle Lyon itselfe, since by what is done about it, doeing, and to be done the place itselfe cannot be valued, and heavens forbid that in any future age, any successor in my familly shall ever consider of it so, as ever to expose it to seall. The place and seat of the house with the two part Land of the Mains, and the third part Lands of the Churchtoune were acquyred and purchased by my grandfather, but shortlie before his death. The other part of the Mains which was the third thereof and the two pairt lands of the Churchtoune have been, of many ages, in my familly. My Grandfather made this purchase from My Lord Gray,[54] att wch time save that the land was special good, it was a place of no consideratione, fitt for nothing else but as a place of refuge in the time of trouble, wherin a man might make himselfe a prisoner; and in the meantime might therein be protected from a flying partie, but was never of any strenth, or to have been accounted a stronghold to endure a seige, or a place capable to hold so many as with necessarie provisions could hold out long, or by salleys to doe much prejudice to an enemie, and such houses truly are worn quyt out of fashione, as feuds are, which is a great happiness, the cuntrie being generally more civilized then it was of ancient times, and my oune opinion when troublesome times are it is more safe for a man to keep the feilds then to inclose himselfe in the walls of a house, so that there is no man more against these old fashion of tours and castles then I am.

And I wish that everie man who hes such houses would *fol. 44.* reforme them, for who can delight to live in his house as in a prisone. And I am much addicted to a general reformatione, and have not a litle propagate that humour in the cuntrie where I live, as generally improvements have been more since the time of the King's happie restauratione then has been in a hundred years before, and every on almost att the instance or exemple of some leader has done more or less.

My father, as he had indeed reasone so to doe, did in the yeare of God 1637 finish the staircaice which he had begunn some years before, and he putt on ane inteer new roofe, upon the Castle and Jamm which before had ane old scurvie battlement and was vaulted in the top and flagged over. He did also build that wch is the present kitchen which had only a chimney with a timber brace carried up with patched straw and clay and full of hazard for taking of fire, as indeed upon many occasions it did, but I was obleidged to make a thorrow reformatione thereof. he built also the brewhouse and woman-house q^{ch} now is and the greatest barne which stands in the north west corner of the stackyeard without so much as a closs or court, so that the first landing or lighting was at the verie entrie gate.

Thus I found it so that I need not condescend upon what is done since, since the knowledge of what was done before will easily bring it to mind by what is to be seen now, only this I must say if ever I live to finish it. The house stands upon a verie stuborne rock, the beating doune of q^{ch} hes been done, and will yet cost much labour before it be perfected, the face of wch when again built up and covered with a wall will not be known, but true it is that the whole bounds of the kitchen yeard and nouricerie below the house and upon the west syde thereof is formed out of a declining rock q^{ch} came out that
fol. 45. farr, and the whole falling walks are cutt out of rock upon the East halfe of them and all filled up and carried ground upon the west halfe. And this I mention the more particularly because all levellings when done are so under cover disguise that it's scarce to be beleeved what work or labour there hes been att the doing of it, besyds the Litle garden, q^{ch} is before the gate where the statues are, was nothing but a litle piece of ground without forme declining to the east, an ugly rock standing up in some places as high as the top of the statu's are upon the west syde. The bowling green no better and the plott upon the south syde of the house worst of all, the utter court beat doune by the force of quarry mells and peiks to render it accessable, the north and middle greens clouts of corn land. The south green a piece of my father's planting and oarchard. The great low gardine A marrish, stuborn clay raised to the hight its now of with carried ground, the offices att the barns no better then a company of small and naughtie cottar houses and a great part of the bounds of Charls Wood on the East syd all spoilt and casten up ground

for the yearly mantinance and reparatione of these earth houses, as necessarly a great dale of good and pasture ground is continually waisted to uphold such ugly cottages. The pend and entrie hard by it was a quagmire as the most part of the enclosed ground besouth it was, the middows an open and common pasture so that before my time it was not known what the mawing of grass or use of hay was att that place

The house itselfe was extreamly cold and the hall was a vault out of q^{ch} since by the stricking thereof I have gained the rowmes immediatly now above it. no access there was to the upper part of the house without goeing thorrow the hall, even upon the most undecent occasions of Drudgerie unavoidable to be seen by all who should happne to be in that rowme nor was there any other to reteer to, till the rowme | wch is off *fol. 46.*
it was changed as it now is, for att that time it was not above fourteen feet broad. However for the first ten years of my life I lived there and had enough to doe for the first seven years of these ten to gett togither as much as did compleitly furnish that house, and were as much strangers to Old Glammiss as if it had not been. And for the first three years of my life wch I only reckon since the year 1660 I could not endure allmost to come near to, or see it, when the verie Mains was possessed by a wedsetter, so, when my wyfe after the end of the first seven years considered that nothing contributs so much to the distruction and utter ruine of furniture than the transporting of it, I was induced by her to make my constant abode att Castle Lyon for some time longer till she gott togither some things necessary to be had before we could think of comeing to Glammiss wch she provyded with so much care as that for our first comeing to Glammiss where I proposed to live for some time as reteeredly as I did att first when I took up house at Castle Lyon having scarce a spare rowme furnished to lodge a stranger in. And tho. it was my resolutione to follow my father's way of living constantly at Castle Lyon in summer and att Glammiss in winter yet the reforming of my house at Castle Lyon wch I was fully bent to doe in the way and manner as it now is, was a work of such difficulty to be done and took up so much more time then att first I apprehended it should that my familly stayed here full three

years before it was possible for me to reduce that place again into any order. Perhaps in the summer time My wife and I and the children might goe doune sometimes, they for their diversione but I to give necessarie directions for the advancing of the work wch I declare had I known of what difficultie it was befor I undertook it I had never enterprised the same. *fol. 47.* But now it most be done, and there were three new windows slaped out and made in the storie of the low hall, and a back stair from it up on the west syde of the low hall, answearing to the old stair there, another back stair from the vestible of the high dining roume or hall to the verie top all digged out of the thickness of the wall, seven closets out of the walls upon the other three corners also The wall of the dining-roume and drawing-roume paived and the new windows thereof and the new roumes gained out of the deepness and hight of the vault of the old hall immediatly above the dining-roume, and the bedroom above the drawing-room reformed with new lights to the south. All wch was done att a great charge and stand now finished, much of the furniture that was there before fitted not the rowmes againe and was all brought to Glammiss, a place not easie to be filled, new things bought for the other so that att this day it stands compleitly furnished and verie fashionable. And before all was quytt finished My familly returned there in the summer time according to our proposed custome. And in summmer 1683 when the roofe of the Quire of the Church of Longforgane was altogether ruinous, it gott a new roofe att the common charge of the heritors, but I took occasione att the same time to reforme my loft and seat of the church and to build a roume off it for a retyring place betwixt sermons.

My Lands of Inshture and Holms were in my minoritie sold off that estate to the new Lord Kinnaird,[55] and it was done att that time when I tho. a child was fined in the time of the usurpatione of Oliver Cromwel when many more were. And it was my misfortune being a child att that time not to be in that capacitie to act against him wch had I been a man I wou'd have done to my utmost hazard. I my selfe feued out the lands of Milnehill for payment of a hunder pond feu duty yearlie. The third pairt lands of Dron for a certaine feu lykeways, and the roume in fforgan called the Byrflet and am readie to feu out more of any pairt of my estate except allenarlie the places of my two special residences.

It may easily be beleeved that what with my busines and *fol. 18.* transactions that doe daylie occurr and what with the working men I have had att Castle Lyon sometimes feuer and sometimes a great many as att present there is, that I have had verie litle spare time. I was never addicted to any kind of feild sport save hunting allenarlie wch kind of Dogs I gott togither of all sorts immediatlie after I cam from Ingland in the 1660 year of God as a plenisher must doe att first soon after I putt of the worst and bred upon the best and verie speedily brought my pack into a verie good and precise kind of running hounds, and by crossing the breed now and then with some other choise dog or bitch have continued the same kind of hounds from the verie first to this verie time, neither did I ever find that this sport does so much dammage to horses as it 's commonly reproached w^{t} and its like my children being so accustomed with these hounds may obleidge me to keep them still, for I beginn my selfe not to follow the sport as much as I was wont to doe.

Now as is before writtin I remaind constantlie from the sixtie yeare of God that I first took up house att Castle Lyon till the yeare 1670, in so much, that dureing that whole space My wyfe never saw Glammiss but once. not that I resolved to continue still to neglect this the ancient seat of my familly, whereabout the greatest parte of my estate lyes, but that being quitt spoiled in both houses and nothing remaining but the bare walls and haveing with great dificulty, trouble, and charge gott togither as much as made Castle Lyon habitable, and not being resolved to spoyl it by the frequent transporting thereof, there we remained till some more was provyded then served our turn att that place. And in the yeare 1670 we came here as new beginners where we past that winter and lodged our selves all in that storry of the old house q^{en} is on the top of the great staircaice, for that storry was only glazed att that time. The nixt summer being impatient to see the ruins of the place, for the east wing of the house was no better then if it had had no roofe att all, so I entered to work and gott on a roof upon it after I had highted the walls of the great round *fol. 49.* and erected two new litle geivels on the syd | wall making out more lights in the second and third storry wch are easie to be knoun att this day by the newness of the work, putting out the grats out of the windows of the third storry lykways with severall altrations of the contrivance within doors too tedious here to sett doune. and whereas the third storry was cumsylled above wch sort of sylling is comonly a nest for ratts I gested it over and gain'd rowms above within the roofe, highted the staire of that syd of the house on turn, so that these roums now above add not a litle to the conveniencie of our present dwelling lodgeing the younger children and such of the wemen servants as are of the best account who have private access by a back stair to these roumes my wyfe maks use of her selfe. To the syd of the house I have clapp'd to a new building wch answears to the three storrys and is covered with lead wch platforme goes off the fourth storry, and is of great convenience and use to us who live for the time in this syd of the house.

It is hardly possible by any descriptione wch I can now make to give any impressione to my posteritie what the place was lyke when I began first my reformationes for there remains nothing of it but the great old house itself allenerly. The old chattered and decayed trees wch surrounded the house, yet there were not many, and the most of these that were, were to the southward, a comon mistake of our ancestors whereas reasonably any thickets or planting that are about any man's house ought rather to be upon the north, northeast, and northwest, neither was the planting wch was here of any bounds The whole planted ground not exceeding four aikers att most, verie disproportionable to the greatness of the place with a verie low wall of dry stone scarce sufficient to hold out any beast There was but on entrie to the house wch was to the southeast with an utter gate att no greater distance then much
fol. 50. about the place where the | bridge is over the ditch hard by the round upon the corner of the gardin from wch to the inner gate of the Court there was a Rasso,[1] and a low wall such as I told you off before in each syd till you com to the gate of the closs or Court, where there was a bridge with a pend over a mightie

---

[1] Probably *ressault*, a French architectural term applied to a recessed erection.—ED.

broad and deep ditch wch surrounded the house upon the inner brink whereof there was a high wall, a gate forenent the bridge and over the gate a little lodge for the porter. There was upon the east syd of the gate houses two roums in lenth wch joyned to the great east round of the house so that you may guess by this how strangly near and untowardly this wall and this gate stood with the house itselfe, upon the west syde of the gate within the wall beformentioned there was [a] row of byrs and stabls and att the tourne, the walls and ruins of a spatious old hall and off it the thing wch they called the chamber of Dess, but upon this I never saw a roofe, upon the inner wall of this there was a too fall and the geival thereof open fitt to receive a coatch wch I supposed never had a door, of this the Inglish garison made a smiddy, upon the end of the old hall wch made the turne there were other buildings where the women house was and lodgings for serving men, nixt to this there was the cheif stable with travesses for horses fitt for to hold seven or eight but the lofting of these was quitt rotten, then did the building turn and joyned to the inmost corner of the weast geivall of the great hall of the house where there was a brew-house and a baick-house wch had been of my father's building. All this before mentioned was within the bounds of that wch you now see is the fore-court where the two greens are on each syde of the pav'd walk a strange confused unmodel'd piece of business and was to me a great eye sore, these houses also upon the east syd of the gate of the | entrie were also in the time of *fol.* 51.
the Inglish garisone consumed with fire, for in the loft they keeped hay where the fire was first keneled, wch is commonly the end of all hay Lofts, and a foolish thing it is to house hay unless a man will be so provident as to build a house particularly for it separat from all others, and without the great inner ditch upon the outsyd of the planting there were two other great ditches on without another, without any direct conveyance there to the river—wch stankt up the water so as that the place by reasone of these ditches appeared most exceedingly marish and weat and was generally condemned for it is supposed to be an unholsome seat of a house. These ditches were the cause off and necessitate me when I built the walls of the gardin bowling-green kitchen gardns and back Court to put

over rough pends where the ditches runn and these pends are visible to this day and I hope though the house stands low, for it stands on a plain inviround on all syds save to the south with runing water w^{h} in my apprehensione is very delightfull yet no considering man will now censure it as a marish place or unwholsome for that cause.

I did upon my first $resol^{ne}$ of the chenge which I have made here make a skame and draught of my whole project, for unless men so doe they will infallibly fall into some mistake, doe that wch they will repent ymselves aftr, and be obleidged to pull their own work downe againe. Therefore necessarie it is for a man to desyne all at once (chalk is no sheers, and the desyning hereof does not impose any necessity upon the projector but *fol. 52.* that he may verie weell prosecut | his designe by pecemale as he can, and by doeing something everie day according to the saying of the great Mathematician *Nulla dies sine linea* and wch is applicable lykewayes to men's business) it will aryse to something in the years time and by the space of divers yeares to some thing more considerable, yet a man by this way prosecuting his designs, wch certainly is the best and easiest, needs extremely to be tempered with patience.

For the first two or three yeares of my time att this place the maist parte of my work was to remove the great and old timber wch I found here and I think I gott about a thousand ponds scotts for it, then all those buildings before descryved were so in my way (as the old timber was) that it behoove to goe away. This destroying pairt wch was necessarly previous to the other during that time was the occasione of my undergoeing a great censure in the cuntrie—especially amongst my owne people, and the working men who were brought in wrought with great backwardness and repining and I have been told that the cuntrie people here when they mett at the church or at bridels or burialls their discourse was commonly enveying against me as a puller downe of what I had never built, whereas indeed beeing without all forme and quyt ruinous excepting only what my father had built, which lykways were so narrow that they were verie inconvenient, the difference upon the mattr was not so verie great for some of them wanted roofs and all the rest behooved to have new roofs and the removing of the whole to a back court apart as they now stand was of more import and advantage to the place then the difference of charge was of value, but at the same time | when *fol. 53.* I was in the mouths of all the commons so condemning me I made an observe wch is verie true, for tho. I have not left of the litle planting wch was here a standing tree but on wch was on of the dooll trees where they played of old att the foot ball upon the green att the burne syde, yet there was not a word of censure for the destroying of the planting wch in effect proceeds from a generall humor in commons who have a naturall aversione to all maner of planting and when young timber is sett be sure they doe not faill in the night time to cut even att the root the prettiest and straightest trees for stav's or plough goads, and many on they have destroyd to my selfe albeit if they stood not in great awe and fear they would have yet done greater harme to my young plantines. I have sometimes discovered by bribs fellows who have cutt off my trees whom I have punished so severly that it greatly terrified others who perhaps would have done the like but for fear of punishment.

Thus then having projected all that I have done att this place I have prosecut my designe every yeare doeing something these thirteene years past and after five or six years being here that I gott all the old house glassed of new and the most parte of the rooms plenished on way or other I did in the yeare of God 1676 with the lessening something of the number of my constant workmen here and adding a good many att Castle Lyon make the alterat^nes^ within the house there as I have before descryved in three yeares time, but to returne to Glammis. tho. it be ane old house and consequentlie was the | more diffi- *fol. 54.* cult to reduce the place to eny uniformity, yet I did covet extremely to order my building so as the frontispiece might have a resemblance on both syds, and my great hall wch is a rowme that I ever loved haveing no following was also a great inducement to me for reering up that quarter upon the west syde wch now is, so having first founded it I built my walls according to my draught and form'd my entrie wch I behooved to draw a litle about from the west else it had run directly thorrow the great victual house att the barns wch my father built and I was

verrie loath to destroy it: verie few will discover the throw in my entrie wch I made as unsensible as possiblie I could. Othrs more observing have challenged me for it but were satisfied when I told them the cause, others perhaps more reserved take notice of it and doe not tell me and conclude it to be an error of ignorance but they are mistaken. I confess I am to blame that designing so great a matter as those reformnes putt all together comes to, I did not call such as in this age were known and reput to be the best judges and contrivers, for I never bestowed neither gold nor mony upon this head, and I look upon advyce as verie necessarie to the most part of undertakers, aud the not seeking and taking counsell is commonly the cause why things are found amiss in the most parte of designs that way, nor have I the vanity to consider my owne judgement as another cannot better, yet being resolved to performe what I have done with litle noice and by degrees, and more to pleas and divert my selfe then out of any ostentane, for I thank God I am as litle envious as any man and am verie
fol. 55. glad to behold things weell ordered and contrived att other mens dwellings and never Judged anything of my owne small endeavours worthie to make so much noice as to call for or invit to either of my houses skd publick Architecturs My work and projects lykways being complexed things and hardly on man being to be found fitt to give advyce in all I never Judged it worth the trouble of a convocne of the severall artists such as masones who's tallent commonly lyes within the four walls of a house, wrights, for the right ordering of a roofe and the finishing the timber work within, gairdners for gardens, orchards &c. I have indeed been att the charge to imploy on who is to make a book of the figure of the draughts and frontispiece in Talyduce[1] of all the Kings Castles, Pallaces, towns, and other notable places in the Kingdome belonging to privat subjects who's desyre it was att first to me, and who himselfe passing by deemed this place worthie of the taking notice of. And to this man (Mr Sletcher[56] by name) I gave liberall money because I was Loath that he should doe it att his owne charge and that I knew the cuts and ingraving would stand him mony.

The old house stands now in the midle with two wings whereof

[1] *Tailledouce*, the French term for etching on copper.—Ed.

that upon east syde coast me a new roof the other on the west syde was founded and furnished by my selfe. all my office houses are placed of either syde of these two wings w[ch] with some other toofall on the north maks up the back closs. | My stables *fol. 56.* after they were fully finished and done new by the malice of a cursed fellow who as Cook after the terme when he was put away upon ane implacable hatred w[ch] he took up against another servant who lay above the stables burnt all downe by his throwing in fire over a partition wall in the night time when everybody was abed into that roume immediately above the watch house w[ch] greatly surprysed my whole family. The flame whereof being a most violent fire, had not by divin providence the East great round been heighted some six or seven feet when I putt a new roof therein, had certainly saised that pairte of the roof of the great house whereby the whole would have been in danger, such crimes being of ane occult nature and allways perpetrat in a most secret way there was great difficultie to make any probatione but I persued the Reskal crimenaly and showed before the Court his guilt by undenyable circumstances and had it not been the ignorance of the Jury who tho. they were no favourers of him yet by a mistake in the wording of y[r] verdict brought him in guilty of the presumptione contained in the lyble but directly of the crime itselfe. The Judge by the influence then of the Justice Clerk The Lord Craigie Wallace[57] being a west cuntrie man and the Reskal Cuningham a west cuntrie man he demured to pronounce the sentence of death w[ch] he most justlie deserved and refused to inclose the Jury againe but he theireafter being still detained prisoner conscious of his owne guilt petitioned for the *fol. 57.* sentence of banishement | and enacted himselfe never to returne to the Kingdome under the pain of death and accordingly was sent away in a ship bound for the planta[ns], but being wrek'd by the way he with some few more saved there lives by swimming, and he being a bold and impudent reskel returned and by chance being seen in Edēn I caused again apprehend him and sent him away by the first ship being prevailed up by My Lord Glencairne[58] and others of the name of Cuninghame not to insist against him for his life since w[ch] time it is not known if ever he returned to Scotland. These stables I restored to their former conditione wch was not all my loss having burnt to me besyds a coatch wch was litle worse yn new and three rich sadles with great difficulty of saving my horses. I lost lykways above fourteen or fifteen pair of pistols some of wch were verie fine and divers good swords for all these were keeped in the nixt roome by him whom the Cook design'd to burne.

There be now an entrie from the four severall airths and my house invyroned with a regular planting, the ground on both syds being of a like bigness and the figure the same with a way upon either syd of the utter court to the back court where the offices are att the north gate the gardners house is apon the on syde and the washing and bleatching house on the other with a fair green lying thereto to bleatch upon and a walk there is planted wch goes round the whole intake, wherein when you are walking you'l behold the water runing
fol. 53. in both syds of the planting. | And upon the west syd where the river is to make the way accessible from the west I have built a bridge and have cutt downe a litle hill of sand wch I caused carrie to such places as were weat and marish. The utter Court is a spacious green and forenent the midle thereof is the principal entrie to the south with a gate and a gate house besyde two rounds on upon each corner, the on is appointed for a Dayrie house and the other for a Still house, and the gate house consists of on roume to the gardine and another to the bouling green, the walls are lined, the roof plaistered, the floor lay'd with black and whyt stone and are verie convenient and refreshful roumes to goe in to from the gardine and Bouling green Ther is in the gardin a fine dyal erected and howsoon the walk and green plots are layed there will be statu's put into it, and there is a designe for a fountain in the Bouling green and on great gate from the gardine and another from the bouling green to the utter court att the southend of wch directlie forenent the gate of the inner court, there is another great gate adorned with two gladiators, from wch the avenue goes with an enclosure on each syd holdne with a plantane of fir trees wch is ane entrie of a considerable bread and lenth leading straight up to the barns and offices there, wch offices stand yet unreformd as they were, but if it pleas God that I live I intend to make them better. there are two

stak yards there, the on opposite to the other, betwixt w^{ch}
there is a wall cross to the avenue and a great gate placed
therein verie pleasant to behold, what I have of further designe
not yet done, time will produce the knowledge of, only upon
the west syd there is a park but a great part of the wall
thereof is ruinous tho. latlie but done, by reasone of the bos-
ness of the stone wch mulders into sand and dust and was gott
upon the river syd a litle below the stone bridge, they were
sought for there because of the great convenience and nearness
of them but all that's done is lost labour. | and paralel to this *fol. 59.*
another park is designed upon the east syd of the principal
entrie and so be time other two parks wch should invyron the
whole house and would be a circumference betwixt three and
four miles about, and planting secured by an inner wall, for
it's better being hem'd after the maner that is don betwixt the
girnal house and the warens. This if it were done, and the
planting any thing growne to a hight wou'd make the seat of
the house verie glorious as invironed with a wood of no less
bounds, but this is a work of a great time and what I shall
not be able to accomplish I hope may be done in the succeeding age, and this park might have four gates, on answering to
each of the four severall entries to the house.

Att the church I have made a loft for my owne use, and
built a litle addition to my burial place both wch contribute
extremelie to the adornment of the church, besyds three other
lofts that I made therein, yet the church stands uncompleit
for the time by reasone of the Laird of Claveres interest in the
paroch who does not contribut his help for makeing other two
lofts betwixt the pillars on the southsyd as weell as it's done
upon the north. And if I can be able to overtake it I designe
to build a tolebooth both for a prison house and for a roume
to hold my courts in wch is a shame should be wanting and
verie inconvenient and having the privilege of a weeklie mercat
tho. it be not in use yet if there were a cross built wch I
designe in the mid of the croft of land att the back of the
malt house, and a square made there for a mercat place I
doubt not but in a short time a weeklie mercat | might be *fol. 60.*
recovered to be holdene there wch would tend extreamlie to
the advantage of the inhabitants.

I purpose lykways to lenthen the avenue with a double row of trees on each syd from the uttmost gate att the barns thorow the land betwixt the barns and the toune straight to the open att West hill and perhaps further. After the forgoing account the doeing of wch things was a yearlie charge and no less trouble I shall likeways hereafter sett downe a particular account of the severall rentalls of my lands and what parte thereof I found in the hands of wedsetters as also what is of new purchase having before told what lands I have alienat and disponed.

Glammiss the narrow circle.

First the rentall of this about Glammiss wch I reserve out of my factors charge into my owne hands consists of the Mains itselfe with the parts and pendicles thereof, the Church toune Balnamoon, Westhill, Welflet, myretoune and bridgend and Litle Cossens. The rentall of wch is litle up or downe of two hunder and sixtie bolls of bear, a hunder and sixtie bolls of meall, a thosand on hunder and sixtie pond money, besyds the custom's, but the most pairt of all this I found wedsett. The Mains itselfe to Wm Gray of Graystone, Sheriff-clerk of fforfare, the toune of Glammiss to James Crightone portioner in Cupargrange, whose sowme is yet unpayed, but with consent I obtained the possessione and pays him his yearlie @ rent. I purchased Westhill and redeemed the Welflet from Mr. Patrick ffithie and his wyfe Katheren Lyon as lykways that house and land in the toune possessed be Agnes Wightone q^{ch} Katheren Lyon had the right thereof in life-rent as the relict of Edward Peettie, a servant of my father's who's sone it's lyk, an she were dead, may pretend a right thereto but might be opposed, for his clame is unjust. Myretoune and bridgend was also wedsett but redeemed from Robert ffotheringhame[59] now of Lawhill a brother to ffotheringhame of Balindean who att that time was heretor of Easter Denoon in this paroch. Balnamoon was all wedsett to Mr. Silvester Lammie[60] minister, so by this account the halfe lands of the Newtoune and Litle Cossens was only free wch is a verie smal part of the rental and so long as those wedsetters continued I had small reasone of
fol. 61. contentment to be much att this place but | those were the first wch I redeemed they being nearest adjacent to my house.

The sowme of the nixt rentall wch make up the charge committed to David Lyon is litle up or doune of eight hundred bolls of meall Two thousand six hunder sixtie six pond thirtaine shilling four penies mony besyde the customes whereof Drumgley a considerable toune was wedsett to John Smith of Gleswall and disponed by him to the Laird of Aldblair from whom I redeemed the same, I mean the two part lands thereof, the third part lands was a part of M^{r}. Silvester Lammie's wedsett with that of Balnamoon. I purchased the lands of ffofartie from William Gray of Grayston as lykways the lands of Graystone and blackhill. The same now had the toune of Arnafoul with the Mains thereof in wedsett wch I redeemed from him. I bought also the lands of thorntoune with its pertinents. I found the milne of Arnafoul and Knockbenie possessed by ffrederick Lyon be way of pensione, wch I know he and his father brook'd all my father's lifetime free, nay did not so much as pay the publick dues but in the time of my curators his possession was challenged for wch he could produce no right or title so wisely submitting himselfe I became his freind and suffers him yet to possess both for the halfe q^{ch} a tenent would pay, but John Lyon of Rochelhill in the same case w^{t} him, without a title, by reasone of his continued possessione avowed the same to be his owne, but because of his obstinacie I dispossessed him after wch time he lived in a miserable condition for some years so piticing him I gave | him cloaths and entertainment att my owne table so long as he lived, and a church to on of his sons Another of them purchased a good way of living to himselfe at Edenburgh, the rest of his children were litle worth. I found Wester Denoon wedsett to John Violent from whom I redeemed it, and have latelie sold this land to John Burn for the pay^{t} of fourtie pond and ten wadders of feu dutie yearlie. I acquired also the superiority of Easter Denoon which pays me ten ounces of silver plate yearlie. I purchased also the lands of Smattone and Bagownie and pertinents thereof for Donald Thorntoune, and Melgime. The newtoune of Glammiss and the accompt thereof is wrong placed upon the foot of ye 60 page for it ought to be here, the roume of Clipethills hes been this long time unluckie by ill tenents never haveing payed the duty. The Mains of Cossens and pertinents thereof

Rentall within David Lyon his commission.

fol. 62.

I justlie possess having payed more of that poor man's debt then that and other pairts of his land wch I have is worth. The lands of Balmuketie were all wedsett to George Lyon of Wester Ogil wch I redeemed. Those lands hold waird of the Marquis of Douglas, and it cost me right deer my compositione I purchas'd a litle pendicle hard by there called Balbegno. As lykways the toune and lands of Reedie in the paroch of Airlie. All the rest of the touns and lands of that paroch were a pairt of my mother's joynture wch I entered inteer to after her death save Cardean and the third pairt lands of Leuros, wch the Earl of Lithgow gott in wedsett for the twentie two thousand merks that was payed to him for his claime after her death, he brooked these lands about two years. I sold the lds. of Bekie, Drumdairne and Carlenwell to Mr. Thos. Wilsone for the payment of a considerable feu duty. *fol. 63.* But he has never payed the same. And being year and day att the horne I have bestowed the gift of his escheat to Mr. John Lyon Sherriff Clerk of fforfare, for this Wilsone is a base unwordie man and deserves to be no better used, but have so accorded with ye Sherriff Clerk for this gift that Drumdairne and Carlenwell and the rent thereof returns to myselfe.

Rentall of Tannadyce and places adjacent.

The rentall committed to the care of Robert Ogilvy is litle up or doun of two hundred fiftie three bolls bear, three hundred and ninetie four bolls meall, two thousand two hunder and fourtie pond money and som yearn and poultrie these lands lyeing att a greater distance being all converted in money. Marquis and Murchillock still wedsett to ffindowry and unredeemed is not included in the rentall, neither is the rentall of Auchnedy in regard its wedsett and unredeemed from Mr. David Lindsay. And in lykmaner the rentall of the lands of Killhill and oyrs is not here comprehended in regard they are wedsett to Mitchell Gray of Turbeg. These two last are wedsetts of the old Sherrif Clerks, with the burden of wch I accepted of the dispositione of these lands.

Now as to the barone of Tannadyce to make a long tale short I found it att my entrie intyrlie in the hands of wedsetters whom I did redeem since wch time I have sold the lands of Muirtone and Nether Bogill to Mr. James Cramond, the lands of Litle Bogillo to Patrick Lyon for payment of a certain few dutie yearlie conforme to the table rentall.

I have also acquyred the lands of Quilke and Kintyrie from Cossens by rights of apprysings and debts exceeding the value.

As lykweyes all the rest of the lands contained in this rentall are now purchased since wch time I have fewed New-milne to M^r. James Small[61] minister | att Cortachie. *fol. 64.*

The Rentall of the lands of Litle Blair and others committed to the care of James Couper on of my fewars being twentie bolls bear, fourtie four bolls meall, sixtaine bolls of oats and two firlots, seven hundred and eightie four pond eightaine shillings money besyds customs. All this litle rentall is of my owne purchase. *Rentall of Litle Blair.*

The Rentall of Auchterhouse and lands in the paroche of Lundie and Tellen is in and about a hunder and twentie seven bolls bear, a hunder and sixtie on bolls meall, three thousand five hunder sixtie nyn pond seventaine shilling four pennies money besyd customs. The haill forenamed lands of this last table rentall is all new purchase. *Rentall of Auchterhous.*

The lands of Castle Lyon according to the rentall is in and about two hunder seventie six bolls wheat, two hunder twentie five bolls bear, sixtie two bolls oats, two hunder and thirtie bolls meall, thirtie six bolls of peas, on thousand two hunder pond money besyd customs, here too I have acquyred the superiority of the lands of Knap, Lawriestone and Bulien and tuo parte lands of Dron. What I have fewed out is mentioned before. *Rentall of the Lordship of Lyon.*

Rentall of Kinghorne is a hunder and seventie six bolls three firlots bear, seven bolls meall, fifteen bolls oats, four hunder and three pond thirteen hunder shillings two pennies money. *Rentall of Kinghorne.*

In this and the other four preceeding pages there is much comprysed in litle bounds wch I am not able to sett down particularlie by the speciall transaction nor to assigne the time when they were done, not having keep'd any Minute book for it as I am now to doe being alwayes satisfied and assured in the time that things was exactly and right done.

I remember besyde many other particular debts wch were never settled upon wedsett rights. There were two cardinal debts, I call them so because I reckoned y^m to be great even so

much as I was not owing the lyke to any on persone. Besyde
fol. 65. The soume of twentie | thousand pond wch My sister who was
married to the Earle of Aboyn had left to her by my father,
she had lykewayes a right to twentie thousand merks wch was
resting to my father by the Earle of Seaforth, yet she had not
all this att first but it fell in to her and was so provyded by
the death of her elder sister Joan. Soon after the marriage to
wch I was verie averse but could not prevaill nor hinder it, she
being at her owne disposal, the E. of Aboyn behooved to have
the money of his toucher wch I payed him att two terms. The
other great debt was just the lyke soume that was resting to a
rich man in Dundee called Provost Watson, who had a right
of @ rent upon the husband pleughs of the toune of Longfor-
gand wch att last I lykways payed.

And it is not to be imagined that I could possiblie pay
these and many other debts, redeem the wedsetts and make
the purchase of lands before mentioned, build and support the
necessary charges thereof, make three several journeys to
London besyd the first before mentioned, make two severall
expeditions to the west cuntrie which I did by public order,
furnish both my houses in the way they are when I found only
bare walls, make a considerable collection of silver plate, main-
taine a great familly, support my law suits, and my owne
necessary travelling staying att Edēn.—many times more then
the on half of the yeare, maintaining my eldest son abroad
tho. I cannot say but that allwayes he hes been so stayed and
moderat as to keep himselfe within bounds, without being in a
considerable debt wch debts I have enumerate in a preceding
pairt of this book, yet it is not the halfe by what it was first
when I entered upon the stage, besyds that I have payed many
fol. 66. woeful cautionries | of my father of wch I never had nor never
will get releife.

I have lykwayes had as no man can be so forseeing as to
delyver himselfe from such contingencies considerable loss by
sundrie merchants who hes broke with mon^{y} and the effects of
bargens of victuall that I have sold and other people who have
been unfaithfull to me in the return of their accompts whereof
I can never be repaired, such as William Couper and ffrancis
Areskin two base and unfamous cheats. Besyds great losses

wch I have sustained by depauperat tenents and great soumes owen me att this day by such who are not yet brok, but are not able to pay me without casting my ground waist. There are some considerable debts owen to me wch I need not here sett down because they will be mentioned hereafter as they occurr in transactions so that I shall now return to the dayly account and jornal of my business and continue the same as close as I can from the day on wch I left.

I have lykways att this day pairtly att Castle Lyon upon my Mains there, and pairtly att Glammiss and att the Newtoune a verie considerable stock of corn and cattel wch would aryse to a great soume of money. 27 day.

I have sett a tack of Robert Lindsays possessions of Litlecoul in Tannadyce to James Guthrie brother to Thomas (Memus) Guthrie wherein it is agreed betwixt us that he is to pay sixtie six pond thirtine shill: four pennies for each year tack Begining the first pay^t^ hereof att Witt. nixt and twentie pond of augmenta^ne^ of the duty yearlie. 28 day. Tacks to James Guthrie.

John Toch hes also gott a tack of another fourth pairt of the Lands of Meicklbagillo for the payment of the duty accustomed, he had the halfe of that soume before and so is now tenent to thrie parts thereof. John Toch.

John Smith is continued by a tack in the possessione of the fourth pairt of the said towne so that its | hoped by his displenishing a pleughs labouring he may be able to pay his debt. John Smith. *fol.* 67.

The toune and lands of Quilke are sett in thrie equall third pairts to John and James Cudberts his sone and James ffairwather, with this imprevement of the duty, that where as before they were obleidged to repair with all their grindable corns to Lochmilne and that the tenent there payed me four bolls meall yearlie for it, These tenents now for ane immunity and freedome from the said milne pay by their tacks yeirlie two bolls bear on boll meall and twelve pond money more then they did. John and James Cudberts and James ffairwather.

Andrew Gray in Balbona having a possessione under me of 200 pond of silver duty yearlie and he being a man verie intent upon suits of law for he had a world of broken plea's I was induced upon hopes that the sparing of him should enable him to prosecute his actions att law. I had the patience to 2 Februarij 1684. Andrew Gray his new security at least to reenter him in prison.

forbear him a lang time till att lenth after he gain'd on suite wch yeilded him more than would have payed me, he made use of most of the effects thereof another way and payed me but a small pairt wch thing provoking me justlie I put him in prison and poynded his corne and cattel in harvest 1683 and he himselfe lay in prison from that time till this day that being prevailed upon by others for his inlargement I signed a warrand to the Magistrats for letting him out of prison and gott a bond from on Mr. George Gray wretter in Dundee wherein he is obleidged to reproduce his persone if alive on the nynth of

fol. 63. Apprill next or pay the sowme | yet resting be Andrew Gray wch after the compt of the poynding was made and cleared the debt was found to be 340 ponds and its wished that Andrew may live and that Mr. George may make no restitune of him.

4 day. Cossens debt to James Steel payed.

The Laird of Cossens was resting to James Steell in Kinaltie 666 lib 13 sh.s 8 p.ns, by an old bond of his fathers wheron infeftment did follow and a decreet of poynding of the ground of Kintyrie. This debt tho. I have now more upon the estait then its able to bear yet in regard that the said James Steell was an old possessor and being lykways addebted to me in 417 lib of bygon dewties, for and preceeding the cropt 82 I was moved out of my free Good will to give him a discharge of this debt and have gott a right from him to this debt of Cossens with the byegone @ rents thereof resting unpayed.

A tack to James Steel younger.

I have also granted a tack to the said James Steell's sone for the accustomed duty for ten years to run after the deceas of his father.

13 day. A tack to John Ramsay with the Kirktoun aickers of Tannadyce.

I have sett a tack of a number of the Churchtoune aikers of Tannadyce possessed last by James Smith To John Ramsay there for the old accustomed dewty together with the malt kill and coble with the use of the victual house so long as I have not use thereof myselfe. This was a house built by my father the lofts whereof in caise the ferme bear was not sold was designed for keeping of the bear so not to let it ly in the tenents hands And below tho. there was never a meall girnel yet if it shall be found necessarie there is a verie good place and roume for it in the furthermost end of the barne Hitherto the kill and coble hes been put to no profitt nor anything placed in rentall for it, but now John Ramsay payes yearlie by his tack 13 lib 6 sh.s 8 p. for it and when the tack expyres the duty may be raised to a halfe or at least a third pairt more.

I have compted with Andrew Wright[62] who is the wright imployed in my building he hes gott in the first place a great dale before now wch shall not | be mentioned or resumed here, and amongst that the rowme he possesses in Longforgone called the Byrflet for payment of a small feu duty, the rentall of it was ten bolls of bear besyds the teind sheave drawne. But to look forward there is contracts standing betwixt us for the work at Glammiss wch is still unfinished as weell plaister work as wright work, and there remains att this day due to him conforme to the fitted accompt five hunder sixtie nyne pond eight shilling. There was lykwayes severall other compts of by work wch are all cleared preceeding this day. 14 day. *fol.* 69.

There is lykewayes ane undertaking of his att the Church of Longforgen wch is be itselfe. Nothing is payed hereof except what he rests by his last discharge of his aiker roume cropt 1682.

Alexander Nicol on of the four tenants of Kinaltie being dead and having run himselfe in the tuo yeares wherein he brooked the roume in some debt to me, and his father James Nicol yet in more debt both in my owne time and in my father's and his children being verie young I was forced to deal with others and so found on Robert Doig who's daughter Nicol had married, and so for love of his grandchild or upon other private reasons undertook the debt and took tacks of the roume wch I put him in and his son James who are bound conjunctlie and sev^llie as it stands plenished, they are oblidged by tack to pay the usuall duty as before and have given their bond for six hunder sixtie six pond thirtein shilling four pennies wch tho. it be short of what was addebted to me by these Nicols first and last, yet it is more then ever I could have receaved from the Nicols unless I had exposed the roume to the hazard of being casten waist. 16 day. A tack of the fourth pairt of the toun of Kinaltie to Robert and Ja. Doigs. *fol.* 70.

I have this day made the Tax Roll of Auchterhouse conforme to the act of parliment for my releife of the present publick burdens. The Tax Roll of Auchterhouse.

There was on David Kidd who lived in the Templebank of Thorntone wch is of dewtie eight bolls bear, eight bolls meall, and twelve pouttrie, he putt into my hands as much more as the @ rent thereof exhausted the rent save sixteine pond that he payed of superplus dutie yearlie. This honest old man dyed without ishue and of his owne good will was pleased not only to discharge the debt w[ch] I did owe him and left my bond to be given up to me but did lykwayes leave any litle stock w[ch] he had on the roume to me, and dyeing in the tale of harvest 1683 the roume became so void of a tenent so I aggried in this moneth of ffebruarij with on James Gordon, who had a litle tenement hard by and I behoov'd in regard the season was farr past to grant him considerable help for the tillage for the cropt 1684 and a quarter of victual halfe beare halfe meall of deduction of the rentall for the said yeare and it was reasonable lykways to quitt him the pouttrie because he [got] not the Tofts, and so having entered in a minute with him he is now tenent in the templebank for the old dutie in a five years tack.

18 day. David Kidd's Legacie.

James Gordon succeeding tenent in Templebank.

James Stevinson Maltman in Glammiss.

I have signed a tack to James Stevinson maltman in Glammiss for the malthouse w[ch] is improven somewhat of the dutie for it was of old twentie five pond yearlie and is now thirtie thrie pond six shill. eight pennies, this was reasonable to be done in regard of late the repar[nes] of the malt house cost me a good dale of money, there is lykwayes obleidged everie few yeares to pay a years dewty of entrie money. This James Stevinson has also gott thrie aickers of the Churchtoune Land in ferming and is to gett tuo more when the entries from the barns is made up thorrow the shade of land the lenth of Westhill, it not being possible to doe it in any certinty att present in regard of a great change of land and of an overturning of the most of these possessions by drawing out the lenth of the avenue that farr, for this I had lykeways thirtie thrie pond six
fol. 71. shilling eight pennie of entrie money.

Brewars in and about Glammiss.

I usually sell a quantity of bear more or less to my own brewars everie year at 13 sh.s 4d of the boll att least more then the current rate, but in regard the bargen was made for the cropt 1683 a month before the begining of January 1684 from w[ch] time this book has its comencement I doe not hear sett down in speciall the particular quantities or the persons names who bought, only the pryce accorded on with those in and about the toune of Glammiss is five pond six shill: eight pennies *p* boll and those few of them who payed readiest money hes 13 sh.s 8d of ease in the boll wch is yet six shilling eight pennies more then the current pryce in common mercats.

I have this day sold to James Stevinson sixtein bolls for readie money and other sixtein bolls att the pryce above mentioned and the bear is ordered to be delyvered to him of the growth of the Newtoun of Glammiss.

I signed a tack to Archibald Black of Patrick Lyons tenement in the toune of Glammiss of tuo aicker and a halfe of in-feild and ane aiker of out-feild for the accustomed dewtie during his and his wyf's lyfe time and twentie pond given by him of entrie money. 19 day.

There was on Thomas Nicoll for some time tenent in Cardean who becam banquerupt and insolvent of whom after much adoe I did att last obtaine securitie for a hunder and fiftie tuo pond wch after all was resting to me, and his brother Ja. Nicoll in Lindertis became good for it by a bond at thrie dayes dait. 21 day.

I signed a tack to David Smairt and Alex. Murison of four aickers of land at the Kirktoune of Tannadyce. 25 day. D. Smith A. Murison.

I have sent tuo hunder pond to M^r^. William Balvaird[63] for My son Pa. his use att Aberdeen as provision for the current quarter for wch he is att his returne to give an accompt as lykewayes the money wch he received att ther going there in the month of No^r^. Mr W. Balvaird.

fol. 72.

I payed to M^r^. John Lambie of Dunkennie a yeares @ rent of his princip^lle^ sowme conforme to his discharge of two hundred and fourtie eight pond of this days dait. March 10 day. Dunkennies @ rent.

Andrew Dall in Dundee is payed of his @ rent of fourtie pond from Wittsonday 1682 till Witt.—83 having gott twelve bolls of the cropt 82 att a lib 6 sh.s 8d. the boll wch comes to sixtie four pond and so twentie four pond more then that yeares interest so that just now his wyfe Margrat Croll hes gott a warrand for thrie bolls and a halfe of meall for sixtaine pond which payes his @ rent till Wittsonday—84. Andrew Dall's @ rent.

Moreover the said Margrat Croll is this day payed of our house compt of small things furnished by her from Dundee by a precept on the grinter att Castle Lyon for ten bolls of oats Margrat Croll house compt.

which is sold to her att 4 lib per boll and the superplus of the said compt payed in money.

There being a hunder and on pond payable out of my lands in the paroch of Glammiss to the minister serving the Cure as a pairt of his Local stipend to witt fiftie five pond out of Graystoune fourtie thrie pond out of Balnamoon, and three pond out of Westhill I have altogither reserved the payment of the whole tho. Graystone be in the factors charge to my owne care and so have this day payed the whole for the cropt 1682 and have also ordered the payment of the like soume for the cropt 1683. This is due to the said Min[r] besyde what is payable by the tenents as in Thorntoune by vertue of ther tacks and is never stated in Rentall.

Mr John Ramsay's @ rent.

I have sent in to Dundee to Helen Summers and her sone M[r]. John Ramsay the soume of tuo hunder pond scotts as the @ rent of thrie thousand thrie hunder and thirtie three pond six shillings eight pennies which was resting to them preceeding the terme att w[ch] my factor is to pay them out of the cropt 1683.

Mr David Cambell his @ rent.

I have payed sixtie pond to M[r]. David Cambell Minister at Menmure as a pairt of the @ rent unpayed by David Lyon of Whytwall of the princ[ll] soume of two thousand merks conforme to his discharge. *fol. 73.*

I have ordered and given money for buying of a salmond net to fish severall pools which hes hitherto been neglected upon the river of Southesque lying to my lands of Tannadyce and Barneyeards and have given a commissione for fishing these watters to John Ramsay for the pay[t] only of the third fish he shall take. This is only for a tryall till I know to what availl it may trewlie extend and I have good reason to take notice of this because that divers thereabouts made a litle too bold to fish my waters and to draw upon my syde, especially the Laird of Findheaven who is such a neighbour as it is fitt allwayes to take narrow notice and to curb his incrotchments to which no man is more addicted then he who by hear-sayes and the stories of old people is much influenced (ffinheaven being the old seatt and ancient inheritance of the Earls of Crafoord) and is apish of the priviledges whereto his predecessors in those lands had never right but assumed it over the neighbours even from Brechen to Cortochie, the most pairt of them being all

The Fishing of Tannadyce and Barneyeards set to John Ramsay.

private gentlemen who thought it not fitt to be heard with him, and my ancestors ther residence never being upon the place never made it ther concern tho. now everie on of the proprietors keep ther fishing and maintain it within ther own bounds.

Sold in Dundee fiftie bolls of bear to on William Ogilvy a brewar att 4 lib 13 sh.s 8 d. the boll which is to be applyed towards the payment of Doctor Yeaman's son's @ rents, and James Lyon his factor is to be compted with that a clear discharge may be gott. 18 day. fiftie bolls bear sold to Wm Ogilvy.

I have compted with Provost Couts for his bargen of the victual of Tannadyce of the cropt 1682 out of the effects of which there was six hunder pond payed to the E. of Panmure of bygane feu dewties of the Tullos. Twelve hunder and odd ponds retained by the Provost towards the payment in pairt of a debt due to him Three hunder pond as his @ rent of five thousand pond resting by bond from Witt. 1682 till Witt. 1683 on accompt of sweetmeats furnished to the house and other things arrysing to upwards of three hunder pond and by our last fitted accompt there is eight | hunder and thirtie four pond yet resting to him. Provost Couts accts cleared of the cropt 82. *fol.* 74.

An accompt also of thirtie five pond eight shillings resting to Bailie Pyper in Montrose for black crap and other things is payed this day. Bailie Pyper's acct payed.

I have sent of this days date a bill to my sone for twelve hunder pond. My Eldest sones bill for money.

Payed to the Smith, John Waker the remnent of the money due to him for the raile erected on the top of the house of Glammiss being two hunder and twentie thrie pond. John Waker the Smith's last payment.

I have set in tack the lands of Eastfield to John Hill there for the ordinarie duty att Auchterhous. John Hill.

I have taken in and cleered James Coupers compts of his intromissione both att Auchterhouse and Litle blair for the cropt 1681 and 1682 so that what @ rents or other things payed by the discharge of these accompts are therein sett doune I doe not think it fitt here to resume them further then that a good many of the @ rents of these debts which are appoynted to be payed by the factor att Auchterhouse and Litle blair as is sett doune in the twelth page of this book are accordingly 26 day. James Couper's Accts.

payed and the discharges lying amongst the instructions of the accompts of these yeares.

James Crighton @ rent.

And to overtake the payment of James Crighton's @ rent w[ch] is a considerable soum yearlie I have given a warrant to James Couper who is the youth's tutor to uplift and receive from the tenents in Dronlaw of their bygone rests as much as with a small ballance w[ch] he was resting by the carelessness of his fitted acct to me maks up a full yeares @ rent being five *fol. 75.* hunder and sixtie pond and commences from Mert. '82 to Mert. '83.

Tax money of Auchterhous compted and payed fiftie bolls bear sold to the brewars att Auchterhouse.

I have this day compted with the ground officer of Auchterhouse for his collectione of the Tax money there w[ch] extends to no more then on hunder and eightie four pond.

Att my comeing att this time from Glammis to Castle Lyon being att Auchterhouse in the way I sold to the brewars there about fiftie bolls of the ferme bear of that place att 5 lib. 6/8d. the boll.

3 day of Aprill. John ffyfe.

I have signed tacks to John ffyfe in Shillhill of Alex. Newtons roume of Kintyrie and the said Alex. Newton being by some malchance run so in debt albeit the roume be extraordinarie weell worth the duty must be taken notice off that he embezel not his goods after bear seed time and his cornes in harvest.

John Bell.

I have also signed a tack to on John Bell in Cerrithill of Archibold Cudbert's roume of the bents.

Bond of releif from the Earle of Northesque.

I sett this doune w[ch] follows for a memoriall least if it please God to call upon me by death that those concerned after shall know that I became obleidged in a bond w[t] the late Earle of Northesque[64] if I remember rightlie to Scugal Lord Whyt Kirke[65] on of the senators of the Colledge of Justice for a certaine soume of money wherein we were both principalls albeit it is really the Earle of Northesque his owne proper debt to evidence w[ch] I have his bond of releif w[ch] lyes in on of the shottles of my cabinet at Edēn. this is fitt to be known and its as fitt to keep in custodie that bond of releife least the first bond wherein I am bond principall with the Earle of Northesque may fall into the hands of a stranger who may procure an assignment to it.

Sicklyke I became obleidged for the Laird of ffinheaven the

same maner of way to Doctor Gleig[66] in Dundee— I cannot particularly condescend on the same but I have a bond of releife and it lyes in the same place w[t] the other, it will be fitt to press Phinheaven to releife me of this engagement, standing in no wayes obleidged to him. *and sicklyk from his brother the Laird of Phinheaven.* *fol. 76.*

I have compted this day with George Ramsay sklaiter for his whole work both att Glammiss and Castle Lyon in the yeare 1682 and 1683 and I find over the partial payments w[ch] he hes received there is yet due to him on hunder and nyntein pond and six bolls of meall, w[ch] I have this day ordered to be payed to him and he has sub[t] the accompt. *George Ramsay Sklaiter.*

I have made the Tax Roll att Castle Lyon, and have committed the collectione yr.of to James Doss, ground officer. *Tax Roll att Castle Lyon.*

I sold to the brewars of Longforgone the matter of fyve chalders of ther owne ferme bear att 5 lib. 13/8d. *p* boll. *Brewars at Longforgone.*

I have ordered the payment to the four constant masons att Castle Lyon of a hunder and six pond thirtein shilling four pennies as the pryce of the new wall w[ch] is built upon the south syde of the southmost greene of the entrie there, being twentie roods thereof. *The masons' pay.*

I being debitor to Heugh Wallace the cash Keeper, I have allowed him retentione of a hunder and fiftie pond starlen being my mertimes terms pensione last past upon his receit in pairt of payment, and resolve sicklyke that he shall have the Whittsunday ensuing w[ch] will goe near to pay him off att w[ch] time compts shall be made and the superplus payed that so my bond may be secured. *Heugh Wallace Cash Keeper.*

10th day. I have at last after much adoe and straining of Andrew Gray obtained security for the remains of what he owes me and so have gott bond from M[r]. George Gray, wreitter in Dundee for three hunder and fiftie pond four shilling payable at Mertimes nixt with halfe a yeares @ rent, but new debt runs on and care most be taken not to suffer two terms to run in on unpayed for he payes of yearlie duty two hunder pond scotts so that att Witt. nixt there falls a hunder pond due.

11th day. I have this day cleared a current acct. with John Duncan on of the late Bailies of Dundee I rest to him of ballance by the said acct seven hunder and fiftie four pond I have | gott his discharge of the @ rent of the principall soume I owe him *Compt cleared with John Duncan. His @ rent payed till Candlemes.* *fol. 77.*

preceeding Candlemas last I sold to him five hunder bolls meall att four pond the boll, the effects of which are to be retained by him for the payment of the ballance of his accompt and of on thousand thrie hunder and thirtie thrie pond on shilling eight pennies of his principal soume att Candlemes last.

500 bolls meall sold to him and twentie by on Thomas Davie.

And to the end that the provision of meall may answer these two payments I have this day ordered Thomas Davie in Longforgane to delyver to him twentie bolls of his ferme meall upon his receit thereof wch is to be by and attour the other five hunder bolls wch is to pay the odd money which the two soumes that he hes payment and retentione of exceeds two thousand pond. And so soon as the delyverie is compleited wee are to adjust the same.

16 day. James Burghs acc^t^ cleared and some sixtie bolls meall bought be him.

I have cleared accompt with James Burgh, timber merchant and owe him by the said accompt two hunder pond and some odds whereof payed to him a hunder pond this day and he hes bought three score bolls of meal at 4 lib. 3/8d. the boll upon which he is to give receits so that according to them he is to be compted with for more or less according to the delyverie and what the same exceeds the soume resting to him according to the ballance of the acc^t^ which he has marked with my owne hand I am to take timber for it at his returne as wee can agrie and if not he is to pay me the money.

18 day.

I have this day cleared and payed off four masons who were brought a purpose from Glammiss to rebuild the wall of the oarchard upon the south syd of the avenue as it is now reformed wch stands me fourscore ponds scotts.

20 bolls bear and 100 b. meall sold to James Bower.

Sold to James Bower[67] in Dundee twentie bolls of bear and a hunder bolls of meall. The first att 4 lib. 13/8d. the boll and the last at 4 lib. 3 sh.s 4d. I have with him and other pairtners in Dundee a share of the shipp called the Lyon and I did owe the ballance of an acct to Bowers father, so that the effects of *fol.* 78. this must goe | In the first place to the payment of that and the eight pairt of the victual is upon my own adventure to Norroway.

Alex^r^. Cran masone.

I have appointed the tenents of Balnamoon to pay in there severall silver dewties to Alex^r^ Cran, masone, towards his payment.

Having compted with James Reed for the excsess of his dewtie payable by him for this tack of the yeards parks, meddows and milne of Auchterhouse payable at Mickelmess '83 and for pittpoyntie the said yeare over his @ rent of four hunder pond, he hes cleared bygons excepting a hunder and on pond and some odd shillings which is to goe in so farr towards the payment of Mistress Hays bygone @ rent att Perth. May 21-22-23-24 James Reed compted with.

My Lady Buchan's annuitie payable att Wittsunday '84 is ordered according to the resolutione and divisione of those things before sett downe amongst my factors. My Lady Buchan's annuity for Wittsunday 1684.

And sicklyke William Geekie's @ rents is ordered to be payed to James Christie in Auchterhouse. Will Geikie's @ rent.

The moss-meall money and compt thereof is fitted and cleared with John Smith in Drumgley moss greive for the yeare 1683 and a new commissione given him for this current yeare. The moss meall of Drumgley in the year 1683.

Mr Robert Hay of Dronlaw having commensed an action against me wherein he alledges that I made a bargen wt him about his land notwithstanding ther was no bargen but a communing and that I possessed the same by virtue of expyred apprysing, yet he does so importune the Lords of Sessione craveing allwayes my oath upon the termes of the bargen when he knowes that I am neither in Edēn nor desyre to be in it ceasing to insist in his actione when I am there that he is now the second time obtained a sentence of the Lords for the payment to him of three hunder thirtie thrie pond three shillings eight pennies as a mean for his subsistence during the dependence thus they out of pitie more then justice are bountifull to him att my charge and at this rate he may pray the actione never to be on end. The first decree was in summer '82 which was accordingly payed, this last is also ordered now to be payed by the brewers wtin the paroch who have gott of my bear out of the effects thereof and when payment is made its fitt to gett not only a receit from him but the decrees and sentences of the Lords. Mr Robert Hay of Dronlaw.

fol. 79.

I was owing to Alexander fforester[68] of Milnhill twelve hunder pond scotts which by a hunder and nine bolls wch he gott of the cropt '82 and retentione of his owne feu dewtie by the feu dewtie of the Knap for the yeares '82 and '83 and the The Last of Mai.

Alexander ffforester. teind bolls payable by him the said two yeares according to a fitted accompt he is fully payed and the bond retyred, but I still owe him by a tiquet two hunder pond. This is also payed.

Laird of Layis @ rent. I have this day given a warrand to the three brewars in fforgane, John Lyon, Alex[r] Watsone and Thomas Davie for four score of ponds each of them which payes the Laird of Leyes @ rent till Witt. immediatlie last past '84.

Some Masons compted with. I have this day compted and cleared with these masons who built the low wall below the great gardine.

Anna Hume's @ rent payed. I have payed Anna Hume two yeares @ rent of her principall soume of 333 lib. 6sh.s 8d. till Mertinmes nixt by a precept on Provost Couts.

June 2 day. Bailie Watson. I have sold a hunder bolls of meall to Bailie Thomas Watsone in Dundee at 4 lib. the boll w[ch] is desyred for his owne payment of 400 lib. which I owe him by bond and is the remainder of the 4000 lib. and @ rents thereof which I was once oweing to him. I have given provisione by precepts to M[r] Patrick Jack for paying my publick burdens due at Witt. 84 for my lands in Perthshyre who is to report the discharge thereof to me from the public collector.

3 day. I have this day ordered the effects of the tuo hundred bolls of oatts sold to Bailie Raitt in Dundee being eight hunder pond to be payed to Andrew Young factor constitute by the Laird of Craigie Kid his curators being five yeares @ rent of 2666 : 13 : 4 which I owe of principall w[ch] payes the @ rent compleitly till Witt. last past 84.
Craigie Kids @ rent.

8 day Sir Tho. Stewart. My Eldest son. I borrowed from Sir Thomas Stewart[69] of Garntilly 3333 lib. 6/8d. w[ch] was occasioned for the most pairt because of My Eldest son's returning from his travels and bills being drawne upon me sooner then possibly I could gett provisione of my owne | as allreadie two severall bills for 1541 lib. and that I expect more from London.
fol. 80.

17 day RobertLindsay. I have this day after compt made with Robert Lindsay in Littlecoul exchanged the bond w[ch] he had of me of borrowed money for 233 lib. 6/8d. payed three termes @ rent thereof retyred the bond and given him a new bond for 800 lib.

M[r] Pa. Lyon of Carnustie. I have this day sent to M[r] Patrik Lyon of Carnustie 160 lib. as a yeares @ rent of 2666 : 13 : 4 commencing from Mertinmes 84 and his current pensione.

I was resting by my tiquet to Drumond[70] present Provost of of Edēn four score ponds wch was the ballance of a fitted accompt betwixt us and its this day payed and my tiquet retyred. 19 day. Provest Drumond.

The sadler, on Ramsay in Edēn his acct payed of 56 lib. 21 day. The Sadler's acct.

I have given provisione to James Nicol in Lindertis for buying of fiftie meat weddars as lykewayes hes ordered him to buy a hunder young sheep for stocking the Newtoun of Glammiss. An order for buying of sheep.

I have also caused provyde what by putting young oxen in stock for old oxen and by what is gott and apprysed over from tenents seventaine for fattening and for the use of my house and will yet stand in need of seven more my stent being four and twentie. Oxen for hoggs.

I have upon the Mains and Newtoun of Glammiss and att Castle Lyon pairtly for my pleughs and pairtly for my work a hunder oxen now standing and this is besyde my cowes and young cattel. A standing stock of 100 Oxen.

I payed to Bailie James Man[71] in Dundee a peice of Cleret wine wch was gott in the year '83 besyd the tunn wch I had from George Kinnaird. 3 day. Bailie Man payed of a piece of wine. *fol.* 81.

I gave provision to Mr Patrick Jack for paying the current terme of Whittsunday last past supply money and other publick burdens on my lands in Perthshyre, and accordingly he is to report discharge. Publick burdens payed in Perthshyre.

I have fraughted a ship for Dunkirk for the exporting to that place my whoal remnant of bear and pease to the number of about six hunder bolls. The particular acct of the voyage and success shall afterwards be sett doune. On Pat. Corser, skipper. Ship fraughted for Dunkirk.

I have sent in with M^r Pa. Jack to Mistriss Gray in Perth 360 lib. as three years @ rent of two thousand pond resting to her by gane att Mertimass last, all her preceeding rent having been trewly ordered by me to have been payed by Bailie Watsone in Perth wch payment she contraverts and affirms that the said Baily left so much of it unpayed tho. the treuth is he broke and went off the kingdome att the same time when on McKewan and his sone in Stirlen served me just so for my wheat three years agoe. But Mistriss Gray having accepted the precept and entered in pay^t therewith, ought not to recure 24 day. Three yeares @ rent of Mrs Gray in Perth.

upon me, especially seeing the said Watsone wrott to me before his departure that he had payed her.

25 day. Coals payed for.

A bark full of coall containing thirtie seven bolls bought and payed att 26 lib. 13 sh. 4d. *p.* chalder. This besyde another parcell brought in the month of Apryll, and the same bark is hyred again to returne.

The Closet w^{tin} my Charter house.

Agried with the four masones in Glammiss for digging down from the florr of the litle pantry off' the Lobbis a closet designed within the charter house there, for wch I am to give them 50 lib. scotts and four bolls meall.

July 1 day.

I have ordered the payment of a years @ rent due to the Laird of Nevay of 4000 lib prin^{ll} sowme I owe him this yeare is before David Sym's factory in who's division the payment
fol. 82. now is appoynted. This is on the Moss-greine of Drumgley.

Straton Apothecary.

I have payed Robert Stratone the apothecary his acct. of 123 lib. which is long owing and such accts are ridiculous, and I pray God help them who have ocassione to be much in there books, since ther drogs and pastiles are sett downe under such strange names and unknown marks that they cannot be weell controlled.

Robert Mitchell chapman.

I have also compleited Robert Mitchell a chapman his acct. preceeding Apryll last wch drew pretty deep and there is another current since.

Robert Sievwright another.

And sicklyke on Robert Sievwright of the same sett, tho. his accompt be not so deep.

5 day. Alexander Thomsone Sadler.

There was also an old accompt due to Alexander Thomsone sadler inflemed upon the expeditiones to the west contrie never cleared till this time by reasone of the rudness and importunity of the sadler, and now agried to extend to 320 lib. for which I have sold to him fourscore bolls oatts att 4 lib. the boll.

Mawers att Castle Lyon.

I have agried with the mawers upon a pennie for the making of my hey conforme to a particular nott thereof in another book for wch they have this year 44 lib. besyde bounties, this is att Castle Lyon for what is att Glammiss is referred to David Lyon not being upon the place.

This day does Corsar's shipp called the providence of Dundee sail, the bill of loadning is for tuo hunder and fourty nyne bolls wheat, tuo hunder and thirtie tuo bolls of bear and fiftie six bolls pease, and commissione is given to Mr. George fforrester to sell the same att the best availl. The shipp is bound for Dunkirk.

Payed to the Laird of Strathmartine his bygone @ rents and a pairt of his prin[ll] soume and a new bond gevin him for on thousand tuo hunder pond, and I presume I have assignment to as many of his debts w[ch] I took with his owne consent as will goe near to compose this soume. Strathmartin his @ rent.

I have payed to Mr. Carstairs, Minister of Inchtur 40 lib as a yeares @ rent of 666 lib. 13 sh.s 4d. w[ch] past to him by bond. This @ rent is payed till Wittsonday. M[r] Carstairs @ rent. *fol.* 83.

Much about this time I went to Edenburgh upon the comeing doune of the Earle of Perth,[72] Chancelour, where I stayed ten dayes.

I payed on Clark a taylour's acct of 107 lib 7s. Clark a taylour his acct payed.

Another accompt payed, on Bowder, a merchant, of 59 lib. Bowder a merch[t] payed.

I sold the lands of Inchkeith to Sir George M[c]Kenzie[73] of Tarbet, Lord Register, and have a few dewty payed to me 40 lib yearlie and a fellow deer. The pryce besyds this few dewty was 2000 lib. 23 day. Inchkeith sold.

Ordered the payment of sixtie four pond to Mr. John Balvaird,[74] minister of Kirkden, as a yeares @ rent of 1066 lib. 13 sh.s. 4d. resting to him of prin[ll] sowme by Peter Adam tenent in Drumgley and that out of the pryce of bear he bought, being a brewar. August 6 day. M[r] John Balvaird his @ rent.

ffollowes the accompt of the sail of the victuall att Dunkirk by Mr. George fforester. M[r] George fforester his acct.

His charge is

ffirst by 196 Razers wheat sold @ 9 lib 10 sh.s per Razer w[ch] comes to 1862 *inde.*	1862	00	00
By 19 Razers wheat sold at 8 lib 15 sh.s which is	0166	05	00
By 285 Razers bear att 4 lib 10 sh.s is	1282	00	00
By 47 Razers peas at 7 livers *p* Ra[r]	0329	00	00
By Cash receaved att Castle Lyon	0048	00	00
By Cash receaved for the brig dealling	0016	10	00
Summa tot.	3703	15	00

His discharge is

ffirst by cash payed the waiters at Dundee	0002	18	00
By customs payed at Dundee	0017	00	00

By the pettie customes and shore dews . .	0009	00	00
By the measuring the cornes	0013	13	00
By the factors charges in selling the corne .	0015	00	00
By the 60 suse [sous] per tone	0163	00	00
By custome to the toune of Dunkirk . .	0030	05	00
fol. 84. By tuo months advance of 1100 livers .	0022	00	00
20 of Agust. By fraught payed the skipper	0386	13	00
By avarage payed him	0015	00	00
By cash payed James Elder for wch he is comptable	0082	00	00
By cash payed the factor . . .	0072	00	00
By exchange of 2875 livers @ 1 *p* cent . .	0028	10	00
By my provisione of 2847 livers @ 5 livers *p* cent is	0142	10	00
The soume of this and of that on the other syde of Discharge is	0999	09	00
The ballance payed in is tuo thousand seven hunder and four livers and six souse *inde* .	2704	06	00

My son his last bill payed. Two horses bought.

I have payed My eldest son's last bill wch was payable tuo months after the drawing thereof of on hundred and thirtie pond sterlin. I have also payed seventie pond sterlin for tuo horses which his servant returned to Ingland for, and these two with the charge of bringing home the horses exceed the returne of the comissione from Dunkirk.

Thomas Broune of Lecoway on of our late factors.

Thomas Broune of Lecoway payed the sowme of five hunder thirtie and three pond sex shill. eight pen. wch the last uinter he gave bond to me for. The reasone of the granting of the bond was a compositione of a great many things I had to lay to his charge while he was my factor wch I chused rather to accept of then to torture my selfe att law with so confused a man.

There is yet an action against him to the value of 333 lib wch he has advocat from the Sherrif court wch at last cannot *fol.* 85. but come upon him.

My sone had of provisione for a litle start he made over to Edenburgh some sixtie dolers.

22 day. The Candlemaker's acct.

I payed the Candlemaker his acct. of the last winter's

candles as my wyfe acknowledges the same of a hunder pond or thereby.

Alexander Hume tylor had an old acc[t] resting to him exceeding five hunder pond scotts for which I at last accorded with him (the delay of the payment being for the exorbitance of the acct.) and caused delyver to him att Dundee a hunder and twentie five bolls of meal w[ch] at 4 lib *p* boll payed the whole accompt.

There being three years and a quarters @ rent due to Andrew Bruce, merchent att Edēn. I have ordered the payment of on yeare by Alex[r] Swin factor att Kinghorne. I have also secured him for the other two yeare and quarters interest due preceeding Lambas last 1684 and have renewed his bond for his prin[ll] soume of eight thousand pond wherein for his satisfaction My eldest son is bond with me. Andrew Bruce security renewed on the 23 day.

M[r] Andrew Reed hes sold the lands of Crachie Milne to the Earle of Southesque. I was moved upon his intreatie to take his bond for 33 lib. 6 ss. 8d. payable at Mertimas nixt being his few dewtie for Wittsunday and Mertimas '83 last past. M[r] Andrew Reed's few dewtie for the yeare 1683.

I was owing to the Collector of the Shyre of Angus, John Auchterlownie of Guynd the mertimas terme eightie thrie and Wittsunday's term eightie four supplie which extended to eleven hunder sixtie four pond or thereby, and this being too much to be owing att once I behooved to cut it short and so sent him seven hunder and sixtie four pond myselfe and ordered the payment of the other four hunder pond by equall portions from my three factors of Glammiss, Auchterhouse, and Tannadyce. September 2nd. Guynd the collector of Forfarshire.

I went to Edēn. to attend the Councill where I stayed two weeks. 3 day.

I payed there the tylor Maxwel's acct. w[ch] extended to 87 lib. or thereby. Maxwel, Tylor.

As also on M[rs] Douglas acct. about 40 lib. M[rs] Douglas Merch[t]. *fol.* 86.

I caused buy about twentie six stone of butter in the wye house and did pay the same. Butter bought.

And I payed on M[c]Gie 36 lib. for a whole intyre glass which he put some time agoe in on of my coatches. M[c]Gie's accompt.

I did add to the work before mentioned of a closet in my charterhouse severall things of a considerable trouble as the 25th day. Slopings in and about the Charter house at Glammiss.

digging thorrow passages from the new work to the old and thorrow that closet againe so as that now I have access off on flour from the east quarter of the house of Glammiss to the west syde of the house thorrow the low hall, and am to pay the masones because of the uncertainty y^r of dayes wages, and just so to the Wright and plaisterer. I bought from Bailie Duncan in Dundee a parsell of tuelve hunder and sixtie dales wch I am about to cause cary to this place just now Togither with two other parsells of dales which came home in the Lyon, a shipp whereof I am an owner in an eight pairt, the compt whereof must be cleared thereafter with the rest of the owners.

Two thousand dales or thereby bought and caried for Glammiss.

The Glazier's acct.

The Glazier's acct. of glass and weir for my new loft at the Church of Longforgan came to in about 60 lib. wch I ordered to be payed by my factor att Auchterhouse, it comprehended lykwayes the reparing of some broken glass windows att Castle Lyon.

Tack dewty of St. James ffair for the yeare 1684.

The toun of fforfare payed into me the tack dewty of St. James ffair which is 53 lib. 6 ss. 8d. yearlie and a yeares @ rent of 200 lib. which they owe me.

October 10th.

The Earle of Northesque[75] and I fitted an accompt, by wch I came debtor to him in five hunder fourtie six pond. The particulars whereof were too long here to narrate only let this serve, that hereby I retyred and am assigned to a debt of Invereightie's owen by Captain Wishart wch debt is on of those I was oblidged to pay for him and is contained in the List. Moreover there is two yeares @ rent payed of Bonner's debt conforme to the discharge wch are all in a bundle within the fitted accompt and in on of the boxes of my cabinet w^t other
fol. 87. of Invereightie's papers.

Coals payed.

I payed an accompt of coals which was a pairt of a loadning which came to the Burnmouth of Invergowrie and extended to fourtie eight pond or thereby, which was some dayes before the removall of my family from Castle Lyon and the remnant of a former accompt.

The hunting att Litle blair.

My sone gott twentie dolers when he went to his hunting in the Stormont att Litle blair.

William Rennay Painter.

William Rennay in Dundee hes gott towards his payment for the painting (such as it is) of the roofs of the Quir of Longforgone 40 lib. and a boll of meall.

30th Octr 1684. George Gullan's accompts.

George Gullan gave in his acct. of debursements of the last winter's sessione whereof the ballance was payed, but there are preceeding debursements of former yeares not cleered till which time ther's no acct. made nor payment of his pensione and his last subsct accompt is to be sought till the same be found.

Bond given for 333 lib. 6/8d. of Catheruood's mothr To on Pa. Corsar.

The said George Gullan by the right of his wyfe hes gott bond from me this day for three hunder thirtie thrie pond six shillings eight pennies to the behoove of a child on ffredrick Corsar a sone of Anna Carmichael (now the wyfe of George Gullan) by her first husband, who fell to the right thereof by a conveyance made by Elizabeth Wilsone Lady pennie-land, and is a pairt of that money which I did once owe to Baylie Catherwood in Edenburgh, the sowme was two thousand six hunder and sixtie six pond. The @ rents now payed to Catherwood's relict till Candlemes 1681. This Lady pennie-land hes right herselfe to a thousand pond of the forsaid debt and her @ rents are payed by my order be Lievtenant Hay who hes the discharge for his instructione, and there is a tiquet given to George Gullan for 60 lib. wch is all that falls due to him preceeding Mert. approaching, and is payable when he delyvers a discharge dewlie subscryved by the persone therein mentioned. The other halfe of this debt of Catherwood's is not yet taken course with in regard the persone who fell to the right thereof hes not made any applicane about it. *fol.* 88.

Mr Robert Blackwood.

I gave bond to Mr Robert Blackwood for four hunder pond payable att Christinmes nixt, and hes his discharge of all merchts accts preceeding this day's dait.

Mrs Hay her fies payed.

Mistris Hay went from my wyfe's service, and had all her bygone fies payed except somewhat whereon I cannot condescend, which she desyred my wyfe to keep for her payable on demand.

Robert Nish Wheelwright.

I caused bring from St. Andrews two sett of coatch wheels where they are only best to be had, which stood me four pond sterlin the sett, from Robert Nish, wheelwright.

1 day of November. Strathmartine's debt payed and my bond retyred.

I was oweing to the Laird Strathmartine twelve hunder thirtie six pond as the remainder of the Lands of Pittpoyntie which I bought of him, which I payed by giving him up bonds of his whereto I had right by assignatione. To Witt. his bond which he was oweing to James Reid in Auchterhouse; To

Andrew Ogilvy in Lindertes and ffrederick Lyon of Arnafoul extending to seven hunder and fiftaine pond four shilling ten pennies. And I gave him precepts, on upon James Reid for 233 lib. 6ss. 8d., on upon James Cristie in the Mains of Auchterhouse, for a hunder pond, another payable by Isobell Cristie, relict of Andrew Ogilvy in Lindertes for 178 lib. 10ss. 8d. w[ch] with 8 lib. 17ss. 10d. payed in money extends to 520 lib. 15ss. 2d. which two soumes does exactly amount to the debt due to Strathmartine and I retyred my bond from him.

10th Nov. Charges of Cossen's buriall payed.

This day I compted with M[r] Silvester Lyon,[76] minister of Killiemuire, who was pleased to be att the trouble when the late Laird of Cossens sicken'd and dyed their to keep an accompt of the expenses and charge he was att in the houss where he lay and of his buriall which came to a hunder pond scotts or thereby and w[ch] is this day ordered to be refinded to him.

fol. 89.

13 day. Marrie and Kattren Pillmer's @ rent payed by M[r] George Gray in Dundee.

Marie and Katteren Pillmers creditors of mine in twelve hunder pond scotts a peice received payment conforme to their discharge from M[r] George Gray, wreiter in Dundee of the soume of three hunder three score two pond four shilling. There was three yeares @ rent resting to Katteren and tuo yeares to Marrie preceeding this Mertimes new past so that the soume now payed overpayes their @ rent and it is to be imputed towards their principall sowme, which must needs be taken course with, with all possible convenience for that they are very inhumaine and rigid creditors, ignorant of themselves and inflamed by some ill-willer.

A debt resting be the toune of fforfare payed.

The toune of fforfare payed two hunder thirtie 3 lib. 6ss. 8d. with a yeares @ rent w[ch] they were resting to me by bond, there bond was delyvered up and discharged.

Given towards my son's goeing to the College.

This money was given in pairt of provisione for my second son's goeing to the Colledge of Aberdeen nixt week.

A horse bought for the stone carts.

I bought a horse for the use of the stone cart att Castle Lyon from John Lyon of Longforgone and am to allow him fiftie thrie pond six shill. 8d. as his pryce.

Mittchell went out of Westhill.

Some weeks before now John Mitchell in West hill being a miscreant unthriftie fellow and an ill payer, I chosed rather to put him out of his possession then to continue him any longer therein, and after compt made with him he is truly resting me besyds his dewtie cropt 84 for w[ch] there are some pitefull cornes in the yeard, the sowme of 205 lib. 5ss. 10d. which if it be possible means are to be used to recover it from his cau[r] who is on James Smith for the present att London, a journeyman and smith.

I have sett his roume for the same dewtie to ffrancis Doig in the Myretoun. and the same is sett to ffrancis Doig.

Having this day compted with James Nicoll my tenent in *fol. 90.* Lindertes for money partlie w[ch] I gave him in provisione att Wittsunday last to buy wedders for the use of my house I find he bought att sundrie times att several places and several mercats, the number of seventie three wedders (besyds fiftein young sheep and two rams) which is all which was bought this year, but it's to be taken notice of that the custome sheep are punctually gotten in besyds. Seventie three wedders bought.

I ended and cleared all accompts preceeding this dayes date with John Jollie Merchant in Edēn. and I am resting him of ballance 466 lib. 13ss. 4d. towards the payment of which I have sold him two hunder bolls of bear att 4 lib. 13ss. 4d. p boll and two hunder bolls of meall att 4 lib. to be delyvered att Candlemes, and to be retentione of the ballance resting to him by the exception of the contract. 17 day. Compts cleared with John Jollie.

Lykeas out of the pryce and effects thereof he's obleidged to retyre to me M[r] Robert Blackwood's bond w[ch] I latlie gave him for 400 lib. payable at Cristinmes and another bond for a lesser soume or not exceeding that in the hands of Bailie Spence in Edēn. And the remainder is not payable till Lambes att w[ch] time if there be any new current compt he is then to have retention of what it shall amount to. The way of M[r] Blackwood's pay[t] and Bailie Spence in Edēn.

John Ross, on of the late tenents in Tannadyce hes att last given a new security for what after all he was resting to me, so that I have gotten bond from him for 145 lib. and Wester Ogill cāur. as lykewayes for the payment of the current yeares dewtie, I designe to sett asyde this bond amongst others for my transaction with Burnsyde. 18 day. John Ross bond designed for Burnsyde.

For fulfilling my promise to Bridgton and his curators every on of us having resolved to take off more or less of his creditors for the concealment of his debt, My share was to have been

John Huntar his debt deu by Bridgton transacted for w^t James Elder and Isobell Crighton who were the persones who stood in the right thereof.

two thousand merks, and I took off ffredrick Lyon in the begining of this current yeare, mentioned on the third page of this book, and now I have transacted with James Elder and his wife Isobell Crighton, who was the relict of on John Hunter to whom | the debt was first oweing, prin^{ll} soume was 666 lib. 13ss. 4d. and no less then 520 lib. of bygone @ rent, all wch I am assigned to, and it will not be amiss that I caus draw a bond of corroboratione to be signed be Bridgton and his curators both for ffrederick Lyon's debt and this presentlie narrated prin^{ll} and @ rent.

fol. 91.

Ja. Smith a crediter of Bridgton's will be resting owing me 300 lib. or thereby.

Bridgton is also debitor to on James Smith, sometime hammerman in Glammiss. This Ja. Smith owes me by bond a hunder pond scotts and he also became cāur. for on John Mitchell in the tack of Westhill whom I thrust out of the possession for ill payment, who after compt was found resting me two hunder and five pond 10ss. 5d. so that I designe if possablie I can by arrestment and other diligences to effect the money oweing to him by Bridgton wch being done to includ this also in Bridgtons' bond of corroboratione, all which aryse to upwards of two thousand pond wherein Bridgton will be debitor to me, which is designed to be foreborne till he come to be major and then to be repayed or then to effect therewith the lands of Scrogiefeild wch is the only roume he hes in the paroch of Glammiss.

A bond of corroboration to be gott from Bridgton and his curators.

Bond given to Ja. Elder for 617 lib.

Att my transactions with James Elder I payed him of all the bygane @ rents and gave him bond, his accompt and mine running just so for 617 lib. 5ss. and I purpose to allow him yearlie retentione of his current dewtie and the pryce of what bear he buys, being a brewar in the toune of Glammiss, till he be fully payed not only of this soume but of 666 lib. 13ss. 4d. due to him by his wyfe, who's the daughter of on M^r Ja. Crighton, this being the sixth pairt of the soume wch I did owe to him, and the portione designed her thereof by hir father.

20 day. New bond given to Bailie Duncan.

I have conforme to my agreement with Bailie Duncan mentioned on the 76th page of this book, cleared all his bygone @ rents wch was resting, payed him 1333. 6. 8d. of his prin^{ll} soume, and given him new bond for 2000 lib. bearing @ rent from Mertimes last.

fol. 92.

Compted with Bailzie Watsone for the hundered bolls of meall sold to him mentioned in the 79th page, and accordingly I reteered my bond from him for 400 lib. wch is the remnant of 4000 lib. I was ones resting to him. Bailzie Watsone payed.

I agried with James Man, Robert Kinloch,[77] and Alexander Raite,[78] Bailzies in Dundee, and sold to them a thousand bolls of bear att 4 lib. 16ss. 8d. p boll. The on halfe of the money payed in hand and the other payable at Wittsunday. I give them twenty bolls of meall to the bargon and they give me a quarter of a butt of sack. 21 day. A thousand bolls of bear sold.

There being great @ rent no less then from Wittsunday '73 till Witt. '84 is eleven yeares resting to Doctor Yeaman's[79] son of the prin^ll soume of 4000 lib. att least I cannot fall upon any discharge mentioning payment since that time, I have within these two yeares been labouring to overtake the payments and have payed to James Lyon factor appoynted by his tutors 1920 lib. or thereby, but have not been able to clear all bygons hitherto. Doctor Yeaman's son's @ rent payed.

I have sent to Sir James Sinclar of Kinnaird -360 lib. as a yeares @ rent of 6000 lib. wch I owe him wch payes reallie and truly till Wittsunday last, tho. he is pleased only to give a discharge for on yeare in generall pretending that there is a yeare more resting to him. Sir James Sinclaris @ rent payed.

I payed an accompt in Herrie Craford's, shop-keeper in Dundee and gott his relicts discharge for upwards of 100 lib. scotts. 24 day. Merch^t accompt payed to Herrie Craford's relict.

I payed to George Gollan the money of my tiquet and retyred it accordingly to the article relating thereto on the 87th page. George Gollan.

I payed Margrat Croll her @ rent upon her husband Andrew Dall's discharge of 40 lib. till Witt. '84. Andrew Dall's @ rent payed.

I payed an accompt of seck in Dundee wch was bought there from merchants being the first hand and not from vintners, there being no seck in my house att this time, in great the acct came toward 60 lib. An acct. of seck payed in Dundee.

fol. 93.

This day my eldest son went for Edenburgh and there was a hunder croune given to his servant John Lyon to compt for to his master. 25 day. My eldest son's goeing to Edēn.

Given to Mr William Balvaird as much money as w^t what

My son Pat. his goeing to Aberdeen.

he gott before mentioned on 89th page as maks up 266 lib. 13ss. 4d. towards my son Pat. his charge for his quarter goeing now to Aberdeen to the Colledge. And to Mr William for his owne use 66 lib. 13. 4d.

Mr Ranken Catechist in Dundee his @ rent payed till Lambes '82.

I have also payed to Mr James Ranken Catechist in Dundee, conforme to his discharge 200 lib. as a yeares @ rent of 3333 lib. 6ss. 8d. wch is in my hand of money mortefied by Mr Pa. Yeaman to those in that office. By which particulars immediately before mentioned my fingers apeared clean and the money is exchanged.

Bear sold to Tho. Steel in Dundee.

Sold att the same time to Tho. Steell in Dundee a hunder bolls of bear att five pond the boll.

27 day. George Innes of Denoon's few dewtie.

I compted this day with George Innes of Easter Denoon for his bygone few dewties commencing from Wittsunday '75 till Wittsunday '84 att 30 lib. yearlie, and his former payments being compted he wes found resting to me 158 lib. 1s. 8d. for wch I have gotten bond but for payment thereof I bought fourtie bolls of bear from him att 4 lib. 3ss. 4d. the boll, and so when he delyvers the merchants receits to me to whom I directed him he is to gett up his bond againe and the ballance what the said fourtie bolls extends to more then the soume contained in the bond, but here I gaine by the pryce that I have sold att in Dundee 26 lib. 13ss. 4d.

1st day of December. Dunkenny his @ rent till Witt. 1684.

I have this day saved David Lyon the trouble of the payment of a yeares @ rent to Dunkenny having given him my selfe provisione, partlie in money and partlie be a good debtor for the doeing of it and he is to report me Dunkenny's discharge, being for the sum of two hunder and fourtie eight pond wch I am to lay up with the rest of his discharges and papers by wch I have it cleerly in prospect to pay him his prinll soume att Wittsunday.

3 day. Payed Margrat Huntair her bond. Katteren Lyon payed.

This day I have payed att my Broking compt wt Margrat Huntair and John Cheplan her son in Lochmilne the soume of 406 lib. I was oweing to them by bond and a deall of bygon @ rents. Payed to Katheren Lyon her annuity due att Mertimes last past.

fol. 94.

3rd of December. Bear of Tannadyce sold to Provest Coutts att 5 lib. the boll.

I have sold to provest Coutts in Montrose my bear of Tannadyce and the fforest and places adjacent att 5 lib. the boll payable at Wittsunday. I am to order my factor for the whole that is there without any reserve and particularly those few who have engaged to delyver bear ower their ferme this bargon, being new, sold it, being altogither needless to bring the same to my lofts att Glammiss and lykwayes to give orders for selling the stra of the corn yeard of Kintyrie and for threshing out the bear to the end it may be carried. I am also to endeavour to cause delyver att Dundee a hundred bolls of bear in case Mr Jollie to whom I have sold two hundered transferr his bargon to provest Coutts.

I have also cleered accts. with provest Coutts for the bear of the cropt 82 (our bargon of the meall mentioned before in this book not holding) for how soon the bear was all delyvered wch he had most a neid for he rejected the other. The effect of this bear served to pay the ballance of the former immediat compt wherein I was debtor to him in a hunder and odd ponds as lykwayes his interest of the prinll soume I owe him from Witt. '82 till Witt. '83 and an account of sweetmeats partlie received for the use of my house amounting to upwards of two hunder pond. The ballance is now by the presented staited subt acct. betwixt us upon his part due to me for a small matter current to the nixt acct. which shall goe toward the payment of the sweetmeat acct. wch as it stands corrected on the margene is not payed.

It is to be remarked that the two hunder pond was not allowed in the last fitted acct. but only in the next being 215 lib.

I payed to Mistris Ogilvy the relict of Mr William Ogilvy minister at Neuburn her @ rent from Mert. 1678 to Mert. '84 of the prinll sum of seven hundered pond or thereby, ffor which I gott her discharge.

23rd day. Mrs Ogilvy her @ rent payed.

I was owing to Heugh Wallace his majestie's Cash Keeper four thousand pond wch since that he was desyrous to have payment because of his purchase of land I carefully complyed therewith and allowed to him retentione of the money of my pensione for his payt.

Four thousand pond payed of debt wch I did owe to Heugh Wallace Cash-keeper.

fol. 95.

To witt Mert. '83 and Mert. '84 and so much of Mert. '84 as completed the soume. The superplus he payed in to me upon wch I discharged these three termes.

My pensione payed for Mert. 1684.

Payed to Craigmillar 580 lib. as the @ rent of 9666 lib. 13. 4 wch I owe to him and that from Candlemes '83 till Candlemes '84. Tho. by his discharge he giv's only a receite of the money because of his adjudicatione now running

Craigmiller his @ rent payed till Candlemes '84.

But that by his former discharge it 's clear there was no more resting.

7 pond sterlin payed to Banackburn.

I payed the secretaries dues to Paterson of Banockburn, keeper of the signet office being seven pond sterlin. It was for a letter under his Majesties hand direct to the treasurer about the Lord Cardross'[80] fine out of the payment of which I yet ly from Sir William Sharp who was Cash-keeper att that time.

Mistris Stewart's house rent payed.

There being yet due to Mistris Stewart 133 lib. 6ss. 8d. as halfe a yeares rent of her house where I lodged some yeares agoe att the Golden Unicorne she is this day satisfied and payed thereof.

Mr Lyell a mercht in London.

There was a years @ rent gott from on John Davison a merchant in Leith who owes me betwixt five and six thousand merks as the pryce of a bargen of meall, of the cropt '82 and who contraire to all honesty, in defraud of the payment, obtained a protectione wh bearing the payment of his @ rents to his creditors he was thereupon atached by a messr with a caption, and this obleidged him to pay the bygon interest wch was given to on David Plenderleith an agent for Mr Lyel, merchant in London and is to goe towards his payment of a considerable debt I owe to him in so farr Baylie Hac did receive also for the use of Mr Lyell 500 lib. scotts or thereby and I waite for an answer from Lyell of a proposall I have made towards his compleit payment.

29 day. The Earle of Southesque his payments.

I have ordered the payment of a debt wch I owe to the Earle of Southesque of a hunder pond sterlin by a precept on provest Couts of Montrose.

A freinge maker payed.

I payed Mrs Stelfoord a woman who makes freinges 50 lib. scotts wch was for an acct. resting to her.

Bailie Spence's payment.

I drew a precept this day on John Jollie for paying and retyring my bond from Baylie Spence conforme to Jollie's obleidgment to me in a contract past betwixt us.

fol. 96.

The pament for the extract of the decreet for our releife anent Heriot's Hospital and The resolutiones taken thereanent.

The debt wherein the E. of Erroll and I stand engaged to Heriot's Hospitall[81] of Edenburgh extending now to about a hunder thousand merks, and being about to extract our decreet of locality upon the estate of the late Earle of Argile of Lands in Kintyr for our releif There falls due conforme to the king's order att three of the hunder to the Clerk of the Commissione two thousand pond wch I have this day advanced, I mean the Earle of Erroll's halfe as weell as my own he not being in toune and for payment thereof have drawen a precept upon the Lord Register out of the pryce of Inchkeith, and have wrĩn a letter to Boyl[82] of Kelburne our factor in Kintyre for the returne of money it being resolved upon by my Lord Erroll and me to refund our selves of the expense of what our decreet of Locality and passing of the sealls shall stand out of the first end of these rents Thereafter to apply the rent soly for the payment of the yearlie @ rent due to the hospital so that by Kelburne's returne I most be reimbursed of this advancement.

It will be fitt lykewayes that we order Kelburne to pay to the Kings Advocat what we gave him bond for, for his pains.

I owe to Sir James Rochhead five thousand merks borrowed in October '75. I find only a discharge of a year and three quarters @ rent granted in the yeare '77. I have sett asyde my second son his pay for the overtaking his @ rents in the first place and then for the pay[t] of his prin[ll] soume w[ch] payment began att Wittsunday last. Sir James Rochhead his last discharge of @ rent was in Oct[r] '77.

I was oweing to John Hamilton, Stabler in the Canongate 50 lib. 10ss. less for the payment of w[ch] I have drawn a precept on my factor Alex. Swin for ten bolls of oatts w[ch] att 5 lib. 6ss. 8d. p boll comes to fiftie thrie pond 6ss. 8d. So John hamilton at the getting of the precept payes in 3 lib. 6ss. 8d. John Hamilton Stabler, payed.

I had of his Majestie the gift of five hunder pond sterlin of the Lord Cardross' fyn whereof I granted the receit to Sir W[m] Sharp[83] upon his tiquet and obleidgement for the same for the payment of w[ch] Sir W[m] gott bond from the Earle of Mar and other of the Lord Cardros freinds, and now the way of payment proposed is that I having given to the Countess of Buchan when I entered first to the Lands of Auchterhouse bond for the paying of her the @ rent of twentie thousand merks yearlie during her lyfetim in consideratioun of her renonciatione of her lyf-rent right | which she desyred might be given in fie to her son the Earle of Buchan and accordingly the bond was conceeded, payment thereafter was made att the Countess desyre of nyn thousand merks thereof to Robert Straton, apothecarie in Dundee who had a wedsett in the North Inch not redeemed with the money for the Countes life, so I gave a Lord Cardros fyn. *fol. 97.*

The Earle of Mar. Countes of Buchan.

new bond in the same termes for the said eleven thousand merks which remained of the twentie and have payed the @ rent thereof previously twice in the year to the Countes whereof the last was att Wittsunday '84, now the Earle of Buchan having assigned his right of fie to the Lord Cardros and he having transferred the same to the Earle of Mar it is proposed that I should accept of discharge of the said debt as payment to me of the forsaid fyn and the Earle of Mar, in prospect hereof hes payed to the Countes of Buchan her @ rent due att Mertemes last '84 being two hundered and twentie pond And is att our returne to town to render the transaction effectuall that so Sir Wm Sharp may gett his obleidgment up, care is to be taken that I be sufficiently discharged of the said eleven thousand merks, especially against Mr Robert Hay, who as a creditor of the Earle of Buchan's hes endeavoured to affect this money.

Being debitor to Sir John Maitland [84] in the soume of 2000 lib. prin^ll and bygone @ rent and he being verie pressing for his money I have this day drawne a precept upon my bear-merchants in Dundee for the payment thereof at Witt. nixt.

fol. 98 [blank].

fol. 99. Followes an account of my busines in the former Method Beginning now the first of January 1685.

1 day of January. Adam ffowelli's @ rent payed.

I payed to Adam ffowelles 120 lib. here at Edēn as a yeares @ rent of two thousand pond I owe to him and that from Lambes '82 to Lambes '83.

Mistris Campbell house rent.

I payed to on Mistris Campbell twentie cros doleres towards the payment of the house rent wch I intend to hold during and till the time of the ensewing parliment.

10 day. My Eldest son

Given to my Eldest son's servant John Lyon five pond sterlin to accompt to his Master.

22. The accompt of the narrow circle.

I am just now busied taking in the accts of the cropt '83 with the tenents in the narrow circle att Glammiss it being in my owne charge.

Helen Symmer her @ rent.

I ordered the payment of 400 lib. as two yeares @ rent due to Helen Symmer and her son Mr Jon Ramsay of there prin^ll soume of 3333 lib. 6ss. 8d. by George Hendersone our factor at Auchterhouse wch I beleeve may be all that is resting preceeding mertimes last albeit he says there is a yeare yet more due to him so that the last discharge must be look'd out att Castle Lyon.

I ordered David Lyon to pay to Jon Maclane 80 lib. as on yeeres interest of 1333 lib. 6ss. 8d. due by me of on Wm Rodgers mortificatione and another yeare by a precept on Tho. Steell in Dundee upon the said Maclane's acquittance.

Rodger's Mortificatione.

I sent over 66 lib. 13ss. 4d. for buying of a parsell of dry sweet meats my wyfe having in store wet sweetmeatts besyde her upon the occasion of the marriage of my neice the Earle of Aboyne's daughter to M'Kenzie of Tarbet the present Lord Register's sone upon the 29 of this instant. This will draw a considerable charge | upon me of cloaths to my wife and children besyds the charge of the wedding wch most be dispensed with for so near a freind.

Money for sweetmeats. My neice her wedding.

fol. 100.

Mr David Lindsay,[85] minister att Maritone payed to me his superplus duty of the wedsett of Westersandiefoord for the yeares '82, '83 and '84 att 6 lib. 13ss. 4d. yearlie.

Minister of Maritone.

There is on Petrie on of my vassells, a fewar in Babrogie who suffered his few dewty to run on ever since I acquyred the right thereof from my author, Campbell[86] of Lunday and is otherwayes much in debt in the cuntry, who's gift of escheat I signed this day in favour of on James Andersone, a confident persone and to the behoove of Bandoch who's back bond I have for being comptable for the feu dewties and in regard that this Petrie had a pretence that his feu dewty was wedsett to him by my author, all wch I designe by the gift is to obleidge him to pass therefra so that the feu duty may be effectuall both for bygons and time coming.

24 day. Petrie of Babrogie his gift of escheat and Bandoch's back bond.

I had a little debt oweing to me by the Souttars, elder and yõr, portioners of Cupar Grange who now turned allmost insolvent. I have assigned my servant Ja. Coupar to this debt and to the bygon feu duty resting to the end that with a debt owing to himselfe he may led an adjudicatione and have gottine his back bond for being comptable and to mak payment to me of the soumes assigned.

Souttar elder and yõr debt assigned to James Coupar on his back bond.

I allowed to ffredrick Lyon 80 ponds as his @ rent from Mert. '83 till Mertimes '84 att his compting wt me this day in his duty payable cropt '83.

Fredrick Lyon's @ rent.

And sielyke I owe to Jon Thorntoun in the toune of Glammiss 333 lib. 6ss. 8d. who's @ rent from Mert. '83 till Mertimes '84 is payed att his compting with me for his duty cropt '83.

fol. 101. Provest Carnagie his charter of Litle Milne.

I subscryved a charter in favours of Provest Carnagie in fforfare of the lands of Litle Milne upon an adjudica^ne wch he hes led against on ffouler, heritor thereof, and out of favour to the provest remitted much of the compositions.

Forrest the glassiers acct.

I payed to on fforrest a glassier an accompt of glass. A part whereof is in the new work and a part intirely repara^nes of broken windows for no small thing does uphold this house in glass. The soume of 46 lib. scotts or thereby by a precept on Jon Smith, Mossgreive in Drumgley.

ffebreware.

My son.

My son's servant John Lyon gott ten pond sterlin att tuo severall times upon his Master's goeing over to the Weems for a visite for which he holds compt to him.

21 day. George Ramsay Sklaiter.

I compted with the sklaiter George Ramsay for his last summers work both for dressing the roofe of the house of Cossens and for thieking the new byres and sheep cott att my barns of Castle Lyon, the accompt of which does extend to 94 lib. scotts for who's payment I have drawn a precept upon Andrew Blyth in the Raws in his duty cropt '84 besyds 3 bolls 1 f. 2 p. meall of bounty due to the said George Ramsay. This is more particularly sett downe in the end of my compt book with the tenents of the cropt '83.

John and Wm Gray's there acct. more particularly sett down in the compt book, cropt '83.

I compted this day with Jon and William Grays who built the wall round the planting att Castle Lyon for that part beginning att the gate upon the north entrie and ending att the burn wch extends to 29 rud of work and including two bolls wheat and five bolls 2 pecks meall wch they have gott from my grinter of the cropt '84. They are now and before payed of the soume of 232 merks as the full pryce thereof, the most part of which is by precept on Tho. Davie in Longforgan who's house they haunted.

fol. 102. Observ^ne anent workmen.

I chuse much rather to pay a very full and competent pryce to all kind of work men then to be in use of waisting meall and malt and allowing them morning drink and four-hours wch was the custom long ago: but that I have worn it out of use, finding too tho. it was much yet these kind of cattell being in use of it considered it very litle.

I did pay 30 lib. for thirtie twelve ell trees for puting up some particere walls in the west quarter of the house of Glammis. I payed lykewayes for the advance of the work for a stone of Glew and four stone of lead wch was principaly designed for running the ballasters and raills of the gate house and stairs thereof presently erecting.

23 day. A small provisione for the work att Glammiss.

I payed 30 lib. as the @ rent of 500 lib. due to the kirk sessione of Auchterhouse and that from Mert. '83 till Mertimes '84 last past conforme to their discharge dated the 22 of ffebrewarie 1685.

30 lib. @ rent payed to the kirk sessione of Auchterhouse.

I have been imployed this week past upon my annuall acct with my tenents here att Castle Lyon and with a great number of workmen whereof there's an absolute necessity of clearing once a yeare to preveen an unevitable confusione wch other wayes would ensue. The thing is chargeable and its effects brings more pleasure then profitt. But this being my weak syde the humeur is prevalent upon me and so I persevere. The particulars being all or for the most part placed in my compt book with the tenents crop '83, here it is observable that we are to the fore with it since that the effects of the cropt '83 have served to answer the charge till Martimes last '84, att wch time I usually make up my acets for the cropt '83, but this yeare was put by my measurs partlie with my being att Edēn and p^tlie^ by my neice her marriage.

28 day. Compts att Castle Lyon.

Resolved upon this as an easier way rather then to obleidge my wyfe still to be att the trouble to apply to me upon everie litle occasione for money and so have ordered six hundered ponds scotts to be payed to her in four equall parts according to the four quarters of the yeare be my factors. Merti. last was the first terme and Candlemes last was the second wch is payed.

fol. 103. 600 lib. scotts payed and to be payed to my wyfe twixt mert: '84 and '85.

Siclyke to teach my eldest daughter a litle management and to know the species of money There is att the same termes and Divisions a hunder pond payed and to be payed to her whereof two termes are past and payed.

My dau^re^ Grisall.

By the multitude of beasts wch my work here necessitats me to keep which cannot be continued otherwayes having no less then 24 oxen in dayly work, besyds a spair ox to each ingeag'd leading stons and forseeing the want of fodder, I have given

Provisione for buying of fodder.

directions and there are 100 bols fodder allready bought and more will be if needful towards the payment of which I have drawn a precept on Gilbert Mores for his silver duty payable to Alex^r Andersone another of my tenents who is the persone I imploy to provyde me the fodder.

38 lib. payed for 100 dales to on Alison in Dundee.

There was 100 dales brought last year for the use of the church the payment of which has been forgott, and on alisone having undiscreetly charged my servants with it who bought them who aught rather first to have acquainted me, upon the knowledge thereof I have immediately ordered the payment by Thomas Steel in Dundee.

Margrat Croll her house compt being presented to me and I ignorant of many of the particulars thereof have sent in to Dundee for her present ayde 33 lib. 7ss. being about the halfe *fol. 104.* of the extent thereof.

March 3rd. My eldest son.

My son's man Jo^n Lyon had this day five pond sterlin to compt for to his master upon his goeing to the Weems.

Jean Leg.

Sold to Jean Leg sixtaine bolls bear for which she hes payed me the money.

4th day. Transaction w^t Burnsyd.

I had a full intentione to have made a finall transactione for the whole debt I owe to Burnsyde, but there was a debt of Invereighties and another of Ardblairs wherein neither of them were able to satisfie Burnsyde in security and I chused rather then to let it ly any longer undone to doe it in a part fully designing to apply the same tuo soumes for satisfying Burnsyde, the remainder for which I have given him instantly bond.

The transactione is as followes

ffirst after clear compt I am debitor to him upon two severall bonds in the soume of .	4142 6 8
Payed in maner following	
(1.) By Robt and Ja. Doigs ther bond the soume of 603 lib. 13ss. 8d. from wch there is halfe a yeares @ rent to be rebated in regard the same is only payable att Witt. nixt w^t @ rent thereafter, so remains .	0585 10 11
(2.) By James Dickeson's bond payable att Mert. nixt with halfe a yeares @ rent 196 lib. 5ss. 6d.	0196 05 6
(3.) By Thomas Nicol in Balmacewin his bond	

payable att Witt. nixt w^t. halfe a yeares @ rent	0161	17	5	
(4.) By John Ross bond due w^t @ rent from Mertis. last 145 lib. 3ss. . . .	0145	03	0	
(5.) By Jon Blair in Thorntone his bond bearing @ rent from Mert. last 127 lib. 4ss. 2d.	0127	04	2	
(6.) By Ja. Steel in Kinnalty his bond bearing @ rent from Mert. last 90 lib. 13ss. 4d. .	0090	13	4	
(7.) By Da. Thomsone of Walkmilne of Glenboy his bond for 76 lib. from wch is to be deducted 2 lib. 5ss. 7d. as halfe-a-yeares @ rent thereof the said bond bearing no @ rent till after Witt. nixt remanes 73 lib. 14ss. 5d.	0073	14	5	
(8.) By David Sampsone in bents milne his bond for 47 lib. 2ss. 6d. and 4 lib. 4ss. 6d. of extent preceeding Mert. last. *inde* .	0051	07	0	*fol.* 105.
(9.) By James Aliburton in Easter toune of Ketens his bond for 76 lib. 9ss. payable att Mert. last with @ rent thereafter *inde*. .	0076	09	0	
The soume of thir bonds comes to on thousand five hundred and eight pond four shillings nyne pennies *inde*. . .	1508	04	9	The old bonds are cancelled. Bond given to Burnsyde for 2633 lib. 6ss. 8d.
The sum due to Burnsyd being 4142 lib. 6ss. 8d. *inde*.	4142	06	8	
The payments by the above written bonds being	1508	4	9	
Rests 2634 lib. 1ss. 11d. for wch new bond is given bearing @ rent from Mertimes last *inde*.	2634	01	11	

Which is to be payed of by Invereighty and Arblair for which they are to be prest and what their soumes is short is to be made up some other way.

I owe to Thomas ffermour in the Cottoune of Auchterhouse 200 lib. scotts. I have allowed him retentione of his ferme bear cropt 84 wch payes his @ rent till Candlemes '85 last past. *Thomas ffermour his @ rent payed till Candlemes '85.*

I have this day taken up James Coupar's accts. of his intromissione with my rents in Auchterhouse and att the same *9th day.*

Auchterhouse accompts cropt 1683.

time carried the ballance of that acct. wherein I was debtor to him to the acct. of the same yeare of Litleblair and pertinents.

G. hendersone factor cropt '84.

He desyred to be excused from any more adoe att Auchterhouse wch is now in the hands of George Hendersone who dwells upon the place and so may do it easier.

Ja. Coupar continued in Litleblair.

He continues tho. in my litle business of Litle blair being every way litle.

Gourdie's debt to be payed and Mr Jo^{n} Crockett to be compted with.

And he has orders what by something in his hands and by what is resting by the fewar and others there to pay a debt wch I owe to Da. Kinloch of Gourdie and the same is calculat to be due att Lambes nixt precisely, and he is also to prepare Mr Jo^{n} Crockett's acct of Litleblair wch was before his entrie,
fol. 106. because he cannot, at least he will not doe it himselfe.

Da. Crighton his @ rent till Mert. 84.

Ordered the Payment of Dawid Crighton in Cookstone his @ rent of 80 lib. upon Alex^{r} Reid and James Nicol who bought bear of Da. Lyons charge of the cropt 83.

1685.

I am obleidged in this place to assigne some reasone why there should be so great an intervall of time of busines and the account thereof. And its shortlie this, that much about the time of the month of March mentioned before, I went to Ed^{r} and forgott my book behind me, it had been an easie matter to have supplyed this, but that about the time of my returne the first appeerance of the rebellion wch thereafter happened broke out wherein every honest man was so concerned that for most pairt they did forgoe there owne private busines as indeed it took me up no less nor nyn or ten weeks, having carryed into the west countrey the militia regiment of Angus and continued their two full weeks longer then any militia of the Kingdome having it in charge to convoy to Ed^{r} the whole spoyll of the rebell Argyll[87]—his stor's of ammunition and warlick provision and a great many prisoners from Glasgow, and the whole train of Artilery both from Glasgow and Stirlen.

Yet it is not to be supposed but ev'ne during the time especially before our actual march into the west countrey something of my busines was done now and then as occasione did offer w^{r}of as it shall occur hereafter some acct. shall be given thereof.

In the month of Apryll my eldest son went to London and

returned in May his charge was litle more nor 1333 lib. 06ss. 8d. or thereabout.

My son's going to London.

I borrowed from Sir George Lockart two hunder pond sterlin wch was imployed for the s^d^ se^all^ uses aftermentioned.

Two hunder pond borrowed from Sir George Lockart.

ffirst fiftie pound thereof was payed for a bill towards my son's charge.

fol. 107.

Another fiftie pound went inteerly to my Lord Cars use for which he will again be comptable to me.

The rest went pairtlie to My own charge being for a considerable time att Ed^n^ and pairtlie was given out to creditors for their @ rents or oỹ^r^ accompts whereof it's impossible to give a particular relatione because of so much elapsed time.

I did sell to Thomas Mill of Muretoun the lands of Easter and Wester Balbeno to be hold'ne feu of the Lordship of Lyon, I had in excambion some eight aikers of Land wch ly upon the east end and above the toun of Longforgon marching with the ministers glib and his bond for tuo thousand two hunder sixtie six pond thirtain shill. four pennies whereof there is no pairt as yet payed.

The seall of the bonds of Easter and Wester Balbeno's.

Att the first eruptione of the rebellione the Treasurer[88] ordered the Cash-Keeper and others to buy great quantities of victual for the use of the Kingis armies if neid were and accordingly Hew Wallace the Cash-Keeper bought from me a thousand bolls meall and five hunder bolls of oats so accordingly there went about to Stirlen wch was appoynted for the place of store on small bark with oatts and another with meall and brought receits of their loadnings back to Dundee with them but before the first bark with the oatts returned with the second loadning, the rebells being totally routed dispersed and discuss'd those commissioned by the Cash Keeper to receive the victuall refused the same so that their being no debateing w^t^ the publick tho. the bargone was clear, my servants put a stop to any further loadning at Dundee, And the second loadning of oatts was lofted at Stirlen and on Jo^n^ Lyon a shoemaker there had my commissione to sell them att the best availl but I shall be a looser about twentie shill. of each boll of wch I would have had if the Cash Keeper had not resiled from his bargone having sold the meall to him at 4 lib. 13ss. 4d. and the oatts att 5 lib. p boll.

Meall and Oatts sold to the publick and for the most part cast 'ne againe.

fol. 108.
The wheat sold to Merchants in Glasgow.

Att my being last time att Glasgow I sold my wheat of the cropt 1684 to Baylie ffarie Walter Buchanan baxter and I am told that Baylie Jonston was also a partner, the tenents fell short of the delyverie the cropt was so very bad the last year so there was scored two hunder bolls delyvered the pryce was 8 lib. 6ss. 8d.

Robert Ogilvy's accompts.

Since I cam home I received Robert Ogilvy my factor his accts. cropt 83 of the lands of Tannadyce and oȳ[rs] within his commissione.

Wheells bought from St. Andrews.

I bought of Nish the Wheell wright in St. Andrews four pair of stone-cart wheells w[ch] stand me about 4 lib. the pair and he having bought from the Church sessione the trees of the Church yeard I thought it best to retaine the money of the wheeles for pay[t] of the pryce of the trees and gave an obleidgement for the same accordingly w[ch] shall be made good being fully determined to rear up upon the west gevall of the church a bell house whereof there will be a particular accompt keep't as to its charge be on of the sessione delegat for that purpose to the end that it may be known w[n] that money now in my hand is all expended and that thereafter it may goe upon a publick acct. tho. if I be not the doer of it upon adventure it would not goe up in this age.

M[r]. James Cramond's few.

M[r]. James Cramond payed his few and teind duty to myselfe cropt 84.

Fraught of lyme and coalls payed by M[r]. Patrick Jack.

M[r]. Patrick Jack had provisione by the few duty of Millhill and Knap for the paying the fraughts of the victuall to Stirlen and the returns with lyme and coalls but the particular acct. thereof is not yet made with him.

Mistris Ogilvy relict of the Minister of Newburn was payed of her @ rent of 700 lib. prin[ll] on of Invereightie's debts w[ch] I undertook att preceeding Mertimes last conforme to her discharge att Ed[r] some time before our western expeditione.

fol. 109.

Immediatly before the march of my regiment into the west which happened in the beginning of June Alex[r]. ffoster of Millhill payed in to me 333 lib. 6ss. 8d. in part pay[t] of a greater soume w[ch] he rests me upon which I gave him receite accordingly w[ch] money and a greate dale more in the hands o on of my servants Thomas Crombie wretter of this book was

333 lib. 6ss. 8d. received from Alex. ffoster.

expended in our western jorney conforme to his particular accompts thereof.

Receaved of John Lyon in Stirlen 133 lib. 6ss. 8d. in pairt of pay^{t} of 127 bolls 2 firlots oatts wch he had commissione to sell att Stirlen. John Lyon in Stirlen.

My wyfe having made this present time the terme to on Isobell Atkinson her wardroper upon an offence done betwixt her and on John Tylor who is also put away which shall be nameless and the acct. being made of all that this woman can pretend to wch is resting unpayed the same does amount to 80 lib. which is payed to her every farthing. Isobell Atkinson's fies.

I have now made the particular acct. with M^{r}. Patrick Jack by wch the fraughts to Stirlen of the meall and oatts and returne of lyme and coalls comes to 277 lib. 13ss. 8d. the provisione wch he gott of money and a discharge to Alex^{r}. ffoster of Millhill for paying him the said soume out of the pryce of the teind bolls payable by him for the lands of Millhill, cropt 84. The ballance of M^{r}. Pa. Jack his acct. payed by an order upon Alex. ffoster of Millhill out of the pryce of the teind bolls cropt '84.

The meall receaved at Stirlen by Hew Wallace the cashkeeper his commissione to Cristofer Russell there extends to 312 bolls and by the exorbitancie of his receaving att 16 stone p load their is of intaik 19 bolls 2 firlots wch in regard aught also to be compted to me. There is of oatts 127 bolls 2 firlots received also by Cristofer Russell by virtue of his commissione from the Cashkeeper. Meall and oatts receaved by Cristofer Russell in name of Hew Wallace.

fol. 110.

A rectificatione of Andrew Wright's claime as follows

ffirst for the two roofes being to be done with the bell cast fiftie three pond six shillings eight pennies.

ffor thatching of them w^{t} open work a hunder pond. The windows cannot be condescended upon till he have occasione of seeing some such clos windows done which being a distinct thing in itselfe there can be no varia^{ne} in it. A double of a memorial w^{t} Andrew Wright for the roofs and finishing of the two summer houses in the low garden of Castle Lyon.

As for the flooring lyning and sylling wch the said Andrew hes placed so liberally and att random in his acct. without considering the quantitie of the houses or the true availl of the thing itselfe in so much that I wounder he is not ashamed, neither am I to have the ground storry floored as he hes supposed so that this article when reduced to 133 lib. 6ss. 8d. is too much.

This soume besyde the windowes is 286 lib. 13ss. 4d. and I am content that the bargen of trees att 133 lib. 6ss. 8d. be applyed in so far for the payment of this work by itselfe and that he mount my four pieces of cannon w[t] carriages on wheells and he shall have eight bolls meall in bountie and four more if my sone pleases.

The trees must be all digged this goesummer and he must be obleidged that the trees fall all as the allow lyes to the east.

Moreover I have this day given eightaine pond in part pay[t] of the total above written.

The four ordinarie measons their acct. preceeding the first of June 1685.

Their last task of the new byre and sheep cott and hey barn w[ch] compleits my whole building there, the two summer houses of the low gardin and the wall betwixt them comes to seven hundered and fourtie pond seventaine ss. four d. and about two chalder of meall conforme to the particular acct. thereof particularly sett down in the compt book of the Lordship of Lyon cropt '83.

As lykewayes there is there sett down all their four compts a pairt w[ch] in all amount to 797 lib. 1s. 9d. so that there meall being all payed they rest to me 56 lib. 13ss. 5d. w[ch] goes to acct. of their payment of the falling walls now in hand.

[All the foregoing written by Thomas Crombie. Succeeding part written by Lord Strathmore.]

fol. 111.

28 *March* 1688.

Here is a long surcease of what I am very unaccountable for; for this three years I have neglected to wreat memorialls of my transactions. But I conceave it is a thing very necessar both for the ease of one's own memory, and ther present satisfaction, to the end when all is recorded posterity may see and be convinced of ther not being unprofitable in there generation, and may be induced by good example to follow the good and to eschew what may be amiss in the management. Tho. I take God to witness it has been and is the outmost indeavour of my life to order all my affairs both for the honour credit and preservation of my family.

The first occasion of my geving up my former method of making my particular not's of my affairs was that in the moneth of Sept. 1685 being sorely straited in my credit by the diligence done by the administrators of Heriot's hospitall upon my estate, I choiced at that tyme immediatly after the rebellion of the late Argyle and upon his forfalture to insist for and clame releif of the debt since my father's undertaking of it was for him The E. of Erroll being joyntly bound was in lyke manner persewed, but at this tym had the ease and advantage of staying at home, and I in persewance of my releif went up to Court w^t the D. of Queensberry Treasurer for the tyme, not having seen the king since his coming to the Crown, and having confidence of his Majestyes favour in that affair. Heriot's hospitall.

But to my great loss my hop's were soon blasted and that which I aimed at turned impracticable. My freind the Treasurer turned out of his employ^{t} so y^{t} after six moneths stay I had enow adoe to expiat almost the cryme of coming w^{t} him and standing by him.

At last my own innocence caryed me thorow, yet I returned *fol. 112.*
and nothing done in that affair I cam for. The interest of the popist party and especially of the new converts growing to that height as to depress all mens pretences and claims which had not a dependance upon ther favour and procurement, in so much that the present Chancellor and Secretary, the Earl of Perth and Melfort[89] tho. the E. of Erroll was a co-cautioner w^{t} me and y^{r} brother in law by marriage of ther sister, opposed my project at that tyme which was this: The E. of Erroll and I upon Argyle's forfaulture prevailed and obtained A locality in his lands and estate of Kintyre for about six thousand merks be year, which was all could be done upon the forfaultur and it was nearer the @ rent of the soume we stood distrest for then any other of his creditors attained to. But it was burdened and affected by My Lady Argyle's life rent of 420 lib. be year as a part of her joynture, and laying at ane untolerable distance from us and in a place so remot, It was still inconvenient for us in case we could better doe.

For this, it was that I projected at my going up to make it my busines to give the King somewhat, whereas others seek from him, and many since that tyme have got great things, for all the forfalture w[ch] happ'ned upon Argyle's rebellion w[ch] in the D. of Queensberry's parliament were annexed to the Crown, were since disjoyned again and giv'ne away.

Thus I say my project was to give the King, ffor I proposed that his Majesty would be pleased to gratify and enable the city of Ed[r] so as that they might become debtors to ther own hospitall in that soume w[ch] exceeded a hunder thousand merks by allowing them some more of the exercese of ther own excyse then at the tyme they injoyed, and also by prorouging the gift of the plack of the pynt for so many years more to run.

That for this the Town might as administrators for the hospitall discharg the E. of Erroll and me of the debt and renounce and resigne the diligences following upon it in our favours. And in the third part that we would dispone to the
fol. 113. King our right to the s[d] lands | of Kintyre to remain w[t] him and the Crown for ever.

This, as befor I told, took no effect at that tyme, and w[t] great difficulty I made my peace so as that the King was pleased to make me on of the extraordinary Lords of the Session w[t] a pension of 300 lib. sterlin.

But a giv'ne over play was never wonn, and when I returned in March 1686, Then and always since I made application to the Chancellour, and by my letters to Secretary Melfort, so that partly by a dutifull complyance in so far as was possible in all publick matters and Judicaturs and partly the Interest and allyance of the E. of Erroll my co-cautioner making the thing more favourable.

That very project above narrated, opposed by them and rejected, has now tak'ne place. The King and we have entered into a tripartite contract, and each of us performed to others what we were thereby oblidged.

And so at last we are delivered from that greivous debt, w[ch] first and last has stood me more by seeking releif of it, then the thing would have been to my part, if I had payed it in the year 1660 when I came from scools.

O miserable and fatall cautionry, ffor my family has suffered more by the engadgements of my father who, good man! thinking every one as honest as himself and tender-hearted to his friends, refused scarce any one who ask'd of him, then at this day I injoy of free estate over the pay^{t} of my present debt.

My eldest son was then w^{t} me at Court and returned home March 1686. at the same tyme, my 2nd son came up w^{t} him and went to his travells in France.

My journey at that tyme and my son's being w^{t} me, including also herein a great dale of furniture, plate, and statues, stood me about fyveteen hundreth pound sterline.

Men who's fortun's are burdened w^{t} debt may when ther *fol.* 114. children are young doe somewhat to less'ne ther debt by making annuall pay^{ts} of some on debt or other, especially if corns, of which our estats most consist give any good pryce. But that has been the misfortune of my tyme that for the most part the pryce of corns one grain w^{t} another has not exceeded ane hundreth merks ꝑ chalder and oft'ne under that, besyds the difficulty of getting merchants and sometyms those prove bankerups. But now the most part of my children being grow'n up to the age and stature of men and women, It's no easy mater to live and to pay @ rents and the publick burdens, and much less to pay debt, tho. I hope by the following acct. in which I resolve to be punctuall by wreating down and here recording all I doe to make it appear that I doe all that can be done, and that nothing is unprofitably bestowed or misaplyed. Besyds that I have reason dayly to adore and magnify the name of my God who out of his infinit goodnes to me more then I deserve and to my family has blest me w^{t} good and vertewous sons and daughters, of good dispositions and frugall and moderat as much as my heart can desyre. Blessed be he who hes made me happy by them and make me thankfull and exemplar to them in what is good. Nor can I deny the great advantage I have by ther mother who's care has been of her children and to stay at home and guide w^{t}in the hous her part. So that thes have been my advantages and are such as have enabled me to doe thos things wch perhaps if others had done, they would be proud off, and wherein my profusenes is or has been, consists in them things which will not dye w^{t} me, But will remain to posterety. I have had the toyle and the care and trouble | of it, may they injoye the *fol.* 115. pleasure profit and contentment of it, many A pound and penny has it cost me at both my houses, y^t as the maintaining of it in good order will indeed be a yearlie charge yet the first doing is as it were the purchas of ane inheritance in proportion to the other, and if this other be not duely performed, the best of policy go's to wrack.

The servant who wrote the former part of this book went abroad w^t my second son, after wch Having six moneths at leave, and in some more disuse of pains and application from that tyme till now I was instant enow and at the head of my own affairs, but delayed making or continuing the record of what I did, trusting the same to my memory. But that now finding myself at a loss therby, and being resolved to sett all down w^t my own hand and not to committ it to a $serv^{ts}$ wreating, who may be here to day and away the morrow, I hope by being punctuall therin, and by what is writ'ne before and hereafter shall make up the loss of thes three years memor's, for from the tyme I left and discontinued my wreating till now it is no less then full three years and some odd moneths.

M^r. dvit, 90. Limner.

I agried with him in the month of feb^y 1688, and albeit I managed it w^t all the care and precaution possible (for some eight years agoe or more for doore and chimney peices at Castle lyon when the reforms of that house were compleeted, and divers picturs then done which are in the great hall of Glams or elsewher thorow the house he had then near about as much of my money) yet the painting of the roof of my hye dinning roume off the great Hall, The ovall of the cheif bed chamber and my chappall which stood him I'm sure more then half a years work, arose to a considerable summe of money.

fol. 116.

I here include all the Chimney and doore peices of both storeys of the west syde of this hous of Glammiss, off the floor of both halls, all together stand me nynety pound sterline, and his bed and boord in the family, wch soume of nynety pound sterline is accordingly payed him and discharged upon the back of the Contract wch I have layed up in my cabinet at Ed^r.

Ane acct yet resting to M^r. dVit.

Besyds this, ther is Twenty pound due to him for the King's picturs wch are fixt in the lyning of the upmost drawing-roume, and some other picturs not as yet payed.

Mistris Moreis and her sister hous painters.

I have also agried with two English women hous painters, who have been a considerable tyme here, The acct whereof when ther work is finished shall be sett down. The most p^{rt} of ther tyme my family has been at Castle Lyon, but when it's here, they have also the benefit of ther meat in the house. And tho. I hold it as a rule to agree w^{t} workmen so as not to have the trouble of feeding them, for in some cases, if they know off no imploy^{t} elsewhere they prolong the work for the benefit of having ther meat bound to their mouth, yet such as thes painters and the more ingenious sort of craftsmen coming from places at a distance, ther is a necessity of being liberall that way.

Observ. concerning workmen.

And ev'ne of masons and wrights wher a man has much adoe, It is expedient to have a headsman over the rest, who must also have something of this nature done to them. Tho. ev'ne it's frequently losed that is done that way, for they are apt enow to receive the favour w^{t}out any rebatement of the pryce of ther work.

And the only way not to be cheated is to have no work. *fol.* 117.

Decr. 4th Robt. Ogilvy's acct. 87.

Tak'ne in Robt Ogilby's acct^{s} of Tannadyce cropt 1687, wherein the pay^{t} of the creditors set asyde for him are instructed to be payed till Whits. 1687. The Newe Colledges Tack Teind duty, and other debursments.

Counts to be made w^{t} W^{m}. Couts.

The victual was sold to John Couts. The acc^{t} of which goes to pay his @ rents and a part of his principle soume. And according to Mr Couts his resats Count is to be made w^{t} him.

Logy Ogilby's bond designed to pay Easter Ogill.

Delivered to the Sherif clerck A bond of Logy Ogilvy now of Balgay, upon wch he is to arest in the Tennants hands and then to perseu a forthcoming. This I designe should go to Easter Ogill to begin the pay^{t} of 666 lib. 13ss. 4d. I owe him, and wch I resolve to compleet, because he is a freind and a gentle craver.

5th day.

Publick dews.

I have draw'ne 3 precepts on my 3 factors for 200 lib. scotts p peice towards the pay^{t} of the publick dues for Mert. last past by the Collector of Angus, w^{t} whom after pay^{t} ane acct. is to be fitted.

W^{m}. Wals bond.

He has also a bond of one Wm Walls in Forfar for 120 lib. scots as his composition for medling w^{t} my boat upon the Loch.

Dec. 10th. At this tyme after some few dayes stay at home, being at Edin. since the end of Sept. befor, I was forced to return to attend the counsell. This was the tyme of the first surprysing newes of the Dutch invasion, and of the P. of Oranges designe of landing in England wch he did afterwards wt wonderful success. It was then scarce when harvest was done that the militia was draw'ne together, and by one detachment after another thes expeditions dwynled into nothing, as every thing else did wch concerned the King's service, all succeeding wt the Prince to a miracle.

My stay so long at Edr being upon this occasion upwards of three moneths drew a good deal of money, besyds the postponing of my own privat affairs at home, and about the *fol.* 118. Terme | And now was the generall confluence of the most part of the nobility and great numbers of the gentry to the Court to attend the P. of Orange. The King having wtdrawn himself and gone beyond seas, but since I am farr from designing any historicall relation here, I only hint at thes extraordinary accidents in relation to my own privat busines.

Amongst others, it was obvious enow to my self a necessity for me to goe. But it being scarce three years since I was ther befor, and London journeys being always very chargeable to me, since I cannot in my humour easily refuse the temptation of buying, I made a shift to putt off going myself, tho. I was nominat by the Counsell as one of thos who should goe to represent the condition of the nation. This I effectuat by tuo devyces. The ffirst was the Counsell in Scotland the King being gone resolved upon ane address to the P. of Orange and having signed it, They pitched on the Lord Glammiss, my eldest son to goe wt it.

They recommended it lykewayes to the Treasury to give him three hundreth pound sterling in order to his journey. But at this tyme yr was no corum in the Treasury and as litle money, so that ther was a necessity for borrowing.

Borrowed from P. Watson. And accordingly ther was borrowed from Provest Watson in Dundee 1333 lib. 6ss. 8d. and having been ow'ne him some money befor The bond was made 2666 lib. 13ss. 4d. which was signed by my selfe, my son and Ld Cars and other freinds at this exige'nt.

Ther was another bond giv'ne to a blank person for 666 lib. 13ss. 4d.

So at this occasion ther was 2000 lib. borrowed for My son's journey tho. it may be hoped that it may be refounded again out of the treasury.

So my son went up w[t] this address in the very beginning of *fol.* 119. this yeare.

The other thing w[ch] puts my stay under a specious pretence is that the M. of Athol[91] being left w[t] a very full commission by the Counsell to command the force presently in Scotland, and other ample powers, when he went away it behooved him to provyde in some measure for the order of the present standing force, and so left it to my care, which I shall desyre to hold a very short while.

Behold the uncertainty of this world and of all humane affairs. The E. of Perth L. Chancellor from being the first minister of State is now a prisoner in the Castle of Stirline, And his doers glad to convoy away the best of his goods, and dispose of them privatly. 1689.

M[r] Cockburn the Goldsmith bought a parcell of his plate to the value of a 1500 lib. sterl. Of this plate I choiced out eleven dishes great and small such as fitted best the table I intend to serve w[t] them, w[ch] weigh about but upwards of eight hundred ounces. The plate of intrinsick value is 3 lib. 4ss. p ounce, I agreed to acct. it and 6ss. p ounce more, some of the dishes being splite new and the rest very litle worse, he puts out the former graving and do's myne of new. This amounts to 3000 lib. scots. for w[ch] I have giv'ne bond payable at Whits. next and he keeps the plate in his custody till pay[t] be made. Ther is also a chaffing dish. Bond giv[ne] to Cockburn, Goldsmith.

I have also bought of Bailzie Brand in Edin[r] a Cabinet for my fyne bed chamber, a very large looking glass for the drawing roume, Table and Hands of Italian paste, very fine, and other two speciall good glasses, I give for all four score pound sterline payable at Whits. nixt.

Adolphus Durham gets of the Cropt 83 Two hundreth bolls bear, he furnisht me from Holland a parcell of cloath damask and Holland cloath for sheets. Ther was wyne sweetmeats and spyces and other things too w[ch] were all to be payed by *fol.* 120. Bear sold to him. Adolphus Durham, his Count.

John Davidson in Leith, who first broke to me and was resting me a considerable soume for meale, y^{r}after he began to pay this debt by parcells, and had he lived I would have got pay^{t}, but unluckily he dyed this last year, after he had undertak'ne the pay^{t} of all thes things to Adolphus Durham, wch I am forced now to make good to him.

Ther was one Calderwood in Ed^{r} I was owing 4000 mks too, he dyed and so the soume was divyded among his children and oy^{rs}. Ther was one Lady Pennyland got 1000 lib. of it.

Lady Pennyland payed, G. Gollan creditor in 500 mks.

This was payed the last year 87. George Gollan by his wyfe got 500 mks y^{r}of to whom I have giv'ne bond a p^{rt}.

Ther is also one Calderwood in Ed^{r} for his own share and others has got bond for the superplus.

Bear sold to Calderwood for his payt.

And he is to get three hundreth bolls of bear of this last cropt 88 towards the pay^{t} of the principle summ and @ rents to be counted at such a pryce as the rest of my bear shall be sold at.

Mr. Thos Learmont Advocat creditor in 1000 mks.

I counted w^{t} Mr Thomas Learmont for his bygone @ rents and pension, wch in all Mert. last amounts to ten thousand merks, for wch I have giv'ne him a bond of corroboration. But accumulations are very dangerous and destructive, so no more plaids of this set. But this was A force. *fol.* 121.

Archbishop of St. Andrews new Tack Bond giv'ne him for 1200 lib. scots.

Tuo years agoe I settled w^{t} the Archbishop of St. Andrews[92] for a new Tack of the Teinds of my Lands of Castle lyon for the pay^{t} of the former tack dutie of 40 lib. stg. yeare, and six chalders of victuall to the minister of Lonforgan yearlie, I gave him bond for the entry wch was agreed upon to be tuelve hundreth pounds scotts.

Da. Crighton entered to the lands of Easter Adamstoun.

I agreed with David Crighton of Adamstoun for his entry to the lands upon his purchase of them from the former Heritor called Johnson. He was to have giv'ne me but 233 lib. 6ss. 8d. of composition while his author was alive, but the transaction not being compleeted the old man Johnson dying in the tyme I obleidged him to give ane hundreth merks more and so signed his charter of confirmation containing a novodamus.

The s^{d} David Crighton payed the entry according to his first agreement, by reporting to me a resale and discharge be Wm Geekie of Baldouries for 120 lib. wch compleets his @ rent till

Whits. last I had also from D. Crighton a Jacobus wch compleeted the first agreement, then for the last I had his ticket for 66 lib. 13ss. 4d. wch I have put in the custody of Wm Crighton his son that he may get sixty lib. of it over w^t^ him to Ed^r^ to give to Mr Mein the postmaster for his pension till Mert. last for his furnishing me the news letters and gazets weekly. The other Ten merks I'll call for upon occasion as I pass that way.

22 Jany '89 Wm Geekie of Baldowrie his @ rent paid till Whits. last. Mr Mein post^mr^ his pension till Mert. last ordered to be payed.

I am owing to the tuo sister Pilmers ane hundreth pound sterlin each. The younger is marryed on Provost Steven in Arbroth and to him I have sold three hundreth bolls meal towards the pay^t^ of his principall soume and acct is to be made accordingly when the pryce shall be agreed upon, the same being to be regulat by what my Ld Panmure gets from his ferms.| I had sold a good tyme agoe a litle roume in the Toun of Longforgan called the Byre flat to Andrew Wright my wright and plaisterer. It was valued at that tyme to him for twenty fyve hundreth merks, and this has all alongs in his Counts been imputed to him in payment of his work here at Glāms till it was exhausted.

300 bolls meal used to P. Steven in Arbroth.

fol. 122. februar the 8th.

So now falling upon ane exchange of it w^t^ the Lands of Easter and Wester Rochel-hill I could not in justice deny to take it back at the pryce he got it at, wch being at a chalder of victuall of ferm for the Byre flat and y^t^ at 2500 mks p chalder made it go farr towards the pay^t^ of the pryce of Rochel-hill. This Rochel-hill is a good roume and of a large bounds, But has not been in the hands of industrious tennents, and might be brought worth four hundreth merks be year, yet I could scarce come to two chalder of victuall for't and a hundreth merks of money, and this being sold at 1800 merks p chalder and taking the Byre flat in the first end of it, allowing also the few duty payable yearlie of 47 lib. 6ss. 8d. and four Wedders of diminution of pryce. The Ballance to be payed in be Andrew Wright was accounted to be seven hundreth thirty three pound six shillen eight pennys, and this he will also pay be his work.

Andrew Wright quits the Byre flat in longforgon and fews the land of Rochel-hill.

So the Byre flat in Longforgan is again myne and the few dutie of Rochel-hill is to be yearlie four Wedders and fourty seven pound six shillen eight pennyes money. And he is to pay his proportion of publick burdens at a hundreth pounds of valued rent.

I have assisted Robt Strachan to build his house.

I was obleidged by a certain paper signed by me when I fewed the lands of Dron 3rd part y^r of to Robt Strachan's father to be at the half of the charge of building him a dwelling house and tho. this obleidgm^t was very scrimp and narrow yet out of

fol. 123.

my good will now at his entering into a | Contract w^t Andrew Wright for building him a house, I have undertak'ne the pay^t of two hundreth pound thereof and four bolls of meal wch shall be accordingly done.

12 feb. Wilson portioner of the Grange of Aberbothrie.

When I sold the lands of Bakie to that infamous rascall Mr Tho. Wilson, I accepted of A debt due to him by one Capt. Wilson in the Grange of Aberbothrie and after some difficulty in't I attained to the possession of the roume wch continued so for divers years. Yet this thing was not to be coveted, so that I granted his son a reversion upon the pay^t of four thousand merks. Nether am I so nyce in the mater but accepts of partial pay^ts Some years agoe he payed 666 lib. 13ss. 4d. y^r of and yesternight eight hundreth pound so y^t now ther remains unpayed only the soume of twelve hundreth pound scots. I continew in the possession of the roume and allows Wilsons @ rent for the money he has made partiall pay^ts of. My factor James Cuper must cleare accts. w^t him about the @ rents of this four thousand merks wch were owen before I setled w^t the son, and for wch the old fellow was put in prison.

At my being here at Castle lyon at this tyme as I had all the last yeares accts to cleire so Had I lykewayes a number of the Tennants to setle in new tacks.

Alex^r Watson younger being to remove at Whits. nixt from his roume in Longforgon, I have set the same to Alex^r Henderson, he has giv'ne me two hundreth merks of entry and has a lyferent tack, yet it is lyke if old Sanders Watson elder remove or dye, this Alex. Henderson may be prefered to this roume. If he be I designe y^t he should pay a hunder merks more And I am upon the mater engaged to Pat. Moreis to prefer his eldest son.

fol. 124.
The setting of Tennants at Castle Lyon.

I have brought one francis Graham in the raws to Alex^r Henderson's roume and raised the rent two bolls of oats.

This roume of Francis Grahams in the Raws I have sett to

John Moreis a young man, and have accepted of ane hundreth merks of entry from him. I was the rather induced to be favourable to him because that his father, grandfather, and forbeirs have been ther since the memory of man, and Francis Graham had possession of it only as marying his mother.

Thomas Davies roume is now set out all in parcells, and I beleeve profitably enow. Androw Wright being now to goe up to Rochel hill quits both the Heritage of the Byreflat and the labouring of the aiker roume wch was formerly possesst by James Moncur. This aiker roume is sett to Patrick Blair, and he payes a hundreth pound of entry money.

David Matthew compounded his entry to his aiker roume in Longforgon for 40 lib. scots.

John Mitchell succeeds to $Alex^{r}$ Givan ther. his entry money is 26 lib. 13ss. 4d.

I ordered James Cuper w^{t} the help of ane hundreth and sixty pound payable be Milhorne to pay to Mistris Hay in Perth 320 lib. scotts as 3 years @ rent of three thousand merks I owe her. James Cuper's provision for this is a ticquet he rests me of the ballance of Ardblair's money, and a bond of James Suters in his custody wch is to be cleered when he reports me Mistris Hay's discharge. Mistris Hay in Perth her @ rent.

fol. 125.

Thomas Dass wife Janet Webster dying, she stood only in the right of the Tack, it is ane aiker roume in Longforgon, so upon a new tack he payes a hundreth pound of entry. Thos Dass entry.

I gave to Margret Croll a precept for fyve bolls meal on James Jack, Tennent of the Easter Bridgend, wch w^{t} 3 bolls of oats got by wifs order out of the lofts makes eight bolls victuall wch at 5 lib. p. boll payes her the @ rent of 40 lib. scots deu for 666 lib. 13ss. 4d principal and the @ rent commences from Whits. '87 till Whitsunday 1688 last past. Andrew Dall's @ rent of 40 lib. payed till Whits. 88.

Laird of Leyes @ rent payed till Whits. 1684 his last discharge was reported by Gilbert Moreis, Tennent in the Raws. Leyes @ rent.

The soume is assigned to Trumble of Bogmill.

I designe y^{t} John Moreis entry money should goe to pay another years @ rent to help to overtake it besyds the continuing Gilbert Moreis in paying the current rent.

I had pity the last year of Ogilvy of Templehall, who was

Templehall's debts to be assigned to Monorgon in p^{rt} of pay^{t} of his @ rent.

straitened by his creditors and cast in prison. I payed Ogilby of Trottock his money, and gave order for paying Kinnaird a brother of Coustoun's, but he going in to England being on of the Troup of Guards and not yet returned, it is not cleered w^{t} him. This pressure on Templehall was much at the instigation of his nyebour Monorgon who has mind for his land, yet since he has made a fair bargain w^{t} him for a roume west in the Cars, and so I am to assigne Monorgon to thes two debts, wch he is to allow to me in p^{rt} of pay^{t} of his by gone @ rents of 2000 I owe him.

Mr J. Campbell.

I owe to the children of Mr John Campbell, Dundee, four thousand merks, and in p^{rt} of pay^{t} of ther bygone @ rents I recovered | *fol. 126.* A discharge of the tutors for eight hundreth pound scots.

bond giv'ne to Fintrie for 800 lib.

I gave bond to the Laird of Fintrie for it wch is a very thriftles way and a consuming.

Mr Ramsay's @ rent in Dundee.

I did lykewayes order Mr Clerck to allow a bill of Mr Ramsay in Dundee to whom I owe fyve thousand mks. for 600 lib. scots wch is 3 years @ rent of the s^{d} soume. This receit of his factor Mr Crocket lyes in Mr Clerck's hand till I cleir accts. w^{t} him.

18 feb. John Jolly counted and cleired w^{t}.

I was owing to Mr Jolly merch^{t} in Ed^{r} of current acct. a very great one, the sum of two thousand four hundreth eighty fyve pound Scots money.

Mr Robt Blackwood's bond retyred and Bailzie Spences debt of 200 lib. originally dew to Hew Blair.

A new Contract w^{t} John Jolly, retention in his own hands.

Bailzie Brand to be payed.

After cleiring the acct. of proceedings and destroying a Contract of Victuall wch was betwixt us in the year j^{m} vjc eightie four By wch then he received pay^{t} of former Counts and by the effects of wch bargain I had delivered up to me as a p^{rt} of his obleidge^{t} two bonds wch he retyred to me, one from Mr Robt Blackwood of four hundreth pound scots, and another from Bailzie Spence originally to Hew Blair merch^{t} in Ed^{r} for two hundreth pound. I entered into a new Contract w^{t} John Jolly for 700 bolls half bear half meal cropt 1688 at 5 lib. p. boll. In the first end of wch he has retention of the soume resting him of 2485 scots, and he is oblidged to pay to Bailzie Brand merch^{t} ther the soume of nyne hundreth and sixtie pounds scots money at Whits. The smal remainder is either payable at Lambmas or in case of any new acct. he is to keep in his own hands.

The two thousand merks I did owe to the Laird of Leyes being assigned to Tho. Trumble of Bogmill w^t the bygone @ rent of it I have in security instructed the last pay^t to have been for Whits. 1685, tho. the discharge be Leyes bears only till Whits. 84. I have just now ordered the payment of two years rent wch will cleir the | @ rent till Whits. 1687 and y^t by one precept on Alex. Watson younger for the soume of 80 lib. and by giving him a bond of John Moreis for 66 lib. 13ss. 4d., and 13 lib. 6ss. 8d. in money wch makes up another year. They are depositat in Alex^r Henderson's hand in the meantyme.

Bogmill's @ rent 2 year of 80 lib. payed wch serves till Whits. 1687.

fol. 127.

I signed a Tack to Mr Low for the smiddie seat of Glammiss ane entrie dew at least of 33 lib. 6ss. 8d. every seven year, if more cannot be had.

March the 4th. Willm Low's Tack.

Having had the misfortune once of one, Francis Erskyne, Kirkbuddo's son to be my servant he malversed to A strange pitch, and prov'd ane infamous rascall wch oblidged me to put him in prison merely to let it be knowne thorow the countrey that he was no more my servant, for after he had been discharged of my service for a twelvemoneths and more he went about and in all places wher I travelled would com̃e and give himself out that he was my serv^t and imployed in my busines, but y^t his money had fall'ne short, and so they w^tout any doubting gave him money, some ten, some twenty dolers, and this he did to divers persons and in divers places.

14 March. Francis Erskyne ane infamous rouge.

After a twelvemoneths abode in prison he broke it and got out, but being in no safety in this country, he thought fitt at last to apply to some whom I trusted, and particularly to Mr P. Lyon of Carnustie advocat. By this tyme his elder brethren dyed and he came to be the Lairds eldest son, and was very desyrous to buy his peace, So I gav Mr. Patrick A factory whereby after dealing with him, he gave bond for two thousand merks payable the one at Mart. 1688 and the other in 1690 year of God, thes bonds are in Mr P. Lyon's name, for wch I have got a back bond declaring the trust of this dayes date, and when the old man his father dyes will persue him w^tout mercy for it.

14 March 89.

fol. 128.

This day the disposition and charter of Rochelhill now to be called Wrightfeild was signed and delyvered to the s^d

15 March.

Andrew Wright.

Andrew Wright and the rights of the Byreflat are to be returned.

And ane acct. twix and Whits. to be stated wt him for the superplus pryce, and all his work.

15 M. 89.

Precept draw'ne upon David Lyon and George Henderson for 150 lib. scots deu at Mertimes last payable to my wife, each of them that soume is three hundreth pound scots.

My wife's annuity of 600 lib. scots.

And sicklyke upon D. Lyon and Robt Ogilby of Coule for 150 lib. scots each of them at Whits. or Midsummer nixt payable to her on resat, *inde* 300 lib. scots money.

This makes six hundreth pound scots to her wch I have been in use to give her upon her privat occasions.

8 May 89. Mr J. Balvaird Stip. and @ rent.

I counted wt the minister of Glāms and ordered the brewar ther to pay him two yeares money stipend to Wit. '87 and '88 as Lykewayes Two Yeares @ rent of his principle soume of 1066 lib. 13ss. 4d. scots money wch payes him till Mert. 1689.

Contract wt Bailzie Arbuthnet.

I contracted wt Bailzie Arbuthnet in Dundee for 250 bolls wheat 200 b. oats and 50 b. peas, in all 500 bolls at 5 lib. 13ss. 4d. p boll payable at Lambas nixt.

Ja. Cuper's money.

I received from James Cuper 2000 lib. for wch I gave bond, But it is in prospect of his buying litle Blair to be hold'ne of me.

Ja. Crystie.

I received 333 lib. 6ss. 8d. from James Crystie in Auchterhous in payt of his bygone rents.

timber bought for Castle lyon.

I bought and payed readie money for 60 raills and 21 great trees, and 200 deals for my houses at the gate of the pond.

June the 9th Mr Clerck.

I sent 1333 lib. 6ss. 8d. to Edr to Mr Clerck towards his payt Count not yet received.

fol. 129. June the 1st Mrs Martyns @ rent.

I gave a precept for paying Mistris Martyne her @ rent for 2 years preceeding Mert. last of 1050 merks principal on Robt Ogilvy my factor of Tannadyce.

The levy cost me 3 horses.

I did outreike two horse in Angus and one in Perthshyre for the levy of horse and had difficulty enow in pleasing the officers, wt ther ryders and arms.

The dun gelding.

I bought a dun gelding from Millfeild and gave 18 lib. for him to my son Pat.

Oyr 2 horses bought at Auchterhous.

I bought other two horses for service the one at 2 lib. ster.

for the sadle and the other at 3 lib. for the cart from G. Henderson.

I gave a precept to Mr Rankyne Catechist in Dundee for a years interest of 5000 merks, being 200 lib. scots, on John Nicoll Mossgreive. 15 June. Mr Rankyns @ rent.

[END OF MS. OF BOOK OF RECORD.]

II

CONTRACT BETWIXT THE E. OF STRATHMORE AND M^{R} DE VET 1688

Att Glammiss the Eighteenth day of Januarie jm vj^{c} ffour scoir eight years. It is agreed upon Betwixt Patrick, Earle of Strathmore on the one Part and M^{r} De Vite Limner, on the oy^{r} pairt As after follows, That is to say That the s^{d} M^{r} De Vite binds and oblidges him to enter to the work presentlie particularlie aftermen^{d} and to finish and perfyte the same with all possible diligence with the outmost of his skill and art of painting and that he shall not goe from the s^{d} work at any time before the same be done without the s^{d} Earles Consent And first the s^{d} M^{r} De Vite Binds and oblidges him to paint the roof of the Chappell as the samen is divyded into three severall pannells so as that the fifteen largest pannels yrof shall containe everie one of y^{m} a full and distinct storie of Our blessed Saviour Conforme to the Cutts in a bible here in the house or the Service Book. And the rest of the pannels to be filled some with the Angels as in the skie and such other things as he shall invent and be esteemed proper for the work And forasmuch as y^{r} are upon the syde walls of the Chappell and rowme within sexteen large pannels, A doore peece and that above the table of the altar the s^{d} M^{r} De Vite Does hereby bind and oblidge him to paint in als full stature as the pannels will permitt the pictures Conforme as they are to be found in the two books abovementioned of our Saviour his twelve Apostles this in the Chappell and in the rowme within that of King Charles the Martyr and of St. Paul and St. Stephan Ane altar piece expressing the Crucifixione and the doore piece the Ascension Each picture to have the name y^{r}of above and at the foot a scroll containing the same words as are exprest in the cutts.

2nd And the s^{d} M^{r} De Vite does Lykwayes Bind and oblidge him to paint, perfyte and finish the roof of the dining-rowme immediatlie off the great hall upon the plaister yrof. this is to be done and is to contain the full historie of some one or oy^r^ of Ovid's Metamorphosis And it's designed by M^r^ De Vite and expected by the s^d^ Earle that the same shall be well done as y^t^ it may be of credit to the one and satisfactione to the oy^r^.

3rd There is Lykewayes to be a rowme for the storie of Icarus in the midle of the plaister of the bed chamber to be done by him.

4th There are lykwayes fyve chimneys and fourteen doore peeces of the high apartment off the hall to be done upon cloath of the bignesse of the pannels and to be fixed within the same and lykwayes in the apartment off the Low Hall yere are four chimneys and eleven doore peeces to be finished and done upon canvaess as s^d^ is, and all these are to be representationes of figures and poeticall fictions or such oy^r^ things as are usuall and proper.

5th The s^d^ Earle is to cause prime the roofe of the Chappel and such pannels of the syd walls q^ron^ the abmēn. pictures are to be drawn, and the roof of plaister in the Dyning rowme so far to prepare it for M^r^ De Vite's work. As Lykwayes to furnish oyle to him for the painting and cloath or canvass for the whole chimney and door pieces.

6th As lykways the s^d^ Earle In contempl^ne^ of the s^d^ M^r^ De Vite's works and in full satisfactione and recompense yerfore Is to be bound and oblidged Lyk as he be the tenor hereof binds and oblidges him and his airs to pay to the s^d^ M^r^ De Vite or to his order or asscyns the sowme of ffourscore and ten pound sterling the one half yerof is to be payed at such times as he shall call or have occasione for it at any time dureing the work provyding that before the pay^t^ of the full half three pairts of foure of the whole work be done and the oy^r^ equall half of the sowmes so agried on shall be thankfullie payd at his finishing and perfecting the same. He the s^d^ M^r^ De Vite is lykwayes to have his bed and board in the familie so long as the same remaines at the place. And it is agreed upon y^t^ the p^tie^ failzing shall pay to the p^tie^ observing or willing to observe his pairt of the premisses The sowme of Twentie pound sterling by and attour the performance of the same. Whiche the s^d M^r De Vite oblidges him for his pairt to doe to the said Earle's satisfactione and contentment. And for the more securite both the sds. pairties are Content and Consent that thir presents be registreat in the books of Counsell and Sessione, or of any oy^r ordinar judicature within yis realme and decerned to have the strenth of ane decreit of any of the judges yerof that letters and exets. neidfull may be direct hereon in forme as effeirs And Constitutes

. . . . . .

Their prors. In Witness whereof (wrin be Mr David Balvaird, servitour to the s^d Earle) they have subscryvit yir pnts. Day, moneth, place and yeir of God above written Before thir witnesses, John, Lord Glammiss and the s^d Mr David Balvaird and John and David Lyons servitours to the s^d Earle and Lord Glammiss.

Glammiss witnes	STRATHMORE.
D. Balvaird witnes	J. DE WET.
Jo. Lyon witnes.	
Da. Lyon witnes.	

dorso. Received att the wreating hereof by me James de Weet twelve pound which with threescor eighteen pound formerly received from the Earle of Strathmore makes in all fourscore ten pounds sterlen wherof I discharge the s^d Earle Att Edēn. 17 November 1688 befor thir witnesses David Lyon and George Dickson servitors to the s^d Earle. J. DE WET.

Da. Lyon witnes.

Georg dickson witnes.

III

ACCOMPT OF JACOB DE WET

Accompt of w[t] money is resting be the Earle of Strauchmoore to M[r] Dewett, Limner	lib.	s.	D.
Imp. the Picture of Diana in the Great Hall .	004	00	00
Itm. the Picture of Europia . . .	004	00	00
Itm. the Picture of Icarus in the Hall . .	005	00	00
Itm. 8 Little Door pieces at 4 Doll. per piece .	007	14	08
Itm. 3 Chimney pieces at 3[lb] sterl. p. piece .	009	00	00
Itm. 2 Door pieces at 5 Doll. p. piece . .	002	08	04
Itm. My Ladyes Picture	005	00	00
Itm. 6 Little Pictures at 3 [lib] p. piece . .	018	00	00
Itm. 2 great Pieces for my Lord and his 3 sonns; as also my Lady and her 2 Daughters .	025	00	00
Itm. 14 Pictures at 5 [lib] p. piece . . .	070	00	00
Sum is	150	03	00
Received of this above written accompt. 2000 marks Scotts w[ch] is, in Sterling money .	111	02	$2\frac{4}{6}$
	039	00	$09\frac{2}{6}$
	lib.	s.	D.
Remaines D. Ballance . .	039	00	$09\frac{2}{6}$

[Note by Lord Strathmore on back of preceding Acc[t]].

	Sterline
1st I would give now after full deliberation For the Roofe of the Chapel . . .	15 00 00
2nd For Our Saviour the twelve Apostles The Kings Father, the two Martyrs, Paul and Stephen the Alter and Door Peices .	20 00 00
3rd The Roofe of the Dining Roome and the Ovell in the Roofe of the Bed chamber . .	15 00 00

4th The five Chimney and fourtaine Door peices at the hye Apartment . . .	12 00 00
5th The four chimney and eleven Door peices of the lower Apartment In regard they are somewhat larger than Above . .	12 00 00
But I am extreamly concern'd for the work of the Chappell and the Roofe of the hye Dinning Roome especially and yrfor will add six pound *inde*	06 00 00
	80 00 00
There is Ten pound more in the Contract and Ten pound in discretion.	
He is to give me his own picture and to draw my sons in Three ovals.	
Oyr deductions from Mr d vits' acct.	
first my wif's picture as many more of that formerly done is but 4 lib. soe he stating it at 5 lib. here is	01 00 00
Then my son's pictur's were on condition and his own wch is not done made 4 picturs at 2 lib. p. peice is	08 00 00
More Kinnaird's pictur is payed for . .	02 00 00
Then thos done in the Chappell are over valued in	. . .
Giv'ne to d' vit a litle befor and att his way going 20 Rex dolers	47 00 00
More to M Moreis wch he was ow'ne her three Rex dolers	08 00 00

When the Earle of Strathmore payed Mr d Vit two thousand merks wch is 111 lib. 02sh 02 ster. He made ane acct. of the particulars, and reckned that this money overpayed him wch he choiced rather to doe then to fall short, considering limning a generous trade, and the Earle himself being ane encourager of artists designed no unjust thing to Mr d' vit and the Earle wishes wt all his heart that Mr d' vit had made as good and profitable acct. of his tyme ever since as he did for the short tyme he was wt the Earle of Strathmore. And to illustrat this here followes the pryces at which he reckned the particular peices of work.

First the two great pictures he acc[ts] at no less then D' Vit states them *inde*	25 00 00
Item the twelve pictures in the hall, few of thes twelv but M[r] d' vit had more or less from the gentlemen who sat, at 4 lib. p. peice *inde*	48 00 00
The other three pictures of the same syze, two of them being but copyes . . .	10 00 00
Six litle picturs at 40 ss. p. peice is . .	12 00 00
The picture of diana and Europia being two chimney peices best done . .	03 00 00
That of Icarus in the hall . . .	04 00 30
Three other chimney peices @ 1 lib. p. peice is .	03 00 00
And Ten door peices at ten shellens p. peice and too deir of that being of no value and litle and narrow is	05 00 00
The *summa* is . .	110 00 00

IV

ESTIMATE FOR REPAIRING THE ORGAN IN GLAMIS

Proposall For repairing the Earl of Strathmore's Organ in Glamss Formerly consisting of 10 Stops which were as follows.

1. Open Diapason Trible 2. Principal Trible 3. Twelft Trible 4. Fifteenth Trible 5. Cornet of 3 ranks 6. Fifteenth Trible	The most of these except the Cornet are about the Organ.
7. Principal Bass 8. Stopd Diapason 9. Fifteenth Bass 10. Nineteenth Bass	None of these that are left is of service being what is of them Brused or split.

the Belloss are quite Spoiled as also the Keys which must be new, and the other Reparations I propose viz.

To repair the Open Diapason Trible.

To repair the Principal Trible.

To repair the Twelft Trible.

To repair the Fifteenth Trible.

To make A Cornet of 3 ranks (a Principal Twelft and Tirza).

To make A Diapason Bass to meet the Trible.

To make A Stop'd Diapson Thorough.

To make A Principal Bass for the Front.

To make A Twelft Bass.

To make A Fifteenth Bass.

The above reparation I propose to make for thirty pound sterling.

James Bristowe.

GLAMIS CASTLE.

[p. 110

NOTES

NOTES

[1] *Mr. Ranken, Catechist in Dundee.* Page 1.

Mr. Ranken studied at St. Salvator's College, and received his degree of Master of Arts from the University of St. Andrews on 27th July 1667. Having taken orders as a Deacon in the Episcopal Church, he was intruded to the church of Benvie, but was unable to maintain his position there against the feeling of the people. He retired to Dundee, and was there appointed Catechist, his salary being provided by the interest on the sum of money mortified by Bailie Patrick Yeaman and placed in the hands of the Earl of Strathmore. The payment of this salary is repeatedly mentioned throughout the Book of Record, and it is noteworthy that his name appears on the first and on the last pages of the manuscript. He survived till 7th April 1729, when he had reached the eighty-second year of his age. His son, John Ranken, was minister of Clunie, and was translated thence to Inchture, where he died in 1737. From the time of the Revolution till 1727 there was only one Episcopal congregation in Dundee, and at the latter date it was divided by Bishop Raitt, one portion having a meeting-place at Yeaman Shore, under Bishop Raitt's ministry, and the other continuing services in the Seagate Meeting-house, under Mr. James Irvine. Mr. David Fife, who was Episcopal minister at Glamis, was called to succeed Mr. Irvine in 1744. Mr. Yeaman belonged to a family that was long connected prominently with Dundee. He was for a lengthened period in the Town Council, and held the offices of Harbour-Master, Treasurer, and Bailie. On 6th May 1675 he mortified the sum of £3333, 6s. 8d. Scots (£277, 15s. 6d. sterling), to pay the salary of a Catechist in connection with the Episcopal Church. By the decree erecting the Cross Church, Dundee, into a separate charge in 1788, this office came to an end, and the new minister took the place of the Catechist, the produce of the mortification being included in the stipend paid by the town to him. On page 74, Mr. Ranken's name is wrongly given as James in the manuscript: it should be Alexander.

[2] *Frederick Lyon.* Page 1.

Frederick Lyon, of Brigton, was the third son of Patrick, first Earl of Kinghorne, and consequently uncle of the Earl of Strathmore. He obtained a charter of the lands of Brigton on 31st July 1622, and represented Forfarshire in the Conventions of 1644 and 1647. After his death in 1660 he was succeeded by his eldest son David (designated Patrick in the Burgess Roll of Dundee, under date 7th March 1663), at whose death the property was heavily burdened. John Lyon, the brother of David, came next into the estate, and it was judged expedient by Lord Strathmore, and others of the Lyon family, to take up the debts that were due from the estate of his lordship's cousin. Frederick Lyon, here referred to, appears to have been one of the principal creditors, and his name is frequently mentioned throughout the volume. John Lyon was retoured as heir of his brother David on 24th March 1685.

[3] *John Lambie of Dunkennie.* Page 1.

The name of L'amy or Lamby has been associated with the estate of Dunkenny since the beginning of the fifteenth century, and it was possessed by a family of that name till early in the seventeenth century. The property then passed out of the hands of the Lambys for some time, and was acquired by David Lindsay, Bishop of Brechin, who only possessed it for a short period. The estate was acquired by John Lambie, mentioned in the text, previous to 1646, having been sold by the daughters of Bishop Lindsay. From the references made on page 22, and elsewhere throughout the volume, the character of this John Lambie will be understood. His brother, Silvester

Lambie, was minister of Glamis from 1625 till 1665, and the son of the latter succeeded to the estate of Dunkennie.

[4] *Laird of Strathmartine.* Page 2.

Patrick Wynton was Laird of Strathmartine at the time of the writing of the Book of Record. The property had been in the possession of the Wynton family early in the sixteenth century, and its members frequently intermarried with the Scrymgeours of Dudhope and other leading families in the locality. On 21st September 1699, Thomas Wynton was served heir of his father, Patrick Wynton.

[5] *The Master of Kinnaird.* Page 2.

The Master of Kinnaird here referred to was Patrick, eldest son of Sir George Kinnaird, who was created Baron Kinnaird of Inchture in 1682. He succeeded as second Lord Kinnaird, in 1689, and his second son, Patrick, became third Lord Kinnaird in 1701. The second wife of the latter was Lady Elizabeth Lyon, daughter of the first Earl of Strathmore. The price of the tun of French wine is given as £312 Scots. As Patrick, Master of Kinnaird, was entered Burgess of Dundee on 20th October 1670, it is probable that he and his brother George were concerned in the importing of wines, which had long formed the greater part of the commerce of Dundee. The house known as the town mansion of the Kinnairds of Inchture stood at the 'Shorehead,' latterly called Fish Street, Dundee, and was removed only a few years ago.

[6] *James Lyon, Litster, Dundee.* Page 2.

James Lyon was enrolled as Burgess of Dundee on 23d February 1672. As there were many of the leading merchants of Dundee connected with the Lyons of Glamis, it is probable that he was related to that family, from the interest which the Earl of Strathmore took in his affairs. Donald Thorntoun of Balbennie was the son of Alexander Thorntoun of Blackness, and succeeded his father in the lands of Foffartie on 20th August 1652.

[7] *Patrick Lyon, minister of Rescobie.* Page 3.

Patrick Lyon obtained his M.A. degree from the University of St. Andrews on 26th July 1670. He was appointed schoolmaster at Kirriemuir, and was admitted as minister of Rescobie on 23d December 1677. Here he remained as minister of the parish till his death in August 1703, aged 53.

[8] *Earl of Airlie.* Page 3.

James Ogilvy, second Earl of Airlie, was the son of James, first Earl of Airlie, and of Lady Isabella Hamilton, daughter of the Earl of Haddington, and was born *circa* 1615. The first Earl had been a devoted adherent of the Royalists, and his son, young Lord Ogilvy, was left in charge of the paternal castles of Forther and Airlie whilst the Earl was abroad. The Estates of Parliament, then dominated by the Presbyterian party, ordered these fortresses to be seized, as the Earl had refused to subscribe the Covenant. A Commission of Fire and Sword, dated 12th June 1640, was granted to the Earl of Argyll, empowering him utterly to subdue and root out rebels such as Lord Ogilvy was then considered. Acting on these instructions, Argyll destroyed the Castle of Forther, but failed to capture the inmates. His unfeeling conduct at this time is referred to in an imaginative manner in the well-known ballad of 'The Bonnie House o' Airlie.' Lord Ogilvy made his escape to England and was present at the battle of Marstonmoor. Whilst returning to Scotland in command of Prince Rupert's men after that engagement, he was captured by a skirmishing party of the Parliamentarians, and imprisoned in the Tolbooth of Edinburgh, in 1644. Here he remained until his old companion-in-arms, the Marquess of Montrose, restored him to liberty after the battle of Kilsyth, in August 1645. He was placed in command of some of the Royalist troops at the battle of Philiphaugh, in September 1645, and was captured after the battle as he was escaping from the field. He was carried prisoner to Glasgow and thence to St. Andrews, and was condemned to death by the Parliament that met there in November 1645. Through the intrepidity of his sister, Lady Helen Ogilvy, he escaped from St. Andrews Castle the night before his execution was to have taken place, she having exchanged clothes with him and remained in prison whilst he passed out disguised. After suffering severely in the Royalist cause, he was at last induced to submit to General Leslie in 1649 under guarantee that his life, estate, and liberty would not be endangered, and soon afterwards he was relieved from the pressure of the Acts that had been made against him. He was appointed to the command of a troop of horse at the Restoration, and was sworn a Privy Councillor. He lived to see William III. firmly established on the throne, and was a member of the Scottish Parliament that met in 1693, though he was excused from attendance on account of his great age and infirmity. His death took place shortly after this date. The Earl of Airlie was twice married, firstly to Helen, daughter of George, first Lord Banff, by whom he had one son and three daughters. The Earl's second wife was Isobel, widow of Lewis, third Marquess of Huntly.

[9] *Lady Lindores.* Page 3.

Lady Marion Ogilvy, eldest daughter of James, second Earl of Airlie (see preceding note), was the wife of James Elphinstone, only son of the first Lord Balmerinoch, who took the title of Lord Coupar in 1607, when he received a charter of the temporal lordship of the Abbey of Coupar-in-Angus. Lord Coupar was born in 1587, and survived till 1669, when he expired without issue, and his title and estates devolved upon his nephew, the third Lord Balmerinoch. A curious story is told regarding the relationship of his wife, Lady Marion Ogilvy, and himself in Riddell's *Peerage and Consistorial Law.* Lord Coupar had been nearly eighty years of age when he married Lady Marion, and she persuaded him to execute a deed conveying his honours and estates to herself and any one whom she should please to marry. This strange document was afterwards set aside by the Court of Session on 28th June 1671, as evidence was given that Lord Coupar was on his deathbed when he signed the deed, and was under compulsion.

Lady Coupar was afterwards married to John Leslie, third Lord Lindores, son of James, second Lord Lindores, and of Mary, daughter of Patrick, Lord Gray. Her son, David Leslie, succeeded as fourth Lord Lindores.

[10] *Alexander Leslie, minister at Ceres.* Page 4.

Alexander Leslie was the fourth son of James Leslie of Warthill, and obtained his degree from King's College, Aberdeen, in 1657. After being chaplain for some time to David, Lord Newark, he was admitted minister of Anstruther Wester on 17th January 1666. In October of the succeeding year he was translated to Ceres, where he remained for seventeen years. On 22d October 1684 he was again translated to Crail, but was deprived on 17th September 1689 for non-conformity and for refusing to pray for William and Mary. He died at Crail on 23d September 1703, in the 60th year of his age.

[11] *Mr. Campbell, minister at Menmure.* Page 5.

David Campbell was the second son of Magister Colin Campbell (born 1577, died 1638), who was minister of the Third Charge in Dundee, and was one of the leaders of the Presbyterian party. His mother was Margaret Hay, who belonged to the family of the Hays of Kinnoull, as is shown by the fragment of her tombstone still preserved in Dundee. David Campbell was born in 1619, and obtained his degree as Master of Arts at St. Andrews on 2d May 1639. He was admitted to the parish of Menmure on 17th December 1644, but was unable to enter upon his duties for nearly a year in consequence of Montrose's rebellion. He survived till June 1696, and was succeeded by his son, James Campbell.

[12] *Provost Watson.* Page 5.

Alexander Watson was the eldest son of Alexander Watson, Dean of Guild in Dundee, and was entered on the Burgess Roll on 23d November 1658. He became proprietor of the estate of Grange of Barry about 1660, and was bailie of Dundee in

1668-9, and Provost in 1670-73. He was Commissioner for Dundee at the Convention of Royal Burghs in 1670, being chosen Moderator of the General Convention. His daughter, Grizell Watson, was married to Gardyne of Lawton, Forfarshire, in 1676, and his son, Thomas Watson, succeeded him previous to 1701. The estate remained in possession of the family till the middle of last century.

[13] *Patrick Strachan, minister.* Page 6.

Patrick Strachan studied at the New College, St. Andrews, and was presented by George, Earl of Panmure, to the parish of Carmyllie in 1659. He was translated to St. Vigeans on 5th November 1665, and continued there till his death in 1693. He had two sons ministers, David Strachan, who was also in the parish of Carmyllie from 1684 till 1709, and George, who was intruded to St. Vigeans after his father's death, but was never settled there.

[14] *Bishop of Dunblane.* Page 8.

James Ramsay, Bishop of Dunblane, was the son of Principal Ramsay of Glasgow University. He was born in 1626, and took his degree at Glasgow in 1647. He was ordained minister of Kirkintilloch in 1653, and was translated to Linlithgow in 1655. He took an active part on the Episcopalian side, and on 29th May 1661 he assisted at the burning of the Solemn League and Covenant in the Market-place of Linlithgow. From this parish he was removed to Hamilton in 1664, and on the recommendation of Archbishop Leighton he was presented to the Bishopric of the Isles in the succeeding year, but Ramsay still continued to be Bishop of Dunblane. On 23d May 1684 he was promoted to the See of Ross, and died at Edinburgh on 22d October 1696, aged 70.

[15] *Countess of Buchan.* Page 8.

Lady Marjory Ramsay, eldest daughter of William, first Earl of Dalhousie, and of Lady Margaret Carnegie, eldest daughter of David, first Earl of Southesk. Her husband, James Erskine, seventh Earl of Buchan, succeeded to that title in 1640; was fined £1000 by Cromwell's Act of Grace and Pardon in 1654, and died in October 1664. The only son of the Countess of Buchan was William, eighth Earl of Buchan, who died a prisoner in Stirling Castle, unmarried, in 1695. The earldom by special charter was inherited by Henry, third Lord Cardross, who is referred to further in Note 80.

[16] *Duncan of Lundie.* Page 9.

The family to which Alexander Duncan belonged, and which is now represented by the Earl of Camperdown, can be traced in connection with Dundee from the beginning of the sixteenth century. Finlay Duncan was settled as a surgeon in Dundee previous to 1550. His son, William Duncan, surgeon, was bailie of Dundee from 1590 till 1608. From him descended Alexander Duncan of Lundie, referred to in the text. He was the son of William Duncan of Seasyde, bailie of Dundee in 1656, and was born in 1652. At an early age he took part in the municipal affairs of the burgh, and having amassed and inherited a considerable fortune, he acquired the estate of Lundie from Colin Campbell, a scion of the family of Argyll, *circa* 1680. Though long a public official, Alexander Duncan died comparatively young, as is shown by the inscription on his monument in the Howff, or old burying-ground of Dundee. This was one of the most elaborate mural tablets in that place, although it has been suffered to fall to ruins. The inscription is as follows:—

'*Humo adjacenti conditur quod morti concesserunt Alexander Duncan de Lundie, qui fato fundus est Aprilis—A. Æ. C.* 1696 *ætat.* 44*; ejusque dilecta conjux Anna Drummond, unica filia M*[ri] *Joannis Drummond de Megginch quæ decessit Aprilis die* —1695, *æt.* 42. *Necnon eorundem liberi Gulielmus, Patricium, Christiana, et Anna, quibus parentes superstitis erant. Item, alter Gulielmus, qui matri non vero pater vixit, et Joannes, filius natus secundus, qui mortem obiit Julii die*—1696, *ætat.* 20. *Mausoleum extruendum curavit M*[r] *Alexander Duncan de Lundie A. Æ. C.* 1718.'

His eldest son, Alexander Duncan of Lundie, was born in 1677, and was provost in 1719. His death took place on 2d January in the latter year, when in the forty-second year of his age. Alexander Duncan, his eldest son, born in 1703, died in 1765, was also provost at the time of the Rebellion of 1745, and the second son of the latter was the famous Admiral Viscount Duncan of Camperdown.

[17] *Earl of Panmure.* Page 9.

George Maule, third Earl of Panmure, was the eldest son of George, second Earl of Panmure, and succeeded his father in March 1671. He was Privy Councillor to Charles II. and James VII., and died 1st February 1686. He was full cousin to the Earl of Strathmore, his father having been brother to Lady Elizabeth Maule, wife of the second Earle of Kinghorne, and mother of Lord Strathmore. To George, second Earl, there are frequent references made throughout the 'Book of Record,' as he was one of the tutors who had charge of Lord Strathmore during his minority. For this nobleman Lord Strathmore seems to have had very profound respect, and he gratefully acknowledges the efforts made by the second Earl of Panmure to repair the injustice done to him by Patrick, first Earl of Panmure, grandfather of Lord Strathmore. (See pp. 24, 25.)

[18] *Patrick Lyon of Carnoustie.* Page 9.

Magister Patrick Lyon of Carnoustie was a distant relative of Lord Strathmore. He must not be confounded with Sir Patrick Lyon of Carse, who was also a relative, and who is known to antiquaries as the author of a manuscript Genealogy of the Principal Scottish Families, which is now in the Advocates' Library, Edinburgh, and formed the foundation of Sir George Mackenzie's well-known work on this subject. Patrick Lyon of Carnoustie was admitted a member of the Faculty of Advocates, and his son, Magister Patrick Lyon, was served heir to his father on 16th March 1699.

[19] *Minister of Kettins.* Page 9.

David Paton, minister of Kettins, was the son of David

Paton, merchant in Dundee, and was born in the burgh in 1624. He was educated at King's College, Aberdeen, and took his degree there in 1644. Four years afterwards he was presented to the parish of Kemback, in Fife, and was translated to Kettins, Forfarshire, in June 1650, where he remained till his death in April 1692. By his will he bequeathed 'the sum of 70 lib. scots and 14 rix dollars' to assist the poor in the parish of Dundee. His son, James Paton, who was born in 1655, became his father's colleague and successor at Kettins, but ceased preaching 1716, though he survived till *circa* 1730. He also mortified the sum of £1000 Scots for the education of girls and young women in Dundee. The date of this Deed of Mortification was 27th October 1726. The first of this family in Dundee seems to have been Andrew Paton, furrier, who was entered on the burgess roll on 10th October 1516, and the succession from him to James Paton can be traced.

[20] *Dr. Edward, minister at Crail.*—Page 10.

Alexander Edward one of the Regents in the Old College, St. Andrews, was promoted to the parish of Denino, Fife, in 1652, and translated to Crail in 1663. The degree of D.D. was conferred upon him in 1673, and he died at Crail on 7th May 1684, aged about sixty-one. He was succeeded by Alexander Leslie (see Note 10, page 118).

[21] *Mr. Nicolson, minister at Errol.*—Page 10.

John Nicolson studied at St. Leonard's College, and took his degree at St. Andrews on 9th July 1655. He was ordained minister of Meigle on 26th March 1661, and was translated to Errol on 4th September 1666. The degree of D.D. was conferred upon him on 4th December 1684. He was deprived on 29th October 1690 for refusing to pray for William and Mary, and he died in retirement about 1701.

[22] *Carstairs, minister of Inchture.*—Page 10.

James Carstaires, son of Thomas Carstaires, Boarhills, took his degree at St. Andrews in 1662, and was admitted as minister of Tannadice, Forfarshire, on 22d August 1667. He was presented to the parish of Inchture by the Archbishop of St. Andrews in February 1682, and remained in that charge till his death in 1709.

[23] *Laird of Craigmillar.*—Page 11.

Sir John Gilmour of Craigmillar was the son of John Gilmour, W.S. and became advocate on 12th December 1628. When the Court of Session was reorganised after the Restoration, he was appointed Lord President, and took his seat on 13th February 1666. He joined the party of the Duke of Lauderdale, and was active in promoting the downfall of the Earl of Middleton, father-in-law of Lord Strathmore. The position of Lord President was resigned by him in 1670, and his death took place in the following year. His title was derived from the estate of Craigmillar near Edinburgh, which had long been held by the Preston family. The purchase is thus recorded in Lamont's *Diary*:—'1660 or therby—Sir John Gilmure, advocat in Edb. bought the lands of Craigmellar in Lowthian, from the Laird of Craigmellar.'

Sir John was married to Margaret, daughter of Sir Alexander Murray of Blackbarony. Their son, Sir Alexander Gilmour of Craigmillar, was created a Baronet in 1668, and the title continued in the family till the death of the fifth Baronet in 1792.

[24] *Lord Carse.*—Page 11.

Sir Patrick Lyon of Carse was second cousin of the Earl of Strathmore, and was admitted member of the Faculty of Advocates on 11th July 1671. He had previously been Professor of Philosophy in the College of St. Andrews. On the decease of Lord Nairn he became an Ordinary Lord of Session, taking his seat, with the title of Lord Carse, on 10th November 1683. He was appointed one of the Lords of Justiciary on 20th February 1684; but as he was an ardent Jacobite he was deprived of both offices at the Revolution. For many years his family had an intimate connection with Dundee. The old Close in that burgh known as Whitehall Close, which is now removed, was the place where his town residence stood, and the sculptured stone, with date 1660 and the arms of Scotland, that latterly decorated the Nethergate entrance to this Close, is reasonably supposed to have been taken from the house of Sir Patrick Lyon when the front land was built about a century ago. Sir Patrick's son, Magister Patrick Lyon of Carse, was retoured as heir to him on 30th October 1695. There is a portrait of Sir Patrick Lyon still preserved in the drawing-room of Glamis Castle, which was painted by Jacob de Witt.

[25] *Sir James Rochhead.*—Page 11.

Sir James Rochheid of Inverleith was the son of John Rochheid, and grandson of James Rochheid, merchant and burgess of Edinburgh. The estate of Inverleith, near Edinburgh, which had long been in the possession of the family of Touris, was acquired by James Rochheid prior to 1652. Sir James entailed his estate in 1692, and was created a baronet in 1704. This title became extinct in the person of Sir James, the second baronet, whose daughter Mary was married to Sir Francis Kinloch, Bart., of Gilmerton. She is referred to and described by Lord Cockburn in his 'Memorials.'

[26] *Sir John Maitland.*—Page 11.

Sir John Maitland of Ravelrig was the son of Charles, third Earl of Lauderdale and of Elizabeth, daughter of Richard Lauder of Halton, Midlothian. He was admitted to the Faculty of Advocates on 30th July 1680, and was knighted and created a Baronet of Nova Scotia on 18th November of the same year. As he supported the party of William III. at the Revolution he was appointed Lord of Session in November 1689, taking the designation of Lord Ravelrig. Having taken his place as Member of Parliament for Edinburghshire in 1685, he remained almost continuously in that position until 1695, when he succeeded his brother as Earl of Lauderdale. He was a strong supporter of the Union, and survived to see it accomplished. His death took place on 30th August 1710.

[27] *Kinloch of Gourdy.*—Page 11.

David Kinloch of Gourdy was the son of John Kinloch, and the grandson of Dr. David Kinloch of Aberbothrie. His father had acquired the lands of Gourdy in Perthshire through his mother Grizel Hay, daughter of Hay of Gourdy, and John Kinloch had a charter confirming these lands to him in 1630. For many years the family of the Kinlochs were intimately associated with Dundee, and held much property in that burgh and the neighbourhood.

[28] *Laird of ffindourie.* Page 11.

Robert Arbuthnott of Findowrie was descended from the same family as that of the Viscounts Arbuthnott, the direct ancestor of this branch being David Arbuthnott, son of Robert Arbuthnott of that Ilk. The latter acquired the lands of Findowrie on 9th February 1574, and granted them to his son David, and they descended in a direct line to Robert Arbuthnott, mentioned in the text. The grandfather of the latter suffered severely during Montrose's Rebellion, and received compensation by order of Parliament. Both Robert and his father (also named Robert) were strong supporters of the Covenanters, and were heavily fined by the Earl of Middleton. When Lord Strathmore led a regiment of Angus horsemen to the west country to suppress the rebels under the Marquess of Argyll in 1685, the Laird of Findowrie was intrusted with a command under him. He was succeeded by his son Alexander on 30th July 1698.

[29] *ffodringham of Bandean.* Page 13.

John Fotheringham of Ballindean, Perthshire, was descended from the Fotheringhams of Powrie, Forfarshire, a race that settled early in Angus, and are said to have derived their descent from Henry de Ffodringhay, who received the lands of Balunie, near Dundee, from Robert II. previous to 1377. When Thomas Fotheringham of Ballindean died in 1670, his eldest son, John, succeeded to the estate, and is the Laird of

Ballindean referred to in the text. He died in 1686, and his next brother, James, succeeded him, but only kept the estate for one year. The third brother, George Fotheringham, was served heir on 31st August 1687. The estate of Ballindean came afterwards into the possession of the Wedderburns of Blackness, and now gives the title to Sir William Wedderburn, Bart., of Ballindean.

[30] *Auchterlownie of Guynd.* Page 14.

John Ochterlony, who was Collector of Supply for the Shire of Forfar, was the representative of the ancient family of Ochterlony of that Ilk. He succeeded his father on 12th April 1676, and was Commissioner of Supply for Forfarshire from 1678 till 1690. In literature he is known from the 'Account of the Shyre of Forfar,' which he wrote for Sir Robert Sibbald of Kipps, and which is now amongst the Macfarlane Manuscripts in the Advocates' Library, Edinburgh. In 1689, when William and Mary issued the order for new elections of magistrates in all the burghs of Scotland, John Ochterlony was appointed to superintend the election in Montrose. In his own account of his paternal mansion he claims to be 'the lineal successor, chief, and representative of the ancient familie of Ouchterlony of that Ilk.' In concluding his 'Account,' he thus refers to his ancestors:—'I will add no more for our Familie of Ouchterlony of that Ilk but what I have said in the generall description of some places we have and had concern in, but that I have ane accompt of the marriages of the Familie these fifteen generations, viz.—1st, Stewart of Rosyth, in Fyffe; 2d, Maull of Panmure; 3d, Ogilvy of Lentrathene, predecessor to the Lords of Ogilvy; 4th, Gray, of the Lord Gray; 5th, Drummond of Stobhall, now Perth; 6th, Keith, Lord Marishall; 7th, Lyon, Lord Glames; 8th, Cunninghame of Barnes; 9th, Stewart of Innermeath; 10th, Olyphant, of the Lord Olyphant; 11th, Scrimgeour of Dudope; 12th, Beatoun of Westhall; 13th, Peirsone of Lochlands; 14th, Carnegy of Newgait; 15th, Maull, cousine-germane to the deceist Patrick, Earl of Panmure. All these are daughters of the above written families. The familie is very ancient, and very great, having above fourteen score chalders of victuall, which was a great estate in those days.'

[31] *Duke of Lauderdal.* Page 14.

John Maitland, second Earl of Lauderdale, was born at Lethington, 24th May 1616, and succeeded to the title in 1645. His name is familiar to every student of Scottish history, because of the prominent part he took in the management of Parliamentary affairs, both in the time of Charles I. and of Charles II. Having been taken prisoner at the battle of Worcester, in 1651, he was imprisoned in the Tower of London for nine years, and was liberated by General Monck in March 1660. He proceeded at once to the Hague, and returned to this country in company with Charles II. at the Restoration. From this period his power in Scotland was almost unlimited. He was made Secretary of State, President of the Council, one of the Lords of the Bedchamber, Governor of the Castle of Edinburgh, and an extraordinary Lord of Session. In 1669, he was appointed High Commissioner to the Parliament, aud after the fall of the Earl of Middleton he obtained the entire control of Scotland. He was created Duke of Lauderdale in 1672, and continued to control that country till the Duke of York was sent to the North in 1680. From this time his influence rapidly declined, his offices were taken from him, and the pensions he had received were cancelled. His death took place at Tunbridge on 24th August 1682. He was buried at Haddington, and the inscription on his coffin in the Lauderdale vault there is thus given by Monteith:

'*In Spem beatæ Resurrectionis hic conditur illustrissimus et nobilissimus Princeps ac Dominus D. Joannes Dux de Lauderdale, Marchio de March, Comes de Lauderdale et Guilford, Vice Comes Maitland, Dominus de Thirlestane, Musselburgh, Bolton et Peterham; saepius ad Parliamenta et Ordinum hujus Regni Conventus tenenda Prorex, a Restauratione Regiæ Magistatis per 20 Annos, solus, pro Regno Scotiæ, Regum optimo, Carolo Secundo a Secretes; Praeses Secreti Concilii, praedicto potentissimo Regi, in Regno Anglia, a Secretioribus Conciliis et ex Cubiculariis Primariis unis; in Scotia ex quatuor Collegii*

Justitiae extraordinariis Senatoribus unus, Castelli Regii Edinburgeni Constabularius et Gubernator, Nobilissimi Ordinis Garterii Eques.

'*Natus* 21 *Maii M.D.C. XVI. Leidintoniæ Obiit* 24 *Die Augusti, prope Fontes de Tunbridge Anno humanæ Salutis M. D. C. L. XXXII Ætatis* 68.'

The Duke of Lauderdale's Parliament referred to in the text was held at St. Andrews in 1646, and the Act to which Lord Strathmore alludes was passed for the purpose of relieving 'Johne Erle of Kinghorne, Johne Lord Lowre, the Laird of Panmure, Sir Alexr. Erskene of Dun, and some uth[r] gentlemen of the Sheriffdome of Forfar,' who had borrowed 6600 merks for the payment of officers and furnishing of amunition for the levy of troops in that county. The Parliament directed that the sum should be taken up by a stent upon the whole shire. The suggestion which Lord Strathmore makes that Lord Halton, brother of the Duke, went shares with him in this impost, is rendered not unlikely from the after conduct of Halton, who was deprived of his office of Treasurer for malappropriation of funds in his charge. The Earl of Brentford (Bramford) was Patrick Ruthven, son of William Ruthven of Ballindean, an eminent officer under Gustavus Adolphus, who was created Earl of Forth in 1642, and was afterwards made a Peer of England, with the title Earl of Brentford, for his valour in support of the cause of Charles I. in 1644. He died at Dundee, at a very advanced age, in 1651. Sir William Binning of Wallyford was Lord Provost of Edinburgh in 1676, and was a Commissioner of Supply for Midlothian from 1678 till 1704. In 1693 he was heavily fined for his concern in the purchase of arms for the Government, having attempted, in conjunction with his partners, to swindle the country, by extorting an increase on the contract price agreed upon, and for attempted bribery. Sir William was married to the daughter of John Dundas of Duddingston.

[32] *Laird of Salton.* Page 14.

Andrew Fletcher, the celebrated patriot and political theorist, was the son of Sir Robert Fletcher of Saltoun, and the grandson of Sir Andrew Fletcher, Lord Innerpeffer of Session. He was educated under Gilbert Burnet, afterwards Bishop of Salisbury, and became Member of Parliament for Haddingtonshire in 1681-2. Here he became so strenuous an opponent of the arbitrary rule of James, Duke of York, that he found it necessary to withdraw to Holland. As he had refused to take the test, he was outlawed, and when he returned with Monmouth in 1685, his estates were confiscated and granted to the Earl of Dumbarton. In the Revolution of 1688 he took an active part, and again represented Haddington in the Parliament of 1702-7. He was opposed to the terms suggested by the English Parliament at the time of the Union, and voted against it. He died, unmarried, at London, on 16th September 1716.

[33] *Bannerman of Elsick.* Page 14.

Sir Alexander Bannerman, descendant of Alexander Bannerman of Elsick who was Sheriff of Aberdeenshire in 1512, was Commissioner of Supply for Kincardineshire in 1678 and 1685. He was created a Baronet of Nova Scotia on 28th December 1682. He was appointed overseer for the election of magistrates in Aberdeen, under the Royal Warrant of 1689. By his marriage in 1670 with Margaret, daughter of Patrick Scott, and sister of Sir Francis Scott, Bart., of Thirlestane, he had a son, Patrick Bannerman, who was Provost of Aberdeen in 1715. Sir Alexander is now represented by Sir George Bannerman, Bart., of Elsick, Kincardineshire.

[34] *Lord Ross.* Page 14.

George, eleventh Lord Ross, son of William, tenth Lord Ross, and of Helen, daughter of George, Lord Forrester of Corstorphine, was an ardent Royalist, was sworn of the Privy Council at the Restoration, and held a commission as lieutenant-colonel of the Royal Regiment of Guards. He was married to Lady Grizel Cochrane, daughter of the first Earl of Dundonald, and had a son, William, afterwards twelfth Lord Ross, and a daughter, Grizel, married to Sir Alexander Gilmour, Bart., of Craigmillar. His second wife was Lady Jean Ramsay, daughter of George, second Earl of Dalhousie, who had also a son and daughter, Charles Ross of Balnagowan, and Jean, wife of William, sixth Earl of Dalhousie. Lord Ross died in 1682, and was succeeded by his eldest son. Though it is not stated that the debt referred to in the text was contracted with the eleventh Lord Ross, there is every probability that it was so.

[35] *Earl of Linlithgow.* Page 15.

George, third Earl of Linlithgow, was the son of Alexander, second Earl, and of Lady Elizabeth Gordon, daughter of George, Marquess of Huntly. He was born in July 1616, and succeeded to the title on the death of his father. As the date of his father's decease is not precisely recorded in any of the peerage genealogies, the time of his succession to the earldom is obscure. Sir Robert Douglas in his *Peerage* states that George, Earl of Linlithgow, had charters under that style in 1669, and this has been accepted as the year of his accession. As his name is entered in the burgess roll of Dundee as Earl of Linlithgow on 26th October 1660, it is evident that he must have succeeded to the title nine years before the accepted date. The third Earl of Linlithgow was a faithful adherent of the Royalists, and suffered severely during the supremacy of Cromwell. He represented the sheriffdom of Perth in the Parliament of 1654-5, but took little part in the proceedings. He had been appointed constable and keeper of the palace of Linlithgow and the castle of Blackness in 1642, an office which had been hereditary in his family from 1598, and which was conferred by royal warrant in 1803 on his representative Sir Thomas Livingstone of Westquarter. At the Restoration the Earl was made a privy councillor, and was appointed colonel of the Royal Regiment of Horse Guards. There is a curious account in Lamont's *Diary*, page 187, of a strange duel that happened at the race-course of Cupar in Fife, betwixt the Earl of Linlithgow and Lord Carnegie on 12th April 1666, in which the Earl was severely wounded. After his recovery he was one of the principal commanders to whom the suppression of the Conventicles was committed, and he acted in concert with General Dalziel and John Graham of Claverhouse. The high position which he occupied in the army is proved by the fact that the Earl of Argyll was directed to serve under him in this task. There is a letter from the Duke of Rothes to the Earl of Argyll, preserved amongst the documents at Inveraray Castle, which is in these terms:—

'*Edinburgh*, 7 *June* 1679.—The fanatickes in the west and vther haveing formed themselves into a dangerous rebellion, whose numbers and force doe daylie incresce, wee have therefore thought fitt to desyre your lordship, with the greatest expedition your circumstances can allow, to disentangle yourself from the expedition for which you are commissionated against the rebellious people in the Highlands, to the end your lordship may, with the greatest diligence you can, repaire to his Majesty's host, and joyne the forces vnder the command of the Earle of Linlithgow, with your friendis, vassallis, servantis, and followeris, weill appoynted and armed, for assisting towards the suppression of this treasonable insurrection. . . .'

The Earl of Linlithgow terminated his military career by resigning his command in 1681, and he was then appointed Justice-General of Scotland. This office he retained till the Revolution of 1688, when he was deprived, in common with his fellow-Royalists. He was concerned in the plot of Sir James Montgomery of Skelmorlie for the restoration of James VII. to the throne which he had abandoned, but he died before any overt action had been initiated. His death occurred on the 1st of February 1690, when he was in his seventy-fourth year. By his marriage with Lady Elizabeth Maule, daughter of the first Earl of Panmure, and widow of John, second Earl of Kinghorne, Lord Linlithgow had two sons and one daughter. The elder son, George, succeeded his father as fourth Earl of Linlithgow, but did not long survive him. The second son was Alexander, third Earl of Callendar. The daughter, Lady Henrietta, was married to Robert, second Viscount of Oxfurd. The Earl of Linlithgow was stepfather to the Earl of Strathmore, and frequent references are made to him throughout the *Book of Record*.

[36] *Earl of Craford.* Page 15.

William Lindsay, sixteenth Earl of Craufurd, and second Earl of Lindsay, succeeded his father in 1676, being the second of the house of Lindsay of the Byres to hold the title of Earl of Craufurd. Unlike his father, who was a strong Royalist, the Earl of Craufurd warmly took up the cause of William III. at the Revolution, and in 1689 subscribed the Letter of Congratulation sent by the Parliament to that monarch. In that year he was chosen President of the Scottish Parliament, and it was on his motion that the Convention of Estates was converted into a Parliament. The Earl of Craufurd died on 6th March 1698.

[37] *Sir George Lockhart.* Page 15.

Sir George Lockhart was the second son of Sir James Lockhart of Lee, Lord Justice-Clerk. He was admitted advocate on 8th January 1656, and as his brother, Sir William Lockhart, had supported Cromwell, and been rewarded with the hand of the Protector's niece in marriage, George Lockhart was chosen advocate to Cromwell on 14th May 1658. The Restoration in 1660 put an end to this office, and Lockhart was compelled to take the oath of allegiance to Charles II., kneeling, before he could gain re-admission to the Faculty of Advocates. His father had maintained his loyalty to the Stewart family and had been replaced on the Bench, and this probably had some influence in reconciling the king to the only law-officer appointed by Cromwell in Scotland. He was knighted in 1663, and his great talents and profound learning soon carried him beyond all his rivals at the Bar. In 1672 he was chosen Dean of the Faculty, and was elected one of the representatives of Lanarkshire in the Parliament of 1681. When the division took place betwixt the Duke of York and the Duke of Lauderdale, Sir George Lockhart sided with the former, and thereby secured Court influence in his favour. On the death of Sir David Falconer of Newton in 1685 Sir George was chosen Lord President of the Court of Session, and was made Privy Councillor and a Commissioner of Exchequer. He has been accused of trimming, since he had held office under

Cromwell, Charles II., James II., and William III.; and it does seem strange that he could have consistently sworn fidelity to each of them. On the other hand it is claimed that it was with a patriotic purpose that he retained his office, and that his position materially assisted the progress of the country. It was his misfortune, however, to meet with a tragic end. John Chiesly of Dalry, near Edinburgh, had been a litigant in the Court of Session, and a decree was pronounced against him by Sir George Lockhart and by Lord Kemnay, awarding aliment out of his estate to his wife and ten children, and Chiesly had been so incensed against the Lord President that he had openly avowed his intention of assassinating him. He had even the hardihood to communicate his intention to Sir James Stewart of Goodtrees, six months previous to the deed, and, though that gentleman endeavoured to dissuade him from his evil purpose, he refused to abandon it. The Lord President was informed of Chiesly's purpose but paid no heed to the warnings he received. On Easter Sunday, 31st March 1689, Chiesly loaded two pistols and took his place in the choir of St. Giles' church. When the service was over the Lord President, with two of his friends, took his way homewards to his mansion in Old Bank Close, and as he was entering his own door, Chiesly levelled his pistol, took deadly aim at his enemy and shot him in the back. The bullet passed through his body, and his death took place almost instantly. The assassin was at once seized, though he made no effort to escape and boasted of his infamous deed. On the following day the Convention of Estates, which had been adjourned on Friday preceding and was not appointed to meet until Tuesday, was hastily summoned, and, considering the enormity of the crime, passed an Act 'granting power and warrand to the magistrates of Edinburgh anent the torturing of John Chiesly of Dalrye, the actor of the horrid and inhumane murder of Sir George Lockart, and of William Calderwood, writer, as accessory therto. In regaird of the notoriety of the murder and the execrable and extraordinary circumstances therof, the Estates do appoynt and authorise the provost and two of the bailzies in Edinburgh, and lykewayes the Earle of Erroll, lord high constable, his deputs, if the said deputs shall please to concurr, not only to cognosce and judge the murder, but to proceed to torture John Chiesly of Dalry, for discovering if ther were any accomplices, advysers, or assisters to him in that horrid and most inhumane act. . . . And the Estates declair that albeit in this extraordinary case they have allowed torture, yet the samen shall be no preparative or warrand to proceed to torture at any tyme hereafter, nor homologatione of what hes bein done at any tyme bypast.' Chiesly did not seek to evade the punishment of his crime, and on the same day—Monday, 1st April 1689—he was hurriedly tried before Sir Magnus Price, Lord Provost of Edinburgh, and condemned to death. He was drawn on a hurdle to the Cross, where his right hand was struck off, and he was thence conveyed to Drumsheugh, where he was hung in chains with the pistol tied around his neck. (Hugo Arnot states that the place of execution was at the Gallowlee, between Edinburgh and Leith.) The right hand of the murderer was affixed to the West Port of Edinburgh, where it remained for some time.

[38] *Mr. Cheesly att Edenburgh.* Page 15.

John Chiesly of Dalry, whose execution is referred to in the preceding note, belonged to a family of burgesses in Edinburgh, who acquired the barony of Dalry in the sixteenth century. His father was Walter Chiesly, merchant and burgess of Edinburgh, and his mother was Catherine Todd, who died 27th January 1679, and was buried in the Greyfriars Churchyard. During his father's life John Chiesly obtained the lands of Gorgie in 1672, and ten years afterwards he had succeeded to the estate of Dalry. It is a curious coincidence that the names of Sir George Lockhart and of his assassin, John Chiesly, should appear on the same page of the *Book of Record*, written six years before the deed was committed; and it is noteworthy that even at that time Lord Strathmore candidly expresses his opinion of the future assassin by calling him 'a bas uncivil raskel.' Rachel Chiesly, the daughter of this atrocious criminal, is known in history as that Lady Grange who was imprisoned by her ruthless husband for a considerable time in one of the islands of the Hebrides.

[39] *Earl of Morton.* P. 16.

William Douglas, Earl of Morton, was the son of Robert, Lord Dalkeith and Earl of Morton, and succeeded his father in 1649. His grandfather, William, Earl of Morton, had obtained a gift of the lands of Orkney and Shetland, in acknowledgment of the large sums of money which he had expended in support of the Royalist cause, but the charter thus granted was repudiated by Charles II., and this munificent gift was re-annexed to the Crown. There are several references throughout the *Book of Record* to the dealings of Lord Strathmore and his father with the father and grandfather of the Earl of Morton. The marriage of the Earl of Morton with Lady Grizel Middleton, sister of the wife of the first Earl of Strathmore, brought the two families into close contact, and Lord Strathmore accuses his mother-in-law of showing undue favouritism toward Lord Morton (see page 28). The only son of the Earl of Morton, Charles, Lord Dalkeith, died when an infant, and the title, at the Earl's death in 1681, devolved on his uncle, Sir James Douglas of Smithfield. The subsidiary title of Lord Dalkeith was renounced by the Earl of Morton in 1672, and was ratified to the Duke of Buccleuch and Monmouth at that date.

[40] *Earl of Midlton.* P. 16.

The career of General John Middleton may be regarded as that of the typical soldier of fortune of the period. He was the eldest son of John Middleton of Caldhame, in Kincardineshire, and of Helen, daughter of John Strachan of Thurton. His father was slain by Montrose's men in 1645, while sitting in his chair within his own dwelling. John Middleton began his military life as a pikeman in Hepburn's Regiment, and served with his troops in France. Returning to England, he joined the Parliamentary army in 1642, obtained the command of a troop of horse, and became Lieutenant-General under Sir William Waller. Shortly afterwards he came north to Scotland, and took service with the Presbyterians under General David Leslie. He was present at the battle of Philiphaugh on 13th September 1645, and took so prominent a share in the defeat of Montrose at that time, that the Scottish Parliament rewarded him with the gift of 25,000 merks. In the succeeding year he marched against Montrose to the north, raised the siege of Inverness, and compelled the Marquess to retreat and capitulate. So complete was his victory at this period, that Montrose was forced to leave the country. It was whilst Middleton was making preparations for this successful expedition that he visited Dundee, and was specially honoured by having his name placed on the burgess-roll on 23d March 1646. Dundee being then a defended town, was regarded as the most convenient rendezvous for the Presbyterian forces, and when the army was remodelled in the following year, under General Middleton's supervision, the 'Dundee Regiment' was specially exempted from the order for disbandment. The Act of Parliament ordering this re-arrangement of the troops is in the following terms:—

'12 *Feb.* 1647.—The Estates of Parliament ordainis these companies of foote q[lk] ar to be keipt vp of Colonell Stuart, the Viscount of Kenmure, Lieut.-Gen[ll] baillie, Earle of cassillis, Lord couper, Earle of murray, and Lord Chancelloris Regiments, and that Regiment in dundie, for making vp of the gen[ll] of artillarie his Regiment of the new modelled forces, —To marche the readiest and straightest way from there quarters To dundie and mak there Randezvous their q[r]. they ar to ressave further orderis for thair farder marche.'

At this period Middleton was still in the service of the Parliamentarians, but in the succeeding year he abandoned them and joined the Royalists. When troops were raised for the purpose of rescuing Charles I., he was appointed Lieutenant-General of Cavalry, and made a diversion in favour of the king in the west country. Thence he marched into England, in company with the first Duke of Hamilton, and fought with great gallantry under him at the battle of Preston (17th August 1648). He was taken prisoner there and sent to Newcastle, but effected his escape, and shortly afterwards he attempted to raise a Royalist army in the Highlands, but was defeated, after a daring struggle, in 1650. When Charles II. marched from Stirling into England at the head of a numerous army, Middleton accompanied him, and was present with him at the battle of Worcester (3d September 1651), where he made the chief resistance to the Cromwellians. In this engagement he was wounded and taken prisoner, and having provoked the resentment of Cromwell by his conversion to the Royalist cause, the Protector committed him to the Tower of London, and endeavoured to have him executed as a deserter from the Parliamentarian army. Middleton succeeded in escaping even from this secure place of confinement, and made his way to France, where he joined the fugitive king at Paris. In 1653 he was despatched to Scotland to command the Royalist troops there, but was defeated by General Monck at Lochgarry, on 26th July 1654. Again he escaped to the Continent, and once more found refuge with Charles II. at Cologne. His services to the Royalists had been so great that he was specially excepted from Cromwell's Act of Grace and Pardon (1654), and he remained abroad until the Restoration in 1660.

So devoted an adherent of the Royalist party might well anticipate honour and reward when the star of the king was in the ascendant; and in this respect he was not disappointed. On 1st October 1660 he was created Earl of Middleton, was appointed Commander-in-Chief of the Forces in Scotland, and Royal Commissioner to the Scottish Parliament. Two years afterwards he was made an Extraordinary Lord of Session, and for a brief period he held almost undisputed sway over Scottish affairs. His administration, however, was disgraced by the grossest tyranny, and his life was spent in scenes of the vilest debauchery and licentiousness. 'Aided by the base subserviency of the Estates,' writes Dr. James Taylor, 'he annulled all the proceedings of the various parliaments that had been held since 1633, and in a brief space of time overturned the entire fabric of the civil and religious liberties of the country, his chief opponent at this time was John Maitland, afterwards Duke of Lauderdale, and the reckless conduct of Middleton afforded him ample opportunity to facilitate his rival's downfall. The Earl seriously offended the King by procuring the passing of the Act of Billeting, by which many of the principal Royalist noblemen were incapacitated from holding prominent offices; and he was suddenly disgraced and deposed from the elevated position which he had held, 'to the joy of the nation,' writes Sir Robert Douglas, 'as his administration had become odious from his severities, and contemptible from his riotous excesses.' By his appointment as Governor of Tangier, in North Africa, he was carried into honourable exile in 1663, and never more returned to Scotland. Ten years afterwards (1673) he was killed by falling from his horse at Tangier.

The Earl of Middleton was twice married. His first wife was Grizel, only daughter of Sir James Durham of Pitkerro and Luffness, by whom he had a son, Charles, afterwards second Earl of Middleton, and two daughters—Grizel, married to William, tenth Earl of Morton, and Helen, married to Patrick, first Earl of Strathmore and Kinghorne. The second wife was Lady Martha Cary, daughter of the Earl of Monmouth, by whom he had no issue. There is an excellent portrait of the Earl of Middleton in the drawing-room at Glamis Castle, in the possession of the Earl of Strathmore.

[41] *Earl of Errol.* Page 16.

Gilbert, tenth Earl of Errol, was the son of William, ninth Earl of Errol, and of Lady Anne Lyon, only daughter of Patrick, first Earl of Kinghorne. He was therefore full cousin of the Earl of Strathmore. On page 16 of the *Book of Record* allusion is made to the fact that the father of Lord Strathmore, John, second Earl of Kinghorne, died from the plague, having been infected by the governor of the Earl of Errol, who was then staying in charge of the young nobleman in Lord Kinghorne's house at St. Andrews. The Earl of Errol was engaged in support of Charles I. in 1648, and raised a regiment for the service of Charles II. In acknowledgment of his efforts, he was made a member of the Privy Council in 1661, and obtained a charter from the king on 13th November 1666, enabling him to appoint by will the heir who should succeed to his title and hereditary offices. He was married to Lady Catherine Carnegie, youngest daughter of James, second Earl of Southesk, on 7th January 1658, but there was no issue of this marriage. He died in 1674, and nominated as his successor his kinsman, Sir John Hay of Killour, who became eleventh Earl of Errol.

[42] *Earl of Aboyn.* Page 17.

Lord Charles Gordon was the fourth son of George, second Marquess of Huntly. His mother was Lady Anne Campbell, sister of the first Marquess of Argyll, and he was born *circa* 1620. He is described as 'a man of great honour and loyalty, who adhered firmly to the interests of Charles I. and Charles II. during the Civil Wars, often exerting himself in their service, on which account he suffered many hardships.' His faithfulness was recognised at the Restoration, and he was raised to the Peerage by patent, dated 10th September 1660, with the titles of Earl of Aboyne and Lord Gordon of Strathavon and Glenlivet. He gained some reputation as an author, although his poems were not printed, but were largely circulated in manuscript amongst his friends in the north. There is a volume in the library at Skene House, entitled, 'A Collection of Severall Satyrs, Lampoons, Songs, and other Poems,' which contains some of his poems, amongst them being one called, 'A Satyre on the Duke of Lauderdale,' which commences in this strain :—

'The scepter and crown,
With the gospell and gown,
Are now turned all to confusion,
The Hector of State
Is the rascall we hate,
And his plots we will treat in derision.'

One of his cleverest pieces is amongst the Fountainhall MSS. in the Advocates' Library, and was published in Maidment's *Book of Scotish Pasquils.* It is entitled, 'On the Tymelie death of little Mr. Andrew Gray, Late Minister of Coul, 1678' :—

'This narrow hous, and room of clay,
Holds little Mr. Andrew Gray,
Who from this world disappears
Though voyd of witt yett full of yeires.

To point him forth requyres some skill,
He knew so little good or ill,
Yet, that his memory may live,
Some small accompt I mean to give.

He had a church without a roof,
A conscience that was cannon proof,
He was Prelatick first, and then
Became a Presbyterian.

For he with Menzies, Row, and Cant,
Roar'd fiercelie for the Covenant.
Episcopall once more he turn'd,
And yet for neither would be burn'd.

A Rechabite he did decline,
For still he loved a cup of wyne.
No Papist—for he had no merit—
No Quaker—for he wanted spirit.

No infidel—for he believed
That ministers by stipends lived,
No Jew he was—for he did eat
Excessivelie, all kynds of meat.

Although in pulpit still he had
Some smattering of the preaching trade,
Yet, at each country feast and tryst
Rav'd nonsense like an Antichrist.

And lest ye think I doe him wrong,
He being short, to be too long,
No more the matter to obtrude
I with this Epitaph conclude.

Here lyes Mr. Andrew Gray
Of whom I have no more to say;
But fiftie years he preach'd and lyed,
Therefore God d—d him when he dyed.'

Lord Aboyne was married to Lady Elizabeth Lyon, only daughter of John, second Earl of Kinghorne, and sister of the first Earl of Strathmore. He died in March 1681. His eldest son Charles, second Earl of Aboyne, was married to Lady Elizabeth Lyon, second daughter of the Earl of Strathmore.

[43] *Earl of Seafort.* Page 19.

George Mackenzie, second Earl of Seaforth, was the son of Kenneth Mackenzie of Kintail by his second wife, Isabel, daughter of Sir Gilbert Ogilvy of Powrie. He succeeded his brother Colin, as Earl of Seaforth, in 1633, and was an ardent Royalist. He was one of the Association which met at Cumbernauld, in 1641, for the purpose of concerting measures to support the cause of Charles I. Joining with Montrose in 1646, he incurred the displeasure of the General Assembly of that year, and was excommunicated by that meeting. In the following year he was included in the list of those to whom clemency was to be extended on condition of their finding caution, and it is probable that it was at this time that Lord Strathmore's father incurred the liability alluded to in the text. If so, this 'cautioneric' must have been undertaken very shortly before the death of the Earl of Kinghorne, and was thus left as an inconvenient legacy to his infant son, afterwards the first Earl of Strathmore. The execution of Charles I. seriously damped the hopes of the Royalists, and Lord Seaforth, together with many of his companions-in-arms, retired to the Hague, which was then and long afterwards the principal Continental asylum for political refugees. He was favourably received by Charles II., who nominated him as principal Secretary of State for Scotland, but he did not survive to exercise the functions of his office in his native land. He died in Holland in 1651, and was succeeded by his elder son, Kenneth, third Earl of Seaforth.

[44] *Laird of Dun.* Page 19.

Sir Alexander Erskine of Dun was the son of Sir Alexander Erskine, and succeeded his father *circa* 1630. He was Commissioner to Parliament for Forfarshire in 1630, and from 1639 to 1641. Though originally a supporter of the Covenanters, strong attempts were made to induce him to join Montrose and the Royalists. Charles I. granted him a pension of £200 yearly 'for the services of himself and his predecessors to the king and his progenitors,' but this seems to have had no effect whatever. The House of Dun was attacked by Montrose, as the following notice in Spalding's 'Memorialls of the Trubles in Scotland' clearly shows:—

'Montroiss seing he is not follouit be Argyll, he leaves the wod of Abirnethie and to the wod of Rothimvreouss saiflie gois he, and thair remanes a while. Fra that he marchis to the heid of Strathspey, throw Badzenocht, throw Atholl, quhair many of these countreis met him and follouit him; and round about cumis he agane into Angouss, quhair it is said he raisit sum fyre, about Covper of Angouss, of landis pertening to the Lord Covper, ane archcovenanter and brother to the Lord Balmyrrinoche. He marchis to the place of Dun, quhair the burgesses of Montroiss and countrie people had put in thair best gudes for saiftie, being ane strong hous, and him selfe a grite covenanter. Bot Montroiss takis in this houss, plunderis the haill govdis and armes.'

Sir Alexander Erskine held a commission as colonel of horse, and was on the Committee of War in 1644-48. Having been captured along with the Master of Gray, Sir John Carnegie of Craig, and Sir James Ogilvie of Newgrange, he was imprisoned with them, but was liberated in February 1646, on finding caution for £10,000 Scots. This evidently was the 'cautionrie' which Lord Strathmore's father had undertaken, and which had not been recovered from the Laird of Dun in 1683. The exact year of Sir Alexander's death is not recorded, but he was succeeded by David Erskine of Dun, who is described as laird in 1669.

[45] *Earl of Traquair.* Page 20.

Sir John Stewart, first Earl of Traquair, succeeded to the estate of his grandfather in 1606. He represented the county of Peebles in Parliament in 1621 and 1625, and was created Lord Stewart of Traquair on 19th April 1628. Charles I. made him Treasurer-Depute of Scotland on 7th May 1631, when that office was resigned by Lord Napier of Merchiston. When Charles came to Scotland in 1633, and was crowned at Holyrood, he raised Lord Stewart in the Peerage, by making him Earl of Traquair, Lord Linton and Caberstoun, by patent dated 23d June 1633. The Earl was appointed Lord High Treasurer on 21st May 1636, and was Commissioner to the General Assembly of the Church of Scotland in 1639. In that same year he was Commissioner to the Scottish Parliament, and dexterously managed the prorogation of Parliament, under the pretext of a declaration of war issued by the king. In 1641 he was impeached as an incendiary by the Scottish Parliament, the charges against him being that he had stirred up jealousies between the king and the Estates of Scotland; had intercepted a letter from certain of the Scottish nobility to the king of France, and had falsely represented it as an act of disloyalty to King Charles; he had influenced the king to refuse a hearing to the Commissioners from the Estates of Scotland, who had gone to London at his Majestie's request; he had falsely reported the proceedings of the Scottish Parliament; had secretly conveyed ammunition by night into the castles of Edinburgh and Dalkeith; and had committed malversations in his office of Treasurer of Scotland. As his punishment was left to the king, and as he was necessary to Charles, no serious result followed his impeachment. In 1648 he took part in the 'Engagement,' and marched with the army to England, but was made prisoner at the battle of Preston, and confined in Warwick Castle for four years. He returned home in 1652, and survived till 1659, dying, it is said, of starvation, through lack of the merest necessaries of life. Lady Traquair was Catherine Carnegie, third daughter of David, first Earl of Southesk, and the sinister motives imputed to her in the text may have arisen from the family feud that existed between the Southesks and the Lyons of Strathmore. 'Veitch of Daick,' alluded to, was Sir John Veitch, Member of Parliament for Peeblesshire, who was an intimate friend of the Traquair family.

[46] *Lord Spinie.* Page 20.

Alexander Lindsay, second Lord Spynie, was the son of Sir Alexander Lindsay, Lord Spynie, and grandson of David, Earl of Craufurd. His mother was Lady Jean Lyon, daughter of John, Lord Glamis, and aunt of the second Earl of Kinghorne, so that Lord Strathmore's father was full cousin to Lord Spynie.

He succeeded his father in 1607, and though there were extensive properties belonging to him in Forfarshire, he chose rather the adventurous life of a soldier of fortune. He joined the army of Gustavus Adolphus, and fought throughout a portion of the Thirty Years' War. He died in March 1646, and was succeeded by his second son, George, third Lord Spynie. The latter was a devoted supporter of the Royalist cause, and, according to Douglas (*Peerage*, vol. ii. page 518), 'After the death of Charles, Lord Spynie ruined his patrimonial estate by raising forces for the service of his son. He accompanied King Charles II. to the battle of Worcester, was taken prisoner there, and sent to the Tower of London. He was excepted out of Cromwell's Act of Grace and Pardon 1654.' Although the Lord Spynie for whom the Earl of Kinghorne was surety must have been the second Lord, it is evident that the conduct of his successor would prevent Lord Strathmore from obtaining payment of the debts due to his father. The third Lord Spynie died in 1672, eleven years before the *Book of Record* was written.

[47] *The Laird of Aldbarr.* Page 20.

James Lyon of Aldbarr was the second son of Patrick, first Earl of Kinghorne, by his wife, Lady Anne Murray, daughter of John, first Earl of Tullibardine. He was therefore the younger brother of Lord Strathmore's father, the second Earl of Kinghorne. The lands of Aldbarr, which had been granted to the famous Sir Thomas Lyon, Master of Glamis, had returned to the head of the family, on the death of John Lyon, son of Sir Thomas, without issue, and they had been granted to James Lyon by his father previous to 1615. James Lyon was Member of Parliament for Forfarshire from 1630 until his death in 1641. Douglas is in error in his account of the Strathmore family (*Peerage*, vol. ii. 565), when he refers to James Lyon of Aldbarr as being dead before 1617, although he corrects himself on the succeeding page, when he points out that John, Earl of Kinghorne, was served heir of his immediate younger brother, James Lyon of Aldbarr, on 6th May 1642. The character of James Lyon of Aldbarr is sufficiently indicated in the text, pp. 20-22.

[48] *Earl of Marr.* Page 21.

John, seventh Earl of Mar, was the son of the Regent Mar, and of Annabella, daughter of Sir William Murray of Tullibardine. His name figures prominently in the history of Scotland towards the later portion of the reign of James vi. It was to him that the King intrusted the guardianship of his son, Prince Henry, and the Earl accompanied the King to England in 1603, when he went south to assume the crown of the United Kingdom. He enjoyed the favour of King James whilst at the English Court, and was made Lord High Treasurer of Scotland in 1615, holding that office for the succeeding fifteen years. He died at Stirling on 14th December 1634. His daughter referred to in the text was Lady Margaret Erskine, one of the children by his second wife, Lady Mary Stewart, daughter of Esme, Duke of Lennox. She was the first wife of John, second Earl of Kinghorne, but left no children. Her death took place on 7th November 1639, and is thus referred to by Sir James Balfour:—

'The 7 of November, this same yeire, deyed at Edinbrughe, Lady Margaret Arskyne, 3d daughter to Jhone, Earle of Mar, Lord Thesaurer of Scotland, Countesse of Kingorne, wyffe to Jhone Lyone, 2d Earle of Kingorne, by quhom shoe had issew diversse childrene, but all of them deyed befor herselue; her corpes were enbalmed, and solemley interred in the comon sepulture of that familey, at the churche of Glamis in the mounthe of Februarij 1640.'

[49] *Earl of Southesque.* Page 25.

David Carnegie, first Earl of Southesk, was the eldest son of David Carnegie of Panbride, and of his second wife Euphame, daughter of Sir John Wemyss of Wemyss. He was born in 1575 and died in 1658. It was thus his lot to witness the Union of the Crowns under James vi., the succession and execution of Charles i., the supremacy of the Parliamentarians, and to terminate his career very shortly before the Stuarts were restored to the throne. He was raised to the peerage on 14th April 1616, by the title of Lord Carnegie of Kinnaird, and in the succeeding year he took his seat as an Extraordinary Lord of Session. He entertained King James at Kinnaird Castle when that monarch re-visited Scotland in 1617, and he was created Earl of Southesk when Charles I. was crowned at Holyrood in 1633. His faithful adherence to the Royalists caused him to be fined £3000 sterling by Cromwell in 1654, and he died at an advanced age in February 1658. As his life is fully related in Sir William Fraser's 'Carnegies of Southesk,' it is not necessary to detail it here. The incident recorded in the text represents the Earl of Southesk in rather a different character from that usually ascribed to him.

[50] *Duke of Lenox.* Page 27.

James Stewart, fourth Duke of Lennox, was the son of Esme, third Duke of Lennox, and of Catherine, daughter of Jervase, Lord Clifton of Leighton Bromeswold. He was born in 1612, and succeeded his father in 1624. As he was nearly related to James VI. the King took him under his special charge and he was educated at Cambridge, and travelled for some time on the Continent. On 8th August 1641 he was created Duke of Richmond, and during the civil wars in the reign of Charles I. he was actively employed in his service. His power in Scotland was very great, as he held the two offices of Great Admiral and Lord High Chamberlain, together with many minor posts. It is said that 'the Duke had the sincerest affection for the King, and was one of the noblemen who offered to suffer in his stead; and the whole tenour of his behaviour to that prince and his extreme regret for his death, show that he was in earnest in offering to be a vicarious victim for him.' He died on 30th March 1655.

[51] *Sir William Bruce.* Page 28.

Sir William Bruce of Balcaskie was the second son of Robert Bruce of Blairhall, and of Jean, daughter of Sir John Preston of Valleyfield. The exact date of his birth is not recorded, but it probably took place about 1630. He was trained in Royalist principles and was very active in attempts for the restoration of Charles II. He is credited with having suggested to General Monck the expediency of calling back King Charles to the throne, and is said to have been the first to communicate the likelihood of his restoration to the exiled monarch. As a reward for his service he was appointed Clerk to the Bills in 1660. Having acquired the lands of Balcaskie in Fifeshire in 1668, he was created a baronet of Nova Scotia, with the title of Sir William Bruce of Balcaskie, the royal patent being dated 21st April 1668. It is evident, from the remarks made by Lord Strathmore in the text, that he had a very low opinion of Sir William Bruce's character. He describes him as 'a contentious and teuch lawer,' and animadverts upon the means whereby he acquired the lands of Kinross from the impoverished Earl of Morton. These lands were burdened with a right of regress to the reversion which apparently the Earl of Morton had given to Lord Strathmore's father when he became his cautioner, and Lord Strathmore anticipated that he would not be able to establish his rights to Kinross against so experienced a litigant as Sir William Bruce. There is now in the charter-room at Glamis Castle a document written after the death of Lord Strathmore by Sir William Bruce, in which he protests that the new Earl of Strathmore had no right of regress to the lands of Kinross. Having acquired the barony of Kinross, he chose thereafter to be designated by the title derived from it. He gained great repute as an architect, and Kinross House (now the property of Sir Graham Graham Montgomery) was designed by him, and though tenantless for many years past, is still a splendid palatial mansion. It was occupied by the Duke of York (afterwards James II.) when he came to Scotland as Lord High Commissioner. Still more remarkable were the designs which Sir William Bruce made for the restoration and completion of Holyrood Palace. It is said that Sir William devised a plan for connecting Edinburgh with what is now the New Town by means of a bridge that was to occupy the site of the present North Bridge, although the scheme was not carried out for many years after his death. Sir William was Member of Parliament for Fifeshire in 1669-74, and for Kinross-shire from 1681 till 1686. He was married to Mary, daughter of Sir James Halkett of Pitfirrane, Bart., and had a son and daughter; the first of these, Sir John, died without issue, and the second, Anne Bruce, was married to Sir Thomas Hope of Craighall, Bart., and carried the estates into that family. Sir William died in 1710, having reached a very advanced age.

[52] *Minister of Longforgan.* Page 29.

Magister Alexander Mylne was the son of Bailie Alexander Mylne, of Dundee, and was born in that burgh in 1618. He received his education at the University of St. Andrews, and took his degree there on 2d May 1639. He was admitted minister of the church of Longforgan in August 1649, and remained in that charge till 1661. In the latter year he was translated to the Second Charge or South Church of Dundee, in which place he continued till his death in August 1665. From him descended the Mylnes of Mylnefield, who were related by marriage to the Wedderburns of Kingennie. By his wife, Agnes Fletcher, he had four sons and one daughter. Two interesting monuments still exist in the Howff of Dundee—which was the orchard of the Franciscan Monastery there, and was gifted to the town as a burying-ground by Queen Mary in 1567. These were erected by Alexander Mylne, in memory of his father and his brother, who are supposed to have both fallen during the siege of Dundee in 1651. The inscriptions upon these stones are as follows:—

'*Patri optimo, Alexandro Milne, sæpius in hac urbe prætura cum laude, defuncto tandem anno ætatis suæ* 68 *Ann. Dom.* 1651. *Vita functo, monumentum hoc Magister Alexander Milne, filius, erigendum curavit.*

Relligio, nivei mores, prudentia, candor,[1]
In Milno radiis enituere suis:
Consule quo, felix respublica; judice, felix
Curia & ædili res sacra semper erit.'

'*Chariss. fratri Thomæ Milne in urbe hac propugnabat vita cum decore functo. Ann. Dom.* 1651, *ætat. suæ* 22. *Monumentum hoc posuit Magister Alex Milne, Pastor Forgonensis.*

Longam fama dabit vitam quam fata
Negabant, nec moriter cvi contigit appetere.'

---

[1] Referring to the motto of Dundee—*Prudentia et Candore.*

[53] *Lady Northesque.* Page 29.

Lady Jean Maule, eldest daughter of Patrick, first Earl of Panmure, was the sister of Lord Strathmore's mother. She was married to David, second Earl of Northesk, who died 12th December 1677.

[54] *Lord Gray.* Page 33.

Patrick, seventh Lord Gray, was the son of Patrick, sixth Lord Gray, and of Barbara, fourth daughter of William, Lord Ruthven. He is known in history by his early title of the Master of Gray, and has earned unenviable notoriety from his duplicity when acting as Ambassador from James vi. to plead the cause of Mary, Queen of Scots, at the Court of Queen Elizabeth. His first wife was Elizabeth, second daughter of John, Lord Glamis, who was Lord High Chancellor, and the purchase of the lands referred to in the text was probably made during her lifetime. As his father survived till 1609, and he himself died in 1612, his enjoyment of the title of Lord Gray was very brief, hence his survival in history as the Master of Gray.

[55] *Lord Kinnaird.* Page 36.

Sir George Kinnaird, of Inchture, was the son of Patrick Kinnaird. He supported the cause of Charles ii. during the Commonwealth, and after the Restoration was rewarded by receiving the order of knighthood from the King's own hand. He represented Perthshire in the Parliament of 1661-63, and took his seat as Sir George Patrick Kinnaird of Rossie, knight, and was sworn a Privy Councillor. His services seem to have awakened even the dormant generosity of Charles ii., for in 1682 he was created Baron Kinnaird of Inchture, with remainder to the heirs-male of his body. Hence Lord Strathmore, writing in 1683, refers to him as 'the new Lord Kinnaird.' He died on 29th December 1689. The present Lord Kinnaird is his lineal representative.

[56] *Mr. Sletcher.* Page 42.

John Slezer, the draughtsman of the *Theatrum Scotiæ*, is well known by name to every Scottish antiquary, although no complete biography of him has been issued. The following notes are founded upon documents in the Advocates' Library, Edinburgh, on papers in the possession of Charles S. Home-Drummond-Moray, Esq., of Blair-Drummond, and on the account contained in the editor's book entitled, *Roll of Eminent Burgesses of Dundee.*

Slezer was a Dutchman, attached in a military capacity during his early years to the House of Orange. He came to Scotland in 1669, and became acquainted with several of the nobility in consequence of his skill as a draughtsman. Through their influence he obtained a commission as Lieutenant of Artillery, and was intrusted especially with the practical superintendence of the ordnance. He was made a Burgess of Dundee on 19th April 1678, and the entry of his name on the Burgess Roll of Dundee is of interest, as being the earliest notice yet found of him in any document. It was about this period that he visited Glamis Castle, upon the invitation of the Earl of Strathmore, and made the interesting sketch of the Castle which appears in the *Theatrum Scotiæ.* It is to this visit that Earl Patrick refers in the text, and as Slezer's work was not published till 1693, this shows that Slezer had contemplated its production many years before its publication. The progress of the work was temporarily interrupted. In 1680, John Drummond of Lundin, brother of the Earl of Perth, was Master of the Ordnance, and he was directed by Charles II. to send Slezer to Holland for the purpose of having new guns cast for Scotland, and also that he might bring experienced gunners or 'fireworkers,' as they were called, to this country. Many interesting letters written by Slezer to John Drummond whilst employed on this mission are preserved at Blair-Drummond, and afford much information as to this branch of the military service. In one of the notes he hopes that his claim on the Treasury for his expenses had been paid, 'for I suspect,' he adds, 'my wife will be as scairce of siller as myself.' This shows that his marriage had taken place before

1680, and as his wife's name was Jean Straiton, a local name in Dundee, she probably belonged to that burgh.

The favour with which Charles II. and his brother, the Duke of York, regarded Slezer's projected volume, induced him to proceed with it upon his return, though the expenses which he thus incurred must have weighed heavily upon him. His former attachment to the family of the Prince of Orange enabled him to procure a commission from William III., in 1690, as 'Captain of the Artillery Company and Surveyor of His Majestie's Magazines in Scotland,' which office he retained till 1705. He had not passed through the critical time of the Revolution without some difficulty. In March 1689, he was appointed by Parliament to 'draw together the canoniers and the artillery,' and had received the command of the Earl of Leven's regiment of 800 foot soldiers at that date; but as he at first refused to take the oath to support the Committee of Estates, he was ordered into confinement, and forbidden to return to the Castle until he had shown his fidelity. With this command he must have complied before his commission as captain was issued.

The first volume of his *Theatrum Scotiæ* was published by royal authority in 1693, and it contained fifty-seven views of palaces, abbeys, and castles of the nobility. Though the book was rightly regarded as a national work, he could not sell enough to repay the vast expense of its production, and therefore, in 1695, he showed a specimen of it to the Scottish Parliament, petitioning them to aid him in completing it by the issue of other two volumes, the sketches for which were then ready. A very peculiar method was adopted by Parliament to remunerate him for his expenditure. A special Act was passed imposing a tax of 16s., Scots money, upon every ton of goods imported by foreign ships trading to Scotland, and of 4s. Scots per ton upon every Scottish ship above twelve tons burthen exporting merchandise, the tax to be for five years (*Acta Parliamentorum*, vol. ix. page 355). During the currency of the Act he received, by his own account, £530 sterling, but when it fell to be renewed in 1698 there were serious limitations put upon it. The first portion of the tax was to be devoted to the support of 'His Majesty's frigates;' handsome salaries were provided for the officials who had to administer it, and Slezer and John Adair, the hydrographer, were both to be paid 'out of the superplus.' To encourage the exporting of coals, foreign ships who carried that mineral were to pay half the usual dues, whilst those carrying other cargoes were assessed at 24s. Scots per ton.

This new arrangement did little towards assisting Slezer, and the arrears both of his claims and of his military pay soon amounted to a very considerable sum. In 1705 he again petitioned Parliament, stating that he was then £650 sterling out of pocket; but his case had not been examined three years afterwards. He then declared that though he should have obtained £1,130 from the Tonnage Tax, he 'had never receaved the value of a single sixpence.' His whole claim then amounted to £2,347 sterling, but it is only too probable that it was never settled. The later years of his life were spent in Edinburgh, and on more than one occasion he was forced to take refuge from his creditors in the sanctuary of Holyrood. His death took place on 24th June 1714, and his widow and second son, Charles Slezer, obtained a portion of his claim up till 1723, but the greater part was absorbed in clearing off the debts which he had incurred during the production of his book. From some of the papers in the Advocates' Library, it appears that James Anderson, the celebrated author of *Diplomata Scotiæ*, was in the habit of advancing small sums of money to him, and he also suffered from the penuriousness of the Parliament, and from the dishonesty of its officials.

The letterpress which accompanied the first edition of the *Theatrum Scotiæ* was written in Latin by Sir Robert Sibbald, but Slezer, without Sir Robert's knowledge, had the articles translated into English. Four editions of this wonderful work have appeared—one in 1693, two in 1718, and one in 1719; and a *facsimile* reproduction was put forth in 1874.

[57] *Lord Craigie Wallace.* Page 43.

Sir Thomas Wallace of Craigie was the son of William Wallace of Failford, and was admitted an advocate before the Restoration. In 1661, when the Court, after the lapse of several years, was reconstituted, Wallace was again admitted as advocate on 4th July of that year. On 8th March 1669 he was created a baronet, and two years afterwards was appointed an Ordinary Lord of Session in place of Sir James Dalrymple of Stair, who was made President. On 9th July 1675, he succeeded Sir James Lockhart of Lee as Lord Justice-Clerk. The incident related in the text affords a glimpse of the method by which justice was administered even in the highest court of judicature in the land. Personal and family influence was brought to bear upon the judges in a manner little calculated to encourage the administration of strict justice, and accusations of bribery and corruption were freely circulated, and in many cases must have been well founded. The instance noted in the *Book of Record* shows how remote family influence could affect the relationship between judge and prisoner. The Lord Justice-Clerk belonged to Ayrshire by birth, and the Earl of Glencairn, who was a Cuninghame, extended his protection even to this disreputable incendiary, because he bore the same name as himself. It is not stated what judge tried the criminal, so that the exertions of Lord Glencairn had to pass through the channel of the Lord Justice-Clerk to be communicated to the acting administrator of so-called justice. This incident confirms the statement made by Mr. James Maidment, that 'no country possessing any pretensions to civilisation ever exhibited such disgraceful instances of judicial depravity as Scotland did, whilst an independent kingdom. The Union contributed mainly to the subsequent purity of the Bench, and the right of appeal to a controlling tribunal, where local prejudices, private feelings, and family influence could have little operation, effectually destroyed the old system of corruption.' In the year when Sir Thomas Wallace became Lord Justice-Clerk, an important dispute betwixt Bench and Bar arose. The point debated was whether the sentences pronounced by the Lords of Session could be appealed to the Parliament. The judge maintained that they could not, whilst the advocates asserted that the decisions of the Court of Session were liable to review by the Parliament as representative of the nation. So bitter was the controversy that the Lords ordered some of the refractory advocates to leave Edinburgh, and several of them, under the leadership of Sir George Lockhart, took up their residence in Haddington. Several ballads were circulated at the time, one of them being a parody on Dryden's song, 'Farewell, Fair Armida,' and is addressed to the Lord Justice-Clerk. It begins thus:—

'Farewell, Craigie Wallace, the cause of my grief,
In vain have I loved you, but found no relief.

An answer purporting to be written by the Lord Justice-Clerk throws the blame of the dispute upon Lord President Stair, and there can be little doubt that no such action would have been taken by Craigie Wallace without the sanction of his superior. Several poems on this subject are printed in Maidment's *Book of Scottish Pasquils.* The Lord Justice-Clerk died at his house of Newton of Ayr, on 26th March 1680.

[58] *Lord Glencairne.* Page 43.

John Cuninghame, eleventh Earl of Glencairn, was the fourth son of William, ninth Earl of Glencairn, and succeeded his brother Alexander, tenth Earl, on 26th May 1670. He was distinguished for his adverse attitude towards the measures whereby James II. sought to introduce Papist customs to Scotland, and his active opposition to the abrogation of the penal laws against Papists brought him into serious monetary loss. At the Revolution of 1688 he declared strongly in favour of the Prince of Orange, and as a Member of the Estates summoned by William, he signed the Act declaring the legality of its proceedings. He raised a regiment of 600 foot soldiers, and was appointed colonel thereof, and he signed the association for the defence of King William in 1696. He was married in 1673 to Lady Jean Erskine, second daughter of John, ninth Earl of Mar, and had one son, William, who succeeded as twelfth Earl of Glencairn.

[59] *Robert ffotheringhame of Lawhill.* Page 46.

Robert Fotheringham of Lawhill is described as brother to Fotheringham of Balindean, and as formerly heritor of Easter Denoon, in the parish of Glamis. Fotheringham of Balindean has already been referred to (see Note 29, p. 125). Robert Fotheringham was married to Agnes, second daughter of Sir John Carstairs of Kilconquhar, the second husband of Anne Bruce, heiress of Sir William Bruce of Kinross (see Note 51, p. 146). The connection betwixt the family of Robert Fotheringham and the Strathmore family is curiously shown by a deed now in the Charter-room of Dundee, whereby Dr. Robert Fotheringham, of that burgh, committed his son James to the curatorship of John, ninth Earl of Strathmore, in 1767.

[60] *Mr. Silvester Lammie.* Page 46.

The Silvester Lammie referred to here was probably Silvester Lammie, Jun., son of the minister of Glamis, and brother of John Lammie of Dunkennie. He studied at St. Salvator's College, and took his degree on 27th July 1661. On 22d September 1665 he was introduced as minister of Eassie, but was deprived by the Privy Council, on 5th December 1695, as a non-juror. Being excluded from the church, he conducted services in the manse till 1701, but after the introduction of another minister to the parish he seems to have desisted. His death took place about 28th June 1713.

[61] *Mr. James Small.* Page 49.

James Small, minister of Cortachy, took his degree as Master of Arts at the University of St. Andrews on 26th July 1670, and was admitted as minister of Cortachy in 1679. He was translated to Forfar in 1687, and remained there until 1716, when he was extruded 'without so much as a shadow of a sentence against him,' and a successor was appointed in the following year. He was living at the close of 1729, though the date of his death is not recorded.

[62] *Andrew Wright.* Page 53.

Andrew Wright, who did the most of the wright-work both at Glamis and Castle Lyon, was long on intimate terms with the Earl of Strathmore, who seems to have had much confidence in his judgment and skill. The timber-work of Glamis

Castle had been committed to the charge of James Bain, who was at that time Master-Wright to His Majesty, and who was engaged in the restoration of Holyrood Palace. After Bain gave up the contract, the Earl seems to have determined to employ Andrew Wright, who was then a mere rural joiner in the town of Glamis, and with him he made a current agreement. So far as can be judged from the accounts preserved at Glamis, Wright had carried on very extensive work for the Earl, and on very easy terms. He undertook all the wright and plaster work for the restoring of Glamis Castle, and his charges were paid principally in kind. For the first portion of work he was to be paid '300 lib. Scots, and eight bolls beare, with as much meall, and his own dyet.' This arrangement suited the Earl well enough whilst residing at the Castle, but was rather inconvenient when the charge for diet had to be paid as board wages. Accordingly, on one of the accounts rendered by Andrew Wright, the Earl makes the following memorandum :—

'The said Andrew must remember that tho' his dyet when the famely is here is not so senceble, yet it is the same thing as when he is boorded, which is *very senceble* to the said Earl when he payed it yesterday, and ought to be more considerat by the said Andrew.'

The next payment of 1000 merks is accompanied by the memorandum :—'From this day and date *no dyet*.' There are several of Andrew Wright's accounts still preserved at Glamis Castle, and the Earl's jottings upon them are rather amusing. In 1685 he had been employed to fix curtains at Glamis Castle, and had charged his time for doing so. Against this entry the Earl placed the following note :—

'*Imprimis*, for puting up hingings—*nothing*, in regard Andrew Wright should give *me* something for learning him to be an appolsterer.'

He had been employed at the alterations which the Earl made at Glamis Church, and to which he refers in the text, and in his account he had charged for the rectifying of one of his own blunders. His Lordship marks on the account opposite this entry :—'Because he made the reeder's seat *wrong*, it is just to give him nothing for making it *right*.'

In his dealings with Andrew Wright, Lord Strathmore showed that uprightness of conduct which was one of his distinguishing characteristics. Recognising this workman as a capable and deserving man, he put him in possession of the farm in Longforgan called the Byreflat, allowing him to pay up the price of it by his work at Glamis and at Castle Lyon. At a later date Andrew Wright wished to exchange this farm in the Carse of Gowrie for the lands of Easter and Wester Rochilhill, and accordingly, on 22d January 1689, Lord Strathmore agreed to exchange the one place for the other—that is, to allow the value of Byreflat, which Andrew Wright had paid, as part payment of the lands of Rochilhill. The balance against Andrew Wright, which amounted to £7,333, 6s. 8d., was to be allowed to lie over and cleared off by work done at Glamis or Castle Lyon. On 15th March 1689, the charter of Rochilhill, which was to be thenceforth called Wrightfield, was delivered to Andrew Wright, and he gave up his claim on the Byreflat at Longforgan. The new name does not seem to have survived the decease of Andrew Wright, as the place is now known by its original designation of Rochilhill.

[63] *William Balvaird.* Page 55.

William Balvaird was the second son of John Balvaird, minister of Kirkden, and was born in 1655. He studied at St. Leonard's College, and took his degree on 23d July 1672. He was recommended for licence on 14th September 1676, and became chaplain to the Earl of Strathmore, having special charge of superintending the education of his second son, Patrick Lyon of Auchterhouse, who was killed at the battle of Sheriffmuir in 1715. In 1684, as the entries on pages 55 and 73 show, he was sent to Aberdeen with his young charge. He was presented to the parish of Kirkden in 1685, when his father, John Balvaird, was translated to Glamis, and he remained in that position until his death in April 1710.

[64] *Earl of Northesque.* Page 58.

David, second Earl of Northesk, was the son of Sir John Carnegie, who was created Earl of Ethie in 1639, and exchanged his title, in 1662, for that of Earl of Northesk. His mother was Magdalene, daughter of Sir James Halyburton of Pitcur, and his youngest sister was the mother of John Graham of Claverhouse, Viscount Dundee. David, Earl of Northesk, was served heir of his father in April 1667, and was married to Lady Jean Maule (see Note 53, page 149), eldest daughter of the first Earl of Panmure, and therefore aunt by the mother's side of the Earl of Strathmore. His death took place at Errol on 12th December 1679, and the following extract from the Records of the Presbytery of Dundee relating to the burial shows how highly he was esteemed in that burgh:—'Dundee, 14 Jany. 1680. This day, while the exercisor was in his gown, going to the pulpit, the Earl of Northesk's corps were handed and lifting, and the canons shutting, and the body of the towne attending the corps, and the ministers invited to the burial, and the corps to be deposited in the church for the night, therfor it was thought expedient to surrcease the exercise this day.'

[65] *Scugal, Lord Whyt Kirke.* Page 58.

John Scougal was the son of Sir John Scougal of that Ilk, and brother-german of Patrick Scougal, D.D., Bishop of Aberdeen. The date of his admission to the Faculty of Advocates is not recorded, and his name first appears as an Ordinary Lord of Session in the Act of Parliament, 5th April 1661, where he is nominated as one of the fifteen Senators of the College of Justice, in the letter sent by Charles II., and dated 13th February 1661. He must have been knighted previous to 1663, as he is described in the Commission for the Restoration of Kirks and Valuations of Teinds, of date 11th September in that year, as 'Sir John Skougall of Whitekirk.' He died in January 1672, and it is recorded that he was honoured at his interment, on the 7th of that month, by the attendance of the judges, accompanied by the advocates and writers in mourning, and having their maces carried before them. On 11th November 1674, Patrick, Bishop of Aberdeen, was retoured as heir of Sir John Scougal of Whitekirk in certain lands at the harbour of Newhaven, together with the office of Bailie of that harbour (*Inquis. Spec.*, Edin. 1213). In Brunton and Haig's

Senators of the College of Justice, page 464, it is stated that James Scougal, Lord Whitehill, was the son of John Scougal, Lord Whitekirk, but this is an error, as from the Retours (*Inquis. Gen.*, No. 7855) under date 22d June 1697, Sir James Scougal of Whitehill, one of the Senators of the College of Justice, is retoured as heir of Sir John Scougal of Whitekirk, his father's brother (*Patrui*).

[66] *Dr. Gleig.* Page 59.

Thomas Gleig was the son of Magister James Gleig, at one time a Regent in St. Salvator's College, St. Andrews, but afterwards for many years master of the Grammar School of Dundee, who was described in the Town Council minutes of his time as 'ane native bairne of the burgh.' James Gleig was an eminent Latin scholar, and several of his poems in that language have been preserved. He was master of the Grammar School for forty-three years, and during this long period the Town Council of Dundee repeatedly made gifts of sums of money to him as tokens of their approbation. In the Council minutes, under date 9th August 1636, it is recorded that the members 'knawing he is of present intention to put Thomas his eldest son to the college, of quhom they have good hopes that he may in progress of time prove profitable to the commonweill,' they would 'freely grant his son ane hundred pounds yearly during his abode in the Philosophy College in St. Andrews.' The anticipations of the councillors in this instance were fully realized, for Thomas Gleig rose to be one of the foremost medical men of the time. He was associated with the proposal, in 1633, for the foundation of a Royal College of Physicians in Edinburgh, and was regarded as a Latinist of very great ability. On 7th February 1657 his name was entered on the Burgess-Roll of Dundee, with which burgh his ancestors had been connected for several generations. In 1649, Thomas Gleig had been third master of St. Salvator's College, where for some time previous he had been Professor of Physic. He professed to have 'endeavoured with faithfulness and painfulness the education of such youths as were entrusted to his charge in the sciences therein taught, and wes careful, so far as in him lay, to have them bred in the principles of loyaltie and dew obedience to the King's Majestie.' For this reason he became obnoxious to the Presbyterian party, to whom the visiting of the Universities was then committed, and as he had been active in promoting the 'Engagement' of 1648, he was violently thrust from his position, and forced to leave his wife and family, and fly to a foreign land to escape the malice of his enemies. After the Restoration he applied to the Estates of Parliament, and a special Act was passed on 9th May 1661, appointing that 'the whole dues and fies belonging to his Charge since he was put from the same in the year 1649, shall be payed vnto him And that he have als good right therto as if he had served.' The date of his death has not been discovered. Amongst the Sibbald MSS. in the Advocates' Library, there is a Latin poem by Dr. Gleig upon Sir George Mackenzie of Rosehaugh, which is as follows:—

'D. Georgius Mackenzie, Eques de Rosehaugh.

'Pingere vis quâ fronte Cato titubante Senatu
Asseruit Patriæ jura verenda suæ.

'Pingere vis Magnus quo Tullius ore solebat
Dirigere attoniti linquam animamque fori.

'Pingere vis quantâ Maro majestate canebat,
Et quali tetigit pollice Flaccus Ebur.

'Pinge Mackenzeum pictor, namque altera non est,
Quæ referant tantos una tabella vivos.'

[67] *James Bower.* Page 60.

James Bower was a member of the important Forfarshire family who held extensive properties both on the Glamis estate and its immediate neighbourhood. They were proprietors of Kincaldrum, Kinettles, Methie, and Innerichtie, and were for many years prominent members of the municipality of Dundee. James Bower entered the Town Council of Dundee in 1684, and continued in office for the suceeding six years. Archibald Bower, the well-known author of the *History of the Popes*, belonged to this notable family.

[68] *Alexander fforester of Millhill.* Page 61.

Magister Alexander Forrester of Millhill, Advocate, was the elder son of David Forrester, minister of Longforgan, and the first of the Forresters of Millhill. He was born in 1666, and was made proprietor of the estate during his father's life-time. Millhill lies to the north-east of Rossie Priory, and was at that time included in the estate of Castle Lyon, which belonged to the Earl of Strathmore. This portion of the estate, as well as the adjoining property of the Knap, referred to in the text, was afterwards acquired by Lord Kinnaird, and now forms a portion of the estate of Rossie. The Forresters, previous to the time of the minister of Longforgan, had held important civic offices in Dundee, James Forrester, ancestor of Alexander, having been frequently Provost of that burgh in the closing years of the sixteenth century, and other members of the family having held conspicuous public positions. Alexander Forrester of Millhill died in 1715, and what has been a magnificent marble tombstone was erected over his grave in the Howff, Dundee, by his sisters, and bears the following inscription ;—

'*Hic requiescit quod mortale fuit M. Alex. Forrester de Milnhill qualis fuerit qui scire velit haec pro verissimis accipiat pietate in Deum caritate in patriam comitate in amicos et benevolentia in omnes eximiam fuisse virtutes que has eruditione multifaria cumulavisse quo minus autem haec satis ducerent in causa fuisse modestiam longe nimiam Mortem obijt mense Oct.* 1715, *aetatis* 49. *Jussu et impensis Marthae et Magdalenae Forrester sororum ejus hic memoram extructum est hoc monumentum.*'

The inscription is now almost illegible. On the lower portion of the stone another inscription relates that Alexander Forrester's brother, John Forrester, succeeded to him, as he had died unmarried. In 1810, the Right Rev. John Strachan, Bishop of Brechin, caused the adjoining stone, which marked the tomb of the ancestor of Alexander Forrester, to be revised, and placed an inscription upon it declaring that Mrs. Helen Forrester, who died 10th April 1788, was the last survivor of the family of Forrester of that Ilk.

[69] *Sir Thomas Stewart of Garntilly.* Page 62.

Sir Thomas Steuart of Grandtully was the eldest son of Sir William Steuart, Gentleman of the Bedchamber to James vi., and of Agnes Moncrieff, daughter of Sir John Moncrieff of that Ilk. He was born in 1608, and was knighted by Charles i. at the Coronation in Holyrood in 1633. He represented Perthshire in the Convention of 1665-67. By his marriage with Grizell, daughter of Sir Alexander Menzies of Weem, he had one son, John, and seven daughters. Sir Thomas died on 10th August 1688, in the eightieth year of his age. He was succeeded by his only son, John, who died in 1720 unmarried, when the estate became the property of Sir George, grandson of Henry, a younger brother of Sir Thomas.

[70] *Drummond present Provost of Eden*[r]. Page 63.

Sir George Drummond was the third son of James Drummond, Laird of Milnab, Perthshire, and of Marion, daughter of Anthony Murray of Dollerie. He was Provost of Edinburgh in 1683 and 1684, at which time he was knighted. It was to Provost Drummond that Sir Robert Sibbald dedicated his book entitled *Hortus Medicus Edinburgensis*, in which he gave a description of the plants in the public garden known as the Physic Garden, Edinburgh. Whilst he was in the Provostship, Sir George became bankrupt, and was forced to take refuge from his creditors in the sanctuary at Holyrood, but was released through the favour of the Earl of Perth, and afterwards represented Edinburgh in the Parliament of 1685-6. He was married, first to Elizabeth Hay of Monckton, and secondly to Helen, daughter of Sir William Gray of Pittendrum, whose brother was married to Anne, Mistress of Gray. Sir George Drummond must not be confounded with Provost George Drummond (born 1683, died 1776), who had a much more distinguished career during the eighteenth century.

[71] *Bailie James Man.* Page 63.

James Man belonged to a notable Dundee family, and was

the son of John Man, merchant, who was frequently Bailie in that burgh. The name of James Man is enrolled amongst the Burgesses of Dundee under date 5th December 1671, and he is there described as a merchant. He began his municipal career as Treasurer in 1675, and from that time till 1691 he was almost continuously a Bailie.

[72] *Earl of Perth.* Page 65.

James Drummond, fourth Earl of Perth, was the son of James, third Earl of Perth, and of Lady Anne Gordon, eldest daughter of the second Marquess of Huntly. He was born in 1648, and studied at the University of St. Andrews, completing his education in France, where he remained till he came of age. On 18th January 1670, he was married to Lady Jane Douglas, daughter of William, first Marquess of Douglas, and this alliance greatly increased his power in Scotland. Having succeeded to the earldom in 1675, he was made a member of the Privy Council by Charles II. in 1678, and adhered to the party of the Duke of Lauderdale. On the fall of that nobleman, he was appointed Lord Justice-General on 1st May 1682, and was admitted an Extraordinary Lord of Session on 16th November of that year. When the Earl of Aberdeen resigned the Great Seal in 1684, the Earl of Perth was preferred to the post of Lord High Chancellor of Scotland, and remained in this office till the death of Charles II. When James VII. ascended the throne, it was anticipated that those of the Romish Church would be likely to find favour with the King, and the Earl of Perth, though he had frequently expressed disapproval of some of the doctrines of the Church of Rome, suddenly declared himself a convert to that creed. An interesting account of his feelings at this time will be found in Sir Robert Sibbald's Autobiography, which was published by James Maidment in the first volume of his *Analecta Scotica.* Whether dictated by policy or the result of conviction, the Earl's change of religion exercised an important influence upon his after life. The Earl was continued as Lord High Chancellor, and the administration of the affairs in Scotland was placed in his hands. Though his attempt to procure the repeal of the penal statutes against the Roman Catholics proved abortive, he still retained the confidence of the King, but his conduct prepared for him a severe retribution after the abdication of James II. The mob in Edinburgh rose against him, and he was forced to fly for safety to France. He took shipping in the Firth of Forth, but having been recognised, he was followed and captured by a few Fifeshire seamen, and was ultimately imprisoned in Stirling Castle. To this incident Lord Strathmore refers on page 95 of the *Book of Record* in these terms:—

'Behold the uncertainty of this world and of all humane affairs. The E. of Perth, L. Chancellor, from being the first minister of State, is now a prisoner in the Castle of Stirline, And his doers glad to convoy away the best of his goods, and dispose of them privatly.'

In Stirling Castle he remained a prisoner for four years, and in 1693 he was banished. Passing through Holland and Germany he reached Rome, where he remained for some time, but was at length summoned to the court of King James, who appointed him governor to his son, afterwards known as the Pretender. The exiled King conferred numerous honours upon him, creating him Duke of Perth—a title which was never recognised in the Scottish Peerage. He died at Paris on the 11th May 1716, and was interred in the chapel of the Scots College in that city.

[73] *Sir George Mackenzie of Tarbet.* Page 65.

Sir George Mackenzie of Tarbat was the elder son of Sir John Mackenzie, Bart., of Tarbat, and of Margaret, daughter of Sir George Erskine of Innerteil. He was born in 1630, and succeeded to the estate on the death of his father in 1654. At this period strong efforts were being made to place Charles II. upon the throne, and Sir George, ambitious to distinguish himself in the Royalist cause, obtained permission from the King to raise forces in the north for this purpose. He served under General Middleton, father-in-law of Lord Strathmore, and with his aid the contest with the Cromwellian party was maintained for twelve months, and ultimately concluded by an honourable capitulation. When the Earl of Middleton was sent as Royal Commissioner to Scotland after the Restoration, Sir George Mackenzie became his chief confidant and most trusted adviser. He was appointed a Lord of Session on 13th February 1661 by the warrant of Charles II. which re-established the College of Justice. It is asserted that it was by his advice that the Earl of Middleton introduced the Recissory Acts, by which the country was deprived of the liberty that had been gained since 1633. It was also through his influence that the Billeting Act, which brought about Middleton's downfall, was introduced, and Sir George was involved in the catastrophe which overwhelmed his patron. The Duke of Lauderdale rose to the supreme place in Scottish affairs, and Sir George Mackenzie was deprived of his seat on the Bench on 16th February 1664. For fifteen years after this date he remained in obscurity, but at length he succeeded in obtaining the forgiveness and favour of Lauderdale. He was appointed Lord Justice General on 16th October 1678, and was sworn a Privy Councillor in the following month. In October 1681 he was the successor of Sir Archibald Primrose in the office of Lord Clerk Register, and was restored to his place on the Bench in November of that year. From that time until the Revolution he had full control of Scottish affairs, and was created Viscount of Tarbat on 15th February 1685, on the occasion of the accession of James VII. It was in consequence of his acute proposal to disband the militia in 1688, that the Revolution was accomplished without bloodshed. The new King, William III., had not sufficient faith in him to replace him in his high position, and he was not restored to his office of Lord Clerk Register until 1692. This post he retained until 1696, at which time he resigned it and retired with a pension.

The accession of Queen Anne again brought Lord Tarbat into notice. On 1st January 1703, he was created Earl of Cromartie and made one of the principal Secretaries of State. He was now advanced in years, and unable to overtake the duties of this onerous office. In the following year he resigned it, and was restored to his former place as Lord Justice General, in which post he remained until 1710. His Parliamentary career was a distinguished one. He represented Ross-shire in the Parliaments and Conventions of 1661-63, 1678, and 1681-82, and afterwards took his seat in virtue of his various offices. He was a strong advocate, both with voice and pen, of the union of the Parliaments, and lived to witness its accomplishment. He died at New Tarbat on 27th August 1714, in the eighty-fourth year of his age. An obelisk, fifty-seven feet in height, was erected by him on an artificial mound near the parish church of Dingwall, to mark the place which he had chosen for his grave. Lord Cromartie was twice married. His first wife was Anne, daughter of Sir James Sinclair of Mey, Bart., who became the mother of John, second Earl of Cromartie, Sir Kenneth Mackenzie of Grandvale, and Sir James Mackenzie, Lord Royston of Session. The Earl was married, secondly, in 1700, when he had reached his seventieth year, to Margaret, Countess of Wemyss, widow of Lord Burntisland, whom he survived nine years. This ill-assorted union gave rise to the following Latin couplet, which was circulated with its contemporary translation at the time of the wedding:—

Fortunate senex nusquam non numine notus
Siccine amore senem te coluere deæ.

Thou soucie auld carle, the world hes not thy like,
For ladies fa' in love with thee, tho' thou be ane auld tyke.

[74] *Mr. John Balvaird.* Page 65.

John Balvaird was born in 1622, and took his degree at the University of St. Andrews in 1642. He was admitted as minister of Kirkden, in Forfarshire, on 13th June 1650, and when he was translated to Glamis, in 1685, he was succeeded by his son William, to whom reference is made in Note 63, page 157. From the time of his induction at Glamis till his death in 1698, he remained minister of that parish. Besides his son William, minister of Kirkden, already referred to, he had another son, John, who was also an M.A. of St. Andrews, and was minister of Edzell in 1684. After his father's death he was intruded as successor at Glamis, and abandoned his former charge, but he seems afterwards to have taken a medical degree, and to have left the ministry a considerable time before his death. There was still another son, called David Balvaird, who witnesses the contract between the Earl of Strathmore and Jacob de Wet (see page 106), and is there described as a servitor to Lord Strathmore. The document bears evidence that it was written by Mr. David Balvaird, so that it is probable that he had taken a degree at some of the universities.

[75] *Earl of Northesque.* Page 68.

David, third Earl of Northesk, was the eldest son of David, second Earl of Northesk (see Note 64, p. 157), and of Lady Jean Maule, daughter of the Earl of Panmure. He was therefore full cousin to Lord Strathmore, their mothers having been sisters. He succeeded to the title on the death of his father in 1677, and died in October 1688. He married Lady Elizabeth Lindsay, daughter of John, Earl of Crawford and Lindsay, Lord High Treasurer of Scotland.

[76] *Mr. Sylvester Lyon.* Page 70.

Silvester Lyon was a native of Kirriemuir, and took his degree at St. Andrews, 27th July 1666. He was admitted minister of Kinnettles on 31st January 1667, and was translated to Kirriemuir in 1669. It is related of him that he preached a very 'zealous sermon against Popery' before the Archbishop and Synod of St. Andrews 'which was reckoned bold and daring.' The name of Silvester Lyon appears in the list of contributors to the Darien Scheme in 1696, to which he subscribed £200 through James Fletcher, Provost of Dundee. He survived till 1st May 1713. His daughter was married to James Rait, Bishop of Brechin.

[77] *Robert Kinloch.* Page 73.

Robert Kinloch belonged to a family whose connection with Dundee can be traced to the beginning of the sixteenth century. He was entered as burgess on 9th June 1670, and was Town Councillor and Bailie frequently betwixt the years 1677 and 1698.

[78] *Alexander Raite.* Page 73.

Alexander Rait was entered as a burgess of Dundee on 11th August 1677, being then apprentice to John Man, merchant. In 1680 he entered the Town Council, and was Bailie in 1681. In 1686 James II. repeated the attempt which his predecessors had several times made to obtain control of the burghs by appointing the magistrates. He sent a Royal Warrant before the election in September 1686 directing the Council to appoint the civic officials whom he named. James Fletcher was the Provost by the choice of the Council, and he refused to implement the warrant, protesting the freedom of the burgesses to choose their own representatives. On 2nd December the King renewed his warrant, and named Alexander Rait as Provost, filling up all the other offices with his own nominees. No attention was paid to this encroachment upon the privileges of the burgh, and a third attempt was made by the King to accomplish his purpose. On this last occasion he appointed Major-General John Graham of Claverhouse (afterwards Viscount Dundee), to be Provost of Dundee, and that energetic soldier assumed the position to which he was called. He presided several times at the meetings of the Council, but in the succeeding year James Fletcher again assumed the office of Provost, and continued to administer it for one year. Graham returned to power in 1688, but after his death at Killiecrankie, Fletcher once more was chosen Provost, and remained in that office till 1698. Like many other Dundee merchants, Alexander Rait was a subscriber to the Darien Scheme in 1696, having contributed £100.

[79] *Doctor Yeaman.* Page 73.

The Yeaman family came from Rattray, near Blairgowrie, to Dundee about the middle of the sixteenth century, and for two centuries after that date they took a prominent part in the civic affairs of the burgh. John Yeaman, to whom reference is made in the text, was entered as a burgess on 18th May 1647, and as he is then designated 'chirurgeon,' he had evidently taken his degree in surgery. His son, who is also alluded to on page 73, was William Yeaman, and was also a surgeon. His name appears in 1696 as a subscriber of £100 to the establishment of a colony at Darien.

[80] *Lord Cardross.* Page 76.

Henry Erskine, third Lord Cardross, was the son of David, second Lord Cardross, and of Anne, daughter of Sir Thomas Hope of Craighall, Bart. He succeeded his father in 1671, and having been connected with the Covenanting party through the families both of his father and of his mother, he strenuously opposed the attempted imposition of Episcopacy in Scotland by Lauderdale. His wife was Catherine Stewart, daughter of Sir James Stewart of Kirkhill, and as she was also on the side of the Covenanters, Lord Cardross was made the victim of religious persecution. In 1674, Lady Cardross had attended the preaching of her chaplain within her own house, and for this offence Lord Cardross was mulcted in a fine of £5000. Of this sum he paid £1000, but being unable to raise the balance at once, he made application to the King for relief from the rest of the fine, but without success. On 5th August 1675 he was imprisoned in Edinburgh Castle, and detained there for four years. He had been pursued with much malignity by Lauderdale's party, and his imprisonment gave them opportunity to proceed to greater extremities. His house at Cardross, which had been shortly before altered and furnished at great expense, was turned into a garrison for the Royalist troops, who remained there for some time, and did much damage to the property. Even whilst he was in prison, an action was raised against him for suffering his child to be baptized by one of the Covenanting preachers and not by the parish minister, and though it was shown that he was then (1677) a close prisoner, and unable to prevent his wife's action in this matter, another fine was imposed upon him. On 30th July 1679, Lord Cardross was liberated, but he had to give security for the amount of fines due by him, and though he made application in the following year to have his forfeited estate assigned to his kinsman, the Earl of Mar, in this he was unsuccessful. From the references in the *Book of*

Record (pages 76 and 77), it appears that £500 of the fine imposed upon Lord Cardross was granted by the King to Lord Strathmore. The Acts of Parliament show that another £500 was given to the Earl of Moray, and Lord Strathmore describes how he applied his share of this gift. Sir William Sharp, then Cash-Keeper, paid the money to Lord Strathmore out of the Treasury, and took bonds for its repayment from the Earl of Mar and Sir Charles Erskine, near kinsmen of Lord Cardross. The Countess of Buchan, whose son, the Earl of Buchan, was unmarried, had a liferent leviable from the lands of Auchterhouse which Lord Strathmore had acquired, and a portion of the annual rent was cancelled by her to clear off that part of Lord Cardross' fine granted to Lord Strathmore. The title and estates of the Earl of Buchan were entailed in such a way that Lord Cardross was heir-presumptive, hence the desire of the Countess of Buchan to assist him in this difficulty. The after part of the history of this fine is rather peculiar. Lord Cardross went to America and founded a colony at Carolina, which was ultimately destroyed by the Spaniards. When he returned, the movement in favour of William, Prince of Orange, had begun, and he exerted himself enthusiastically in support of it. He accompanied the Prince to England in 1688, and became a prominent member of the Orange party in the Scottish Parliament. In 1693, Lord Cardross raised an action against Sir William Sharp's heir for repayment of the fine of £1000 as having been illegally imposed. Sharp, to defend himself, demanded that the Earl of Moray should repay the £500 he had received, and that the Earl of Strathmore should deliver up the bond of £500 which he still held. The case was brought before Parliament, and in June 1693 an Act was passed directing that this should be done. Unfortunately Lord Strathmore had ceased keeping his diary at this date, for it would have been interesting to have seen how he regarded this curious complication. Lord Cardross was made General of the Mint, and enjoyed the favour of King William during the remainder of his life. He died on 21st May 1693, before the Act of Parliament referred to had been passed. Though he had had an adventurous career, he was only forty-four years of age when he died.

[81] *Heriot's Hospitall.* Page 76.

George Heriot, the founder of Heriot's Hospital, is supposed to have been a descendant of the Heriots of Trabroun in East Lothian, and of Ramornie in Fifeshire. He was born in Edinburgh in June 1563, and was trained as a goldsmith in the workshop of his father. He began business in Edinburgh as a goldsmith and money-lender, and in 1601 was appointed jeweller to James VI. When the King went to London, Heriot followed in his train, and took up his residence in Cornhill, opposite the Exchange, following his double pursuit as goldsmith and money-lender. Here he was married for the second time, his wife being a daughter of James Primrose, Clerk to the Privy Council, who was ancestor of the Earl of Rosebery, but she did not long survive this union, dying on 16th April 1612, and leaving him childless. It was probably this latter circumstance that led him to conceive the idea of founding an hospital similar to Christ's Hospital in London, and by his will, dated 3rd September 1623, six months before his death, he left the residue of his property, after the payment of several legacies, to the city of Edinburgh 'To found and Erect ane publick pios and charitable worke within the said Burgh of Edinburgh To the glorie of God ffor the publict weill and ornament of the said Burghe of Edinburgh And for the honour and dew regaird Quhilk I have and beeres to my native soyle and mother Citie of Edinburgh forsaid And In Imitation of the publict pios and religious work foundat within the Citie of London, callit Chrystis Hospitall thair To be callit in all tyme coming. . . . Hospitall and Seminarie of Orphans for educatione nursing and upbringing of Youth being puir Orphans and fatherles childrene of decayit Burgesses and freemen of the said Burgh destitut and left without means.' It is supposed that the sum left for this purpose amounted to not less than £50,000 sterling. With this money ground was acquired, and Heriot's Hospital was erected. The surplus money not required for the carrying on of the Hospital was lent at 6 per cent. interest, and it seems from the *Book of Record* that the Earl of Erroll and Lord Strathmore had become cautioners for a considerable sum to the trustees. The method taken to pay off the interest on the cautionery is fully explained on pages 76 and 89, and is referred to in the Introduction.

[82] *Boyl of Kelburne.* Page 77.

John Boyle of Kelburne was the eldest son of David Boyle of Hawkhead, and of Grizel Boyle, the heiress of Kelburne. He represented Buteshire in the Convention of 1678, and in the Parliament of 1681-82 and 1685. He was appointed one of the Tacksmen of the Excise in 1684, and died on 7th October 1685. By his marriage with Marion, daughter of Sir Walter Stewart of Allanton, Lanarkshire, he had two sons and one daughter. The elder son, David, was created Earl of Glasgow on 12th April 1703.

[83] *Sir Wm. Sharp.* Page 77.

Sir William Sharp of Stonyhill was the son of Archbishop Sharp, and of Helen Moncrieff, daughter of the Laird of Randerston. He was Commissioner of Supply for Midlothian, in 1678, 1685, and 1686, and represented Clackmannanshire in the Parliament of 1681-82. His death took place previous to 1693, as is shown by the Act of Parliament of that year already quoted (see Note 80, page 169), and was then represented by his nephew Sir William Sharp of Scotscraig. The property of Scotscraig on the south bank of the Tay, near Tayport, was acquired by the Archbishop, and some of his structural alterations upon the mansion bear his arms and the insignia of his ecclesiastical office. His son Sir William was created a Baronet in 1683, taking the designation of Scotscraig.

[84] *Sir John Maitland.* Page 78.

Sir John Maitland of Ravelrig has already been referred to (see Note 26, page 124). In the earlier entry, the debt owing to him in 1684 is set down at £1333, 6s. 8d., and a note on the margin at a later date, in Lord Strathmore's handwriting, states that this debt had been paid. The amount referred to on page 78 has probably been made up by an additional sum borrowed from Sir John, and discharged in the manner described on that page.

[85] *Mr. David Lindsay.* Page 79.

David Lindsay was the eldest son of David Lindsay, minister of Rescobie, Forfarshire, and was admitted as minister of the parish of Maryton, near Montrose, on 3rd July 1673. He remained in this charge until his death on 17th December 1673. There is no reference in Scott's *Fasti Ecclesiæ Scoticanæ* to Lindsay having taken his degree as Master of Arts, but as Lord Strathmore styles him 'Mr. David,' it seems likely that he had been laureated.

[86] *Campbell of Lunday.* Page 79.

James Campbell was the only son of the seventh Earl of Argyll, by his second marriage with Anne, daughter of Sir William Cornwallis, and was created a Peer in 1626, whilst quite young, his title being Baron Campbell of Kintyre. Ten years afterwards he obtained the barony of Lundie in Forfarshire, which property had come into the Argyll family, through the forfeiture of Robert, Lord Lyle. He entered the service of Louis XIII. of France and greatly distinguished himself in the Spanish Wars. On his return to this country he was created Earl of Irvine and Lord of Lundie by Charles I., on 28th March 1642. The lands of Kintyre, which had been granted to him by his father, were sold to his brother, the Marquess of Argyll, and it thus curiously happened that Lord Strathmore had a claim upon Kintyre through the forfeiture of the Earl of Irvine's kinsman in 1685, and a right to his estates of Lundie by purchase at the same time. The Earl of Irvine died in France, previous to the Restoration, and as he left no issue the title became extinct.

[87] *The Rebell Argyll.* Page 84.

Archibald, ninth Earl of Argyll, was the son of Archibald, Marquess of Argyll, and of Lady Margaret Douglas, daughter of William, Earl of Morton. His history is too well known to require repetition here, and he is only noticed to call attention to the connection betwixt him and Lord Strathmore. The hapless rebellion, in which he was concerned with the Duke of Monmouth in 1685, was speedily suppressed, and the unfortunate Earl was executed at Edinburgh on 30th June 1685.

[88] *The Treasurer.* Page 85.

William Douglas, third Earl and first Duke of Queensberry, was the son of James, second Earl of Queensberry, and of Lady Margaret Stewart, daughter of the first Earl of Traquair. He was born in 1637, and was made a Privy Councillor when in his thirtieth year. On the death of his father in 1671 he succeeded to the earldom, and was made Lord Justice-General when Viscount Tarbat became Lord Clerk-Register. On 11th February 1682 he was created Marquess of Queensberry, and the right was accorded to him to use the double tressure in his coat-of-arms, as carried by the Royal Family. On 12th May of this year he resigned his office as Lord Justice-General, and was made Lord High Treasurer, that office having been under commission for fifteen years before that time. Several important offices were committed to his charge about the same time, and on 3d February 1684 he was created Duke of Queensberry, and stood high in favour when Charles II. died. The accession of James VII. made little change in his position, as he was continued in the high offices which he had held under the deceased monarch. Like others of the Scottish nobles of his time, however, he became a martyr to his religious convictions. The Earl of Perth, who was Lord High-Chancellor (see Note 72, p. 163), had secured the favour of the King by changing his creed, but the Duke of Queensberry frequently testified his objection to the revival of Romanism, and his enemies succeeded in turning the King against him. In 1686 he was deprived of his offices, and retired from public life, refraining from taking an active part in the movement that produced the Revolution. He acquiesced in the conferring of the crown upon William and Mary, but he refrained from taking office under the new sovereigns.

[89] *Earl of Melfort.* Page 89.

John Drummond, Earl of Melfort, was the younger brother of James, fourth Earl of Perth (see Note 72, p. 163). He shared in the favour of his brother, and was appointed General of the Ordnance in 1680, Treasurer-Depute in 1682, and one of the principal Secretaries of State in 1684. In the following year, when James VII. ascended the throne, he was continued in the latter office, and was created Viscount of Melfort, in Argyllshire. In 1686 he was raised in the Peerage with the title of Earl of Melfort, and he continued as Secretary of State till the Revolution. Leaving the kingdom, he joined King James in France, and was created Duke of Melfort and Marquess of Forth. Sentence of outlawry was pronounced against him in 1694, but he remained at St. Germains, having full control of the exiled king's affairs until his death, which took place in January 1714.

[90] *Mr. dvit, Limner.* Page 92.

Jacob de Wet was a Dutch artist, who came to this country probably with the Dutch carver, Jan Van Sant Voort, in 1674, and they were both engaged at the decoration of Holyrood Palace. This work was completed in 1686, and Lord Strathmore entered into a contract with de Wet on 18th January 1688, employing him to execute a number of paintings for Glamis Castle, many of which are still in existence there. The details of this bargain will be found in the second and third papers in this volume (pp. 104-9).

[91] *Marquess of Athol.* Page 95.

John Murray, second Earl of Athol, and afterwards first Marquess of Athol, was the son of John, first Earl of Athol, and of Jean, youngest daughter of Sir Duncan Campbell of Glenurchy. He was born in 1635, and succeeded to the title on the death of his father in June 1642. When the Earl of Glencairn mustered an army to withstand the Cromwellian invasion in 1653, the Earl of Athol, then a mere youth, joined him with 2000 men, and with his aid the Royalists were enabled to resist the conquest of Scotland at that time. In consequence of his patriotic but unsuccessful efforts, the Earl was specially excepted from Cromwell's Act of Grace and Pardon in 1654. He continued faithful to the Stewart cause, and was rewarded after the Restoration with many honours and offices. He was sworn a Privy Councillor in 1660, and made hereditary Sheriff of Fife, was appointed Lord Justice-General of Scotland in 1663, Captain of the King's Guard in 1670, Keeper of the Privy Seal in 1672, and an Extraordinary Lord of Session on 14th June 1673. Through the death of the Earl of Tullibardine in 1670, he succeeded to that title, and on 17th February 1676 he was created Marquess of Athol. In the early portion of the Duke of Lauderdale's administration, Athol was his intimate friend and confidant, but the severe measures which the Duke adopted towards the Conventiclers, though at first a source of profit to the Marquess, ultimately caused him to sever his connection with Lauderdale, and to join the Duke of Hamilton against him. In revenge for this desertion the office of Lord Justice-General was taken from him, but he retained the other posts to which he had been appointed. He presided in the Parliament of 1681, and was one of the principal agents in the suppression of Argyll's Rebellion in 1685. At this time he seems to have had a very wide commission from the Privy Council as to the command of the forces in Scotland, and Lord Strathmore was under his orders whilst in the west country. To him the Marquess had committed the charge of providing for the army. Though Athol had so long supported the Royalist cause, he was an active promoter of the Revolution, and visited the court of William and Mary expecting preferment, as he was nearly related through his wife to the new king. In this he was disappointed, and his attempt to secure the post of President in the Convention of Estates in the Episcopalian interests, in opposition to the Duke of Hamilton and the Presbyterians, was also unsuccessful. Shortly afterwards he retired from public life, and spent the remainder of his days at Blair-Athol. He died there on 7th May 1703, and was buried in Dunkeld Cathedral, where a magnificent monument was erected to his memory bearing the following inscription :—

D. O. M.

Hic subter in Hypogæo, in Spem beatæ Resurrectionis, conduntur cineres illustris Herois, Joannis, Marchionis Atholiæ, Comitis Tullibardini, Vicecomitis de Balquhider, D. Murray, Balvenie et Gask, Domini Regalitatis Atholiæ, Balivi hereditarii Dominii de Dunkeld, Senescalli hereditarii de Fife et Huntingtour, Stuartorum Atholiæ, et Muraviorum Tillibardini Comitum Hæredis; qui, utroq; Parente, Joanne Atholio et Joanna Filia D. de Glenurchy, nondum decennis orbatus, a Rege Carolo II. reduce, ob gnaviter adversus Rebelles, dum adhuc Juvenis XVIII. circiter Annorum, navatam Operam, summamq; exinde in Bello et Pace constantiam et Fidem, multis Muneribus accumulatus est; Quippe erat Justiciarius Generalis supremæ Curiæ in Civilibus, extra Ordinem Senator, Cohortis prætoriæ Equestris Præfectus, Parliamenti interdum Præses, Sigilli privati Custos, ab Ærario, Scaccario et a Conciliis, Vicecomes Perthensis, Locum tenens Comitatus Argatheliæ et Tarbat, et denique, a Rege Jacobo VII. nobilissimi Ordinis, Andreani Eques factus est. Obiit 7 Die Maii 1703.

[92] *Archbishop of St. Andrews.* Page 96.

Arthur Ross, youngest son of John Ross, minister of Birse, was admitted minister of the parish of Kinnairney in 1656, translated to Old Deer in 1663, and thence to the parsonage of Glasgow in the following year. In 1674 he was consecrated Bishop of Argyll, and was promoted to the See of St. Andrews in 1684. He was the last who held that Archbishopric whilst Episcopacy was the established religion of Scotland. It is said that his violent temper did much to prevent the maintenance of Episcopacy after the Revolution. He died in 1704.

INDEX

INDEX

Printed by T. and A. CONSTABLE, Printers to Her Majesty,
at the Edinburgh University Press.

Scottish History Society.

THE EXECUTIVE.

RULES.

1. THE object of the Society is the discovery and printing, under selected editorship, of unpublished documents illustrative of the civil, religious, and social history of Scotland. The Society will also undertake, in exceptional cases, to issue translations of printed works of a similar nature, which have not hitherto been accessible in English.

2. The number of Members of the Society shall be limited to 400.

3. The affairs of the Society shall be managed by a Council consisting of a Chairman, Treasurer, Secretary, and twelve elected Members, five to make a quorum. Three of the twelve elected members shall retire annually by ballot, but they shall be eligible for re-election.

4. The Annual Subscription to the Society shall be One Guinea. The publications of the Society shall not be delivered to any Member whose Subscription is in arrear, and no Member shall be permitted to receive more than one copy of the Society's publications.

5. The Society will undertake the issue of its own publications, *i.e.* without the intervention of a publisher or any other paid agent.

6. The Society will issue yearly two octavo volumes of about 320 pages each.

7. An Annual General Meeting of the Society shall be held on the last Tuesday in October.

8. Two stated Meetings of the Council shall be held each year, one on the last Tuesday of May, the other on the Tuesday preceding the day upon which the Annual General Meeting shall be held. The Secretary, on the request of three Members of the Council, shall call a special meeting of the Council.

9. Editors shall receive 20 copies of each volume they edit for the Society.

10. The owners of Manuscripts published by the Society will also be presented with a certain number of copies.

11. The Annual Balance-Sheet, Rules, and List of Members shall be printed.

12. No alteration shall be made in these Rules except at a General Meeting of the Society. A fortnight's notice of any alteration to be proposed shall be given to the Members of the Council.

PUBLICATIONS.

Works already Issued.

1887.

1. Bishop Pococke's Tours in Scotland, 1747-1760. Edited by D. W. Kemp.

2. Diary of and General Expenditure Book of William Cunningham of Craigends, 1673-1680. Edited by the Rev. James Dodds, D.D.

1888.

3. Panurgi Philo-caballi Scoti Grameidos libri sex.—The Grameid: an heroic poem descriptive of the Campaign of Viscount Dundee in 1689, by James Philip of Almerieclose. Edited, with Translation and Notes, by the Rev. A. D. Murdoch.

4. The Register of the Kirk-Session of St. Andrews. Part i. 1559-1582. Edited by D. Hay Fleming.

1889.

5. Diary of the Rev. John Mill, Minister of Dunrossness, Sandwick, and Cunningsburgh, in Shetland, 1740-1803, with original documents, local records, and historical notices relating to the District. Edited by Gilbert Goudie, F.S.A. Scot.

6. Narrative of Mr. James Nimmo, a Covenanter. 1654-1709. Edited by W. G. Scott-Moncrieff, Advocate.

1890.

7. The Register of the Kirk-Session of St. Andrews. Part ii. 1583-1600. Edited by D. Hay Fleming.

8. A List of Persons concerned in the Rebellion (1745), transmitted to the Commissioners of Excise by the several Supervisors in Scotland, in obedience to a General Letter of the 7th May 1746, and a Supplementary List with Evidences to prove the same. With a Preface by the Earl of Rosebery and Annotations by the Rev Walter Macleod. Presented to the Society by the Earl of Rosebery.

9. Glamis Papers: The 'Book of Record,' a Diary written by Patrick, first Earl of Strathmore, and other documents relating to Glamis Castle (1684-89). Edited from the original manuscripts at Glamis, with Introduction and Notes, by A. H. Millar, F.S.A. Scot.

In Preparation.

John Major's De Gestis Scotorum (1521). Translated by Archibald Constable, with a Memoir of the author by Æneas J. G. Mackay, Advocate.

The Diary of Andrew Hay of Stone, near Biggar, afterwards of Craignethan Castle, 1659-60. Edited by A. G. Reid, F.S.A. Scot., from a manuscript in his possession.

The Records of the Commission of the General Assembly, 1646-1662. Edited by the Rev. James Christie, D.D., with an Introduction by the Rev. Professor Mitchell, D.D.

'The History of my Life, extracted from Journals I kept since I was twenty-six years of age, interspersed with short accounts of the most remarkable public affairs that happened in my time, especially such as I had some immediate concern in,' 1702-1754. By Sir John Clerk of Penicuik, Baron of the Exchequer, Commissioner of the Union, etc. Edited from the original ms. in Penicuik House by J. M. Gray.

Sir Thomas Craig's De Unione Regnorum Britanniæ. Edited, with an English Translation, from the unpublished manuscript in the Advocates' Library.

The Diaries or Account Books of Sir John Foulis of Ravelston, (1679-1707), and the Account Book of Dame Hannah Erskine (1675-1699). Edited by the Rev. A. W. Cornelius Hallen.

Papers relating to the Military Government of Scotland, and the Correspondence of Robert Lilburne and General Monk, from 1653 to 1658. Edited by Mr. C. H. Firth.

A Selection of the Forfeited Estate Papers preserved in H.M. Register House.

Court-Book of the Barony of Urie. Edited by the Rev. D. G. Barron, from the original ms. in possession of Mr. R. Barclay of Dorking.

REPORT OF THE THIRD ANNUAL MEETING OF THE SCOTTISH HISTORY SOCIETY.

The Third Annual Meeting of the Society was held on Tuesday, October 29th, 1889, in the Professional Hall, George Street, Edinburgh,—Professor Masson in the Chair.

The Secretary read the Report of the Council as follows:—

"The Council has to congratulate the members on the continued prosperity of the Society and on the increased interest which is taken in its publications. The full number of 400 members is kept up, in addition to 36 public libraries subscribing, and there are 32 candidates waiting for admission.

"Two volumes have been already issued for the current year, and there is yet a third due, the 2d part of *St. Andrews Register*, which is passing through the press as rapidly as the difficulties of the work permit.

"Lord Rosebery's presentation volume—*The List of Rebels of* 1745—is also well advanced, and will be probably published, with a preface from his Lordship, in the course of next spring.

"The publications of 1889-90 will be (1) Mr. Archibald Constable's translation of *Major's History of Scotland*, with an introductory memoir by Mr. Æneas Mackay, and (2) *The Glamis Papers*, edited by Mr. A. H. Millar, of Dundee.

"Other works in preparation or in contemplation have been mentioned in previous reports. Among these *The Diary of Sir John Clerk of Penicuik* has been already transcribed; and the translation of Sir Thomas Craig's *De Unione Regnorum* will be shortly put in hand. The Keeper of the Advocates' Library, where the manuscript reposes, has kindly undertaken to be responsible for the editing of the text, and Professor Masson will furnish it with an Historical Introduction.

"The Council has now to thank Mr. R. Barclay, of Dorking, Surrey, for giving the Society an opportunity of opening out a new field. With his kind permission the Rev. D. G. Barron, Minister of Dunnottar, has undertaken to edit the *Court Book of the Barony of Urie*, now in Mr. Barclay's possession. The entries in this book begin with the year 1604 and go down to 1747, with, however, an unfortunate gap of 28 years, from 1639 to 1667. Although there may be many of these Baron Court Books extant, only the merest extracts have been printed; and this volume, apart from its illustrations of the manners and customs of the district, is interesting for its references to the general history of the country.

"The Council has also accepted with much pleasure a generous offer on the part of Mr. C. H. Firth to edit for the Society a selection of papers from what is called the Clarke collection of MSS. preserved at Worcester College, Oxford. The greater part of this collection, though catalogued and described, has never been printed, or even used by any historian. The papers were put together by Sir William Clarke, Secretary to the different commanders of the English army in Scotland from 1651 to 1660. They relate to all matters connected with the military government of Scotland, and the organisation of the army of occupation during that period. There is an abstract of all orders and warrants issued by Robert Lilburne and Monk, from 1653 to 1658, complete in four volumes. Two more volumes contain the letters of Lilburne and Monk during the same period to the English government; and there are other volumes, consisting almost entirely of papers relating to the finances of the Scotch army, and the taxation levied in Scotland. There are, besides, many volumes of miscellaneous papers and correspondence.

"Mr. Firth believes that an adequate series of selections from these documents would require probably not less than three of the Society's volumes. He is at present engaged in preparing for the Camden Society papers from the same collection, chiefly relating to an earlier period, 1647 and 1648, and a few others belonging to the time of the Commonwealth and Restoration, but Mr. Firth will reserve for our Society all that has a special reference to Scotland.

"The Rev. Walter Macleod has recently examined, on behalf of the Society, a mass of forfeited Estate Papers, preserved in H.M. Register House. These papers consist of petitions, reports, rentals, letters, and accounts, and afford not only much interesting information with regard to the family history of the forfeited persons, and some curious facts in connection with the rebellion of 1745-6, not to be met with elsewhere, but amply illustrate the political and social state of the Highlands, especially in regard to the tenure and management of land, the education of the people, and the condition of the poor, at the time of and subsequent to the rising. They furnish trustworthy information regarding an important period of transition, about which comparatively little is known, and on matters of peculiar interest at the present time. Of such a mass of documents, specimens only can be at present put into print. It is proposed that the selection made should be limited to the illustration of the history of the estates owned by proprietors whose names appear in the 'Lists of Rebels.' A volume of such selections would serve as a valuable sequel to Lord Rosebery's work.

"In accordance with the rules of the Society three members, the Right Rev. Bishop Dowden, Sheriff Mackay, and Professor Kirkpatrick, retire from the Council. It is proposed that

Bishop Dowden and Sheriff Mackay be re-elected, and that Mr. John Russell be placed on the Council in lieu of Professor Kirkpatrick."

The Treasurer, Mr. J. J. Reid, then submitted a financial statement, showing that while the year commenced with a favourable balance of £244, 19s. 5d., it closed with a balance of £314, 7s. 1d. He proposed that a sum of £304, 1s. 1d., lying in the bank on deposit receipt, should be constituted a reserve fund.

The Chairman, in moving the adoption of the Reports submitted by the Secretary and Treasurer, commented on the work of the Society, and referred more particularly to the papers which Mr. Firth had kindly offered to edit. "Than the years from 1651 till close on the Restoration of 1660, there was perhaps no period of Scottish history about which they had so little information. It so happened that throughout that period Scotland was part and parcel of the English Commonwealth. They could not help that now, but they should like to know all the facts." Mr. Hay Fleming seconded the motion, which was adopted, together with the Treasurer's suggestion as to the formation of a reserve fund. On the motion of Mr. J. H. Stevenson, Advocate, a vote of thanks was then given to the Chairman and other Office-bearers.

ABSTRACT OF THE TREASURER'S ACCOUNTS

For Year to 1st November 1889.

Charge.

Balance from last year, ...	£214	19	5
15 Subscriptions in Arrear for 1887-88 (18, less 3 irrecoverable), ...	15	15	0
400 Subscribers for 1888-89, at £1, 1s., . .	420	0	0
36 Libraries, at £1, 1s., ...	37	16	0
Copies of previous issue sold to new Members, .	14	3	6
	£732	13	11
Interest on Bank Account and Deposit Receipts,	8	4	9
Received from a Member on account of Postages,	0	0	4
Sum of Charge,	£740	19	0

Discharge.

I. *Incidental Expenses*—						
Printing and posting Circulars, .	£7	3	11			
,, Report and List of Executive, . . .	2	12	0			
,, Report of Second Annual Meeting, . .	1	18	0			
,, List of Members, etc., .	1	10	0			
Stationery (including Receipt-book and Cash-box), ...	3	18	0			
Postage of copies, ...	20	12	7			
Making up, and delivery of copies,	16	16	0			
Copies of *Pococke* and *Cunningham*,	1	1	0			
Hire of Room (Dowell's), . .	1	1	0			
Postages of Treasurer and Secretary,	3	1	11			
Clerical work, ...	8	0	1			
Charges on Cheques, . . .	0	16	1			
Advertising, . . .	0	13	0			
Messenger, . .	0	5	0			
				69	8	7
Carry forward,				£69	8	7

Brought forward,				£69	8	7
II. *Nimmo's Diary*—						
Composition, presswork, and paper, ...	£38	1	6			
Proofs and corrections, . .	4	15	6			
Binding and back-lettering, .	18	9	0			
Transcripts, .	6	0	0			
				67	6	0
III. *Mill's Diary*—						
Composition, presswork, and paper, ...	£75	8	0			
Proofs and corrections, . .	14	8	0			
Lithographing, drawing, and wood-engraving, ...	18	0	0			
Binding and back-lettering, .	18	9	0			
Typographic copy and transcripts,	8	0	0			
				134	5	0
IV. *The St. Andrews Register*—						
Composition, presswork, and paper (in addition to £82, 7s. paid last year), ...	£51	5	10			
Proofs and corrections (in addition to £26, 3s. paid last year),	17	5	0			
Photographing of MSS. etc., . .	8	11	6			
Binding and back-lettering, .	18	7	0			
				95	9	4
V. *The St. Andrews Register, Vol. II.* (*expenses to date*)—						
Composition, presswork, and paper,	£37	5	0			
Proofs and corrections, . .	8	4	0			
				45	9	0
VI. *Clerk of Penicuik's Diary*—						
Transcripts, . . .	£8	8	0			
				8	8	0
Total Expenditure,				£420	5	11
Carry forward,				£420	5	11

		Brought forward,	£420 5 11
VII. 6 *Subscriptions in arrear*, . . .			6 6 0
Balance due by the Treasurer—			
Deposit Receipt, dated 26th October 1889, . . .		£304 1 1	
Bank Balance with Interest, .	£168 5 10		
Less Cheques issued but not presented for payment, viz., £156 6 4			
0 12 6	156 18 10		
		11 7 0	
Cash in hand, . .		1 1 0	
		£316 9 1	
Less 2 Subscriptions for 1889-90, paid in advance, . .		2 2 0	
			314 7 1
		Sum of Discharge, .	£740 19 0

Edinburgh, 19*th November* 1889.—The Auditors have examined the Treasurer's Accounts for the year ending 1st November 1889, and find them correct and properly vouched, with a balance of Three hundred and fourteen pounds seven shillings and one penny at the credit of the Society.

(Signed) RALPH RICHARDSON.
WM. TRAQUAIR DICKSON.

www.ingramcontent.com/pod-product-compliance
Lightning Source LLC
Chambersburg PA
CBHW020356030726
47496CB00007B/2167

* 9 7 8 3 3 3 7 1 1 5 5 8 6 *